Murder In Broadway

An Inspector Vignoles Mystery

Stephen Done

British Library Cataloguing in Publication Data:
A catalogue record for this book is available from the British Library
ISBN 978-1-9164010-2-0

1st reprint (with amendments) 2019

The Vignoles Press
Stephen.done@gmail.com
FB: The Vignoles Press
www.inspectorvignoles.ukwriters.net

Set in Garamond
Cover design & layout: Bill Citrine
Editor: Peter Elson
Printed in Poland by booksfactory.co.uk

Author's Note

Murder In Broadway is not so much a 'whodunnit' as a 'whydunnit'.

Although it can be read as a stand-alone thriller, it forms the conclusion to the events that commenced in Cold Steel Rail, and those who have read that book will have a suspicion of who might be behind the killing in this story... The two books were conceived as one major work under the umbrella title of The Hornet's Beauty. Perhaps one day it may appear in that form as a single (big!) book.

The locations are authentic, with appropriate tweaks to suit a work of fiction and trains run strictly to a timetable to suit the plot...

The book notably features Broadway railway station which has been gloriously recreated by the Gloucester Warwickshire Steam Railway (GWSR) from an almost completely derelict site. Readers are encouraged to support this fabulous heritage railway and witness it for themselves. (For those who love fish and chips, the GWSR run the brilliantly titled 'Cheltenham Fryer'...)

Thanks to David Holmes GWSR Retail Manager for support and reference material that helped this book get written.

All characters are pure fiction, with a number of real personalities and racehorses to add historical verisimilitude.

This book is dedicated to all those readers who have supported The Inspector Vignoles Mysteries over the ten books that have brought us here. Thank you.

Stephen Done
New Brighton, June 2019

Chapter One

Mr Peter Krast turned the key then tested the handle to check the door was locked. Long years of habit made it impossible not to make the almost instinctive action.

He stared morosely at the glossy black-painted door with its polished brass fittings. Nervously checking to see if there was anyone near to observe his actions, he clicked on a pocket torch and carefully inspected the door jamb with his leather-gloved fingers and peered closely at the escutcheon to see if there were any marks to suggest the lock had been picked or forced.

He made an impatient sound, a cloud of breath ballooning around his mouth in the damp night air. 'I can see nothing! There was nothing this morning, so why now?' His heavy accent still betrayed a central European origin as he muttered the words aloud.

Krast turned about and again furtively looked up and down Royal Well Place as if expecting to find someone lurking in a darkened doorway. The short street was deserted save for an ugly ginger tomcat trotting confidently across the rain-slicked road. Krast's Jewellers lay on one of the quieter streets that rarely attracted the crowds Cheltenham welcomed in the days leading up to the biggest racing meet of the calendar and most foot traffic had tailed off to nothing before five-o-clock closing approached.

He turned up the fur collar on his black overcoat and pulled his curious hat of European styling lower on his head as if these twin acts would offer comfort. His thick-lensed glasses were starting to bead with the soft rain pattering down. At that moment he was dazzled by the lights of a large motor car that swung in from St George's Place. It took the corner at speed and recklessly encroached onto the wrong side of the road as it did so, the twin headlight beams fracturing into confusing splinters of light through the rain droplets on his lenses. Krast feared the driver was steering directly towards him and instinctively threw an arm before his eyes, his mouth opened in alarm.

The car adjusted its course and arrogantly swished past without slowing. Krast caught a glimpse of a woman in the passenger seat. She had full lips glossed with lipstick and was wearing one of those crocheted Dutch-style caps popular amongst the fashionable ladies at the moment. He thought the driver had been in uniform, perhaps RAF or Navy, but they sped by so quickly he could not be sure.

It was time to get walking and not loiter on the street in the rain like a fool. His train was due out of Cheltenham St James. His footsteps echoed on the emptying streets. Or were they the sound of someone falling into step behind...

*   *   *   *

The horses slowed to a canter and gathered into a loose group, slowly easing to a walk as they ended the evening gallop. The mercury was dropping fast as the cold air pooled in the bottom of the vale. Derek Coldicott, trainer and owner of Acre Vale Farm observed mutely as the ten racehorses approached, their riders now sitting more upright and relaxed, hands gently patting the steaming necks of their beasts as they muttered almost inaudible words of praise and encouragement into alert, twitching ears.

Coldicott gave a nod of his head, then pushed himself away from the white-painted fence and started walking back towards the stables. It was a familiar routine, and indicated their ride was over for the day. Horse, rider and trainer could all retreat from the icy rain starting to patter on the ground. Coldicott was not a man who wasted words. Even when he secured a win, he restrained his celebrations to a nod of appreciation to the jockey and a clutch of words to the press. Understatement was his style, and he preferred to reserve judgement on a horse until he'd gathered all relevant information and mentally processed this alongside his own acute observations. Training racehorses was demanding, and experience told him not to rush to conclusions. He needed to hear from the stable lads and lasses who would soon be rubbing down each horse and able to report any niggles or signs of stress from their charges they knew so intimately. The riders must also pass on everything they'd learned from the gallops, expertly advising how each flighty racehorse was responding, what mood they were in and how race-ready they believed them to be. Only then would he decide how each of these precious beasts was performing. He owed it to the owners to offer the most accurate and honest assessment, even if it was not always to their liking. More often than not, the news was disappointing. All they ever wanted to hear was that their expensive beast was a dead-cert winner. Trainers learned to develop tough skins. A bawling out or a complaining voice down the telephone line was an all-too frequent conclusion to a long day of work.

As the sound of many hooves clattered on the yard and voices called out as riders dismounted, Coldicott felt his heart sink as he caught sight of a familiar figure.

Lord Buckrose... The sight of the dapper figure in his Harris tweeds, breeks and deerstalker pacing around the edge of the yard with one of those extravagant cigarettes with the gold rings around them in his kid-gloved hand was enough to make his heart sink. Buckrose wasn't due until tomorrow morning and Coldicott had prepared himself for a full and frank assessment then, but not before. He cursed silently, before hastily button-holing a rider and asking him how Money for Nothing had performed. He grunted acknowledgment of a positive assessment, took a deep breath and strode over. If nothing else, he could deliver his demand for the mounting collection of unpaid bills to be settled a few hours earlier than expected.

* * * *

Krast just made it. The train guard was alert to the fact one of the regulars was tardy this evening and stood with a door held open on the single coach that formed the evening push-pull auto-train service to Honeybourne. The guard neatly stepped in behind Krast and signaled the little train away with a sound of the gong that rang in the engine cab via a rope strung through hooks beside the carriage roof.

Appreciating that the 'Coffeepot,' as it was affectionately known by its handful of regulars, was not prepared to depart without him was heartwarming and this simple act made Krast feel better than he had all day.

The diminutive green locomotive that was going to propel the coach to Cheltenham Spa (Malvern Road) station before changing direction and pulling them north-eastwards, was one of the regulars and Krast recognised the crew. Not that he'd ever spoken with either men, of course. He was not much given to fraternising with workers and tradesmen. Nonetheless, he found it reassuring to see their familiar faces.

On board, everything was as it should be and unremarkable in its shabby familiarity. He slumped onto the dusty moquette bench seat of indeterminate colour under the dim reading lights, the luggage rack above sagging with rain-dampened coats. The usual passengers were doing what they usually did; reading their favourite papers in virtual silence save for the odd muttered expression about the 'bad weather,' 'the Government not having a clue' or how a football team was not doing well. None of these comments were cues to start a conversation and aside from the odd nod of a head, twitch of a paper or grunt of vague agreement, companionable silence was maintained. There was nobody onboard whose face was unfamiliar. His fevered imagination alone had conjured up those echoing footsteps...

Krast sat back in the cushions for the run up to Broadway, removed his glasses and started polished them with an expensive silk handkerchief to remove the rain spots. He liked this action. It was calming. Now, away from his shop, he had time to think more clearly about what had happened and perhaps more importantly, what he was going to do about it.

Someone had broken in the shop. No, that was not strictly correct. Someone had *entered* the premises, but there had been no breaking nor forcing of locks, no smashing of windows. Perhaps most disturbing of all, they had been inside his enormous safe and all without recourse to explosives or leaving so much as a single scratch that he could find. They'd even closed the safe door after them and scrambled the tumblers of the lock to make it secure. Safe? Secure? Bah! What a bad joke. Krast, forced a bitter grimace as he considered this startling fact.

Hard though it was to understand, somebody had been poking around, opening boxes and little cloth bags containing valuable rings and earrings or expensive luxury watches imported at great cost from Switzerland. They'd been searching for something specific and not looting the place. This was no 'smash and grab' as the tabloid papers liked to characterise such raids. However, they had not found whatever it was they wanted, because they had taken nothing. Not one item appeared to be missing. It beggared belief. He paused in his polishing as this startling fact once again hit home.

To go to all that trouble and not even take the prize diamond necklace or the valuable tiara which formed the centrepiece of his race-week window display? It was baffling.

Krast gently rubbed his eyes before replacing his glasses. He felt tired. The strain of the day was taking its toll. He closed his eyes and listened for a few minutes as locomotive number 1424 gently pulled away in response to that resonant clang of the guard's gong. They had changed direction and the short train was now boldly chuffing its way into the pitch-black night of the Cotswold hills.

He really should be relieved he'd lost not one shilling of stock - not that a shilling would buy anything in his establishment! He was holding an unusual level of stock in expectation of over-excited racegoers flush with winnings in their pockets bringing in their wives and girlfriends so they could extravagantly splash their cash. It happened every year and he'd learned to invest heavily in advance to ensure his display cases were filled with alluring items. If he'd been called out in the early hours by the constabulary to be greeted by a scene of wanton destruction left by a gang who'd raided his bumper haul of jewellery he would have been mortified, but not surprised. Theft was a constant worry in his profession and the insurance premiums never got easier to meet. However, instead of relief that all his stock was intact, he felt perplexed, and the acute level of anxiety was now making his heartburn flare.

Someone had wanted something specific and was prepared to go to great lengths to get it. Not only that, they had tried hard to not betray their presence, which was going to make it hard to report his suspicions to the police. What could he tell or show them? Nothing was missing, nothing damaged! He'd suffered no loss except his own sense of security and peace of mind. No, he could not call the police, and yet tonight he felt like a marked man.

Krast wondered if Mr Jeffries, his senior sales assistant, was aware of what had happened. Jeffries had not said a word all day. Miss Jephson had also shown no indication she'd noticed anything was not where it should be. Miss Jephson was always careful about how she handled the precious stock and surely would have spoken up if something was amiss.

Their silence was unsettling. Were they *pretending* not to notice?

Krast didn't like to think such black thoughts about two trusted employees, but Jeffries held a key and knew the code for the safe and could easily gain entry in the night. They both knew where everything was and could work quickly and efficiently and leave virtually no trace. But if theft was their intent, then surely there was no need for either to sneak in at night. They had ample time and opportunity to purloin whatever it was they wanted during the day.

Neither Jeffries nor Jephson could be responsible. And besides, *nothing was missing*! Why did this fact make his head ache so much? What crime was he trying to blame them for?

Loss or no loss, Krast had seen signs of the search. Subtle details, discernible only to someone who spent their working life in the same place. Items fractionally not as he'd left them; boxes stacked neatly, but in a different sequence. His photographic memory and obsessive desire for neatness and order made him certain, but despite these tiny mistakes there was no doubt that this had been the work of experts. He could be sure there would be no finger prints and trying to convince a sceptical policeman that he knew a pile of jewel boxes was stacked in a different order to how he'd left them on Saturday night was not going to wash.

What was gnawing at Krast was the disturbing thought that there was *one* specific thing for which the intruders might have been looking. They could have expected to find it in the safe. It was the logical place. If this was the case, then one reassuring detail was that this was something that neither Mr Jeffries nor Miss Jephson knew anything about. He'd made sure that neither had ever heard mention, let alone seen it. If this had been the motive, then it made sense why everything was left in place.

The problem was, Krast was not exactly sure where it was either...

* * * *

Sidney Pearson was one of the stable lads at Acre Vale and immediately sprang into action the moment the riders dismounted. There was a lot to do towelling down, then covering the horses with their blankets before watering and feeding them their carefully monitored dietary allowance. There was the drying, cleaning and storing of all the tack to attend to once the horses were feeding. Each lad or lass had their specific tasks to perform and accompanied by only the briefest exchanges of words or the occasional joke. Professionalism was key to the business, and Coldicott's reputation was based on results and an impressive record of training winners. He expected the same level of determination and attention to detail in everyone he employed and preferred the stable work to be undertaken in a quiet and determined manner.

The evening was already cold, and Pearson was feeling the damp creeping into his bones as he prepared to lead Chicory Blue into her stall. This mare was his favourite and she was in good shape for the coming Gold Cup, although if the running was as hard as the weather forecast suggested, it would not suit her. Pearson was delighted that Mr Coldicott now trusted him enough to look after this fine beast along with the other rising star of the stables, A'kira Kungota. He would be overseeing both horses on their respective race days later in the week. If either managed a win, he might see a welcome bonus come his way. His wages didn't go far, and he was always looking for a way to improve his lot. Getting the inside track on the form of the horses could be valuable if you knew how to use the information wisely.

Above the usual low murmur of sounds from the busy yard, Pearson caught the raised voice of Mr Coldicott. The trainer was standing some distance off and apparently in hot dispute with Lord Buckrose. Perhaps the wealthy owner was making unrealistic demands for his horse at Cheltenham. Money For Nothing was young, yet showing himself a decent runner and fancied by the bookies in the first three in The Broadway Novice's Steeplechase on Wednesday. It was one thing to show promise amidst the novice's, but the horse was a season off finishing even in the chasing pack in the Gold Cup. However, the talk around the stables suggested Lord Buckrose was desperate for his horse to run in this Blue Riband race. This was not the first time that trainer and owner had crossed swords on the subject.

Pearson knew it was bad form to stare let alone listen in, but after he'd guided Chicory Blue into her stall, he deliberately walked slowly across the yard to collect A'kira Kungota and took a longer gander at the two men whilst doing so. He might glean a little more inside information and who knows what someone might pay him for this 'gen'. It did no harm to remain alert. Trainer and owner were each giving as good as they got, and it appeared a heated discussion. However, moments later, as he led his horse back to the stalls, Pearson noticed they had settled their differences in double-quick time and parting with a polite handshake. A trainer had little choice but to take the demands of their paymaster on the chin and Coldicott knew when to tactfully withdraw.

Lord Buckrose stomped into the wet night, his customary bonhomie and sugary charm put aside for now. Pearson thought it odd the lord didn't drive his Bentley, or whatever impossibly expensive motor he owned, right into the yard but chose instead to take his chances walking through the muddy yard entrance and out of sight onto the approach drive. There was no accounting for these aristos! All mad as hatters from what Pearson had observed and working the Coldicott stable he'd encountered enough of them to form an opinion.

*　　*　　*　　*

The train pulled to a stop and someone got out at the pretty station of Toddington. Krast watched as the guard stepped onto the platform to check the train was clear to depart and without bothering to flap his furled green flag, stepped back aboard and clanged the gong like the call to dinner. With the briefest of toots on the whistle, the 'Coffeepot' chuffed into motion.

At Broadway, Krast was the only passenger to disembark, as usual. Rain was still falling and the wind, an almost constant companion on the Cotswolds in March, was soughing through the tall stand of Scots pines that were such a distinctive feature of the stations along this line. The sound was like that of waves washing on a pebbly beach.

Krast stood for a moment taking shelter beneath the over-reaching canopy that protected the modestly proportioned brick waiting room and Gents toilet block on the 'up' platform. He was unsure whether he wanted to hurry home. The intruders might have paid his house a visit whilst he was at work and this thought was disturbing. If a thousand pounds of jewellery stock was of no interest, then they were very particular and surely going to be disappointed by his house contents. However, that nagging voice inside reminded him that there was that *one* thing that might have piqued their interest. But how could they know about it? He'd acted with considerable discretion to ensure that almost nobody knew of it, let alone its whereabouts. Unless, of course, the owner had been indiscreet? It would be utterly foolish, but not impossible.

There was a series of soft beats from the engine as it gently hauled the solitary coach on towards Honeybourne, the wheels tick-ticking on the track joints. The signal arm clonked back to 'danger' as the signalman, high in his box some distance away, gave a cursory glance at the tiny figure with his distinctive hat standing on the platform. The signalman needed to update his log book and it was that time of evening when he knew he had a ten-minute gap before the next heavy goods from the Midlands was due. Time enough to empty the dregs from his teapot and get another brew on the go and he needed to step outside to the lavatory. British Railways ran on tea almost more than it did on coal and the signalman was no exception - but there were consequential calls of nature.

This unremarkable series of commonplace events conspired to ensure that the signalman, despite having a commanding view of the station, did not observe the last moments of Peter Krast's life.

Chapter Two

PC Malcolm Wentworth approached the waiting room door with trepidation. A dead body was not something he'd ever encountered. He'd seen the occasional sheep ploughed into by a speeding vehicle on one of the myriad twisting lanes across the rolling hills, but a dead man was a new and unnerving experience. All the more so, as the position of the sprawling figure lying face down in a position such as you might see in an Am-Dram Society Agatha Christie, suggested the death had been violent.

'He looks a gonner, Trev. You were right to call me in,' Wentworth stood in the doorway and played his torch beam over the body in what he hoped looked like a professional manner. The early morning March sky was overcast and the waiting room unlit and cold as the grave. 'However, I first need to establish that he is, in fact, officially dead.' Clouds of vapour issued from his mouth as he spoke. 'Call a doctor here at once, if you please.'

The stationmaster blinked. 'I reckon he's beyond needing a doctor, Malc.' The two men knew each other well, it being a small village and they sometimes played a game of dominoes in the Horse & Hound.

'Ah, now then Trev, you're forgetting that only a doctor can *medically* confirm what we both can see plainly for ourselves. It is a formality, but it needs doing all the same and in light of the seriousness of the situation I'd best make sure I follow correct procedure.'

'Of course. Everything must be done properly,' Stationmaster Trevor Roberts then issued the order to a young porter. 'Tell Dr. Quinn it is imperative he attend immediately! Jump to it!' Roberts was nervously fiddling with his hunter watch that hung from a gold chain from his waistcoat. 'Most distressing... I hardly know what to say... A dead body in my station. I never thought I'd live to see the day.'

'He didn't, that's for sure.'

PC Wentworth had now ventured closer and was peering intently at the corpse. The eyes were open and staring sightlessly at the prettily patterned tiled floor, his glasses lying a few feet away where they had landed as the man fell. One of the lenses had cracked. 'Do we know this gentleman?' He squatted to get closer. 'His face is familiar, although without those glasses...'

'Er, yes.' Roberts had edged closer to look at the face with its frozen expression of disbelief and the strange spots and livid stains where blood vessels had popped. 'The hat as much as anything else identifies him.' He indicated where the headgear in question had rolled under one of the benches. 'His name is Krast.'

'The jeweller? I reckon you're not wrong there.' Wentworth reached forward and tentatively pushed the shirt collar to one side with a finger. He then risked touching the waxy skin and made a face as he rapidly pulled his finger back. He stood up, knees cracking as he did so and took note of the hat and then nodded agreement. 'Peter Krast. Lives up the Fish Hill end of the High. His house has six windows and a door, just set back a bit.'

'Nice place if that's the one I'm thinking of. He had no family as I know. That's to say, I've never seen him with anyone who looks like family.'

'No wife, that's for sure. A confirmed bachelor I'd say.' Wentworth was starting to make a few jottings in his notebook. 'Might be tricky finding a next of kin. For identification purposes.'

'We've just identified him.'

'We have, but by rights we need a family member or close friend. To do things by the book.' The constable sighed. 'But our identification will suffice for now I suppose... Right! I need this area cordoned off and secured as a Scene Of Crime.' Roberts could almost hear the capital letters as Wentworth puffed out his chest and appeared more confident now that he'd discovered there were no nausea-inducing wounds or pints of blood on the floor. 'It might just be natural causes, but until the doctor tells me why he's dead, I'd best assume the worst.'

'Must you? Assume the worst?' Roberts looked agitated. 'It appears to me as though he's toppled over. A heart-attack. He could have stumbled into here feeling unwell. Perhaps for a sit down until he felt better...but it was not to be.'

'I'm not so sure, Trevor. I'm no expert, but I do not like the look of those marks on his neck. They strike me as odd. As though something was tied very tightly around his neck and then, you will notice that his eyes are wide and staring like he's been choked, and those red spots are worrying me. I also observe that his tie is loosened, and the top button of his shirt is missing as if ripped off when the collar was pulled apart with force. Mr Krast does not appear the sort of gentleman who walks around with a missing button and a tie in disarray.'

'He could have done that as the heart attack set on...He grabbed his throat and...' Roberts stopped. 'But yes, you could be right...' The stationmaster looked glumly at the dead man sprawled on his clean floor as if he were a casually discarded item of lost property that needed tidying away as quickly as possible. 'We could lock this door? That would ensure nobody entered whilst also preventing unnecessary alarm amongst our passengers.'

'I agree. Please hand me the key and I shall personally ensure the door is secured and remains so until further investigations take place. I then need to telephone this in to my sergeant and await instructions. I will personally maintain guard outside until reinforcements arrive!'

'Will this take awfully long?'

'Hard to say. But best part of today, I'd guess. Why?'

Roberts made a pained expression. 'We have a lot of traffic coming though for the festival. An army of policemen stomping about investigating a corpse is not quite the image we wish to promote. No offence, of course.'

'None taken.'

Both men stepped outside and closed the door.

PC Wentworth sniffed the air, glad to be outside. 'This hard frost is going to play havoc with the going. It won't suit the horses...'

'I heard there was snow forecast.'

'Hmm. There won't be much racing today then.'

Both men nodded sadly and inspected the ominous clouds. The imminent cancellation of a day's racing seemed to touch them deeper than the demise of Peter Krast. 'Try to keep a lid on all this as best you can, eh? I cannot countenance any *unpleasantness* here with so many racegoers passing through. We have a special due any moment.' Roberts glanced anxiously at his watch.

'At least he's out of sight.'

'Thank God for small mercies...' Roberts cleared his throat. 'I'm sure we could offer you a cup of strong, sweetened tea. I know I need one...'

'That would be most welcome!'

Chapter Two

The Broadway police were out in full strength. PC Wentworth had been joined by Sergeant Wilcox, and so the sum total of the local force was sitting on the Great Western Railway bench outside the waiting room, the door to which, remained locked. Mugs of tea were steaming in their hands as they awaited the arrival of the railway detectives.

Sergeant Wilcox had overseen the visit from the local doctor. Wilcox in a rash moment of over-confidence had agreed with the stationmaster that in all probability this was death by natural causes. This optimistic misconception changed when Dr Quinn solemnly declared that, 'Krast had died due to strangulation. A rope or similar ligature was thrown around his neck and drawn tight with considerable force from behind. Once on the slab, I fully expect to find bruising on his back or upper arms as the assailant brought considerable force to bear, levering against his back.'

Their worst fears were confirmed; this was now officially a murder case. Wilcox had silently questioned if he and the somewhat unimaginative Wentworth were really cut out for the job and wisely decided they needed outside help.

'We need to bring in the CID.' Wilcox declared whilst Doctor Quinn packed his bag and prepared to return back to his practice.

'Scotland Yard, Sarge?'

'Quite possibly... However, as the deceased travelled here by *train* (a fact we have satisfactorily established), *and* he undeniably died on railway premises and, (I venture to hazard) was killed by someone waiting on said railway premises, *and* -.' He paused for effect. 'The perpetrator possibly used the *railway* to effect their escape, (a fact not yet established), I feel it only proper the British Transport Police should be called in.'

'Put like that and it's not a constabulary matter.'

'Precisely. And they have a Detective Department!'

'They do? That settles it.' PC Wentworth was not in the least bit dismayed by this decision. He'd never quite recovered from a shameful episode last summer when he'd joined an impromptu kick-about with the local kids living in the railway houses adjacent to the station. His ambitious sliced shot towards the chalked goal posts had smashed through a pane of glass in the ladies waiting room and he'd hurriedly slunk off, allowing the children to take the blame. It had been an outrageous dereliction of both duty and responsibility. It had not been long before the truth was out and his scandalous behaviour marked a particularly low point in local policing within the village.

Wilcox spent some time in the stationmaster's office on the telephone. Eventually, the matronly voice of the telephone exchange operator advised him that she was connecting him to The Detective Department in Leicester Central railway station.

A few minutes later he replaced the Bakelite handset on its stand and breathed a sigh of relief. The detectives were on their way and he'd been given a clear set of instructions to follow whilst awaiting their arrival. It felt like a weight had lifted from his shoulders. There was also the professional thrill of having a ringside view of these experts in action. Just wait until he told the wife this evening!

There was plenty to do between swigging tea. The news of a body at Broadway station was spreading across the village as it woke up and prepared for school or work. A group of women and children from the railway cottages close by were gathered on the opposite platform, gossiping with arms folded across their chests whilst trying to get a glimpse of the body. PC Wentworth had made it clear that unless anyone was catching a train, they were not welcome to cross the bridge onto the 'Up' platform, much to the dismay of the local children.

Somehow, a member of the press had already got wind of this scoop and motorbiked over from Gloucester and was trying to get an official statement. This request had been firmly rebuffed by Wilcox, and the young man simply resorted to noting down idle tittle-tattle, which became evermore gory as the minutes ticked by and collective imaginations exaggerated the snippets of facts known to the villagers.

There was a flurry of activity when a forensic team and photographer arrived, having been summoned by the far-reaching influence of the yet-to-arrive detectives. This impressed PC Wentworth. 'They click their fingers and look who turns up. They've come down from Stratford. Closest team available, they said.'

'Yes, we're dealing with professionals here. The Detective Department is clearly run like a well-oiled machine. You should look and learn!' Sergeant Wilcox was nursing yet another mug of tea as he watched the fingerprint man dust silvery powder around the waiting room door handle whilst an underfed individual in a long rain mac was quietly assembling his photographic gear and eying up the bacon sandwich in Wentworth's hand.

Chapter Three

Chief Inspector Vignoles would not describe his team as a well-oiled machine. Not since the start of the year, anyway.

He was staring out of the carriage window watching coils of dirty smoke drift lazily across water-logged fields edged by scrappy hedges studded with the dark skeletons of leafless trees. Spring was likely to be late this year.

He watched as the engine momentarily slid into view as it throatily chuffed towards Honeybourne and thence to Broadway, their destination. The fireman appeared to be battling with a tender of poor coal on his engine, perhaps causing the fire to clinker and burn badly. Whatever the reason, they were making heavy weather of it. If only that was all Vignoles had to deal with...

Come to think of it, his Department was not unlike a recalcitrant steam engine. It got up steam and could be induced to run and might even reach its destination, but it did so only after significant effort and attention from the driver. And Vignoles was the over-worked driver of this extended analogy.

Even a sickly locomotive could be induced to perform tolerably if both footplate crew worked in harmony to manage the situation and reacted to the subtle nuances informing them of what was going wrong. Vignoles pulled a wry smile at his own reflection in the glass. He and his fireman, otherwise known as Detective Sergeant Mellor, were hardly working in tune with each other. They were like the proverbial chalk and cheese and Vignoles was calling on his reserves of self-control to resist tearing into the man.

Not that DS Mellor was a slacker. He was bright as a button and seemed to possess almost boundless energy. There was no denying he put in the hours. Mellor was efficient and competent and Vignoles never had to ask twice for something to be done. It was just the way he did it...

Vignoles knew he was not being reasonable, yet try as he might, Vignoles sensed that for all his abilities as a copper, Mellor was not quite the right man for his team. Mellor was like that enticing summer signing for a football team, who, based on past form, looked to be the next big thing for the club, but once signed never fitted in and the balance of the team became skewed, leading inevitably to the player moving on after a lacklustre season or two. Vignoles silently wondered how soon he could induce Mellor to submit a transfer request.

The root of the problem was that Mellor had not even been an enticing prospect, let alone Vignoles's choice. The selection of a suitable DS to take over from John Trinder, now promoted to the rank of DI and sent into the wilds of North Wales, had rumbled into January and Vignoles had ended up locking horns with his tormentor, Chief Superintendent Badger over the appointment. Vignoles had anticipated there was going to be a difference of opinion and steeled himself for a rough time of it and argued for his own choice until blue in the face. But Badger was having none of it.

'A woman? You cannot be serious, Vignoles? The idea is utterly preposterous.'

'Benson's track record is exemplary...'

'That is irrelevant; a skirt cannot be a DS.'

'That she's a woman is irrelevant, surely? Benson consistently excels in all she does and makes significant decisions that solve cases. That's all the 'relevance' I require.'

'She's a WPC! Women are *not* DS material!' Badger had slapped the desk decisively. 'Dear me, no, no...' Badger had looked astounded, almost lost for words. 'They file things and do so efficiently, that I accept; they type far better than us and make far better tea and provide biscuits...' He'd flapped his hands dismissively. 'They look pleasing to the eye and are excellent at comforting the bereaved and distressed. One far prefers a woman to offer solace to an upset mother or child, of course.' Badger almost looked pleased at this generous demonstration of magnanimity. 'All skills that have their place, but girls are simply not cut out for the kind of work needed in a DS.'

'WPC Benson is not a 'girl' and has been at the heart of all our investigations for many years often facing up to the dangerous perpetrators of crime and has handled herself admirably. She is fearless.'

'And there hangs another problem. What would the newspapers say if they got wind of us letting a woman face mortal danger? What if she were badly hurt - or worse? My God, Charles, the balloon would go up then! We'd be hung out to dry in double-quick time. Believe me we'd be for the high jump putting a woman in the firing line. No, this is foolish nonsense. All very Liberal-minded I'm sure, but this wooly idealism about equality is not for the dangerous world of front-line policing. For Heaven's sake, we face knife-wielding lunatics and villains with guns.'

Vignoles was not sure the last time Badger had faced anything more dangerous than a stiff round of golf but remained silent. 'This is not the proper place for a woman. Put this idea aside and we'll say no more about it.' Badger gave a conciliatory smile. 'Now, as you know, I have *exactly* the man you need ready to step up to the mark! He's the tops.'

So, Mellor it was.

Vignoles sighed and turned from the window and observed the man in question. He was certainly a live-wire, with a knee bobbing with nervous energy and restless, roving eyes. 'Brim full of vitality and sharply observant,' would be Badger's assessment and perhaps not inaccurate, but Mellor didn't always know how to best channel his energies. He seemed habitually restless, and even now, was chain-smoking with almost angry inhalations on his cigarette.

As a Londoner born and bred, Mellor didn't like the countryside very much. This had become obvious when he'd fielded a telephone call early that morning as they were both entering the office to start their day.

'We've got a shout, guv! A stiff...Some old geezer,' this said between puffs on a 'fag' as Mellor would insist on calling them. 'Found flat on his face in a waiting room, first thing.'

Vignoles had tried hard not to wince at the casual and slang-riddled description. 'Does this particular 'old geezer' have a name?'

'Yeah, but it's foreign. Crass, Crust or summat like that.'

'Neither sound especially alien to my ears. The least you could do is confer the dignity of the correct name on the deceased.' Vignoles was trying to be patient and ended up sounding pompous. This didn't help his mood. 'Why does this gentleman's unfortunate demise require our attention?'

'Because he's been snuffed out on a railway station!' A pause. 'Sir.'

'Any indication as to how?'

A long exhalation of smoke preceded Mellor's reply. 'Yeah, a local doctor gave him the once over and reckons he was strangled. Attacked from behind and left for dead in a darkened waiting room. Probably killed last night the doc reckons and only found when the station woke up this morning.'

'Then we'd better take a look. Remind me, where did this incident occur?' *I know darned well you didn't tell me, but you're going to learn to pass on pertinent information,* Vignoles was seething silently.

'Broadway! The only one I know is in Ealing. Apart from in New York, of course.' Mellor actually started to hum 'Give My Regards To Broadway.'

'Then I hope the caller clarified the location. It would not do to sail to New York in vain...'

'It was a sergeant in the local constabulary who rang it in. Said it was down Cheltenham way. Out in the sticks.' Mellor shrugged his shoulders dismissively and pulled a face. 'Never heard of it.'

'Then the village in question probably lent its name to the more famous but considerably younger cousin in New York,' Vignoles replied tartly. *The less said about the dismal example in west London, probably the better.*

Mellor was already thumbing through the Shell road atlas on his desk to find the location. 'It really is in the bleedin' middle of nowhere.'

'By 'nowhere' you presumably mean the Cotswolds. A lovely part of England.'

'All fields and trees and...animals.'

'Cotswold sheep don't bite.'

Mellor realised he was being mocked. 'I never feel quite at home in the country. Too dark at night and full of inclement weather and wet grass for my taste.' He actually shivered.

'You'll survive. Plot a path there and we'll get on the way. It's a fair haul.'

'The Rover has a full tank and ready to roll.'

'We're taking the train.'

Mellor looked crestfallen and slapped the book shut.

Vignoles stood up and reached for his hat and coat. 'Come on, I've an idea what connections will get us to Stratford-upon-Avon. Get Blencowe to double-check connections onwards from there. Tell him to rustle up something special if necessary. If this is murder, we need no delay. Blencowe can telephone Stratford to advise us of the plan.'

*　　*　　*　　*

His car was pulled off the road on the grass beside the Stanley War Memorial. Lord Buckrose was seated and leaning against the bronze plaque listing the fallen in the Great War whilst he finished a cigarette. He'd been buffing his shoes using the cleaning set he kept in a draw-string bag in the boot of the Humber. The soles were thin, but ten minutes of assiduous work with the kit and they sparkled like new if you didn't look closely and spot the seam starting to unravel. Throwing the cigarette butt aside, he stood up and delved into the suitcase that lay open in the boot. Just the one fresh shirt. He needed the others cleaned and pressed without delay. A clean and sharply ironed shirt, even if the collar was rubbed, was essential. Despite the rawness of the early morning, he hurriedly unbuttoned the shirt he was wearing and tossed it into the boot. He put on the last fresh one and immediately looked and felt more like Lord Buckrose. He had a small mirror glued onto the inside of the lifted lid and by bending his knees could see enough to form a decent Windsor knot in a striped silk tie.

He ignored the tweed hunting jacket he'd worn yesterday and selected his Saville Row charcoal grey that matched his trousers and shrugging this on as he stood up and stretched. He'd judged correctly that the road leading down to the sleepy village would see little traffic and until now nothing had passed by whilst he'd prepared himself for the day ahead. If a vehicle appeared, experience taught him to be confident; act natural, as if slipping on a fresh shirt and polishing your shoes beside a war memorial in the bitter March air was the most natural thing to do. A man acting confidently rarely attracted undue attention. He checked his watch, fished out a square of silk, skillfully folded it and pushed it into the breast pocket. He opened his silver monogrammed cigarette case and with a rueful expression confirmed he only had three of the expensive Sobranie cigarettes left. He would need to restock. *Another outlay he could ill afford...* He slipped the case into his jacket then took a crumpled Player's from the pack squashed into the tweeds he'd worn yesterday evening at the stables. This was his usual smoke. Cheap and cheerful, reserved for when not being observed. Such attention to detail was important. It required a few pounds of investment assembling these essentials; the tailored suit, the cufflinks, the silk tie, the silver case and the extravagant cigarettes, but it was worth it when offset against the fortune he was chasing. He just needed to restock his depleted wallet. The banks would soon open and he must tackle the tricky challenge of exuding an air of confidence that bordered arrogance whilst drawing on a suspect account.

Or would he get the good news he was eagerly craving? He was anxious to place that telephone call and hear how things were shaping up. He was fretting about the delay. Why was that man keeping him waiting? Had something gone awry?

Action was the best remedy for worry. Lord Buckrose closed the boot lid and gave the car a quick appraisal. Unsatisfied with what he saw, he slipped on his driving gloves and took a rag from underneath the passenger seat and gave the dullest spots a quick burnish, then ran the cloth over some brightwork to add lustre to a car showing her age. The gentry often drove humble cars when they didn't need their chauffeur-driven Rolls or Bentley, but there was still a line between a decent hard-working runabout and an old banger fit for the scrap man. He stood back and squinted at the results. It would pass muster from distance and in low light. A shower of rain wouldn't go amiss. Rain darkened the colour and the water droplets flattered ageing paint. He sniffed the air and looked at the grey clouds and sensed sleet or even snow. That would be perfect, even if it meant he froze in the car at night. However, he'd best park her down a side street in Cheltenham and he could always take the train to the races. As he started the motor a cloud of oily exhaust erupted at the rear. Or should he hire something more suitable?

'A sprat to catch a mackerel!' Lord Buckrose spoke words aloud to the freezing air and then laughed as he pulled away. If the telephone call he was going to make brought him the news he was expecting, he could buy himself a Bentley - in cash. He could buy two! He laughed uproariously like a man who'd had a tremendous weight lifted from his shoulders.

*　*　*　*

'Nearly there, gents.' The guard slid open the compartment door. 'I've walked the length of the train and advised passengers we shall be making an unscheduled stop of less than one minute at Broadway and they are not to alight. If you could come through to my compartment? I shall let you out there, then immediately flag the train off.'

Mellor looked relieved and stood up. He was like a caged animal.

Stepping onto the platform, they were greeted by stationmaster Trevor Roberts who appeared flustered and anxious in equal parts, and by a small crowd of eager onlookers wanting to get a glimpse of the visiting detectives. It was immediately obvious that despite being a generously proportioned station building with an impressive awning running the full length and a sturdy covered footbridge, this was little more than a sleepy wayside halt masquerading as a big station. It was improbable that the village had ever witnessed such drama.

Mellor glowered at those observing him and at the school girls giggling excitedly with flushed cheeks. He made it clear they needed to 'stand back and let us through,' the order bellowed in an uncompromising manner. The detectives and stationmaster climbed the wooden stairs of the bridge as the train coughed asthmatically as it continued towards Cheltenham, where the fireman could finally give his fire a thorough clean and hopefully fill the tender with decent Welsh coal before the return trip.

'The er...body is over the bridge. In the waiting room,' Roberts explained.

'Forensics on site?' Mellor barked. He was confidently leading the way despite this being his first time on the station.

'The finger print gentlemen are just finishing their investigations and there is a man with a camera on site. We kept this side of the station cordoned off as best we could. There was a train for Stratford that saw no passengers, and then there was the 'Coffeepot', but as the solitary early morning regular user of that particular service is...er...deceased, there was no one getting on or off to disturb the crime scene.'

'Did you just say *coffee pot*?' Mellor stopped in his tracks.

Stationmaster Roberts coughed apologetically. 'The local auto-train service between Honeybourne and St James. That's what we call it.' He looked embarrassed. It sounded parochial and perhaps a little foolish when explained to important detectives in their smart suits, long coats and nice hats.

'They sell coffee onboard?' Mellor looked confused.

'I think you'll find it's an affectionate term bestowed upon the Great Western steam railmotor that once operated along this line and my guess is the name stuck,' Vignoles stepped in.

'Quite correct, Inspector,' Stationmaster Roberts was impressed Vignoles knew something of their line. 'It had an upright boiler that burbled away as though it was brewing coffee.'

'Jesus wept...' Mellor muttered under his breath as he stepped onto the platform. 'Right, gents. What you got for us?' He directed the question towards the forensics team and the two local coppers standing guard with mugs of tea at the ready. All heads turned in response.

Sergeant Wilcox stepped forward and a brief exchange of names and handshakes followed. 'In here. He's exactly as found.'

Mellor followed Wilcox into the small waiting room, Vignoles took time to take in the immediate surroundings, before joining them.

'Can we have some light? I can't see a bleedin' thing!'

'I've been advised the gas mantles have been playing up and one of them kept going out and filling the room with unburnt gas. As a consequence, the station staff left the waiting room unlit last night. They're expecting new mantles anytime soon. Until then, we're in the dark,' Wilcox explained.

'Still using gas? That went out with the bleedin' Ark in London...' Mellor was not impressed. 'This room was pitch dark all night?'

'Correct.'

'And unlocked?'

'Also correct.'

'Anyone could come in here and not be seen?'

'I'd say that would be a correct assumption.' Wilcox felt as though he was being interrogated.

Mellor was pacing around the sprawled figure of Krast. 'Give me your torch,' he clicked his fingers towards PC Wentworth, who hurriedly handed it over. Mellor played the beam over the glassy eyes of the corpse. 'Guv, what's that mark on his neck?'

'Looks like it was made by a ligature of some kind.' Vignoles called the photographer over. 'I presume you photographed his neck in detail?'

'Yes, sir.'

'We need the prints pronto. We still need to find a place to stay, so get 'em delivered to the stationmaster, marked for my attention.' Mellor barked the order.

'Understood, sir. I'll go and process the film now.'

Vignoles turned to Wilcox. 'What did the doctor say about these marks?'

'He suggested that death was through strangulation. From behind, and with force. He wants to have a look at the man's back to see if there is bruising. He identified those red spots as burst blood vessels and his eyes are red for the same reason.'

'Have you identified the deceased?'

'Peter Krast. A jeweller. He has a shop in Cheltenham.'

'Ah ha, there you go! Got a bob or two tucked away, I bet! There's your motive.' Mellor looked pleased.

'He lived in Broadway?' Vignoles pressed on, ignoring his DS.

'He did. I have his address written down and that of his premises in Cheltenham. It being a working day, I expect the shop staff are wondering what's become of the old gent. Poor blighter...'

'Family?'

'None that we are aware of. PC Wentworth and I are of the opinion he's a bachelor.'

'When was the body discovered?' Mellor asked.

'At six o'clock this morning when one of the porters was checking the station over.'

'Did the doctor give any indication of when death occurred?'

'He reckoned early yesterday evening. He was stone cold after being here all night which makes it hard to be more accurate, apparently.'

'Do we know what time he arrived at the station?' Vignoles asked.

'We understand he took the 5.55 out of St James that stopped here at 6.37.'

'That fits. Killed on his way home from work...' Mellor was making notes and then asked for the name and address of the porter who had discovered the body. 'Were any keys found on the body?'

'No, sergeant.'

'Then he was attacked to get his shop and house keys. Very lucrative...'

'Especially if he had his safe key on the same fob.' Vignoles and Mellor exchanged glances.

'You think he was jumped by someone wanting to get in his shop and turn it over?' PC Wentworth asked.

'Looks that way.' Mellor was emphatic. 'No witnesses?'

''Fraid not, sergeant. The station is quiet and it being a rainy night, those on duty were indoors, not looking onto the platforms.'

'Odd nobody found him earlier?'

'Not really, sergeant.' Stationmaster Roberts replied. 'We have few stopping trains in the evening and even fewer people waiting to board or get off. We can check if anyone bought a ticket or was waiting, but a cold and blacked-out waiting room would not have been inviting.' He coughed apologetically. 'We find that most passengers tend to congregate on the 'down' side then cross the bridge only when they see their train approaching.'

'I need names and addresses of everyone on duty yesterday,' Mellor replied. 'Times on and off. We'll be interviewing everyone and so they must make themselves available. No excuses.'

'I'll see to it,' and the stationmaster hurried off. He seemed relieved to have something to do.

'Has anyone contacted the shop?' Mellor continued to fire questions.

'We wanted to wait for your arrival before taking further action.'

'Then we don't know if has been done over? Or if there's another stiff lying there?' Mellor was horrified.

'No...' Wilcox admitted.

'Best get onto his shop, toot-bloody-sweet. We can't have word of mouth reaching them before we turn up,' Mellor faced Vignoles. 'We need to take a gander around his gaff as well. I wouldn't be surprised if it hadn't been turned over.'

Vignoles, who had been quietly making his own inspection of the room without appearing to take much notice of the exchanges, agreed. He was holding a shirt button in a gloved hand. 'Telephone the shop and advise them of the unfortunate turn of events - assuming the shop staff are present and unhurt. They must close the shop both in deference to the situation and to preserve what may be a crime scene. They must not leave until we interview them nor must they touch anything in the shop. We'll go straight there. And bag this. I suspect it matches the others on Mr Krast's shirt.' He handed the button over.

Mellor walked out onto the platform to look for a telephone box.

'It would be quicker if I ran you both to Cheltenham in my police car,' Wilcox offered. 'Stopping trains are infrequent, despite the heavy rail traffic that passes through.'

'I'd appreciate that. Not just quicker, but as Transport Police, I think it wise to have an officer from the local force present. The shop will be off railway property and technically outside our remit.'

Wilcox gave a nod of approval. He was keen to spend more time with the detectives.

Vignoles stepped out of the gloomy waiting room onto the platform. 'The ambulance crew have arrived,' observing the two uniformed men with a folding gurney on wheels standing underneath the roof canopy protecting the gated entrance and the gap between the station building and the footbridge. 'Once the body has been removed, could I ask that PC Wentworth stands sentry outside Krast's house until our return from Cheltenham?'

'Of course.' Wilcox looked at Wentworth. 'Is your bike handy?'

'Yes, sir! I'll go straight away.' He saluted and turned to leave.

Vignoles caught the attention of the man wielding a soft brush and a tin of aluminium powder used for tracing finger prints. 'I need you to hang fire. Take a break and grab some tea and toast. You may well be needed at the deceased's shop and at his home.'

Chapter Four

The shop was painted a glossy black with gleaming door furniture and everything was commendably clean. Even the windows sparkled, despite the fresh raindrops splattered on the panes. KRAST JEWELLERS Est.1945 was emblazoned in gold leaf across the signboard. It exuded an air of wealth and luxury and conversely presented an off-putting and faintly intimidating air to those with modest bank balances.

The door was locked and a 'closed' sign displayed, but in answer to a sonorous bell a young woman with red-rimmed eyes opened the door. She looked cautiously through the gap created by a hefty brass security chain she'd left in place.

'Please do not be alarmed. Police.' Vignoles proffered his warrant card and made the introductions.

'Thank goodness!' The chain was released, and the door opened. 'We've been so worried! Mr Jeffries has been calling Mr Krast's home all morning and even his local railway station and we still don't know what's happened and... Oh dear!' She stopped and blew her nose.

A tall, skeletal man in his early 50s hovered close. 'Mr Jeffries. Colin Jeffries.' He held out a hand. 'I am Mr Krast's senior sales assistant, and this is Miss Jephson. Can you please tell us what has happened? We've heard some truly alarming rumours, but surely they cannot be true...?'

'I regret to inform you that Mr Krast is dead,' Vignoles replied. He saw no reason to delay the stark facts from these two a moment longer.

A short sob from Miss Jephson and more use of the hankie.

'He was attacked on Broadway station last night. It was a violent assault.' Mellor was studying Jeffries' reaction as he delivered the shocking details.

'How dreadful.' Jeffries made a sign of the cross. 'Poor Peter...' He lowered his eyes.

'We found no keys about his person,' Mellor continued. 'It is our belief he was attacked so the perpetrator could take these and gain access to the shop. Has the shop been turned over?'

Jeffries cleared his throat. 'If by that you imply, have we been robbed, then the answer is an emphatic no.'

'Are you quite sure?' Mellor was taken aback.

'Yes, quite sure.' He sniffed in a contemptuous manner.

Whilst this exchange took place Vignoles was observing the reactions of the two sales assistants and running his expert eye over the glass cabinets filled with necklaces and gleaming rings bearing sparkling stones and the rows of wedding bands in velvet lined cases. All looked in order. 'You set everything out each morning?'

'Every evening we carefully put everything away in their correct boxes and place them in exactly the same storage place. We then repeat the reverse exercise each morning.'

Mellor muttered something under his breath suggesting he thought this a waste of time and effort.

'There is a safe in the back office. Common sense and the exacting requirements of our insurance company demand we take such measures,' Jeffries felt the need to justify their actions. 'All but the most valuable items are stored in the safe.'

'It looks like you've put everything out this morning as usual?' DS Wilcox asked, feeling he should make his presence felt.

'I unlock in the morning and Alice and I then set the shop out as we always do,' Jeffries replied. 'We had no reason to suspect anything was amiss and opened up. It was only when Mr Krast failed to arrive or telephone in that we sensed something was wrong.'

'Is he often late?' Mellor fired back.

'Almost never. He does, exceptionally, receive a telephone call or private visit at his home from one or other of our more, er, *discreet* customers, and that can sometimes cause him to forgo his usual train.'

'What sort of customers are those?' Mellor was intrigued.

'Those that like to keep their business *very* private, as I have already explained.' Jeffries sniffed in a haughty manner. 'We deal with some important clients who do not wish to draw attention to themselves.' Jeffries drew himself up tall and was starting to put up subtle defences against overly-inquisitive questions.

'This is a murder enquiry. We need to know everything and anything and this talk about discretion won't wash.' Mellor was bristling.

'I could not tell you more even if I so wished. Neither Alice nor I are privy to conversations that take place in Mr Krast's home. Obviously.' He gave a supercilious smile that would freeze a hot spring in Iceland.

Vignoles was silently wincing at Mellor's approach. It was too early to turn on the heat and risk losing their co-operation. He stepped in. 'The circumstances of Mr Krast's death are such that we shall need to look over the sales transactions of the last few months. This will require you to share information about all your customers. This is routine. You can rest assured that everything will he handled with discretion.' Vignoles was trying to soften these opening gambits and took a small step between Mellor and Jeffries. 'Have you noticed anything missing, no matter how small? Obtaining the keys to the shop would appear the most compelling motive for the attack.'

'Nothing whatsoever. If I had discovered even one item missing, I would have called the constabulary immediately.'

'Miss Jephson? Alice...' Vignoles smiled gently at the young woman and deliberately used her Christian name.

She shook her head. 'It's all as it should be.' She gave Jeffries a nervous look as his withering stare bored into the side of her head. 'We follow a strict order setting out and putting away each piece. That ensures nothing is overlooked...'

'As I have already explained...' Jeffries interjected.

'You'd know straight off if something was missing?' Mellor interjected.

She nodded her head and fiddled with her handkerchief, hands shaking slightly. Mellor then peered into a locked cabinet filled with gleaming jewellery, but not before running an approving eye over the figure of the young sales assistant. She had good legs shown off by an expertly tailored dress moulded informatively to her body and ending just below the knee.

'How did he...die? Was it very awful?' Jephson asked.

'There is no easy way to put this. Mr Krast was strangled. I'm no expert, but I think it might at least have been quick.' DS Wilcox explained, the rich burr of his local accent knocking the edges off the bleak description.

'Oh!' The handkerchief was redeployed.

'No jewellery is missing, so what about cash, personal papers or uncashed cheques?' Mellor asked Jeffries.

'I've had no cause to look over the office paperwork this morning, although everything looks in order and the float in the cash register is correct.'

'You must have a tidy sum of cash over night?'

'Actually, we don't. Saturday afternoons we make a drop in the Night Safe of the Cheltenham Savings Bank to clear the shop of takings and on busy weeks we do the same every evening. The float is a modest twenty pounds. Hardly worth killing for...'

'You have access to the safe?' Mellor continued.

'Mr Krast and I have a key each.' Jeffries said this the air of a man pleased to be entrusted with such responsibility.

Vignoles signalled to Mellor. 'Go through the paperwork and the safe contents with a fine comb with Mr Jeffries.'

Mellor perked up. He was keen to prove the arrogant Jeffries wrong. It was impossible to believe the shop owner had been murdered, his keys taken and the shop remain untouched. 'Open it up and let's have a gander.' The two men went into office.

Vignoles walked behind the sales desk. 'All is as it should be, Alice?'

Miss Jephson nodded.

'Have there been any unusual visitors, letters or telephone calls in the last few days?'

'In what way unusual?'

'Oh, I expect you get all kinds in here. Not the exactly the clientele one would expect in a grocery store, for example.' He smiled with a twinkle in his eye. Miss Jephson was not going to be much use unless he could get her to relax. Removing Jeffries and Mellor into the back office was his opportunity. 'A small number of regulars I expect, but most will be first-time enquirers, is that correct?'

'Yes, sir.'

'And I expect you get a few mooching around with no money to spend but happy to look and waste your time whilst keeping you on your toes?'

Jephson laughed and her face improved considerably for doing so. 'Oh Lordy, yes. I have to keep smiling sweetly and show them everything and yet I know it is quite futile.' She giggled. She was starting to unwind after the initial shock. 'After a while one gets quite good at spotting them and...' She gave a glance towards the back office. 'I confess we sometimes don't even let them in if we don't like their look. We keep the chain on the door most of the time. It sounds awful I suppose, but you get so you can tell who can buy and who can't before they even enter the shop.'

'Please explain...' Vignoles gave a beaming smile of approval.

'Clothes can be a giveaway, although one must be careful as they can mislead too. The horsey set around here often wear old gear stained with mud and grass and come in with muddy boots, but still buy the most expensive items!' She giggled. 'Some of the richest people dress quite shabbily at times, although you can usually tell the clothes were expensive when new. Of course, there are others who scream wealth with their bespoke tailored gowns, suits and coats and the triple rows of river pearls and a waft of delicious perfume...'

Vignoles nodded approvingly. She was an observant young woman.

'Eyes are a good indicator.' She was starting to get into her stride. 'Even how they enter the shop gives you an instant impression. If you can't afford to buy anything, the way you carry yourself is a give-away.'

'You would make a fine detective!' Vignoles looked at Wilcox, who nodded his head in agreement. 'Has anyone set you on alert recently?'

'Not really...'

'No odd balls? Someone who struck you as a potential strangler...' Vignoles deliberately make light of the appalling truth to try and keep this witness at her ease.

'Cripes, no! We had a rich toff with a monocle and smelling like a flower shop who came in to inspect our most flamboyant engagement rings, but he was hardly the murdering type! Quite typical of the sort you see in Cheltenham in the build-up to the racing. He said if he had luck with a horse, he'd make an honest woman of his best gal.' She giggled.

Vignoles could imagine the type. Time to change tack. 'Yesterday evening. What time did you leave?'

'Half-past five on the dot as usual. Mr Krast usually stays a little longer after Mr Jeffries and I leave.'

'And later in the evening, you did what?'

'I went straight home. I live with my parents. It's about a fifteen-minute walk. I was rather chilled and damp when I got in and so I changed. We then had our tea and we watched television together. I turned in early as I have a book I'm enjoying, and it was lights out by ten-thirty. Not a lot to tell!'

'You parents can confirm that I suppose?' It was Mellor back again.

'Of course.'

Mellor was looking disappointed. 'All as it should be back there, guv. Least ways, everything neat and orderly and Jeffries *says* nothing's been filched.' He shrugged his shoulders. 'Whatever they were after, it was not here. I reckon we'd best get up to his house.'

Chapter Five

'Colin Jeffries has an alibi for last night?'

'He does. Home to his sick wife, same as every evening for the last year or more. She's got cancer and often bed-ridden. She rarely leaves the house.' Mellor was checking his note book. 'They ate, he washed up, listened to the wireless until a neighbour called in about eight o'clock and then all had a cuppa together for an hour. They were in bed by ten or thereabouts.' Mellor sounded disinterested as he recounted the story. 'I'll get his missus and the neighbour to confirm it all, but he hardly looks a prime suspect.'

'What if he snuck out later? Once his wife was asleep? Maybe she takes a sleeping draught?' Wilcox, who was driving, was eager to offer his own contribution.

'Possible... But it won't work for the murder. His alibi won't get him on Broadway station early enough to bump off Krast. Even if he could, why risk killing the old man in a public place?' Mellor replied.

'Neither he nor Miss Jephson are promising suspects for a night-time raid, let alone his murder,' Vignoles replied.

'You say that, but what about the girl? I mean, she's got a *television*. On shop girl wages?' Mellor spoke with all the moral outrage of a man who could not afford one himself.

'Hardy a crime to rent a television, sergeant. She lives with her parents. I imagine they acquired a set for the Coronation, like many others did. And besides, she does not have a key to the shop nor the safe.'

'And nothing was stolen...' Wilcox added.

This startling fact that seemed to fly in the face of brutal murder and missing keys, silenced them all for the remainder of the drive back to Broadway.

Wilcox swung the car to a halt outside a house built of Cotswold stone with matching stone tiled roof and pretty diamond paned leaded windows. Roses and a wisteria waiting for the kiss of sun before blooming, draped along the eaves and around an oak front door which stood ajar, at the top of three shallow steps.

PC Wentworth was anxiously hovering on the top step and rushed towards them, throwing a nervous glance into the dark of the interior.

'Glad you're back! I've got them inside. Caught them red-handed I did!'

'Caught who?' It was Wilcox who replied, although all three climbing out of the car were formulating the same question.

'A couple. Pair of kids really. In the house they were and acting suspiciously. Said the door was open when they got here. A likely story! I've got them handcuffed together so they couldn't run off.'

Wilcox strode purposefully inside, hotly followed by Vignoles and Mellor.

The pair in question were seated side by side on a heavy wooden settle in front of a stone fireplace that had a heap of cold ashes and a partly burnt log in the grate. They looked more like embarrassed school kids than cold-blooded killers.

Wilcox addressed his constable. 'Start by telling your side of the story. Then these two can tell the detectives their version.' He was at pains to make the shared policing arrangement work.

'I cycled here as instructed and was preparing to stand guard until your arrival when my eye noticed something not quite right, and upon closer inspection saw the door was not locked and pulled tight...'

'It was ajar?' Mellor interjected.

'Correct. I pushed the door wide with my gloved hand, not wishing to add my dabs to a potential crime scene and stepped inside, playing my flashlight about as I did, it being somewhat dark in here as you can judge now for yourselves due to the small windows and poor light outside due to the inclement weather...'

Mellor sighed impatiently. *Get on with it!*

'...I heard voices and a scuffling and found these two attempting to leave the building via the kitchen door - which was locked, and they could not make their escape. I asked them why they were here and upon who's authority and was unsatisfied with their answers. Bearing in mind the gravity of the situation concerning the owner of said property, I duly apprehended them.'

'And who are these two?' Wilcox asked the constable, but he was glaring at the young couple huddled uncomfortably together, a look of recognition dawning on his face as his eyes grew accustomed to the gloomy interior.

'Mr Ian Twister, 19, goods porter and resident of this village, and Miss Elsie Gable, 18, carriage cleaner and resident in Bishops Cleeve.'

'Twister! I've known your dad since we were at school together. You'd better have a darned good explanation. Explain yourself, and no funny stuff!' Wilcox then indicated with a glance he would like Vignoles to take over.

'What were you doing in Mr Krast's house?'

'The door was not locked,' Twister snapped back.

'We only have your word for that. Either way, it remains private property. An unlocked door is no excuse to enter a dwelling without permission.'

'We never touched nothing! We're not thieves.'

'Came in to look at his wallpaper, did yer?' Mellor was sarcastic. 'Try again.'

'We meant no harm, honest we didn't. We're not trying to take nothing that's not ours.' Elsie Gable piped up.

'Then you *were* trying to take something?' Mellor snarled back.

'Are you aware that Mr Krast has been killed? He was murdered at Broadway station yesterday evening,' Vignoles added gravely. They both remained silent, but the young woman nodded her head. 'Then you will appreciate why we find your presence in his house suspicious. This is a murder enquiry and you should answer our questions honestly no matter what your reasons for being here might be. Lying under these circumstances is a punishable offence.'

There was silence, broken only by the measured tick of a Grandmother clock in the corner.

'You believe there's something of yours in here?' The warning over, Vignoles was gentle with his query.

The couple exchanged glances, their hands clasped together, a gesture made the more poignant because of the handcuffs forcing them together. 'The old gentleman, Mr Krast. He has - *had* -,' Gable stumbled over what should be the correct form. She started again after taking a gulp of air. 'We asked him a few weeks ago if he could help us and he said yes, and then time went by and we heard nothing from him, and we got anxious and then... then we heard he was dead and we...' Gable blushed and stared at the floor as if wanting it to swallow her up.'Me and Else are engaged. Not exactly, but we will be. Just as soon as the old man hurries up and gets it finished.' Twister stopped. 'But of course, he can't now...'

'Get *what* finished?' Vignoles asked. 'Neither of you are making sense.'

'We need an engagement ring. When we've got it, we're going to announce the engagement and get the banns read.'

'We're respectable, despite what you're thinking,' Gable found her voice again.

Mellor made a strange laughing sound.

'We're not bad people!' Gable snapped. 'We heard what happened this morning and it's awful, of course it is. Absolutely horrid.' Gable shook her head in disbelief. She started trembling.

'What was Mr Krast doing for you?' Mellor was exasperated.

'He was making us a ring.' Twister replied.

'Really?' Mellor had seen the price tags in the shop.

'Really!' Gable gave Mellor a defiant stare.

'Upon learning of the death of Mr Krast this morning, why did you suddenly feel compelled to enter his house? That strikes me as both curious and unwise,' Vignoles was puzzled by this pair. Gauche, clumsy and yet something innocent about their manner.

'We were scared someone might have broken in and taken everything. We came to find out if it looked like the house had been robbed and when we saw the door was open, we decided to nip inside and get our ring back.' It sounded lame and Twister knew it.

'Surely it would be at his shop?' Vignoles asked.

'We never went to his shop.'

'We're hardly the sort who could go into that kind of place,' Gable added. It was a point even Mellor couldn't argue against. 'I work in Cheltenham some of the time and I've walked past a few times. They have a big chain on the door and that awful man with the stern face stops people like *us* going in.'

'If you did not go to his shop, explain the arrangement you claim to have made with Mr Krast.'

'We've seen him in the village and also at the station every day. He takes the auto-train regular as clockwork,' Twister explained. 'You get to know who everyone is and what they do in a village this size.'

'You knew he was a jeweller?' Mellor smiled like a shark.

'It's not a secret.'

'You took it upon yourselves to approach him, privately?' Vignoles was starting to feel sceptical. These two were hardly the kind of discreet customers they'd heard about from Jeffries.

Twister shrugged his shoulders. 'I asked him one morning whilst he was waiting for the train. Asked if he could make us a ring. We had a stone, but no ring for it to go on. Nothing special, of course. It looks good, but it wasn't real.' He looked apologetically at Gable. 'It was paste, that's what Mr Krast called it. Funny word if you ask me.'

'It's awfully pretty!' Gable's face suddenly lit up despite her trauma at being handcuffed and grilled by grim-faced detectives. 'I'm just a carriage cleaner and don't go around wanting something I can't have. I don't need more. It's perfect enough for me...'

'Let me get this straight, you had in your possession an attractive but low-value stone and asked Mr Krast to set it on a ring? At an appropriately low cost?' Vignoles asked.

'Two guineas *is* a lot for me...' Twister replied.

'And he was taking ages! He said he was doing it as a favour in his own time at home,' Gable added. 'We knew he had it here because he told us, and then Ian called me this morning about what happened and of course that means lots of investigations and everything and it might be months before we ever got it back.'

'Or never. I was scared it would be put in a bag of evidence and locked away in a police station and forgotten.' Twister added, bitterly.

'What were you both doing last night between six and seven o'clock?' Vignoles asked.

'Was that when Mr Krast was killed?'

'Just answer the question, Twister!' Wilcox snapped.

'I was working. We had an important delivery to transfer in the goods shed,' Twister replied. 'Off a lorry and into a box van. We needed to handle and store it carefully, so it kept us busy until late.'

'There were others there?' Mellor asked.

'Of course. The stuff was too heavy for me alone.'

Mellor wrote down their names. 'And you, Miss Gable?'

'I went straight home. I'd been working at St James all day and took the five to six 'Coffeepot' to Bishops Cleeve. My mum can tell you when I got home and that we all sat down for beef stew and sliced bread. We had tinned prunes and custard for afters. I stayed in. It was not a night to be out.' She gained in confidence as she spoke with the realisation that her alibi was strong.

'That means you travelled with Mr Krast?' Wilcox queried.

'I don't know about that. I didn't see him.'

'Where were you sitting on the train?' Vignoles was interested. 'Is it not a single coach?'

'Right at the front. That is, the front when we left, because it reverses direction later.'

'You did not see your jeweller friend and take the opportunity to ask him about when your ring might be ready?' Vignoles pressed the point.

'I never saw him. I was reading. I'd bought a new magazine and it had a feature on wedding dresses...' She blushed. 'I was so interested I didn't take any notice of anyone else and it's only a short journey.'

Wilcox glanced at Vignoles and nodded that this last part was factually correct.

'Unlock them, constable.' Vignoles issued the order. 'You have their names and addresses?'

'I have, sir,' Wentworth replied. 'I know Master Twister and his family. Due to the seriousness of the situation I felt I had no choice but to hold them here pending questioning.'

'You did the right thing. Now, Twister, I suspect you left your work without leave and doubtless will receive a severe dressing down from Stationmaster Roberts. We'll leave it like that - for now.' Wilcox as the senior officer of the local force, took over. 'If we find the diamond ring during our investigations it will be returned to you in due course, but not a moment before. If either of you can offer help that will lead us to whoever killed Mr Krast, then make sure you share it with us. It would go a long way towards forgiving your foolish actions this morning. We're going to be looking harder at your story and if we find one thing amiss, I'll throw the book at you. Now hop it!'

The couple gratefully stood up, rubbing their wrists to ease the circulation and headed for the open door. 'It was Elsie's day off, actually...' Twister added over his shoulder.

'We're working non-stop from tomorrow at Winchcombe on account of the races,' she added. 'It gets busy with the extra trains.' The distant whistle of a locomotive passing through the station sounded from the bottom of the village as a timely reminder that the line was handling a lot of traffic.

'I couldn't give a monkey's arse, now bugger off!' Mellor wanted to turn his attention to the house.

Chapter Six

Lord Buckrose parked his car beside a row of ramshackle coal merchant's huts on the approach road leading to a fan of dreary sidings embedded in layers of compacted coal dust. He strode purposefully under the *porte cochere* of Cheltenham St James station, walking into the grandiose booking hall with the haughty air of a man who boasted lineage back to the Black Prince. His hawkish eyes were taking everything in. He oozed confidence and a whiff of understated arrogance. Or perhaps that was his expensive aftershave, applied before leaving his car. A porter leaning on a barrow felt the need to straighten up and adjust his cap, although His Lordship gave the lad barely a moment's glance.

Buckrose approached the bank of varnished wooden telephone kiosks and slid a door open, closing it firmly behind and fished out a pile of grubby coins that smelt of metal and sweat. He pressed Button A, dialled, then leaned casually in the corner so he could keep a beady eye on the activity outside. It looked as though an important train was being made ready for departure, as a good number of passengers were entering the concourse, many of whom were smartly dressed and accompanied by trolleys of cases hauled or pushed by porters eager for a tip. This suited Buckrose. A busy station and an important departure were the perfect scenario. He would blend easily with the clientele and was unlikely to attract attention, whilst the booming Tannoy now firing into action would ensure nobody could listen in on his conversation.

He pressed Button B and started talking. He used all his mellifluous charm and shamelessly name-dropped. '...do you know Lord Shenston? No...? Decent fellow... Look, if we strike a good deal, as I feel sure we shall, I consider it only right I let you into a secret...Yes... Could prove most advantageous to a chap like yourself... The Duke has a number of very interesting items that he might allow me put your way... Took me into his confidence that he was looking for a *discreet* outlet. Absolutely hush-hush of course! I'd be in awfully hot water if he knew... Did I mention the conversation I had with the Queen Mother? No...? She quite had me in stitches...' And so it continued. More coins pushed into the slot and the clock hands moving around as the time drew closer for the imminent departure of the 'Cheltenham Spa Express'.

Buckrose however, was now spending more time listening than talking. His face paler and lips drawn into grim line. When he did speak, his slick and easy charm sounded forced. He still tried dropping in the odd reference to Royalty and other impeccable connections he claimed to maintain, but the conversation was not going his way no matter how hard he tried. His voice took on a steelier edge as he tried to hide his impatience. Buckrose was finally left holding the receiver after a chilly 'be seein' yer,' down the line. Once the connection was cut, he uttered a short curse before quietly replacing the handset on the holder. He stood upright and fished out a packet of his trusty Players. *Sod the Sobranies. A* stronger fix was needed, and he lit up in the cubicle.

A minute or so later Lord Buckrose regained some of his *savoir faire,* thanks to his ability to rise above the irritations and setbacks that came with his line of business. No matter how frustrated he was inside, outwardly, he was once again calm. He approached the ticket barrier and arrogantly brushed the request to see his ticket aside with a muttered response about 'his man having it,' and marched down the platform leaving the ticket inspector to hide his embarrassment as he faced an ageing *grande dame* in a silver fox and massive hat. Buckrose had no plans to board the crack express but the walk along the platform and another smoke would clear his head, away from the bustle of the concourse.

He looked at the freshly washed carriages and his eye was drawn to two beautiful women seated at a table laid with a white cloth, set with polished glasses and plentiful silver cutlery. A lamp glowed on the table between them. He tipped his hat and was delighted at the lipsticked smiles he received in return. The fairer of the two was wearing a heavy necklace of amber that glowed in the lamplight. On another day he might have tried to talk those from around her neck and into the palm of his hand, never to be seen by her again following a pleasant afternoon dalliance in a hotel room... Another time. Buckrose had more pressing demands right now. He walked on and observed a pair of fine gun dogs being coaxed into the guard's section of one of the coaches. The guard nodded politely and touched the brim of his cap. All as it should be.

Buckrose stood near the engine, breathing in the clouds of delicately scented steam mixed with the bracing air. It enveloped him and this momentary cloak of invisibility was welcome. With a cigarette jutting from his mouth he jammed his hands in his coat pockets. He'd left his driving gloves in the car and the air held a nip that was making his fingers ache. He noticed that the engine was named 'Chepstow Castle'.

Whose pile of rocks was that? He had a skill for memorising the castles, mansions and manors of the great and the good. He considered it polite to have at the tip of his tongue knowledge from where his many acquaintances hailed, even if the monuments in question were now ruins or, Heaven help us, hospitals for the insane or dreary local Corporation offices surrounded by unimaginative parks where once splendid gardens had been nurtured.

There was a distant peep on a whistle like a referee starting a rugger match. The driver waved a hand in response as 'Chepstow Castle' gave a generous toot in return then produced prodigious jets of steam from the front end, completely blocking everything from view and smothering the gleaming engine. Deep breathy huffs and puffs and a lot of ear-splitting hissing followed, and the mighty train started into motion, the beat steadily increasing as clouds of steam were pushed forwards to create an ethereal wall of vapour. It was a wonder the driver knew where he was going. Worse than a white-out in fog! Buckrose debated whether this was a metaphor for his own present troubles. Eventually the steam cleared as the hissing subsided and blocks of smoke now lifted from the chimney in time with the beat. The fastest train in the world was on her way.

Buckrose watched, but his thoughts were far removed from the stirring sight before him. His telephone conversation had not delivered the result he'd anticipated. Delays...Forced to wait even longer! There was nothing else to do but top up his rapidly depleting fighting fund. He'd half-expected this, but it was still a bitter draught to swallow.

Chapter Seven

The search of Krast's house was inconclusive. There were no obvious signs of disturbance. Krast had been a tidy man. If someone had been inside - and the opened front door suggested as much - they had carefully searched for something specific rather than indulge in the usual wild ransacking. But what were they after?

Vignoles and Mellor were stumped. However, one item they had not located, was the ring the young love birds claimed should be there. Was this significant? Neither detective could summon up the conviction that a piece of worthless cut-glass helped explain Krast's murder.

Mellor sent for the forensic team and set them to work, instructing the photographer to make general shots of each room. There was an oddly deflating sense that none of this would yield useful results.

'Box up his papers and the contents of his work table. Sift through everything, including his shop paperwork and see if there's anything buried in there that gives us a lead.'

'That could take a while...' Mellor replied.

'Call the office and summons Lansdowne here, first thing.' Vignoles appreciated the work involved. 'Ask the Cheltenham Constabulary if they can spare us a uniform to do some of the leg work - that will help keep us sweet with the local boys over jurisdictions.'

'I could telephone in the request, inspector? I'm sure they would assist, especially if I have a talk with them...' Wilcox added, helpfully. 'And you've got Wentworth as well. I'll assign him to assist until you say otherwise.'

'Thank you. Mellor - take over the back office of Krast's shop, that way you can keep an eye on the staff whilst you work. I want a full stock-take. I see no reason to take Jeffries' word that nothing is missing.'

'Righty-ho.'

'And check his alibi.'

'Changin' your opinion about Jeffries, sir?'

'We do this by the book and only put a tick beside his name once cleared. We can then search elsewhere for a suspect. He claims to go home every evening so you should find him in later.'

'A surprise call, eh?' Mellor seemed to like the idea.

'But go easy; if his wife is as ill as he says, she doesn't need you being heavy-handed.'

*   *   *   *

Vignoles returned to Broadway station with Wilcox. He could start interviewing the handful of staff that worked there. On the short drive down, he looked at the wide street on a hill that gave the village its name and the implausibly pretty buildings made from that honey-coloured local stone that seemed to almost glow as if illuminated from inside.

The village appeared untouched by the news of the brutal murder. A horse quietly drank from a trough. A general store had lights on inside but appeared to have no customers. The postman's bright red Morris Minor van was parked beside the main thoroughfare and he was idly chatting with a local over a gate. A big Atkinson furniture delivery lorry was negotiating a corner and leaving a trail of diesel exhaust.

Vignoles stepped out of the car at the station and tactfully suggested that Wilcox return to his usual duties if he had work pressing. They could meet in the evening and talk the day's events over a beer or two. Wilcox took the hint and after suggesting a suitable pub to gather in later, sped off in his little car.

Vignoles needed a quiet pipe and a think before he started the questioning. Aside from the obvious hope that someone saw a potential suspect, what was he hoping to learn? Indeed, what had he learned so far? The case was proving tricky to tease apart, but a sign this could prove an interesting case. It was like tipping the pieces of a huge jigsaw out of an unmarked box. A complete confusion at first, but with patience and care one could slowly piece together parts of the picture. He just needed to work out whether the railway staff were pieces of uninteresting 'sky' or something more engaging. Probably pieces of 'railway line'. That could be useful at least, because lines led somewhere...

A six-wheeled tender locomotive was shunting wagons at the far end of the station and this was sufficient motivation to pull him through the entrance gateway onto the platform. He was craving warmth on his back from the weak sun trying to break through the steely clouds and he stepped from under the extended roof awning onto the open platform now suddenly bright with sunlight. He filled his pipe with Redbreast tobacco from a tin and watched as a long goods train trundled by on the 'up' line hauled by an impressive goods locomotive coated in the stains, dribbles and liberal dusting of oily smuts that betrayed its unglamorous life. It was an attractive beast despite the lack of cleaning, and whilst memorising the short number on the cast brass plate on the cab, Vignoles decided he needed to find time to brush up his knowledge of these 'Western' engines if he was to be here for any time.

Was he going to be here long? The case was serious and quite opaque. No suspect and no witnesses. Motive, at this stage was reduced to the stealing of a set of keys - but to what purpose? So far, nothing had been taken - or perhaps a better way of casting it, nothing that anyone was willing to admit to.

He puffed contentedly on his pipe and chewed all this over as the heavy train rumbled northwards. The killing of Krast was not a crazed drunken assault by a gang of idiot youths, nor a domestic flare up that spiralled out of control. In spite of Mellor's enthusiasm about the missing keys, robbery was not looking a promising angle. The keys might have fallen out of his pocket before the assault. Stranger things had happened and in all his years with the police, Vignoles had not once heard of a mugger willing to strangle a man to death for his wallet - let alone a bunch of keys.

They needed to learn more about Krast. Perhaps he had a secret life? But being killed for bedding someone else's wife was not a motive Vignoles could easily accept based on what he'd learned of the man so far. Nonetheless, there had to be something at the heart of this dark mystery that was worth killing for.

Vignoles was glad he'd put Mellor onto Jeffries. Mellor was irritating, but his tenacious terrier-like qualities might flush out a lie from this cool customer. Jeffries had shown little emotion nor even surprise upon learning that his boss had been strangled. Did Jeffries know more than he was admitting? And there was the inescapable truth that Jeffries had both the time and knowledge to hide or manipulate records so they would be fooled into believing nothing was missing. Had Jeffries contrived to have Krast killed to make it look like a violent robbery in order to hide his own actions? Vignoles was struggling to see how this might play out, but they needed to test the man and see if there was a chink in his armour.

And what of Miss Jephson? Mellor had claimed she was suspect for no worse crime than having access to a television set, but Vignoles was struggling to share this viewpoint. However, even the most unlikely people were capable of duplicity and he ought at least dig a little deeper. She may not hold keys to the shop or safe but might have gained access to these long enough to make a mould in Plasticine modelling clay to enable someone to fashion duplicate keys. But even if this piece of Cold War subterfuge were true, why then kill the old man to take his keys? Even with a length of rope around Krast's neck and a knee in the small of the back, Vignoles could not convince himself she had the strength to be his killer. A word with her mother would probably confirm the alibi and Alice Jephson could be struck off the suspect list.

A little engine on the 'down' line now gave a short 'toot' and propelled some wagons forward with a gentle clatter of buffers.

What to make of the most obvious suspects, Twister and Gable? Two foolish and impetuous lovers. Or twin-murderers?

Vignoles puffed his pipe and shook his head. Even if they had it in them to murder the old gent, why had they not gone straight to his house that evening? Waiting until daylight and after the balloon had gone up so the chance of discovery was probable seemed foolish and nonsensical. And where were Krast's dratted keys? Neither had them about their person when discovered in the house and both had denied all knowledge of their existence. The keys had not been found in house or garden. If their story was true, and there was something so disarmingly gauche about it Vignoles felt inclined to believe it, then the loss of one paltry piece of paste jewellery could never in a month of Sundays be motive for murder.

The Collet goods engine had now delivered an ex-Great Western Railway horse box into the short unloading bay at the platform end, some distance beyond the footbridge. These interesting wagons were often kept in fine external condition and the sunlight was striking the paintwork and making the colour glow in a most attractive manner. Vignoles noticed that it was still painted in the chocolate brown of its former owner and a faded gold crest with the letters G.W.R. in a roundel remained visible. The fireman was now clambering between the box and his locomotive in readiness for releasing the engine so it could back away.

Wait a minute, was that Ian Twister? The young man had stepped out from behind a small shed on the platform. Had Twister hoped to conceal his nefarious house-breaking exploits by acting as though he'd been idling the morning away behind a lamp hut? Twister by name and a twister by nature...?

The engine had drawn away and two young men now stepped out of the horse box close to Twister. They greeted each other warmly. The stable lads left the door to their little compartment open, perhaps to let in some fresh air. One lad was releasing the heavy locking bars on the wide side doors of the compartment holding the horses. Whilst he was doing so, Twister was passing on information that involved a lot of gesticulating and pointing towards the 'up' platform waiting room. Everyone looked suitably surprised, one shook his head in disbelief, but then hurried along the platform towards where Vignoles was standing. As the lad passed, he gave Vignoles barely a glance, staring instead towards the scene of crime and paying scant heed to where he was walking such was his fascination with the news of Krast's murder. The Collet engine now clanked through the station at a terrific pace, eager to get back to the goods shed at the far end of the station.

Vignoles decided he would start his interviews with a second attempt at Twister.

'Morning gents...'

Twister made a grimace then tried to disguise it by blowing on his hands. The stable lad was emptying a galvanised pail of water between the dock edge and the horse box. He straightened up and gave Vignoles a suspicious look.

'Can I help?'

'You have a horse in there?'

'That's the idea.' He put the pail inside the wide door opening without looking at Vignoles. The head and flanks of a beautiful chestnut horse with a white blaze was now visible and the outlines of two others deeper inside.

There was a strong but not unpleasant smell of warm beast, straw and pine wood emanating from the box. A hoof clumped on the decking and the horse waggled its long head. The lad perhaps regretting sounding sarcastic, elaborated. 'We've brought three down.'

'Are they running in The Gold Cup?' Vignoles puffed contentedly on his pipe, wanting them to feel at ease.

'Not this one.' He nodded his head towards the chestnut. 'She's to run in The Broadway tomorrow. She's young.'

'The Broadway?'

'The Broadway Novice's Steeplechase.'

This did not elucidate Vignoles, who knew only the minimum about racing, but he nodded sagely. 'She looks a fine beast. What's her name?'

'Money For Nothing.'

Vignoles smiled. 'Let's hope that's not an accurate assessment!' They laughed.

'She prefers the going hard, so this freezing weather might suit her. Unlike some of the field. One of the others behind is a Gold Cup runner, but I'm not sure the conditions are right. Mr Coldicott is worried about Great Eliza.'

'Who is Great Eliza?' Vignoles queried.

'It's a horse.' Twister had stepped closer. He'd initially hung back, unenthusiastic about another encounter with the detective, but his curiosity was piqued. 'It froze like iron last night after the rain and they reckon the same again tonight. With this east wind and possibly snow on top...' He grimaced. 'That would kill the racing.' It sounded like he knew what he was talking about.

An interesting turn of phrase, thought Vignoles 'Proper Cotswold weather?' He held out a gloved hand to the lad. 'DCI Vignoles. I'm investigating a murder that took place here last night. In that waiting room across the tracks.' He gave Twister an enigmatic sidelong glance.

'Joe Biggs.' They shook hands. 'It's a shock what happened. Ian just told me.'

'And what did you tell your friend, Mr Twister?' Vignoles kept his voice free of any emotion. He fished out his pipe and started to fill it.

'Same as he just said. That a man was killed when he got off a train last night.'

A man. You didn't give him a name, in spite of knowing who he was and being caught inside his house... Vignoles allowed a silence to fall between them. Biggs shuffled his feet and put an unlit cigarette in his mouth and offered his pal one. Twister was glad of the excuse to proffer a lighter and the young men filled a few seconds of unease with the lighting ritual.

'You travel with the horses, Mr Biggs?'

'Yep.' A puff of smoke. 'Me and Sid today. You saw Sid going into the village to get us some grub before the van arrives.'

'Which van is that?'

'We're taking the horses to Stanway House by road. They're sending over their vehicle. We've not come far, but Mr Coldicott likes his horses to settle into the area for a day or so. And the toff who owns Money For Nothing is superstitious and wants his horse to detrain in Broadway seeing how she's running a race of the same name.' Biggs and Twister both grinned at the foibles of racehorse owners. 'We just do as we're told!' and he laughed. 'But the two behind, they're in for the Gold Cup proper, and it's a chance for them to adjust to the conditions and settle before the race on Thursday.'

Vignoles turned to Twister. 'You have known each other long?'

'I know all the stable lads. Joe, Sid and the others. I help them unload. I've worked with horses all my life and its best to have someone who's comfortable with them, so I get this line of work as a rule.'

'Lucky you were here then.' Vignoles gave a puff on his pipe.

Twister looked uncomfortable and stared at the platform.

'Do you sleep in there?' Vignoles asked Biggs.

'One person can stretch out on the bench seat and grab a quick forty winks, but one has to stay alert the whole time. That's why two travel. You need to keep an eye in case a horse gets spooked.'

'Valuable creatures...'

'Not half! If one gets worked up they can kick and throw themselves about and get hurt.'

Money For Nothing nudged the empty pail with a hoof, and it toppled over.

'Yes, yes, I'll fetch you some more!' Biggs gently chastised the horse just as he might a small child. 'I need to get on...'

'Don't mind me.'

Biggs opened a door to a narrow compartment at the far end of the horse box and hauled out some fodder. Vignoles turned away and signalled Twister that he should follow him out of earshot of Biggs. 'About this stone that you and Miss Gable are so fond of.'

'What about it?' He sucked on his cigarette.

'If it has no monetary value, why was it worth entering a dead man's house to retrieve it?'

Twister inspected his cigarette. 'I wouldn't know the first thing about diamonds.' He shrugged his shoulders. 'Elsie likes it and that's all that matters. I didn't want her to be upset if we lost it.'

'How did you come by it?'

Twister threw his fag end away. 'She found it. Someone lost it on a train.'

'Go on.'

'She's a cleaner and found it down the seat cushions. Could have been there years. I mean, there's no way anyone could have found out whose it was.'

'A fake gemstone is hardly cause to put up lost and found notices,' agreed Vignoles.

'Have you found it?'

'Not so far, but we have not completed our search.' Vignoles changed tack. 'Whereabouts were you working here last night? Between five and eight o'clock?'

'I was down the goods shed, with Frank.' He threw a thumb over his shoulder in the direction of the engine that had recently passed. The locomotive was now about the size of a model Hornby train and standing outside the goods shed in question. 'We've got tons of stuff needed shifting. The races cause us a lot of extra work. You can't believe what gets shipped in this week.'

'Surely race-related goods would go to Cheltenham Racecourse station?'

'Supplies for the race punters. But the line is filled with extra traffic in and out for three days or more. The stations along the line have to stock up on the usual necessities. The line can't handle the usual daily goods, especially coal, because of all the specials coming and going. There's not enough capacity.'

'I see.' Vignoles was finding Twister a surprisingly willing interviewee. 'You said you finished late?'

'Just in time to sprint over to the 'Arms' with Frank for a pint before last orders.'

'Frank has a name?'

'Cotton.'

'And Frank Cotton can confirm your story?'

'Of course. I bet the signalman saw us legging it to the pub!'

'And neither of you saw anyone acting suspiciously in and around the station?'

'We were inside working our socks off and didn't have time to be looking at what was outside. It's too far away to see much anyway, especially in the dark.'

Vignoles thanked Twister and walked back down the platform. He needed to look elsewhere for the whoever killed Krast.

Chapter Eight

Slatter's Emporium on Grimsby Street on the fringe of Bethnal Green was the complete opposite of Krast's Jewellers. It was desolately shabby, with brown painted windows either blanked by water-stained sheets of plywood or rendered opaque by countless years of London soot and rain. In the few places it was possible to peer through the filthy shop window the sight that greeted a curious enquirer was both depressing and uninviting. Rows of dead flies on their backs edged swathes of moth-eaten velvet that might once have been a bottle green but now faded to varying shades to grey. This cloth was crudely drawing-pinned to the window-back that also supported glass shelves displaying a motley collection of clocks and porcelain figures, many with crudely repaired breakages or missing limbs. A tray of dispiriting gold rings of little value promised even fewer delights within the Emporium itself, beyond the solid wooden door dropping on its hinges and which made a ghastly screech like a bad-tempered banshee whenever someone was brave enough to venture inside. A tin tray of mis-matched champagne coups on the serving counter rattled frequently as trains on their way in and out of Liverpool Street Station rumbled in the deep cutting just across the narrow street or passed overhead on the massive lattice steel bridge that slashed across the filthy London sky just yards from the roof tops as they snaked their way through Shoreditch High Street.

Grimsby Street was indeed aptly named, in as much as it was grim, odorous and filled with smoke from the passing trains although any connection to the North Eastern fishing port was hard to fathom. The cobbled street was poorly lit by gas lamps and frequented only by those brave enough to venture down this Dickensian backstreet.

The proprietor, Ernie Slatter was one of the more notoriously successful fences in East London and he'd chosen the location from which to conduct his nefarious business with care and consideration and perhaps even the air of hopeless neglect was as carefully managed.

Nobody unwilling to make a deal of dubious legality made the mistake of entering. The few that did were met with the unsmiling glare of Slatter and the musty stench of stale air, cheap tobacco, blocked drains and rising damp. It was always dark inside, made all the more so by the work light Slatter always had flooding his workbench. Just a cursory glance was enough to ensure any innocent enquirer would hurriedly apologise for their intrusion and back out, wrestling to get the door closed as they did.

And yet, in spite these reasons to steer a wide berth, there was a steady trickle of visitors, especially in the darker hours. These were persons who knew how to tackle the screaming door and were immune to the intimidating glare of Slatter seated behind his counter, the light illuminating his face dramatically and accentuating the taught skin of his skull.

The Debt Collectors were two such men. Louis Kane and Jesse Abel were arguably London's most feared hit men. They commanded the highest fees and tackled the trickiest tasks and, in so doing, generated a begrudging respect tempered with loathing for their sadistic methods amongst Britain's most dangerous criminals. It was unwise to mess with The Debt Collectors. It was better to have as little to do with them as possible and never make the mistake of reneging on a deal. They prided themselves on always extracting something from those foolish enough to have fallen behind in their extortion payments or proving 'forgetful' about where they had squirrelled away a certain gang member's cut from a bank job. Whatever the complaint, when The Debt Collectors came knocking it was imperative to offer something without hesitation.

'In cash, in kind - or your life. The choice is yours!' as Kane delighted in repeating to those foolish enough to invite a visit and appear tardy in their response.

Slatter glanced up as the door howled the customary warning note and felt his heart miss a beat. He was not aware he'd screwed up a deal in as many years as he could remember, but when Kane and Abel entered your shop your insides instinctively froze. He put the soldering iron back on its rest, the air hot and pungent with the smell of flux and solder. 'Gentlemen...' his voice was gravelly with years of chain smoking. 'To what do I owe this dubious pleasure?' His eyes were watchful beneath bushy eyebrows.

'Afternoon, Ernest...' Abel stopped in the centre of the small shop and looked around. 'I always look forward to stepping into your delightful emporium! It never fails to leave me quite...speechless!'

'And you're rarely that, Mr Abel. Always willing to pass the time of day, ain't yer...' Slatter risked a quiet chortle. He was desperately trying to think of what might have brought these two unsavoury characters calling.

'So droll...' Abel extracted a handkerchief that looked all the whiter in contrast to the Stygian gloom of the shop. He blew his nose, although more from affectation than necessity, and kept it pressed close. 'Your shop is always so fragrant...'

'So 'ow's tricks?' Kane strode up to Slatter and offered a strong, broad hand. Slatter noticed that a finger was missing the upper section. The wound looked angry and not fully healed. He tried not to show he'd noticed and shook hands, but Kane was observant. 'Someone was not happy with the service I rendered...'

'That's not like you,' Slatter squeaked. 'You're the best in the business.'

'Such flattery... Fair makes my head spin.' Abel flapped his handkerchief like an 18th Century fop.

'Nah, that'll be the flux up yer nose,' Kane retorted. 'What you up to? Fixing up some old rubbish as per usual I see.'

'Fixing a joint in this silver kettle, since you ask. It received some harsh 'andlin' whilst being liberated from its former owner. A new joint will improve the resale, no end.'

'Got to keep an eye on the bottom line, Ernie.' Kane walked around the counter and into Slatter's working space without being invited. There was not much room and Slatter had to push his chair on little castors hard up against the back wall and look at Kane at an acute angle.

'So 'ow can I help you? Fancy a cuppa? I woz gonna put the kettle on...'

'I wouldn't let anything you brewed up in this pigsty touch my lips,' Abel replied.

'A man could catch his death in here...' Kane curled a lip as he spoke and leaned against the counter, effectively barring the exit. He started to idly fiddle with the many tools and oddments littering the worktop.

'It's not really a social call today, dear boy.' Abel blew menthol smoke from a fresh cigarette across Slatter's face from the other side of the counter. 'We need a quiet chat. Man to man.' He winked. 'Could do with a bit of information...'

'Talk don't come cheap. Not 'round' ere.' Slatter replied.

'Of course not. You have a business to run, as do we...'

'Give us straight answers and we'll see you right. You can trust us.' Kane had picked up a brown glass bottle and was gently swirling the contents around.

'That's acid. Careful you don't go spilling it.'

'Nasty stuff.' Abel made a face. 'I know what it does and how it hurts.' The hand holding his cigarette showed a trace of melted skin below the starched white cuff.

'I prefer to just use it for cleaning.' Slatter was still trying to sound unperturbed, but he sensed the menace building in the room.

'We're interested in a rock. A very hot rock. A most particular and lovely one that once seen is not easily forgotten - by an expert. And we'll be the first to say it, you know your stuff. One of the best in the game.' Abel leaned casually on the counter top, one eye magnified by his ridiculous monocle.

'What makes you think I'd remember the one you're interested in? I see hundreds in a year.' He was trying hard to keep his voice disinterested. A train passing through Shoreditch Station set the crystal coups rattling on their tin tray.

Kane leaned closer. 'Worth a mint this one. A King's fortune. Now, as it happens there was some...shall we say, bovver last year and it went missing. Most unfortunate. It had painful consequences, so we feel a pressing need to secure its return. At any cost.'

'You screwed up?' Slatter was so astounded he laughed. 'I never thought I'd see the day you two messed up.'

'I can't see what's so funny.' Abel itched the damaged skin.

'No offence...All right, so you lost the diamond, but what's that to do wiv me?'

'You *do* know about it then?' Kane growled.

'I didn't say that!'

'A little bird told us you had a gentleman in here hawking something interesting. So interesting, you've been putting feelers out to test the water...' Abel was turning on the charm, his magnified eye watching Slatter's face intently. 'But the same little bird told me you found the water rather hot.' Another puff of smoke in his face.

'Nothin' wrong in that. Very sensible.' Kane nodded sagely. 'Ernie Slatter knows not to dive straight in without dippin' a toe first. That's how you've stayed alive so long.'

'You know me. I don't muck folk about. I play fair...'

'Right you are, Ernie! Now do yourself a favour and let us take this dangerous little item off your grubby little hands and we can advise a certain gent in the Scrubs as to where he'd like us to secure his rightful property. In return for a full and proper fee...' Kane had unscrewed the top on the acid bottle and was giving it a cautious exploratory sniff. 'He'll see yer right.'

'I ain't got the Hornet. Honest I don't! I wouldn't touch it even if I had.'

'Then it was 'The Hornet's Beauty'?' Abel smiled. 'Our sources were correct, as ever. Now do be a good fellow and hand it over.'

Slatter shifted uncomfortably on his chair, finding it hard to keep a beady eye on Kane leaning over him and avoid the smoke being deliberately blown into his face by Abel.

'For the avoidance of any doubt, we're representing Mr Reggie Smailes, who as Kane explained, is currently residing at Her Majesty's Pleasure at Wormwood Scrubs...'

'Smailes?' For the first time Slatter sounded worried. His Adam's apple bobbed.

Abel made a rueful expression. 'He has quite a temper...' This said whilst rubbing his damaged arm. 'And seems to enjoy the company of some *awfully* rough men...'

'He's not best pleased that his prized rock went walkies, neither. Wants it back. He'll pay handsomely. He's all heart, behind that vicious exterior!' Kane grinned.

'Pay?' Slatter looked interested. 'How much?'

'Ten percent of the finder's fee.'

'Fifteen.'

'That means you've something to trade...' Kane retorted.

'Nuffin's for free! I don't have it, but I can ask, and I want payin' for my trouble.'

The bottle of acid was slammed down on the desk and Kane quick as a flash pinned the weedy form of Slatter against the back wall. 'Stop stallin' you scrawny bastard! We'll see yer right. Now where's the stone?'

'Uuugh...'

Kane slightly relaxed his grip so Slatter could speak. 'Don't...have it! He took it!'

'Who?'

'The toff...Lord...Bu-Buckrose. Wouldn't leave it.' Slatter's eyes were bulging as his face started to turn an unpleasant shade of red.

Kane backed off, but kept his face close to Slatter's, fist balled and ready to lash out. 'You'd better not be lying!'

'It's the truth!' Slatter was coughing and rubbing his throat. 'He took it wiv 'im. I offered a hundred nicker surety but he wasn't having none of it.'

Abel gave the man a long stare, trying to read the shifty eyes that kept flicking from side to side. 'Think on, old chap. Do the right thing. All you have to do is hand over that nice little stone...'

'He took it, I tell yer!'

'Who's this Buckrose?' Kane hissed.

'I dunno. A toff. Well-dressed and speaks all lahdy-dah...'

'How did he get the Hornet?'

'Said he conned it off a jeweller in Cheltenham. Straight up, that's all I know!'

'What's the deal?' Kane was keeping his simmering anger under check.

'Said he'd call me from a kiosk every couple of days to see what I could raise for it. I had to find a match for the Hornet, as that way he could swap the stones and we sell the proper one, with a 60-40 split.'

'Forty percent of a million - give or take. Nice... You're not as dumb as you look.' Kane grinned at Slatter, as a shark might at a seal pup. 'I never knew you was so good with numbers!'

'Mr Slatter never ceases to surprise. But what's worrying me, is where is the cut for Mr Smailes in that neat little arrangement? I fear Mr Smailes is going to be dreadfully upset when he hears about Ernie's private little plan that overlooks the rightful owner,' Abel's voice was light and sugary. His eye widened behind his monocle as he ended the sentence and it fell onto his chest with a soft sound.

'No, no you got that wrong. I-I didn't know who's it was. I knew it was special, but not that it was the Hornet. I found out later...'

A silence fell. They were expecting more. A train chuffed throatily down in the cutting. A whistle wailed. The glasses shook.

'You don't just rush into something as good as that. I made a sketch… looking down a microscope. It's in my book in the top drawer…' He waved a hand. 'Take a gander!'

Kane opened the drawer and extracted a small watercolour sketch book with a leather binding. He flipped it open. Each page had a meticulous line drawing of a diamond with every facet illustrated and any colour indicated by washes of paint and pencilled notes about aberrations and occlusions in the stone that affected the appearance. 'Strewth…you did these?'

'Of course. Only the most valuable that pass my way. Not worth it for run of mill stuff. Each diamond is unique and has qualities that identify it just like a fingerprint.'

'How could you swap The Hornet for a substitute?'

'I could find something to fool the ordinary man in the street, but not a pro. A pro knows how to *look*. Using lights and high magnification. But given time I could find summat near enough. I sketched Buckrose's diamond whilst he waited as he wouldn't leave it. I needed something to work from. It was later, after he'd gone, I started to realise…'

'That you were cheatin' Reggie Smailes?' Kane sucked air between his lips. 'Unwise…'

Abel took the sketchbook from Kane and studied the page in question. 'Quite beautiful. Such workmanship… It would be a pity if you lost the ability to draw like this…' Abel ripped out the page with the Hornet's Beauty on it then tossed the book onto the counter.

'I was just asking around, nuffin' more! When I made the deal it was before I knew what it was.'

'I didn't catch you seeking our advice. Tut tut,' Kane stood upright and looked down at the little man. 'Ah well. You've given us something at least.' He suddenly grabbed the hot soldering iron and thrust it close to Slatter's face, forcing the man to press his head as far back as he could against the row of shelves behind his chair. 'You're still a lyin' toe rag!'

'No-o…' The red tip glowed barely an inch away from Slatter's eyes, forcing him to close his eyelids which were already starting to hurt from the intense heat.

'When you get a call from your Lord what's-his-name, you make sure you tell us. Right? Con the stone out of him and hand it over. Pull a fast one and you won't ever see another diamond. Or see anything else, for that matter...' Kane tossed the soldering iron aside, clattering onto the counter and immediately the glowing red tip setting the discarded sketch book alight.

The Debt Collectors departed whilst the terrified Slatter hastily tried to extinguish the flames.

Chapter Nine

Mellor rapped on the door and waited. Moments later the gaunt face of Jeffries appeared. He looked mildly irritated rather than surprised.

'I'd like to ask a few more questions. If I may?' The pause, although momentary, was enough to suggest a hint of implied coercion.

'Now? You've have had more than enough time all day.'

'It's a nippy old night! I if could just step inside...' Mellor put a size ten shoe towards the opened door and made it hard for Jeffries to refuse entry.

'My wife...She's not well...We don't have many house callers.' Jeffries looked uncertain. His stiff and haughty manner momentarily deserting him.

'It was Mrs Jeffries I would like to speak with.' Mellor gave a perfunctory smile. He was trying to do as Vignoles had requested, but Mellor didn't like Jeffries, having formed the opinion the man was emotionless and unsympathetic. He wasn't going to be brushed off with heart-rending stories of sickness.

'Oh...' Jeffries dithered. 'I cannot see how she could offer anything material towards your investigation...'

'Colin? Who's that?'

'Just a policeman, dearest!'

'Bring him in here then! Don't loiter on the doorstep letting the cold air in...' The shrill voice was strong and did not sound like that of a bed-ridden invalid.

Mellor and Jeffries went into a back kitchen which was oppressively hot and made clammy with dampened air from the washing drying on a wooden rack lofted above the roaring stove on a pulley system. The room smelt of Reckitts Blue, embrocation and other less savoury smells buried underneath. The smell of sweat and sickness.

Mrs Jeffries was a contrast to her husband. Her face was round and puffy. Her arms were bare, which perhaps explained the intense heat, and the visible flesh was flabby and rubbery, reminding Mellor, uncharitably, of Corned Beef. She was installed in a wing-backed chair with her feet raised on a pouf and partially enveloped by an eiderdown, but any part not swathed in this covering looked like a collection of so many cushions, creating voluminous rolling curves. An open tin of Crawford's biscuits decorated with a Christmas image of Victorian characters wassailing under a gas lamp lay close to hand, and the scattering of crumbs across her ample bust suggested she had already made many a dip into the tin.

'And who are you, young man?'

'DS Mellor -.' He showed his warrant card and explained his presence.

'Cor, I don't get many visitors, so this makes a change!' She didn't quite smile, but her look was not hostile. 'What's Colin done then?' She held a straight face for a moment then let out a raucous laugh that set the rolling hills moving, whilst her husband cringed in the corner.

Mellor was already perspiring and thinking he might also feel unwell if he stayed in this hot and airless space much longer. The bulk of Mrs Jeffries seemed to fill the room and made him feel claustrophobic, a sensation not helped by the presence of a small table and two upright chairs as well as the festoons of washing bearing down from above. He was motioned to one of the chairs by Mrs Jeffries, who clearly ruled the roost. Her husband perched uneasily on the other.

'I apologise for the intrusion. I presume your husband has told you about the murder of Mr Krast on Monday evening?'

'He did. But I never met him. Don't even know what he looks like. I don't think the old snob wanted to fraternise with the likes of me...'

'Now that is most unfair. Mr Krast was a reserved man. He was not one for socialising...' Jeffries intervened, but his wife wafted a hankie in the air as if to signal he remain quiet before blowing her nose with it.

Mellor ploughed on. 'There is police procedure to follow and we must ask certain questions in murder investigations no matter how unlikely they might appear.' He pulled out his notebook and resisted the desire to wipe perspiration from his brow.

'Well, I'm hardly likely to have killed him! I mean look at me!' Her eyes wide with disbelief. She started to laugh then put the hankie to her mouth and coughed a number of times, it sounded painful and made her flesh quiver and Mellor wince.

'You are confined to the house?'

'Not confined. I do get out. Sometimes, on a good day, but I never go far.'

'My wife usually restricts her visits to our neighbours.'

'I need to confirm the statement your husband made about his own actions yesterday evening...'

'Colin?' She coughed again. 'You can't seriously think he's responsible for killing the old boot? He has enough trouble swatting flies! Ha ha!'

'Don't be ridiculous, of course I didn't kill Mr Krast!' Jeffries snapped. 'Now don't you go getting worked up as it just makes your cough worse.' He gave Mellor an admonishing glare.

She flapped at her husband in an irritated manner and dabbed her mouth a few times now the coughing fit was over. 'This is most entertaining. Do go on, constable...'

'...Detective Sergeant.'

'My apologies, *Detective Sergeant.*' Mrs Jeffries gave him a cheeky wink. She'd spotted the flicker of irritation on his face over her mistake. Recognising that he'd been found out did not put Mellor at ease.

'Mr Jeffries, perhaps you could tell me once again your movements from leaving the shop yesterday? For the benefit of your wife.'

'Must I?' He sighed with exasperation. 'This is a complete waste of time.'

'I need you to do as I ask.'

'Oh, very well. I left the shop. That is, I left Krast Jewellers, where I work, just so you can be quite clear we are talking about the same place, at five-thirty on the dot. It was damp and unpleasant out and neither Miss Jephson nor I wasted time hurrying in our respective directions towards home. I was back here just before six...I cannot be more precise as I had no reason to consult my watch. But it was no later than six. Is that not correct?' He looked at his wife.

'I was dozing. I fall asleep so easily these days, Detective Sergeant.'

Jeffries looked annoyed that his wife did not confirm his statement. 'I can assure it was just before six and I took off my wet top coat and hat, changed from my work suit which I hung in the wardrobe and then started to get the evening meal ready.'

'I remember he woke me clattering the pans. Colin is good like that.'

Mellor was uncertain whether she meant he was good at cooking or clattering pans. It probably didn't matter. Consulting his notes from the statement he'd taken yesterday afternoon, it tallied.

'We ate our evening meal and then we listened to the wireless.'

'What did you listen to?'

'The Archers, followed by the news and the sports round up and Family Favourites.'

'I like that Michael Brooke,' Mrs Jeffries added. 'He sounds such a nice man, although I get frustrated sometimes as I nod off and miss some of the songs. But I managed to stay awake on Monday...'

'Did one of your neighbours call by?'

'That's right, Julie came over. Julie Miller. She's an absolute angel. Don't know what we'd do without her. She bakes meat pies and makes soup or stew three or four times a week because of course my husband is in the shop all day and it is so tiring for me to stand in the queues in the shops.' Mrs Jeffries was now looking tired. The stimulus of his visit had shaken her up, but the effects were already wearing off.

'Where does Mrs Miller live?'

'Two doors down at number 20. She came and sat in with me and we chatted. Colin was washing the dishes, weren't you?'

'As I always do.' His voice was unemotional.

'We had that awful play on the radio, droning away in the background it was. It's a serial and I was getting awfully fed up with it, so I was glad of Julie's company to be honest.'

'If you are sufficiently interested and it helps cement my alibi, I can confirm that I was attempting to listen to part seven of 'The Barlowes of Beddington'.'

Jeffries looked smug as he waited for Mellor to dutifully note this down.

'I was getting drowsy and by nine Julie was back home and I was going up to bed. I need so much sleep these days...'

'What did you do after your wife went up to bed, at nine?'

'As I've already told you, I sat in the front room and read the paper until ten, when I turned in myself.' He gave Mellor a cold stare.

Mellor tapped his notebook with his pencil a moment. 'What will you do now?'

'Prepare our evening meal once you have finished asking these pointless questions.'

Mellor allowed a wry smile. 'I meant in regard to your job.'

Jeffries shrugged his shoulders and looked at the tired Lino on the floor. 'Try to find other work. I have been with Mr Krast for twenty years. It is a highly specialised aspect of the retail sector and finding work commensurate with my extensive experience will not be easy...' He puffed his narrow chest out and gave his wife a glance, but her eyes were heavy and drooping and she had that far away stare of someone on the verge of sleep. 'I might not find another placement in the jewellery trade. Not in Cheltenham...' He tailed off sadly. 'Travelling any distance each day would be hard.' He smiled wanly, then stood up. 'My wife is tiring. I would appreciate it if we could terminate this interview now.'

Mellor stood up. There was nothing here.

Mrs Jeffries stirred herself awake with a jolt and gave him a surprisingly warm smile and a little wave. 'Was nice to talk...'

Mellor left the house. Jeffries closed the door behind with barely a 'good night.' As the dark and cold hit Mellor he felt a wave of gloom wash over him. It was his job to stick his nose into other people's lives but sometimes he felt like an ignorant pig doing so. Jeffries was an uninteresting man trying bravely to pretend he was something more than an underpaid sales assistant with a very sick wife. His future looked bleak and the idea he would deliver that hammer blow himself by killing Krast was idiotic. His alibi for the time Krast was strangled was cast iron. It was time to get back to Broadway and report to the boss.

A few steps later he paused outside number 20. Why bother them? It was pointless. Mrs Miller would simply repeat what he'd heard, and yet the professional detective inside told him that every angle should be closed down, every loose end tied up. He knocked.

The chatty and gregarious Julie Miller did indeed confirm what he already knew and he learned a lot more about Margaret Jeffries' cancer and her interminable treatments and hospital visits and about the nurse who came around once a week, and the pies she baked to 'help poor Colin, who bless him, tries his best but was not really cut out for nursing,' and on and on and on...

Mellor wondered how he was going to escape. Julie Miller clearly thrived on having someone to talk to. To talk *at*. A fresh pair of ears to bombard with her tittle-tattle was all the encouragement she needed. He'd long since put his notebook away.

Mr Miller was seated quietly in the front parlour in front of a hissing gas fire. Apart from shaking hands upon arrival and stating that he 'hardly knew the Jeffries,' he'd beaten a safe retreat with a cup of tea and taken refuge behind the paper. Sensible man.

Mellor finally extricated himself and made his excuses. Etiquette demanded he bid the man of the house goodnight and he left Julie to get back to preparing their considerably delayed evening meal and put his head around the front parlour door. To his surprise, Mr Miller waved him in.

'Close the door and take a pew a minute.'

Curious, Mellor did as he was asked.

'You've heard more than you needed from our Julie.' He gave a chuckle. 'She's a chatty soul but without a bad bone in her body. Can't see bad in anyone. If the Devil himself came calling I swear she'd offer him a scone and a cup of tea and then tell us all he's been misrepresented and was a lovely man!' There was a twinkle in Miller's eye. 'Trouble is she can't always get a proper perspective.' He waved a nicotine-stained hand. 'The point is Detective, I go to my darts night on a Monday. Regular like.'

A pregnant pause. Mellor felt he was expected to react to the obvious implication embedded in this unremarkable statement but was failing to find anything to say.

'I go out later as I don't drink much and just want a couple of games and a bit of a natter with the boys before last orders. It being a Monday and with work the next day...'

'This is relevant...?'

Miller leaned forward and spoke quietly, as though he didn't want his happy wife to overhear. 'Mr Jeffries was out on Monday night. Every Monday night in fact... same time, same night.' He tapped the side of his nose. 'I'm not casting aspersions, but I wonder if he or his missus told you that?'

Mellor remained silent a moment. 'Where was Mr Jeffries going?'

'Opposite way to me, so can't say what his destination was. But he's been doing the same this past three months. I'm not saying he's in the wrong and he's likely just nipping out for a pint. And who'd blame him? I'm not trying to get him into trouble you understand, it's just that my wife and poor Mrs Jeffries are of the opinion he spends every night at home.'

* * * *

Mellor stood on the platform at Cheltenham (Malvern Road), which was closer to the Jeffries house than St James, hands thrust into his coat pockets and deep in thought. What did it matter that Jeffries liked a quiet pint on a Monday evening as his dying wife lay asleep upstairs? It was an innocent explanation and perhaps Colin Jeffries preferred not to admit this little indulgence to his wife. Would she chastise him for leaving her alone or admonish him for drinking or would it make her feel guilty that so many of his evenings were spent alone whilst she slept? It must be a lonely time of the evening. Did Jeffries simply want to do something on his own without the need to tell anyone or justify his actions? Jeffries lived his life utterly circumscribed by his six-day-a-week job and the relentless daily demands of a terminally ill wife. It must take a heavy toll on a man.

His train hissed alongside the platform, the scent of the steam reminiscent of baby oil in warm bath water and combined with the heat emanating from the engine, reminded Mellor of that stifling room filled with medication and impending death. He shuddered and climbed aboard the red and cream coach. He slipped into a smoking compartment and returned to considering what he'd learned, aided by a fresh fag.

Jeffries had a strong alibi for the time they believed Krast was killed. Slipping away some hours later did not seem to have any relevance, especially as it was a weekly occurrence, but there was the inescapable fact Jeffries had failed to accurately describe his Monday evening in two separate interviews related to the murder of his employer. It was odd. An innocent explanation had been proposed by Mr Miller, but if it was innocent then why had Jeffries not mentioned it? What was Jeffries eager for the police not to discover?

There was no reason why Mellor should assume Jeffries' actions were innocent. He'd not warmed to the man and was in no mood to be indulgent.

Chapter Ten

The Lygon Arms in Broadway was an impressive building. Built as a coaching inn from dressed local stone it stood four storeys high and possessed four gable ends facing outwards whilst the mullioned windows with their many square panes of old glass allowed an inviting light to spill into the darkness now enveloping the High Street.

Even Mellor appeared impressed. He'd managed, with some verbal arm-twisting, to secure small rooms for Vignoles and himself on the top floor. 'There's almost enough space to stretch your arms wide without touching each wall. And don't stand up straight or you'll clonk yer head. Still, we're lucky to get anything. There's a lot of demand when the racing's on, but as it was cancelled today, they lost a few bookings. The weatherman is still twitchy about the next days and two reservations cried off fearing the whole meeting will be a flop.' He was explaining as Vignoles and Wilcox stepped inside the grand entrance of the inn. 'I told the landlord this was a murder investigation and if didn't let us have the rooms until we'd wrapped this case up, we'd set up our enquiry office in the middle of his front lounge and see how he liked it then! Talk about scaring trade off,' Mellor chuckled.

Vignoles was not sure if this was a true account or told to impress Wilcox. Either way, it worked, as Wilcox nodded approvingly and laughed. 'Geoff's a good man, but he's got an eye on his profits. Racegoers can be profligate spenders.'

'If they've got anything left to spend,' Vignoles replied.

'The type who stay here are flush enough, win or lose. Now, gents, what are you having?'

Vignoles was already walking towards an oaken table surrounded by an odd assortment of comfy chairs close to a log fire. It was a quiet and dimly-lit corner and would suit their purposes admirably. 'Mellor will get these in. We're guests in your village and must repay the hospitality. Pints all round. We need to improve the good innkeeper's balance of payments.'

Mellor dutifully dug into his pocket and hauled out some change. He gave the local bitter a suspicious inspection as he brought the brimming glasses to the table.

'It won't poison you.' Vignoles saw his sergeant's long face.

'It's Hook Norton,' Wilcox added. 'Lovely ale.'

Mellor gave it an exploratory sip and waggled his head in a non-committal manner.

'He's used to London water,' Vignoles added for Wilcox's benefit. 'Have you learned anything more from Krast's house?'

'Not as makes any odds, guv. As you saw, the place had not been turned over and nothing stood out as missing - but how to tell when everything's in place?'

The others agreed.

'I got his papers together and skimmed through 'em, but nothing jumped out. They'll need a proper fine-tooth comb job to make sure.'

'Look for a will. We need to know who inherits his business and house,' Vignoles explained.

'Jeffries is not expecting to inherit anything. He seemed gloomy about his employment prospects when I interviewed him earlier,' Mellor responded.

'Understanding who benefits is vital. We need to see what Krast's bank account looks like.'

'A tidy sum in there, I bet,' Wilcox observed.

'Worth killing for?' Vignoles paused. 'But *only* if the killer can access the account and draw down the funds.'

'Being named in the will would help...' Mellor added.

'Yes. Gaining legal access to his money and indeed the business, looks a credible motive. Theft from the shop or his home can be scratched off. Be alert to the possibility the will is a forgery.' Vignoles was enjoying his pint and it was helping start the cogs of his mind whirring. 'Finding Krast's will is vital and talk to his solicitor to see if he smells a rat.'

Mellor agreed. 'That could explain why we can't find anything missing. The assailant took his keys and searched his gaff and shop to find Krast's will, but not to take anything else. The safe would be the obvious place...' Mellor seemed to be developing a taste for the Hook Norton and nearly finished his pint. 'They swap the real one for a forgery, retreat and wait for the reading of the will...'

'Dog walkers!'

'Eh?' Mellor was surprised by Wilcox's outburst.

'Someone walking a dog might have spooked the intruder in the house. They ran off and left the door open. Maybe someone saw them leaving? Dog walkers would be out on a wet evening, even if nobody else would be.'

'We need a door-to-door search,' Mellor was keen.

Wilcox nodded. 'PC Wentworth can walk the Snow Hill area and down the High. He knows just about everyone and can get them to open up.'

'Good. Don't forget the perpetrators needed to get from the station to his house. Was this on Shank's pony or in a motor? I want to know if anyone saw anything unusual. Cars with alien plates or unfamiliar faces out for a stroll.'

'We'll start first thing.'

'What do we make of Elsie Gable and her diamond?' Vignoles threw this out. He'd been chewing over other aspects of the case whilst the two sergeants talked.

Mellor puffed his cheeks out. 'A bit fishy, but I can't see either of 'em strangling the old fella.'

'Then getting caught in the house the next morning. That was plain stupid. Why not be in and out the same night in the dark?' Wilcox agreed. 'Elsie seems a sweet kid and Twister is no killer. He's not that sort.' He drained his glass.

Vignoles was lighting his pipe. 'I feel the same about both of them. I'm not considering either for murder, but something still niggles me. But Gable is innocent. She took the same train as Krast, which sounds significant, but she got out before he did. I telephoned Bishop's Cleeve station and they remembered her. That fact alone makes her alibi so strong it hardly justifies a follow up...'

'I could call by tomorrow and ask Mrs Gable if she can confirm her daughter's story?' Wilcox offered.

'Thank you.' Vignoles drained his pint. 'I'd be a lot happier if you found that diamond ring. Where the devil is it?'

Mellor shrugged. 'Not seen hair nor hide... I reckon there's something wrong about Jeffries. He was telling us porkies about what he was doing on

Monday night.'

'Explain.'

'I went to his house. It's a trek from the shop, but walkable. Jeffries didn't seem surprised I'd come knockin' unannounced.'

'He's either read up on police procedure or he's been up to no good and was half expecting the visit?' Wilcox responded.

'Maybe... I met his wife and she is an invalid. Looks in a poor way. Anyway, they both pretty much gave the same story that Jeffries was home by six. He warmed up food made by their neighbour, Julie Miller. They ate, listened to the radio until this same Julie swung by and chatted to his wife for an hour whilst Jeffries read the paper and tried to listen to a radio play he was following. His wife, as per usual was in bed by about nine.'

'Jeffries is thereby out of the time frame to have killed Krast,' Vignoles responded.

'Where's the problem?' Wilcox looked confused.

'It's after nine that the wheels start to fall off his wagon. I asked him again if he went out Monday evening and he swore he didn't. However, I thought it best to double-check and called into the Miller's house and after getting a long-winded story that confirmed everything about Jeffries and his wife for early evening, it was Mr Miller who told me that every Monday for the last few months, Colin Jeffries has been slipping out of his house not long after nine.'

'He goes out to do what?'

'Mr Miller reckons a quiet pint on his own.'

'Not killing anyone...'

'No, guv. But Miller doesn't actually know what he's up to. I'm not sure how this fits, maybe it doesn't, but I don't like the fact he's avoided mentioning it.'

Vignoles nodded. 'Twice over. I can't see a link, but it needs following up. He's not the killer, but is this a conspiracy, with Jeffries acting a role away from the 'coal face,' so as to speak?'

'We should tail him.'

'Not sure we can spare the resources based on this one anomaly...We'll keep Mr Jeffries' late night excursions under our collective hats for now and stay alert to possibility it is significant as the case unfolds.'

Chapter Ten

'Now, how did the killer, or killers, get to and from the station? Was it by train, in which case we need to study the timetable and see if there are witnesses on board -,'

'- won't be easy as some are long-distance.' Mellor interjected. 'We'll never trace them.'

'- or was it by car, bike or on foot?'

Wilcox stood up. 'But right now, we need another pint. And this is on me!'

Chapter Eleven

Vignoles found DS Mellor, WPC Lansdowne and a youthful constable from the local force hard at it in Krast's shop on Royal Well Place. Mr Jeffries was in attendance, with a look of insufferable pain on his face as they systematically combed through the paperwork in the back office and commenced the stock take. Miss Jephson was demurely seated behind the sales desk in the shop, at a loss what to do.

Mellor was surprised when Vignoles called WPC Lansdowne away from the tedious job of checking each item against a substantial stock list, explaining he needed her for an interview with Elsie Gable at Toddington, where she was working cleaning coaches that had brought racegoers in for the day.

'A WPC will help win her confidence and talk more freely.' It was an explanatory statement that Mellor could not counter. He grunted acknowledgement, took a bundle of papers from Lansdowne and turned back to the task in hand. He might not like it, but he was not one to shy away from the frequently tedious work policing involved. Vignoles appreciated this aspect of his new detective sergeant.

The increase in the number of passenger trains, many of which were long-distance specials pulled by a dizzying selection of fine express engines, was immediately obvious. St James was humming with people and filled by steam and excited chatter and the patter of many boots and shoes on the concourse tiles. The perishing Cotswold cold had left a silver-grey riming of frost over everything and made the distant hills look pale and ghostly, ensuring that much of the talk was about whether the racing would take place. The cancellation of the previous days' sport had sent a shiver of concern through the collective masses. Many had wisely elected to spend the morning in the comparative warmth of Cheltenham its brightly lit shops and cafes until such time they got word that racing would commence. Even the most optimistic punter knew that it would take a few hours of winter sun to offer any chance of the race officials declaring the ground fit for racing.

Chapter Eleven

Each platform was filled by lines of emptying coaches, some with locomotives trapped at the platform ends awaiting to be released. Vignoles took a quiet delight in watching the station staff and the crews of these splendid former Great Western engines bustle about in an air of ordered chaos. The sight of a gleaming 'Clun Castle' which had recently steamed in from the deepest West Country hauling away a rake of empty coaches before propelling them slowly onto a coal siding was incongruously delightful. Another train of racegoers had been brought down from the West Midlands by another 'Castle class' locomotive named 'Defiant', which now rested quietly before the buffers. A short conversation with a train guard saw Vignoles and Lansdowne ushered to an empty rake due to be hauled up line to Toddington, where it would be shunted into a siding for cleaning in readiness for the return journey that evening. Vignoles harboured a hope of 'Clun Castle' on this short journey to Toddington but had to content with 'Evenley Hall,' although she made a sprightly run of it. The weather might be cold, the case proving a puzzle, the room in the Lygon Arms like a cell and he was away from his lovely wife, but there were compensations for an enthusiast like Vignoles. He jotted the names and numbers on a page in his notebook.

Whilst 'Evenley Hall' shunted the empty stock at Toddington, they were led down to the platform end by a helpful porter, guided over a barrow crossing spanning a number of tracks and towards a series of lengthy sidings spread across a broad expanse of flat land bearing two goods sheds, which struck Vignoles as surprising for what seemed like a small township. Each siding was occupied by rakes of coaches and there was little space free. 'Squeezing a quart into a pint pot' came to mind. Wooden steps, like truncated step ladders, stood below the end doors of the nearest coaches to allow cleaning staff to board. A trolley heavily laden with pails, mops and cleaning materials stood by on the uneven ground of hard compacted ash.

'Mrs Devlin is in charge of the cleaning gals. You'd best speak to her first. She has her eye on everything and misses nothing.' The porter seemed reluctant to go closer and made his excuses.

A scrawny woman in a smock coat with a headscarf wrapped tightly around hair scraped into a tight bun was standing with a clipboard in hand and a stub of a cigarette jammed in the corner of her thin-lipped mouth.

'Yes?' There was no smile in her eyes.

'Mrs Devlin? DCI Vignoles, WPC Lansdowne of the British Railways Detective Department, Leicester. We need to speak with one of your girls.'

'What she done? Thieving, is it?' Devlin narrowed her eyes and her face took on an even harder edge. 'No-one told me about this. I'd have sorted her out without you lot traipsing down here.' She looked the kind who immediately thought the worst of people.

'There is no suggestion of any wrong-doing,' Vignoles replied. *Aside from entering the house of a murder victim, but we'll put that detail aside for now.* 'We are investigating a serious incident at Broadway station on Monday evening and wish to follow up a line of enquiry. Is Miss Elsie Gable working today?'

'Gable? Not one of the usual suspects...' Mrs Devlin retorted. 'But I'll take no nonsense from her! Nor any of them! If she's been causing trouble -.'

'She is helping us with a private matter.'

'Is she now?' Devlin shrugged her bony shoulders. 'Well, she's busy finishing this one,' and Devlin indicated the nearest coach. 'I can't spare her as we've got another three rakes due in.' This statement went some way towards explaining her brusque manner and the sound of 'Evenley Hall' propelling yet more coaches into place supported her protestations. 'You'll have to come back later - seeing as its private.' However, her eyes held a glint of interest. She wanted to know more and Vignoles was sure she would make it her own business to find out once they left.

'This is a murder enquiry and as Detective Chief Inspector of the British Railways Detective Division I expect full co-operation from *all* railway servants,' Vignoles explained.

'Murder?' Devlin gave her cigarette some attention. 'What? Elsie Gable, mixed up with murder?' She looked genuinely surprised.

'She is not a suspect. This is a routine enquiry.' *At least, I think it is...* 'If we may...?' Vignoles indicated the steps leading up to the opened carriage door, some feet above them.

'Five minutes. I can't spare more. This rake gets moved to Winchcombe when they send the engine for it - whether you're onboard or not.'

She bustled along the corridor ahead of them leaving a scent trail of soap suds and cigarettes and came to a halt beside the compartment where

Elsie Gable was on her knees washing the Linoleum floor.

'Gable! Two coppers to see you - about a *murder.*' She snorted contemptuously as if this was a complaint about dirty towels. 'You'd better not have got yourself into trouble young lady or you'll be out the door! And keep it snappy, as we're not paying you to be gabbing all day.'

'Of course, Mrs Devlin. I'm nearly done here...' Gable looked up at the faces peering down at her and her expression reminded Vignoles of a startled rabbit.

Vignoles introduced Lansdowne. 'Please take a seat Miss Gable and we'll sit opposite. You'll get neck ache looking up at us like that!' Vignoles tried to make light of the situation to put the young woman at ease.

Gable plopped her floorcloth into the bucket and sat on one of the bench seats. Vignoles let Lansdowne sit, then gave Devlin a stern look. 'If you don't mind...?' He closed the sliding door with a firm clunk and watched Devlin flounce off, probably to the next compartment. He would keep his voice low to frustrate her eager ears. 'We want to clear up a few details. We won't keep you long.'

'Oh, golly gosh...' Gable glanced nervously towards the corridor. 'Is it about yesterday? I'm dreadfully sorry about that.' She was trembling. 'I just can't imagine what made us go inside. It was so foolish. It will never happen again, I promise.'

'I sincerely hope not,' Vignoles agreed.

Lansdowne took over. 'I understand you're soon to be engaged, to Mr Twister?'

'We should have announced it by now, but we need to get a ring...'

'I understand Mr Krast offered to create a setting for a stone you already had in your possession?' She smiled encouragingly.

Gable nodded. 'Ian arranged it all. I think the old man was a bit sniffy at first, what with being accosted on the station platform...'

'But you won him around?'

She blushed. 'I think I might have, actually. When he met the two of us the day after, Mr Krast seemed more agreeable to the idea.' She giggled.

'That was kind of him,' Lansdowne replied. 'The stone - where did you get it?'

Gable fell quiet. She looked embarrassed and fiddled with a button on her tunic.

'I need you to tell us. The truth, please.'

'I found it.' She spoke softly and gave a nervous glance towards the corridor.

'Where?'

'In a carriage. Like this one. I was cleaning it.' Her neck was turning blotchy pink. 'It was a rake brought down from somewhere up North. Cheshire or mid-Wales, I can't remember exactly, but it was some distance away and in a right state. It needed a good going over and so I even dug down between the gaps at the seat backs.'

Vignoles slid a hand between the seat and the cushioned back of the one he was sitting on. 'Here?'

'That's right. We usually don't bother when we're rushed like today. But sometimes you find a shilling or two... A set of coaches can produce quite a haul.' She gave a nervous laugh.

'The stone was between the cushions?' Lansdowne questioned.

'I stuck my hand down and ran it along to see. Well, you can't *see*, only feel with your fingers. There was this tiny lump. Really hard and a bit sharp. I thought it was grit. Nothing interesting. I pulled it out and was going to toss it straight out the window without looking, but then the light caught it.'

'Can you describe it?'

'Just like a diamond! All sparkly. It was gorgeous.'

'How big?'

'Like so...' Gable indicated a size that Lansdowne considered more than generous for a cut diamond.

'You decided to keep it?'

Gable chewed her lip. 'Is that really bad? But it's not stealing, not really... We'd never find the owner...'

'Did you try?'

'No...'

Lansdowne gave a reassuring nod. 'Strictly speaking, it was *not* yours to keep, but that is not our concern right now.'

'We're supposed to hand everything in to Mrs Devlin. Any money and other lost property is handed over.'

'What happens to the money and other valuables she collects?' Vignoles asked. He suspected he knew the answer. Gable shrugged her shoulders. 'No idea.'

'So, you thought, why hand this to Mrs Devlin and never see it again?' Lansdowne sounded sympathetic.

'I knew instantly it would be perfect for an engagement ring.' She smiled wistfully and looked at Vignoles. 'Have you found it?'

'Not yet. What did Mr Krast think when you showed him the stone?'

'He said it was nice, but actually quite poor quality and worth nothing.' Gable looked offended. 'But what do I know?'

A lot less than Krast, that's for sure. Was he taking this young woman for a ride? Vignoles decided to keep his suspicions quiet.

'Where were you Monday between five and eight o'clock in the evening?' Lansdowne asked.

'Here until six. We knocked off and I went straight home. I wash my hair on Monday's after we've eaten and sit and dry it by the fire.'

'Can anyone confirm that?'

'Mum and dad. They were home all evening.'

Vignoles stood up, 'We won't keep you any longer. Thank you for your time.' He tipped his hat as they left the compartment. Mrs Devlin was hovering close, an expectant look in her hawkish eyes. Neither he nor Lansdowne said a word of any consequence to her as they exited the coach.

Chapter Twelve

'What did we learn from Miss Gable, sir?'

They were seated in a quiet corner of the Bayshill Inn, not far from Krast's Jewellery shop. They needed sustenance and after tucking into fish and chips eaten out of newspaper wrappers in the jewellery shop, much to the horror of Mr Jeffries, Vignoles decided a drink would help lubricate their minds. They'd left the young PC sent down by Sergeant Wilcox in charge at the shop, reassured by the knowledge the PC had sensibly arrived pre-armed with a packet of sandwiches and a flask of tea.

'We learned that her story is plausible and on the balance of probability, true. I believe she's still of the opinion the stone is of no financial value.'

'But you think differently?' Mellor asked.

'I do. You've seen Krast's shop and the stock he handled. I see no reason for him wasting his time on a piece of cut glass for two youngsters with little money. However, they convinced him to take a look at the stone, probably by being persistent and irritating, and once he saw it realised its true worth. He was happy to take on the project then.'

'She stumbled on a genuine diamond?' Lansdowne exclaimed.

'That would explain Krast's willingness to take it off them. I suspect he delayed making the simple setting for the stone because he was trying to hoodwink them.'

'Swap it for a cheap one? The cheating little bugger!' Mellor perked up. This was more like it. The case was developing an edge. Darker motives starting to be uncovered.

'If this diamond was special then it would be worth his while exchanging for a similar one of lower value.'

'It could take time to get a close match...' Lansdowne added.

'Precisely. And Krast was going to need time to find a way to sell the original diamond. This could be a lengthy and tricky process.'

'He needed someone with serious spending power.' Mellor added.

'Is the diamond market not regulated? Could he sell such a valuable stone without proving he had title to it and offering provenance? A buyer would insist on that, want to understand how it came to be cut and by whom and how Krast came to have it.'

Mellor gave Lansdowne a strange look. 'How come you know so much about the diamond trade? You dark horse...'

'Just common-sense. I'm no expert.' She looked mildly irritated by Mellor.

'I think Lucy's right,' Vignoles responded. 'Krast would need to trade illegally, and unless he knew what he was doing, could get into a very dangerous situation. Crooks dealing at this level are going to be clever and duplicitous, with considerable power and influence.'

'Mobsters? Underworld gangs?' Lansdowne questioned.

'Yeah...The sort of lowlife who'd take the rock for themselves and save themselves a packet by not paying up. The threat of violence and intimidation until he handed it over...' Mellor lit up and blew smoke upwards in a satisfied stream. 'Or simply bump Krast off and pocket the stone. Job done.'

'We should give this consideration, but not become fixated on it. We have no proof of any of it.' Vignoles interjected. 'Or do we...? Has the trawl through Krast's papers thrown up anything interesting?'

'Not that I can find. It's an insight into the life of those with the money to flash on expensive jewellery, but nothing suspicious.' Mellor supped his pint then gave his cigarette attention before elaborating. He approved of his new guvnor's love of a pub as a makeshift office. 'All 'Lord and Lady This and That' and dealings with Bond Street jewellers and other suppliers of fine silver. A different world from what we know... But I haven't found anything that helps.'

Vignoles was not surprised. 'Anything suggesting a motive for murder?'

'The stock take shows everything as it should be when cross-checked with the lists Jeffries holds, and he's a meticulous cove. Everything neatly recorded, as you might expect.'

'Which reinforces the idea Jeffries and Jephson are in the clear. There was nothing from the house that drew your interest?'

'I'm nearly through, but it's awfully dull fare. House bills, deeds to his house and a few legal papers from his solicitor,' Lansdowne replied. She took a sip from her glass of tepid white wine.

'Give those legal papers attention,' Mellor instructed. 'Legals are always worth the effort.'

'As you wish...' Lansdowne didn't feel inspired.

Vignoles put his pint down and started to fill his pipe. 'So, we've drawn a blank but before we jump to making wild conclusions and hypotheses as yet unproven, we should review everyone we've interviewed and see if anyone has a credible motive to kill Krast - or have him killed.'

'Colin Jeffries,' Mellor led off. 'We should confirm his situation now Krast is dead. Getting his employer killed seems a dumb move unless he is either in with a gang trying to take the diamond...'

'He hardly seems the sort to be linked with a criminal gang...'

'Agreed. Or, he stands to inherit and when we find the will we can see for ourselves. Seems unlikely, but Krast was a lonely soul and maybe his staff are his surrogate family?' Mellor blew a stream of smoke out and sat back in his chair. 'Either way, he couldn't have done the old man in, but maybe he was working with others and his Monday night visits are related?'

'We need to investigate further, but he feels more like an accomplice, at best.' Vignoles concurred. 'We discount Miss Jephson?'

'She's now out of work and out of pocket and has a strong alibi.' Mellor smiled into his pint. 'Feel a bit sorry for her. Sitting around all morning looking lost...'

'You've changed your tune,' Vignoles gave his DS a sly look.

'How?'

'If I asked you to double-check her alibi you wouldn't complain, despite being a waste of time.' There was no harm in Mellor appreciating that little passed Vignoles' hawk eye. The DS had certainly noticed that Alice Jephson was young, pretty and single. Lansdowne looked like she was going to laugh and hurriedly sipped her wine.

'Best to be sure!' Mellor returned the comment with a straight face. 'What about the odd couple?' He moved the conversation on.

'Elsie Gable strikes me as a straightforward character. She seems fundamentally decent.'

'Except she snuck into Krast's house!' Mellor fired back at Vignoles.

'The door was open...'

'A likely story!'

Vignoles puffed his pipe. 'We can't prove that point either way, but we didn't find Krast's keys in the house nor about their person and the door showed no signs of being forced. I can imagine Gable was encouraged to step inside by Twister. Which brings us to Ian Twister. What do you make of him?'

Mellor weighed up his reply. 'I've seen plenty of trouble makers and whilst Twister is a bit of a lad, he's no killer or gang member.'

'We strike them off. The station staff on duty that evening all have alibis, including Twister. The only fly in the ointment is the missing engagement ring. Have you found any evidence Krast even had it? Something in writing, a scribbled note...?'

'Nothing.'

Lansdowne agreed with Mellor.

'Double-check. Go back to the house. I need to understand what Krast did with it; a name or telephone number of someone he might have shown it to. A diary entry...'

'You think the diamond was the reason he was killed?' Lansdowne asked.

'It's a distinct possibility. But it's also small and easy to conceal or mislay, so we cannot ignore the idea it's just tucked inside an envelope or lost in the pile of a carpet. It could be right under our noses and totally irrelevant. I want to see evidence of this blasted thing before we get too excited about it being the root cause of all the trouble.'

'We take Gable's story on face value?' Mellor sounded sceptical.

'Gable wouldn't know real from fake - I know I wouldn't. Gable convinced me she found it between seat cushions.'

'The true owner may not have realised they lost it on the train,' Lansdowne suggested. 'A mortifying loss, but where would they start to look?'

'Even if the loss was discovered not long after leaving the train, what are the chances they could identify the exact compartment and convince a stationmaster to call down the line and have the train searched? And let's not ignore the possibility that whoever lost it might not want anyone else to know they had it...'

'It was 'hot' when it was lost?' Mellor asked.

'Pure conjecture, but I don't remember a call to arms to find Lady Whatever's lost diamond with a suitably hefty reward for the finder.'

Lansdowne shook her head.

'Me neither.' Mellor finished his pint before continuing. 'Who knew about Gable's fake diamond?'

'I reckon she and Twister kept it quiet. She'd want to show it to her family and friends once it's on her finger. That's how it works with an engagement,' Lansdowne looked at her own left hand and the diamond ring her fiancé Frankie Wainwright had presented her one warm summer evening in 1953. 'Not a word from me, not even to Jane or my mum! I wanted it to be a surprise.'

'You two still not tied the knot, after all this time?' Mellor gave her a cheeky wink. 'He gettin' cold feet?'

'I don't think that's your business, sergeant.' Her green eyes glowered.

'Just askin' luv...' Mellor raised an eyebrow and exhaled a plume of smoke.

Lansdowne looked put out and fiddled with the ring on her finger. It wasn't Frankie getting cold feet so much as a lack of time and opportunity. Reconstructing West Germany was going to be a mammoth task and his abilities specialising in re-building bombed bridges and railway infrastructure were in constant demand. What had started as a short-term position had developed into a long-term commitment whilst he studied for his Architecture degree and clocked up valuable hands-on experience. Frankie was proving a natural in reconstruction work and his services were eagerly sought, with some tempting work offers once he'd qualified. He was turning into quite a 'catch'. Perhaps it was Lansdowne who was now having doubts. He'd asked her to join him in West Germany and settle down... start a family before it was too late. But that meant giving up her job...and her independence...

'We are not here to discuss WPC Lansdowne's private affairs,' Vignoles intervened. 'Twister and Gable are planning an engagement and either of them could have bragged about their lucky find around their respective villages. Broadway is a small place and I suspect Bishop's Cleeve even smaller.'

Mellor stood up. 'Then we need to ask more questions. We need to sniff out someone with an unhealthy interest in her chance find.'

Vignoles realised Mellor was urging them to drink up and get on with the investigation. An admirable work ethic, but Vignoles wanted another pint and time to finish his pipe. Besides, wasn't it his decision when they left?

He drained his glass and stood up.

Chapter Thirteen

Lord Buckrose adjusted his tie using his reflection in a shop window, tweaked the lie of his hat and gave his coat a smooth with a gloved hand. He looked serviceable, although the overcoat would benefit from a steam press. The creases where he'd not folded it perfectly were an irritation but perhaps would shake out with wearing. However, these minor quibbles aside, he knew he looked the part.

He checked his watch. This was a glorious thing of silver with a black dial. Swiftly pocketing this from where it lay on a poolside towel in a swanky hotel in Cannes had been one of his wiser moves. It never lost a second and seemed to ooze wealth and status at a glance. The silver tie pin with the sapphire on the end was a similarly purloined extravagance. Bank tellers and indeed, bank managers, always fell for a gentleman with a watch costing the same as a small semi-detached in Harlow and with a sparkly jewel flashing before their eyes. At least, he hoped they did.

He took a breath, steadied his nerves and confidently strode into the bank. Leaning on the polished counter top as if he was a regular, he pulled out his cheque book with a carefully practised flourish and gave the middle-aged lady bank teller the full force of his disarming smile whilst hoping he'd proffered the correct one for this bank. With three different accounts at three different banks to juggle, it would be an embarrassing mistake.

As Buckrose engaged her with a few opening gambits about the coldness of the weather and his concerns about the 'going' during the festival. She was softening up nicely. 'Some extra funds for the racing, y'know? Costs a bally fortune with the luck I have, ha ha!' He hesitated before writing in the amount. 'I have a horse running later...Costs a fortune, but I've managed to bag a promising young jockey called Piggott to ride her...'

'Really? I've heard he shows a lot of promise. I do hope you get a win!'

'So do I. The trainer's fees need paying,' he laughed easily. 'Serves me right for giving it such a silly name...'

'Yes?'

'I called her Money For Nothing. And that's what I got.'

'Perhaps today your luck will be in.'

'Thank you. Now, here's the thing, I'm down from my estate in the North East...' He was taking the cap off an exquisite fountain pen in preparation of filling out the cheque. 'I'm sure your manager will allow me to draw out a little extra to help things along? I don't like to travel with too much ready cash about my person, because one never knows these days. So many louts and those awful Teddy Boys stalking the streets...' He paused in mock horror. 'You don't have *those* sort here do you?'

'Not in Cheltenham, sir! It is perfectly safe. We're a respectable town.' Another warm smile.

'Thank goodness.' He started to write 'twenty pounds' but paused deliberately to look the teller in the eye. 'Not that I expect any trouble in the Royal box of course. I'm invited tomorrow...' He gave an almost childishly soft laugh. 'Although, between you and me...' and he gave her an outrageous stage wink, 'Her Majesty and the Duke are quite a giggle. When the Queen gets to the races, she really let's her guard down and is quite the entertainer, and then the Duke! His stories are legendary...' He checked to see that his words were hitting home. 'I should not have let that slip...most indiscreet.' He gave her a secret look of horror and dropped his voice. 'You didn't hear it from me, but Her Majesty is attending the Gold Cup. I'd get into the most *awful* hot water with the Duke if he knew I'd been blabbing that about!'

The bank teller shook her head. 'I won't say a word.' It was clear she was dying to hear more.

He signed with a flourish.

The teller was looking doubtfully at the cheque.

'I always sign as Lord Buckrose, I never use the family name. We go back to Norman times y'know? Lord Buckrose of Sledmire to be exact.' He dropped his voice to almost a whisper now, 'it's a Devil of mouthful I know.' He tapped the side of his nose. 'The manager will understand. Actually, my title comes with a sizeable chunk of the East Riding, so it won't bounce.'

The teller went bright red. 'I-I did not think for a moment...' She hurriedly opened the cash drawer and started counting.

'Think no more of it, my dear.' He drew a silent sigh of relief. He was itching to snatch the money and stuff it in his wallet and race out of the bank and up to the racecourse, but instead adopted a look of bored indifference as the notes were carefully counted out whilst he started to tell a horse related anecdote about a minor Royal.

Chapter Fourteen

Vignoles had enjoyed a swift ride to Broadway aboard an unusual working made up of an empty rake of coaches and a clutch of horse boxes. These needed to be taken up line and stored out of the way at Broadway until the end of the day's racing. Number 7312, the eager 'Mogul' type engine at the front, made light work of the train and had cantered along with its chuntering exhaust beat echoing the thundering hooves of the oddly-named racehorses it would carry home later that day.

Vignoles stood on Broadway platform as the locomotive efficiently propelled the train back onto a siding and cleared the 'up' line in readiness for the Wolverhampton-bound express. He waited with pipe in mouth to watch, as he knew to expect something rather special at the head of this train. 'Glastonbury Abbey' hurtled through the station at a speed belying her Edwardian birthdate in a whoosh of spinning driving wheels and frantic connecting rods and a chatter of coach wheels on rail joints. It was but a fleeting glance, but Vignoles appreciated seeing one of the last three 'Star' class engines in service and wondered if he would get the chance again.

As the last of the smoke drifted away leaving a pungent but pleasant smell of hot oil and burnt coal, he pondered his next move. The absence of witnesses to the killing of Krast was nagging at him. Was it one, or more persons involved? He needed to at the very least establish that basic fact. Were they tall, short, thin, fat? What kind of clothes were they wearing? Male or female, for that matter. He urgently needed something to work with, and hence was back at Broadway.

Whoever killed Krast had to have got on and off the station either unseen or in such a manner they attracted no attention or failed to register in the memory. They might have alighted from a train and departed later in the same manner, but after studying the timetable and noting the significant gaps between the infrequent stopping services, this would have meant waiting for a long time on the platform after killing Krast. Even with a fortuitously darkened and unlocked waiting room, the chance of being observed was far too high and it was improbable to believe anyone would take such a monumental risk. The stationmaster confirmed the train that brought Krast to the station waited barely a minute before steaming away and collected no passengers. There was insufficient time for Krast to be strangled and the same train used as a getaway.

That meant the killer or killers must have walked on and off the station, if not exactly in broad daylight (it being dark and drizzly on Monday evening) then at least in view of the station staff - if anyone had looked. Mellor's enquiries had drawn a blank. Nobody had seen anything. How was that possible? Vignoles had been in this job long enough to decide it was worth a second approach, but from a slightly different angle.

This somebody had failed to lodge in the collective brains of the local station staff. Perhaps because they were colleagues or friends and thereby not considered to be suspicious and worthy of mention? The other explanation was that any potential witness had been distracted and consequently saw nothing. This idea was finding favour with Vignoles, because careful analysis of the statements Mellor had collected had enabled Vignoles to place each member of the station staff around the time the 'Coffeepot' had deposited Krast on the platform and up to about half-an-hour on either side. The few staff working that evening had all been inside their respective offices or busy inside the goods shed and signal box. It had not been a night for idling on the platforms or gazing out of rain-spattered windows into the night.

The obvious potential witness was the ticket clerk. He would have the best view of anyone, guarding as he did, the only public entrance onto the station. Reading through ticket clerk Harry Knight's statement, Vignoles decided he wanted to have another crack at Mr Knight, who was on duty and seated behind his desk. Vignoles approached the glass window with the cut out to aide speaking and the handing over of the Edmundson railway tickets.

'Mr Knight, you told DS Mellor that on Monday evening there was a gentleman making enquiries about delivering a horse to the station.'

'That's right, Inspector.'

'Is this a typical enquiry?'

'Quite normal. We have horses coming and going all the time and down Toddington, Laverton and at Racecourse, of course.' He laughed at his repetition of the word 'course'.

'Ah, yes, I noticed the horse dock here. Why is it so popular to unload at Broadway? It's some distance from the racecourse.'

'You might be better off asking the trainers that! On race days the majority do go straight to Racecourse station, but remember, not all horses are for the racing. We've got the fox hunt that starts from here and people travel some distance to ride in that. It is considered a great honour to be invited. We've got a meet this Saturday, and you'll see two hunters arriving here on Friday. Then there's the point-to-point meets and the hunts. Some of the horses for these go up to stables along the vale or to one of the big manor houses.'

'Then you are kept busy making booking arrangements?' This confirmed what Biggs had told Vignoles yesterday, but he wanted to keep the man talking. The more a witness talked, the better the information gathered.

'If the owners or trainers are in with the gentry on the estates, they get use of their stables, and some of the big houses and farms around here even have gallops to give time for the horses to settle in and ready themselves for the big day.'

'It's quite a business!' This was not so different from Leicestershire, where hunting in particular produced a quantity of equine traffic. 'Who was making the enquiry on Monday evening?'

'I didn't know the chap. His was a new face to me.' Vignoles was filling his pipe as Knight was speaking and nodded encouragingly. 'But we get so many from far and wide... I can't know them all.'

'Did he offer a name?'

'Not that I remember...but let me check in my ledger in case I jotted it down.' Knight walked away from the ticket window and stood with his back to Vignoles as he flipped through a large book on the far countertop. He spoke over his shoulder as he did so. 'Monday...7th... Ah, yes, now you see I had to refuse the request to accept a horse on the day he wanted, which was this Thursday, because that being Gold Cup day we were already at capacity.' He had turned to face Vignoles, but remained where he was standing, some distance from the little window. 'I suggested he tried Laverton, although I didn't hold out much hope for the same reason, as they are preferred for the big races, despite having more docking space to offer.'

'His was a race horse?'

'I presumed so at the time...' He approached the ticket window again. 'But it's funny, now I think about it, he contradicted himself. Said the horse was a racer, but later I'm sure he was talking about riding with Saturday's hunt.'

'That's not likely?'

'Absolutely not! Imagine the stir it would cause at the meet! A thoroughbred racehorse. It would be utter madness.'

They both laughed.

'Did he say it was his horse?'

'He was a trainer working for the Earl of Buckrose. Or was he a Lord? I can't remember...a titled gent, anyway. Apparently, His Lordship is well in with the family at Stanway Hall and -,' Knight stopped and the leaned closer to Vignoles and lowered his voice a notch. 'He told me to promise not to tell anyone, but under the circumstances, and what with you being a detective, it won't hurt to say, but he was telling me how this Buckrose gentleman was looking forward to joining Her Majesty in the Royal Box during the Gold Cup... He owns a number of good horses apparently, and of course the young Queen is most knowledgeable on the subject...'

'And has few of her own...' Vignoles puffed his pipe, good-naturedly.

'I happen to know M'as-Tu-Vu is coming in tomorrow. Straight to Racecourse station.' He gave Vignoles the sort of look that suggested he should be impressed. 'There's a good chance Her Majesty is going to be here, as it's her horse.'

Vignoles wasn't remotely interested in Royal gossip, nor particularly in horse owners or breeders, but what was grabbing his attention was the realization that all this discussion about bringing in a horse could have been the perfect distraction. 'What time did you have this discussion with Buckrose's trainer?'

'About 6.30.'

'About the same as when the auto train to Honeybourne stopped here?'

'Yes, that's correct...' There was a flicker of concern on Knight's face. 'The auto train stops here at 6.37 and I remember hearing it pull in and depart.'

'Heard it, or saw it?'

'I remember the sound. The gong the guard clangs to set it on its way to Honeybourne.'

Then Knight had his back turned whilst giving attention to this enquiry just as Krast was getting off his train. 'Was there anyone waiting on the platform or wishing to buy a ticket?'

'No. At that time of evening and with nothing else due apart from the local, it would be unlikely. We only have the one regular getting off that service...' Knight stopped. 'It's not properly sunk in yet. Poor Mr Krast. I don't like looking across the tracks. It gives me a strange feeling...'

'I can appreciate that. But back to Monday evening. You saw nobody else, apart from the enquirer at that time?

'Can't say as I did.'

'How did you leave this enquiry about his Lordship's horse?'

'I offered to put a call through to Laverton, which I duly did, and they surprised me by saying that they might be able to squeeze one more horse in. I rang off and told the gent the good news. He was most grateful, and I then offered directions as how to get there as he seemed a little non-plussed about the geography. It is a winding route and not easy if you're an out-of-towner.'

'You were sure he was not local?'

'He was from down London way. A Southerner with a posh accent.'

'Mr Knight, could you call Laverton and ask if they have accepted a horse on behalf of this Earl of Buckrose?'

'If you wish...' He turned away again and busied himself with the telephone, his back once more to the platform. After a brief greeting and a short explanatory conversation, his tone of voice answered the question. 'Most odd, sir. They've not heard from him. They held the space and awaited a visit or a telephone call to confirm the booking, but nothing! How uncommonly rude. After all the trouble I went to, he could have had the common decency to take up the offer.' Knight looked put out.

Vignoles however was feeling more motivated than he had since he'd arrived. 'Can you give me a description of this man?'

Five minutes later, after making detailed notes and getting Knight's agreement that if he could call upon the services of a Police artist they would sit with Knight and attempt to sketch a likeness. It now looked as though there were two perpetrators. One to distract, Knight whilst the other crossed the bridge and lay in wait for Krast. It was an audacious and bold plan.

It struck Vignoles that the modern-day felon appeared to be learning that the less they looked and acted like felons, the easier it was to get away with murder.

Chapter Fifteen

Paddington Station was buzzing with the noise and chatter of commuters, shoppers and sightseers all moving one way or the other and invariably in opposite directions, ensuring they created maximum confusion and turmoil. Some individuals stood like rocks amidst this swirling river of people with newspapers, umbrellas or cases in hand as they peered at the departure and arrivals boards or contorted their faces whilst trying to decipher the echoing messages broadcast in the sweetly enunciated tones of the station announcer. From the frequency of her amplified pronouncements and the puzzled expressions on those listening, it would appear there was a seemingly inexhaustible supply of trains about to either arrive or depart from a platform different from that originally declared, whilst some, inevitably, were running late.

Steam drifted upwards from the around the many Brunswick green engines proudly bearing polished copper and brass work. Their chimneys capped in burnished metal as were safety valve covers formed into elegant shapes as if products of a Bosnian street trader not the artisans inside Swindon Works. Many locomotives bore nameplates that shone in the lights suspended from Brunel's great over-arching train sheds and these read like pages from school history books; the names of Kings, Castles and unremembered manorial halls somewhere in deepest Dorset or Wales.

However, it was to Gloucestershire the two gentlemen were headed and appropriately, the engine now backing down to couple onto the line of coaches was named 'County of Gloucester,' not that either gentleman bothered to look. They were more interested in finding a quiet compartment in the first class section and eyeing up the location of the dining car.

'This is becoming a regular jaunt. Twice in three days.' Observed Kane as he settled back into the plush deep blue cushions.

'Strictly speaking old chap, this is a different route, albeit to the same destination,' Abel responded with a casual wave of his gloved hand. 'We shall change at Bristol. Always pays to vary one's habits.'

'Agreed. I don't like people to second-guess our movements,' Kane was lighting a cigarette, the missing upper section of the ring finger of his right hand clear to see as he flicked his Zippo lighter into action. The wound had healed but the cold weather made it throb, reminding him of their recent failure and the physical price they'd had to pay. 'Best make this the last. We need to sort this out good and proper or things might get awkward.'

Abel leaned forward to light his menthol cigarette from the same flame. He settled back into his seat and wriggled his back as he did so to itch the irritation of the acid burns across his shoulders. Failure to deliver on a promise was not taken lightly by their paymasters. Acute physical pain was considered just punishment for their failings. Both men knew their track record and ruthless ability to follow orders had saved them from concrete boots and a swim in the Thames. Kane and Able could administer punishment without mercy and devise especially imaginative and unpleasant means of destroying or terminating the lives of those they hunted, so they'd taken their beatings and mutilations with a stoicism that privately impressed, and chilled, their tormentors.

Kane knew what his partner in crime was suffering as he struggled to get comfortable. 'We screwed up.' He shook his head in disgust and swore. His sense of mortification was absolute. This was not their style and the hurt burned deeper than the acid on Abel's back or when the meat cleaver sliced through the skin and bone of his finger.

'Agreed, dear boy. I wonder if we were too casual?' The agonising itching of melted skin served as a constant reminder. 'We took our eyes off the ball and acted in haste. I feel the disappointment harder than I feel these maddening burns.' His monocle dropped from his eye and lay against his Jermyn Street tailored suit.

'We were distracted by the girl. We should 'ave gone straight for the mother. Full force...' Kane held his right hand up and inspected the stump of finger. 'Could be worse, I can still use a gun.' He chortled.

'What's done is done. I'm more peeved that so far, we've drawn a blank.'

Kane nodded agreement and watched as the train guard walked past their window along the platform with an urgent spring to his step. He was going for a last word with the engine crew, confirming the number of carriages and the estimated weight of the train. They would soon be off.

'We've eliminated the jeweller from our enquiries.'

'And drew a blank in so doing...'

'Annoying. Risky business doing him in and all for nothing. But not a completely wasted journey.'

'Elucidate me?' Abel was screwing his monocle back in place. 'A negative hardly draws us closer to getting the Hornet back. I'm unclear what our plan should be once back in Cheltenham.'

'Details, details...' Kane took a long drag on his cigarette and as he did so, sensed a quietness descend around the train as the moment of departure arrived. 'County of Gloucester' gave a sonorous whistle and then a series of rapid sharp barks from the double chimney that hinted at a short wheel slip, then the train creaked into motion. The pace rapidly increased as the powerful 4-6-0 found its feet and the driver opened her up.

'We've got to work with what we know. Be logical and methodical.' Kane fished out his notebook and flipped through it to find a specific page. 'We know Krast had the stone. Fact.'

'I'll go with that. Our friend in Bethnal Green told us his name.'

'Looks like this Buckrose talked Krast into letting him get his mitts on the diamond. We dunno who this posh geezer is, but he blabbed more than he should to that rat, Slatter.'

'But who *is* Buckrose? I've made no headway in Debrett nor The Dictionary of National Biography. The name crops up connected to some minor landed gentry, but the man himself and his family have evaded me. I could explore a few other angles, but I'm loathe to declare our hand.' Abel made a smoke ring in the space between them.

'Wise move. We need to keep a low profile. His Lordship's a proper Scarlet Pimpernel.'

'A charlatan!' Abel looked outraged.

'But clever with it. He's done a decent job - so far.' Kane gave a wicked wink. 'I think he's a pro.'

'It will make the hunt all the more challenging...'

Kane was consulting his notebook. 'We know Krast got 'The Hornet's Beauty' and had it in Cheltenham or Broadway. But he gave it away...'

'Foolish man...' Abel spread his arms wide. 'Why return? The horse has bolted?'

'Neat analogy. Two reasons: We're returning because Buckrose let slip he has a racehorse and if you bothered to take an interest in the back pages, you'd find there's an 'orse with his name attached. Registered with some shady tax-avoiding off-shore syndicate in Jersey, but the name Lord Buckrose slipped out in the racing talk about Money For Nothing. Given enough time I'm sure I could find out who the syndicate really are and where they live.'

'But we're in a hurry.'

'We are. I'm thinking his Lordship's got the hot rock with him, or at least knows where it is, and before he passes it on, we need to relieve him of it.'

'With some friendly persuasion...' Abel glanced at his polished leather doctor's bag on the seat beside him.

'And seeing as Buckrose's horse is racing in the Cheltenham Festival...'

'He'll want to watch?'

'He's bound to be town and my guess he wants to hob nob with all the rich and famous on Gold Cup day. We'll find him. Drawn like a horse fly to a fresh pile of horse shit!' Kane snorted contemptuously. 'I want to sort this out good and proper.' Kane gave his mutilated hand a glance. 'It's caused me enough aggravation already.'

'And the other reason?'

'When I was squeezin' the life out of the old man and whilst he could still speak, he accused me of being in his shop. Said he'd found us out. Knew we'd been in an' searched it.'

'But we hadn't!'

'No...but when you're pleading for your life you tell the truth. So, when he says someone was in there, I believed him. Someone beat us to it. Probably Buckrose, who maybe stole it, not cajoled it. Either way... there's something not right. We need to get back and ask some awkward questions.'

The 'County of Gloucester' gave a long whistle as it raced onwards, billows of steam tumbling past the window as the carriage wheels maintained a relaxing rhythm on the rail joints and the telegraph wires slung between poles looped past the window in a mesmerising rising and falling motion.

'Agreed. I say, a day at the races! Splendid.' Abel's mood had visible lifted. 'Now, how about a little 'stiffener' in the buffet car before lunch?'

Chapter Sixteen

Vignoles, Mellor and Lansdowne had convened in the Lygon Arms for sustenance and to review the day's work. The table near the roaring fire was becoming their office. There were worse places.

'I think I have something.' Vignoles explained. 'Not a lot but needs checking.'

'More than we've got...' Mellor ruefully admitted.

'Mr Knight, the ticket clerk at Broadway, appears to have been distracted by an enquiry on Monday evening just as Krast was stepping off his train. A gentleman wanted to book a slot for bringing in a racehorse on Thursday. Knight didn't take the enquirer's name or address as they ended up moving the potential booking to Winchcombe Station. However, Knight provided a good description and we might even get a decent likeness if an artist sits with him. Better still, we have a name.'

Mellor and Lansdowne immediately sat upright.

'The Earl of Buckrose or it could be Lord Buckrose. Knight was unclear which, but he spoke with a man who claimed to be the trainer of Buckrose's racehorse.'

'But he was a phoney?'

'That is a possibility, as the trainer gave a confused impression about whether it was a racehorse or for riding to hounds and never followed up the reservation at Winchcombe despite appearing eager to secure it. Not a lot, but at least we have a name and title and something to work on.'

'But if it is a front, then there is no such person...' Mellor responded.

'Indeed not. But we first need to establish if this was a legitimate enquiry or a ruse to distract Knight. The timing feels significant.'

'I could try the library in Cheltenham tomorrow?' Lansdowne suggested. 'Titles are well-documented as a rule and relatively easy to trace assuming the library has a decent stock of reference volumes.'

'Telephone Blencowe and get him or Benson on this. I suspect it will be a wild goose chase and just a smokescreen. We need you here following other lines that might prove more fruitful.'

'Righty-ho.'

'How do you see this trainer fitting into the case, guv?'

'The enquiry was alleged to be urgent and involved Knight in some discussion and a telephone call to Winchcombe station. When I questioned him about it, I noticed he stood at the far side of his office with his back to the window and any view on to the platforms. I suggest it was a shaggy dog story to buy time whilst an accomplice slipped on and off the station.'

'And strangled Krast...' Mellor seemed to like the scenario. 'You have a description?'

'Well-spoken with a southern or London accent. Typical country clothing of tweeds and hat. Soft skin, blue eyes, one watering. Confident and an off-hand manner.'

'Something to work with. We do need a likeness. I'll make enquiries with Sergeant Wilcox. Maybe there's an artist around here? It's that sort of a place; all arty and chocolate boxy...' Mellor made it sound like a fault.

'What did you learn from Krast's solicitor?' Vignoles drank deeply from his pint as he looked at his sergeant.

Mellor seemed to be weighing up his response whilst he attacked his own pint. 'His solicitor is one Alan Jephson.' The expected raising of Vignoles's eyebrow followed. 'Father of Alice...'

'The young woman who works at Krast's jewellers?' Lansdowne asked.

Vignoles gave his sergeant a beady look. 'Then there *is* a connection...'

'Only as much as he put her name forward to old Krast for a Saturday job. Hardly cause for concern.' Mellor suddenly sounded defensive.

'Which grew into a permanent position...'

'She proved competent.'

'The family can easily afford a television on a solicitor's salary...' Vignoles grinned.

Mellor brushed this aside. 'I imagine so, but either way, Miss Jephson is not a suspect, as we've established, even if her father does handle the legal side of Krast's business.'

Vignoles supped more beer and left this hang a moment. 'Who benefits from Krast's death in the will?'

'Nobody. He left ten quid to the Cat's Defence League and similar sums to various charities in the area. What's left in his bank account - if anything after costs - goes to a cousin in Czechoslovakia, but only if they can trace him. Mr Jephson was not sounding optimistic on that point, having never had any dealings with the distant relative. He is not aware the cousin has ever visited Britain.'

'But sarge, he's a jeweller in well-to-do Cheltenham. There must be a healthy balance in his account?' Lansdowne piped up.

'Nope. He's in debt. Hocked to his eyeballs. Stoney-broke... I went to see his bank manager, Mr Carshalton, and discovered his house is held as security on loans to the top of his borrowing limit. Carshalton told me he was getting twitchy about Krast's ability to pay. The house will be taken by the bank and sold at auction and once the lawyer has taken his fees and then funeral costs and what not there won't be a brass farthing.'

Vignoles and Lansdowne exchanged surprised looks. 'That is unexpected. His shop exudes an aura of wealth and success. However, it is expensive stock and a few misjudged purchases, a bad debt or two and he could lose more money in days than we'd see in a lifetime.'

'Precisely.' Mellor made a pained expression. 'Trouble is, that's all very interesting but if nobody benefits from bumping him off, then why do it?'

'A motiveless crime?' Lansdowne looked puzzled.

Vignoles had his pipe alight. 'Bad debts and a desperate need to bankroll more purchases of stock suggest a man liable to make bad choices. Did Krast get into trouble with a loan shark?'

'When I was working in Paddington we heard about some pretty nasty sorts in that line. Not people you wanted to cross. Failure to meet their extortionate demands brought retribution. Beatings, fingers lost. Or decapitated corpses on the railway tracks.'

Lansdowne shuddered.

Vignoles could imagine. 'He'd failed in a repayment and brought dangerous attention upon himself?'

'Someone came looking to put pressure on him?' Mellor made as if he were strangling himself.

'I can understand leaning on him to extract payment. Perhaps going too far, and killing him, but why not then take his stock and sell it on? I mean, they wanted money - not a corpse. The killers got no material benefit and a potential death sentence around their necks.' Lansdowne was not convinced.

'Fair point...' Mellor went back to his pint.

'I think a bad debt from unscrupulous crooks lies at the heart of this, but there's something else we're missing. They wanted something that was *not* in his shop nor in his house, but which made the risk worthwhile.'

'But let's not forget, stolen jewellery can be hard to fence. Especially when a whole lot is lifted at once from a single shop. We'd put the alarm out and everyone would be on high alert and only the dumbest fence would handle the stuff,' Mellor explained.

'The stock would become too dangerous to touch?' Lansdowne queried.

'Yep. They'd have CID, the Met and their Flying Squads down on them in no time.'

'Why London?' Vignoles queried.

'Didn't you say that geezer talking about his horse was from London or thereabouts? It's the most probable outlet. London is where all the hottest stuff is most easily fenced.'

'A reasonable supposition based on what we know, but beware hanging too much on that until we can be sure it's not a red herring.' Vignoles replied. 'OK, if Krast was broke and couldn't pay, then no amount of intimidation was going to extract more money. Not the amounts you imagine they were seeking, at least. There must be something else they wanted. Something we've neither found nor identified.'

'Which makes it something that's going to slip under the radar and be easier to sell on...something not on the inventory.' Mellor looked excited. 'The old fella was trading in stolen property. That must be it!'

Vignoles put his pint down with a thump. 'Colin Jeffries told us that Krast dealt with particularly discreet enquiries at his home.'

'He did. And Twister did a private deal, sidling up to the old man in the street. I thought that was iffy since the start.'

'The local lad from the station? Could he be in on a racket?' Lansdowne asked.

'Could be... Sneaking in the house in broad daylight to recover a piece of worthless paste; it sounded a bit far-fetched.'

'Maybe, maybe...' Vignoles was thinking. 'Twister could be part of a chain. Their story of an engagement ring just an excuse for trying to get hold of some far 'hotter' property from the premises before we turned up.'

'Sounds more convincing than the shaggy dog story they sold us.'

'Then Miss Gable is not quite the innocent bride-to-be after all?' Mellor seemed to be relishing pointing this out as payback for his guvnor ribbing him about Miss Jephson. Vignoles acknowledged that possibility with a wry smile.

'The best lies always contain some truth,' Lansdowne picked up the story. 'Finding a lost gem stone could be Miss Gable's way of dressing up the lie that she actually collected consignments from an agreed pickup point. Items slipped down the back of a seat in a pre-arranged compartment... Twister asking for a private commission is just a cover for a liaison for a hand over?'

'Presumably they've done it number of times. How often can they get engaged?' Vignoles drained his glass.

'That's just the story they've sold us *this* time because we're on to them!' Mellor seemed enthusiastic, so much so he collected their empty glasses. 'We need another.'

'My round,' but as Vignoles as handing the money over, the barman called across the room. 'Detective Inspector Vignoles? There's a gentleman on the phone.' He clasped his hand over the mouthpiece. 'Urgent...' The barman winked.

Vignoles walked across to the far end of the bar whilst Mellor went to get their glasses refilled.

'Vignoles...'

'There you are. In the pub?' It was the Badger. His irascible chief superintendent from Marylebone House.

'One needs refreshment even in a murder enquiry.' Vignoles eyed the pint being pulled. He was probably going to need it.

'Then make sure you keep your mind clear as I'll cut straight to the chase. I hope you're celebrating getting this unfortunate business cracked, because I need it cleared up double-quick time.'

'Well...'

'No ifs, no buts Vignoles. We cannot have a killer at large! I need him banged. I trust you have a suspect in your sights?'

'We now believe there may be two perpetrators...'

'I don't care if there's a ruddy pack of 'em! Get them locked up - and I don't care how you do it. Use whatever force and manpower you require. Get these maniacs out of harm's way and we'll argue the finer points afterwards.'

'I intend to close the case as quickly as I am able, but it's not straightforward.' Vignoles could almost feel the crackle of pent-up frustration down the line.

'I don't doubt, but I've spoken to the top brass in the Gloucestershire force and their Super is a hundred percent with us on this and ready to mobilise every man and car at their disposal to haul in anyone you consider suspect.'

'I see...' Although Vignoles was far from seeing. He was long used to be harangued by the Badger, but this almost fanatical sense of urgency was unsettling.

'I don't think you do,' Badger had an uncanny ability to voice Vignoles' silent thoughts. 'Keep this under you Fedora. Her Majesty the Queen is coming down the same bloody line your murder took place on. Passing through the same station on the Royal Train. She detrains at Bishops Cleeve -.'

'I know of it.'

'Her Majesty is attending the Gold Cup. If the Palace get wind of this affair the visit could be called off and it will be all down to us dragging our feet! The reputation of the Detective Department rests on you being able to satisfy the Palace that there is no mortal risk to the Queen...'

'Heaven forbid...' Vignoles tried not to sound sarcastic. Badger was surely exaggerating for effect.

'I'm glad you appreciate the urgency!'

'I've heard the weather is threatening to cancel the racing...'

'That might be a fortuitous bonus, but you cannot assume anything. Good God, we run the risk of panic and having the papers in uproar and questions asked in Parliament! We cannot slip up. You may call upon whatever resources you require. You have your instructions. I expect a satisfactory report by tomorrow evening.' The line went dead.

Chapter Seventeen

There was a high level of readiness within the police stations of Gloucestershire that morning and a casual observer may have noticed there were more bobbies pounding their beats or cycling the streets than usual. In the back offices and at the front desks of every police station, senior officers and desk sergeants were ready and waiting to spring into action and apprehend a suitable suspect just as soon as they received a call. The problem was, no matter how much haranguing and back-beating Chief Inspector Badger gave DCI Vignoles, and no matter how eager the other senior officers across the county were to help, there was nobody to arrest. The simple fact of the matter was policing involved long, hard, painstaking slog; Endless worrying away at scraps of evidence; exploring dead ends and vaguely formulated ideas; searching, asking and seeking for the next tiny clue. There was no escaping the painstaking care required and all anyone could do under the circumstances was rope in extra personnel to knock on yet more doors that morning in the hope that someone offer up a vital lead.

PC Wentworth and WPC Lansdowne were working down Broadway's appropriately wide High Street, one on each side and both armed with a copy of an artist's impression of the man ticket clerk Knight had described. Ten uniformed constables had been driven in early that morning from Cheltenham to do the same, working inwards from the outer corners of the village, as part of Badger's drive to see resources thrown at this man-hunt.

The reproductions of this artist's impression were the only new tool they could call up in their desperate search for Krast's killers, but a likeness of any kind offered a crumb of comfort that progress was being made. However, it still took an optimistic man to believe these pictures were going to result in suspects being arrested and locked behind bars before Her Majesty detrained at Bishop's Cleeve that lunchtime. One could but hope...

The drawing was a work of art and betrayed the hand of an artist heavily influenced by that master of the perfectly judged black line, Eric Gill. Vignoles wondered if style might win over substance, as the undeniable artistic flair on show might not necessarily aide jogging the memory. He considered it too pleasing to the eye for its purpose. However, it was all they had, and he could not fault the late-night artistic endeavour of Miss Marjorie Wolfe.

It had been Sgt Wilcox who'd had the idea that the Gordon Russell Furniture Works in the village employed talented designers and one of these might be able to turn their hand to a likeness. It proved an inspired suggestion and Mellor had wasted no time chasing down Miss Wolfe, who lived only a few streets away. The artist had reacted with only mild surprise tempered by amusement, when Mellor and Wilcox had come knocking on her cottage door later that evening with Mr Knight in tow. The ticket clerk was still dressed in his British Railways uniform with peaked cap on his head, having come straight from work. They must have made an odd group, but the artist was unflustered at having her quiet evening disputed by policemen in their heavy brogues and a character that reminded her of 'Mr Parks' from Nesbitt's 'The Railway Children' which she'd read as a young girl. If he proved half as amusing and likeable, then the evening would pass amiably.

Wolfe's little cottage was filled with candles and oil lamps and elegant furniture, most of which had all the pared-back lines of the Government approved 'Utility' range the Gordon Russell works had become famous for in the post-war years. These modern designs sat a little incongruously however, within the low beamed agricultural worker's cottage with thick stone walls and quarry tiled floor.

Miss Wolfe noticed Mellor casting his eye over a coffee table in the centre of the small room. 'One of my designs.'

'Yeah? Looks all right ...'

'Thank you. I was pleased how it turned out. We made beautiful hand-crafted pieces before the war, following the finest Arts and Crafts philosophy.

Mellor knew nothing about art nor furniture and was eager to press on. 'I can see you can turn your hand to a coffee table, but what about a face?'

'I trained in figurative drawing and it remains my first love.' Her smile was captivating her male audience as was her long velvet skirt and figure-hugging roll-neck sweater that gave her the look of a jazz loving Beatnik. 'I still practice life-drawing and make wood cuts when away from my day job.' She indicated a series of framed prints and drawings of lithe and very scantily clad young women lying in the sun beside gently flowing rivers. Knight was transfixed. Wilcox meanwhile was wondering if the anatomically accurate woodcut of two naked men standing thigh deep in a pool of water and proudly staring back at the viewer contravened laws of decency.

'My brothers...' There was a mischievous twinkle in her eye that made Wilcox turn beetroot red and seek to disguise his confused reaction by a fit of coughing.

'It is just the face we're interested in, Miss Wolfe. Get this wrong and we're chasing nothing. D'you think you can draw a likeness from Mr Knight's description?'

'That does rather depend on Mr Knight's powers of memory and observation.' Knight was enjoying the limelight, appreciating he might be able to offer significant help in tracking down Mrs Krast's killer. This went some way to offsetting his embarrassment that it was his inattentiveness that might have allowed a murderer to slip under his nose.

'I remember his face clear as day. You give me a try...'

* * * *

Door to door enquiries were repetitive and more often than not disappointing, however it just took one positive reaction to their questions to make it worthwhile and both Lansdowne and Wentworth were holding on to his fact in the face of a bitterly cold wind whistling down from the hilltops.

'Police. We're making enquiries in relation to the death on Monday evening of Mr Peter Krast the jeweller. Did you see anyone acting suspiciously that evening between the hours of...?'

'...Perhaps you saw a man looking something like this...?'

'Do you recognise this man...?'

'No idea, mate.'

'Never seen him, sorry luv...'

'Can't help, I was visiting my aunty Mabel in Stratford...'

The apologies and excuses for not being able to help mounted up. And too many doors didn't open. Empty houses that resonated to the sounds of knocking. Then there were the women with crying children in their arms looking frazzled and annoyed at the intrusion and barely giving attention to the question let alone a measured response. There were those so deaf it was hard to know if they understood what they were being asked, and of course the dogs. A village apparently filled with barking and ankle-snapping dogs.

All standard fare, but Wentworth was enjoying it all the same. He knew nearly everyone he encountered and had to resist the temptation to stand gossiping and give too much away about the investigation, whereas for Lansdowne it was just a case of following procedure as attentively as possible, trying to assess if each potential witness was being honest or if they were withholding information. Experience told her that people were either over-keen to help and said more than they actually knew in the hope they would appear helpful good citizens, or were reticent, either from a lack of confidence or a fear of being branded an informer and potentially drawing unwanted attention from undesirable characters. A door to door enquiry was surely a living masterclass in observing and understanding human behaviour.

A lorry driver was lighting a cigarette whilst leaning against the side of his vehicle pulled to the side of the expanse of grass at the lower end of the High Street. The grass fronds were silvery white with hoare frost and the driver's breath formed billowy clouds around his face as he smoked. Lansdowne approached, her feet crunching noisily on the ice-stiffened blades.

'Excuse me. Might you have seen this man on Monday evening? Around six o'clock,' Lansdowne asked, for what must be the twentieth time morning.

'Let's have a closer look, darlin'.' The lorry driver jammed the cigarette in the corner of his mouth and squinted at the print. The wintry sun was bringing no warmth to the wind that twitched at the paper. 'What's he done then?'

'We're investigating a murder at Broadway Station on Monday evening. We'd like to speak with this man.'

'I was here around that time, but I was busy driving my wagon and a face in the dark is hard to take in. I was keeping my eyes on the road.' He handed the picture back to Lansdowne with a wink.

'I understand.'

The driver seemed reluctant to get back in his cab and back on the road and made as if to say something but then seemed to think better of it and tried to disguise this by drawing on his cigarette. He could think of worse things than helping this pretty WPC with her enquiries, but what could he offer? Lansdowne meanwhile was suddenly feeling weary. She was cold, her feet ached and she could do with a hot cup of sweet tea and yet there were more doors to knock upon before she could allow herself to take a break. Perhaps she could coax more out of this man. She sensed there was something else he wanted to say.

'You deliver around here regularly?'

'All the time, darlin'. It's the furniture works, see. I pick up tables, chairs, bedside cabinets that kind of stuff. I'm here most days...'

'This picture was drawn by one of the artists working at the factory.'

'You don't say?' The driver gave her a warm smile. He was wondering if she was up for a drink after work...

'You must be familiar with most of the people you see around the village? I imagine you would recognise their cars and vans...'

'Yeah, you bet.' He liked the confidence she was placing in his abilities. 'There's not much road traffic. It's busier today mind, with all the horse boxes and racegoers motoring in, but usually the roads are almost empty.'

'This man might have come here by car, with another accompanying him.'

The driver took a pensive drag on his cigarette and used this as an excuse to take a longer look at Lansdowne. If he was especially helpful, she might agree to that drink... 'I saw a car I didn't know. An Alvis. It had a Cheltenham plate. Is that any use?'

'What time was this and where did you see it?'

'I picked up a load from the factory and shuttled it down to the goods shed at the station.'

'Broadway station?'

'Yep. The men in the goods shed helped unload the stock ready to ship on by rail to London. It was all nice radio cabinets for Heal's. They've got someone who puts the electrical gubbins inside the cabinets down West London way, then flog the radios for a small fortune. They sell mountains of 'em before Christmas! Very nice...' It was unclear whether he was referring to the radio cabinets or Lansdowne.

'And the car...' She made of point of ignoring his lecherous gaze. It was nothing new and whilst having no intention of teasing him she knew her looks were encouraging him to proffer information.

'I'd done with unloading and was driving down the slip road from the goods yard to head on home when I saw the car. Turning out of the station slip road on the other side it was. They have different access roads. One each side of the bridge.'

'I've seen the set up.'

He appeared impressed this blonde ponytailed WPC knew about the access road layout. Pretty, and smart with it. He'd best play his cards carefully... 'I got a decent look at the car as I waited for them to turn. They headed off up this way, so there's a chance they came up the High.'

'What was the license plate?'

'AD1735. It comes with the job maybe, but I see a plate once and the numbers stick. I knew instantly that was a Gloucestershire reg on account of the AD.'

Lansdowne made a note, her fingers moving awkwardly with the cold. 'Did you see the driver?'

'There were two in the car.' He paused a beat.

'Tell me what you saw. It could be important.'

'I've a decent memory, but I could be wrong and send you off on the wrong track.' He wanted to stay in her good books.

'Let me be the judge of that. Was one of the car occupants this man?'

He took another look at the drawing, taking more time. 'He was driving.'

'You're sure?' Lansdowne felt her heart speed up.

'If not him, then he looked similar.'

'And the other?'

'Well, here's the odd bit. It struck me at the time but I put it aside as a trick of the eye with it being dark and thinking about getting home to me pie and mash and not realising there was a need to take notice...'

'Go on.' Lansdowne felt he deserved an encouraging smile.

'The other man seemed to be wearing a balaclava. You know, covering all his head except his face, and as they turned, he seemed to be taking it off, but the driver then blocked my view.' He shrugged his shoulders and tossed his cigarette butt into the gutter. 'Listen, love, that last bit could be me imagining stuff...'

Lansdowne was scribbling it all down. 'I need your name and address...'

'I'll do you a swap! Your address, for mine...' He gave her a cheeky grin.

Lansdowne gave him a firm but friendly look of admonishment. 'Just yours, thank you...'

* * * *

'Did you believe him?' Mellor was questioning Lansdowne.

'I think he was genuine. There's the usual caveats that it was dark and a fleeting glimpse, but the timing is spot on for two men leaving after killing Krast.'

'Caveats? You swallowed a dictionary, Lucy?' She said nothing in response to Mellor's mocking tone. 'Still, *caveats* or not, the guvnor reckons there were two perpetrators. This smart Alec in the picture and another piece of work who did the killing. He was probably in dark clothes, so wearing a balaclava makes sense. Sergeant? Can we get a trace on this car?'

'I'll call into Cheltenham HQ and get them on to it right away!' Wilcox responded. 'I believe they have a Rolodex of car registrations they use for that purpose.'

'Good. We've got one face and the make and reg of their car. We're closing in...'

'But we still don't know why they killed Krast! It worries me when we've got no clear motive.'

'Now don't you worry your pretty face about that. There's time to sort the whys and wherefores once we get them banged up in the slammer! Now, I need a cuppa, so be a darlin' and run along an' sort one out...and bring some biscuits!'

Lansdowne glared at Mellor but said nothing. He outranked her and creating an atmosphere was not going to help them solve the case.

Chapter Eighteen

Kane threw his cigarette butt away to fizzle in the frosted fronds of the yellowing grass beside the sloping approach road leading to Broadway station. The pines sighed and whispered on the embankment, beyond which, an engine hissed whilst carriage doors opened and slammed shut. The air was bitter, and Kane hunched his shoulders and dug his hands deeper into his coat pockets. He narrowed his eyes to slits, but not to guard against the cold. It took more than a drop in the mercury to discomfort this cold-blooded agent.

His attention was keenly focussed on the row of railway houses that stood at right angles to the station building. Four modest properties with upstairs bedroom windows with a perfect view of the forecourt and approach road. He was trying to recall an indistinct memory from Monday night.

Kane and Abel had become aware of an intensification of the police presence and of the gossiping and chatter about the startling death of the jeweller, prompted by lurid headlines in the newspapers. A BBC radio broadcast van had been seen driving into Broadway and this had served to stoke the interest further. It was to be expected, but Kane was starting to feel concerned. The circle was inexorably tightening around them and they did not have long before they must to cut their losses and leave.

This bleak thought rankled all the more as they'd taken a lot of care in their strategy and finessed it well. The house had been given a good going over without hitch on Monday night, but despite being a masterclass of meticulous exploration they'd not found what they wanted. Perhaps it had been in the shop safe after all... It was frustrating, that even when his eyes were bulging with fear and his lungs bursting with the desire for oxygen, that fool Krast had refused to tell them where the diamond was. He'd taunted Kane that he knew they'd been through the shop. Someone else was muscling in and whilst he had an idea who it might be, it was unsettling to know they were not working alone.

However, they were professionals and like anyone at the top of their game they analysed their work, looking for weaknesses or mistakes that might betray their presence. The Debt Collectors hadn't survived this long by luck alone and it was self-evident they'd got something wrong - and it needed fixing.

It had been a deliberate ploy for Abel to drop the name Buckrose into the conversation with the ticket clerk in the hope it might elicit a response, for theirs had been a two-edged visit; to force Krast into telling Kane where The Hornet's Beauty was by applying unpleasantly persuasive methods and a 'fishing exercise' by Abel to see if others had encountered this elusive lord, who might be able to lead them to the missing diamond if Krast refused to cooperate.

It had been a dangerous evening's work and all they'd gained from it was discovering that Buckrose probably had the diamond and was good at covering his tracks. They'd read in the paper he had a horse in the Broadway Novice's Steeplechase today, but that aside, they knew sod all about him.

They would track Buckrose down, but how long did they have? Kane was concerned they'd offered too much information on Monday. How long before the detectives connected Abel's talk of Buckrose with Krast being bumped off? If they could have got their mitts on the Hornet the same night and headed back to London this wouldn't matter, but they were back in the area and there was work still to be done. Worse still, Kane suspected they'd been observed arriving and departing the station on Monday evening.

Kane had been dressed all in black and with an ex-Commando balaclava over his head and beneath a hat. Nobody could have seen his face, but he would have looked suspicious. And then there was the car. The Alvis was back from where they'd borrowed it and it was unlikely the owner was even aware it had been taken, but Kane had a feeling he'd seen a face at an upstairs window in one of the houses overlooking the station forecourt and they would have had a grandstand view.

The train departed noisily as Kane approached the station. The surroundings helped prompt his memory. He was sure he remembered which house had the partially drawn backlit curtains. He could bring to mind a fleeting image of blonde hair cut to a pudding basin style, looking out between the curtains. The same Richard III hair cut was now visible beneath a striped bobble hat on the head of a young lad idly kicking a football against the side of the station building.

'You like football?'

'You bet, mister!'

'I wanted to be footballer when I was your age...'

'Who'd you play for?'

'I didn't. The war got in the way.'

'Rotten luck!' The lad maintained his steady kicking of the ball at the wall, apparently blissfully unaffected by the icy air. 'What's your team?'

'Chelsea.'

'Oh...' Kick. Kick. Kick. 'Mine's Bristol City.'

The lad allowed the ball to drift towards to Kane who expertly returned it against the wall for the boy to once again maintain his relentless kicking. It was a little moment of bonding.

'You live here?'

'Yep. Blue door's ours.'

That confirmed Kane's suspicions.

'You must see everything. All the trains coming and going...' As he spoke the local train in the station chuffed into motion on its way towards Cheltenham.

'Yep. Got all the numbers. That's 4578 departing now.'

'Is that the number of the train?'

'Engine. Engines haul trains. Nobody takes *train* numbers...' The lad sounded contemptuous of his ignorance. 'Train reporting numbers are the big white letters and numbers in a frame fixed on the smokebox front. They're boring...' He let the ball go towards Kane again and anticipated the return.

A smart boy who notices things, Kane silently observed. 'My mistake! I bet you're the sort of lad who remembers car registration plates?' Kane hoped his expression was not too severe.

'Yeah...I know all the area codes!'

'I didn't doubt it...'

'And I know all the makes of car.'

I bet you do, you nosey, bloody brat... 'You can see everyone coming and going from that window up there?'

'Maybe...' The boy didn't seem interested in the way the conversation was going and concentrated on his ball skills.

'I heard someone in the village say there was an accident here on Monday evening.'

'Who'd you talk to? It was no accident. *Murder* more like!' The boy grinned excitedly.

Kane trapped the ball and held it under his foot. 'You don't say?'

'It's true!' The lad's eyes opened wide. 'Killed, he was! Right over there on the platform...'

Kane gave a wicked grin as he gently rolled the ball back. 'What? Here in the station? In the middle of the night?' Kane turned to face the boy and in so doing noting there was nobody in sight.

'No! Mr Roberts the stationmaster says the police think it happened about six-thirty. Obviously, the police don't know *anything*, 'cos the man who was killed he got off the auto train and I checked my new Timex watch and it came in dead on six thirty-seven. He couldn't have been killed before he got off, so it stands to reason it was later than they said.'

'You're a bright lad.' *And a thorn in my side...*

'It's the most exciting thing that's ever happened here!'

'You must be annoyed missing all the excitement...' Kane ensured there was a playful quality in his voice, exploiting the boy's youthful insensitivity. They were now passing the ball between them via a rebound from the wall.

'How d'you mean?'

'Not seeing the killers come and go!' The cold had a tendency to highlight the scar down his cheek, so he laughed to soften his face. The boy fell silent however and now ceased his relentless kicking of the ball against the wall, no doubt to the relief of the ticket clerk on the other side. Kane lit a cigarette. His glove masking his missing finger. 'Something up?'

'Nuffin...' The boy suddenly rolled his shoulders as if only now appreciating how cold it was and he shivered. The ball rolled from under his foot. 'I have to go in now.'

Kane placed a polished brogue on the ball. He leaned a little closer, eagle eyes peeled to ensure they were still unobserved. 'Did you see something?'

The boy shook his head. He didn't want to talk to this strange man anymore.

Kane could dimly recall a face between curtains; the slight figure holding something in one hand. It could have been a model...a model aeroplane. The boy had probably been glueing it together or adding enamel paint whilst keeping half an eye on the station. 'What plane are you making? A Spit or a Hurricane?'

'Spitfire...How do you know that?' The boy's eyes were wide with either wonderment or unease.

Kane had gauged it right, but it had been little more than a guess. 'Good planes, Spitfires.'

'The best!'

'You saw anything else. Apart from the train arriving?'

'You a detective?'

'Now that would be tellin'...' Kane raised an eyebrow in a playful manner, hinting that the boy had guessed correctly. 'If you saw anything, you let me know. And *only* me. Understood?'

'Wha...? You mean...it might be the killers I saw?'

'Depends *what* you saw...'

'There was a car.'

'I bet you know what make it was...'

'Obviously! It was an Alvis. And there were two men inside.'

'How about a free kick? I'll place the ball...' Kane made a play of getting the measure of the imaginary goal but was checking if they were still unobserved. 'What did they look like?'

'Couldn't see. One was all dark. In black clothes and hat and the other looked like one of the horsey people we get around here.'

'You told anyone else about this?' He was still measuring up his free-kick.

'None of the policemen asked me...'

Kane thwacked the ball high and hard and watched it sail over the station building.

'My ball!'

'Darn it. Misjudged.'

'Why did you do that mister?'

'Just a little reminder. Clever boys who see too much need to be careful.'

'Eh?'

Kane dropped a box of matches on the ground and as he bent down to pick them up his face was closer to the young lad. He hissed the words. 'It's very dangerous telling people things. The wrong sort might hear, and you don't want them coming to see you...'

'I never told no-one!'

'Make sure you keep it like that. Not a word!' He growled the words, as his eyes burned into those of the frightened lad. It took only a moment, but the boy was left in no doubt that this menacing man meant business. Kane straightened up and smiled warmly, looking the picture of innocence, whilst one of his shoes, the sole studded with steel segments, pressed with all his weight and force on top of the boy's thin Clarks shoe. 'Talking out of turn can be very *dangerous*.'

Tears were welling and a sobbing sound came from the boy's constricted throat as his toes felt the searing pain.

'Keep yer trap shut - or there'll be worse!' A wink that could freeze blood.

'Highnam Grange' hauling the Cardiff-Birmingham express wailed as it hurtled through the station, masking the strangulated sound that issued from the young lad's throat as Kane released his foot and casually walked away with an innocent wave of his hand.

But he was troubled. That know-it-all kid had seen them and knew enough to cause problems. But it was daylight and too many people about to do more. Could he risk the boy saying nothing long enough for them to conclude their business here? His hands jammed in his pockets mimicked strangling the life from the boy's scrawny neck...

Chapter Nineteen

'I think I've found something.' Lansdowne approached Vignoles seated behind Krast's desk in the back office of the shop. This felt like the hub of Krast's circumscribed world and it made sense to use it as the base for the investigation. It was not as if anyone was clamouring to reopen and start trading and there had been no word from the solicitor about the obscure cousin in distant 'Mittel Europe'.

Jeffries and Jephson had been told to stand down and keep away but to remain near a telephone in case they were needed. Vignoles wanted both on a short leash for now, especially Jeffries. No policeman worthy of his badge liked a man who lied in a murder investigation.

'What is it, Lucy?'

'Not much, but this name and number don't tie in with anything else I can find in Krast's papers.' She proffered a fancy ticket for a restaurant in Cheltenham. It was printed in a blue ink on heavy white card and had the look and feel of a high-class establishment. The admission price was steep even with the 'complimentary glass of champagne' factored in. Exactly the sort of social event a jeweller might wish to be seen at - even if he was mortgaged to the rafters. Krast had been trying to maintain his illusion of wealth to the last.

'On the back, sir...'

In the clear and distinctive hand they now recognised as Krast's, were six words.

Lord Buckrose
Acre Vale
G & T

'Acre Vale...any ideas?'

'I've been studying a map and asked Sergeant Wilcox and he's pretty certain it must be Acre Vale Farm. A large establishment at the top end of the Vale of Evesham. It's not a farm in the cows and sheep sense; they train racehorses.'

Mellor looked up from the papers he was studying. 'A livery stable?'

'That kind of set up, sarge.'

'And that name Buckrose again...' Vignoles' interest was piqued. Aside from the obvious hubbub around Cheltenham in association with the race meeting, horse racing seemed to be permeating this investigation in a subtle, yet inescapable manner.

'I took the liberty of putting in an exploratory phone call to Acre Vale Farm and learned it is owned by a Mr Coldicott. He also trains the racehorses. The young woman I spoke to said that she thought Lord Buckrose was an owner of horse stabled there.'

'Does she know where Buckrose lives?'

'She does not have access to that information.'

'Not surprising... but good work.'

Mellor had joined them and was looking at the card. 'Knight said the man wishing to arrange delivery of a horse was working for a Buckrose. He claimed he was the trainer...'

'But it does not sit right. Somebody as easy to trace as a racehorse trainer is apparently working in tandem with a professional killer and then leaves whopping great clues to his identity at the crime scene?' Vignoles looked dissatisfied. 'That name Coldicott is nagging me...I've heard it somewhere.' Vignoles jammed his unlit pipe into the corner of his mouth and flipped through his note book. 'Got it! I spoke with a groom unloading horses at Broadway station. Coldicott was mentioned as the trainer of the horses.'

'When was this, sir?' Mellor queried.

'Tuesday. The lad was accompanying three horses trained by Coldicott. There's room for four in a railway horse box such as that, so why not bring all four at the same time, instead of calling down to the station on Monday night and try to make a hasty arrangement? It would be poor time and financial management.'

'Because this supposed last-minute arrangement was nothing more than a ruse to allow the killer on to the station?'

'Agreed, but we come back to the vexing question of why would a noted trainer of racehorses put himself in view like that? Knight did not know the man making the enquiries, and yet Coldicott presumably already made arrangements for the three horses to be delivered on Tuesday and there was every chance he would be recognised. If he owns a training establishment in the Vale of Evesham there is a decent chance Knight would recognise him.'

'I'll quiz Knight on whether he knows Coldicott by sight.'

Vignoles nodded assent to Mellor's suggestion.

'Or, someone was playing false with names and facts to create a diversion?' Lansdowne suggested.

'That is more probable. They did their research so their conversation with Knight did not elicit immediate suspicion. Coldicott could be innocent of any complicity.'

Mellor was staring at the card. 'Try this for size: let's assume Krast likes a flutter on the gee-gees and maybe knows some of those in the race business? Trainers, jockeys, an owner or two?' He was sounding out an idea and Vignoles was listening. 'He's at this swanky event. The sort of evening to attract the well-to-do and well-connected and quite probably some of the racing set. He might have met this Lord Buckrose on the night and got talking horses...'

'And diamonds?'

'Those as well...' Mellor shrugged his shoulders. 'Why not?'

'And then what?'

'Sir? I wonder if G & T has significance? I can't see why he'd note down the drink he was ordering,' Lansdowne offered. They all chewed this over for a moment.

'Gable and Twister...' Vignoles grinned.

'Has to be!' Mellor slapped the card against the desk. 'They said they spoke to Krast in early January. This invite could have remained in his coat pocket in the week or so following New Year and he used it to make a note...'

'About what? Gable and Twister and a livery stable and a gentleman called Buckrose. What does it add up to? Come on sergeant, get that brain of yours working and develop that story to link all this together.'

'Ok... so Krast gets a diamond worth a King's ransom from G & T some days after his drinks party. Just handed to 'im on a plate and out of the blue by two innocent kids. Now, he's in serious need of some readies, so he hits on the idea of swappin' the real sparkler for a substitute. But that's easier said than done. He's got to do some nifty dealing - and well under the radar - because, like Lansdowne said, he can't do this officially.' Mellor gave the WPC a wink in acknowledgement. 'Now, he remembers this Lord Buckrose from the New Year's Eve party. Who knows what they talked about on the night, but maybe there was something about the toff that convinced Krast to get in contact and tell him about his discovery?'

'Buckrose might have had ulterior motives...' Vignoles was chewing this over. 'Using his title and standing in society to hook and reel Krast in. Was he trying to position himself to effect some kind of fraud - then was given an opportunity too good to miss?'

'I reckon he might have! Buckrose must have sold Krast enough lies to make the old man think he could help fence something too hot to handle over the counter.'

Vignoles' brow clouded. 'However, we believe someone claiming to represent Lord Buckrose was also helping cause a diversion whilst their accomplice killed Krast, presumably to get his keys and enter his house and shop to nick the real diamond. Does that fit?'

'It could...Krast and Buckrose talk. They're working out a deal...but Buckrose is impatient and he's a double-crossing thief, so he takes matters into his own hands. Kills the old man, takes his keys and helps himself to the diamond. Hence the reason we can't find it.'

'I could work with that, but it is all supposition,' Vignoles agreed. 'That means Buckrose is not working alone...'

'There's this Coldicott fella. He trains Buckrose's horse. Is he in on the scam?' It was Mellor's turn to look unconvinced.

'We're getting closer, but everything is still too hazy and based on speculation alone. Badger won't accept any of this. We need facts.' *And someone to arrest...* Vignoles was all too aware of Badger's orders. 'Mellor, chase up that Alvis. Tell the Cheltenham lads to give us an immediate answer! Lansdowne, call Blencowe and see how he's getting on with this Lord Buckrose. I need an answer, either way. Is that today's paper? Toss it over, Mellor. I want to study the sports pages.'

Mellor was about to dial the County constabulary but stopped and gave his boss a questioning look.

'Trainers and owners are usually listed on race cards published in the paper,' Vignoles was filling his pipe. 'And I suspect Buckrose and Caldecott are both in town...'

Ten minutes later and a few points had been clarified.

'The Alvis was stolen. Borrowed might be more accurate. An elderly Doctor owns it. He and his wife were having a meal with their neighbours. They were unaware of its little jaunt until the constables turned up at their door. The car was parked at the end of their long garden on a quiet road.'

'Easy to drive away unseen and unheard?' Vignoles replied.

'Yep.'

'Careful and confident. I deduce from this that our killers are skilled operators.'

'Anything on Buckrose?' Mellor asked Lansdowne.

'Blencowe said there is no trace of a Lord Buckrose or any similar title. The House of Lords are unaware of the title. A Buckrose appeared once or twice in relation to the activities of other families in reference books, but this was over three hundred years ago, and also crops up as a geographical location but never as a titled family. Blencowe is still awaiting a reply from the College of Heralds, but he's not expecting them to say different.'

'Then Lord Buckrose *is* a fraudster...'

'And putting in a lot of time, effort and money to appear convincing. He actually owns at least one racehorse according to the race card here.' Vignoles was firing up his pipe.

'Yeah? I expected that to be just hot air...' Mellor was surprised.

'He owns Money For Nothing which is trained by Coldicott. I saw the horse being delivered to Broadway by a groom called Biggs, aided by Ian Twister.'

'Twister? That's got to be more than coincidence?'

'He works at the station. It's his job...' Vignoles responded.

'Do you think the name of the horse tells us something?' Lansdowne observed with a wry smile.

'Almost a coded message that all is not as it appears.'

'Buckrose is a player, guv. And he's good.' Mellor was lighting a 'fag'. 'Gotta be. What sort of man could con a bent jeweller out of a valuable diamond?' This observation was accompanied by a stream of smoke jetted towards the ceiling. 'That must take some doin''

Vignoles puffed on his pipe. 'You think the meeting on New Year's Eve between Krast and Buckrose resulted in Krast handing over the diamond he'd received from Twister?'

'I do.'

'But if Lord Buckrose does not actually exist, then the man talking to Knight could be one and the same?' Vignoles used his pipe to point at the artists' drawing.

'That man could be Buckrose. We need to identify the balaclava'd gent working with him now...'

'Before we get carried away, let's not forget that if Buckrose had already talked the diamond into his possession he would surely just melt away into the night and never been heard of again. Krast could do nothing.'

'The cuckoo has flown the nest?' Lansdowne observed.

A stunned silence fell punctured only by the sound of Mellor drawing heavily on his cigarette.

'I've got Badger screaming for an arrest, so we need to talk to this Buckrose and to Coldicott. They're both going to be at the racecourse today and tomorrow.' Vignoles tapped the newspaper preview of the day's racing. 'Buckrose is likely to be a smart and slippery fellow. It takes guts to broadcast your presence to the world at the height of a murder investigation, but he seems confident. We challenge him, but I'll be the first to admit we are not on solid ground and don't have a scrap of evidence to call him in for a formal interview.'

'And no reason to arrest Coldicott.'

'Let alone suspect him of any crime. Having said that, we'll bang the two of them in a cell on the slightest pretext, if only to keep Badger off my back!'

'Do we have the authority? I mean, we're the railway...'

'From what Badger yelled at me last night, I'd say we've got the authority to stop the Gold Cup running if we must!' The memory of Badger's nagging voice on the telephone line made Vignoles reach for the telephone. 'The race meeting is likely to have a strong police presence but putting everyone on high alert and pulling in reserves won't hurt...We can get the local men to do any arresting, to ensure county constabulary noses don't get put out of joint!'

Chapter Twenty

Cheltenham Racecourse station was heaving. Two lengthy trains were in at the same time, facing in opposite directions. The Brunswick green locomotives were snorting and champing as if at the bit, just like the horses everyone was so eager to watch.

'Caerphilly Castle' was readying herself to hurry north whilst 'Lympney Grange', appeared to be giving her crew a difficult time. The engine looked in dire need of an overhaul, her paintwork faded and work-stained with dribbles of limescale hinted at a priming boiler. She looked a tired old beast perhaps reluctantly retrieved from a siding at the back of her engine shed to take charge of this extra Race day special. The blower was on and the unpolished chimney streaming filthy smoke above the heads of the elegantly dressed passengers disembarking whilst the fireman rattled and clashed fire irons around in the firebox. The driver leaned on the cab side sheet waiting, unhappily, for the signal to restart them on their way into Cheltenham. 'Limping Grange' might be a better name. At least it was not far to go.

The ever-present Scots pines soughed softly on their embankments as a weak sun finally broke through the iron-grey clouds and faces turned upwards and smiles broke out as the first kiss of warmth was felt on chilled cheeks and reddening noses. The weather mattered and the chatter intensified...

'It'll thaw if we get a decent break in the clouds...'

'I can see a spot of blue... so that means Chicory Blue is the horse for me!'

'You reckon Four-Ten won't like the going...?'

'It could turn to mud if it warms...'

'I'm fancying Tingle Tangle in the Cotswold Steeplechase...'

The disgorging passengers moved up the exit ramp edged by white wooden fencing and towards the racecourse entrance, the little shield-shaped enclosure and stand tags flapped in the wind, pinned alongside expensive brooches or metal pin badges declaring membership of any number of associations or regiments.

All human life seemed to be here, crushed into a chattering throng heady with the competing aromas of aftershave and perfume, tobacco smoke, crushed grass and damp earth and the pervasive animal smell of horse and dung. Under-pinning all was the slight tang of burning Welsh coal issuing from the two iron horses in the station. Uniformed police constables made themselves deliberately visible with benign smiles fixed to their faces but each in a state of high alert. They had been told to present a welcoming appearance yet be watchful for anything unusual. Plain clothes police brought in from neighbouring forces mingled and tried not to look like coppers. Everyone aware the hour was fast approaching when the Royal party would arrive.

They were watching and waiting...but for whom?

And how to identify a threat? They were surrounded by a fabric sea of top coats and belted mackintoshes, hats, scarves, bald heads and wind-tousled hair. There were faces in all their varieties with glasses or without, the fat and the thin, tall and short, the rich the poor, the profligate and the thrifty, the sober and those already heading towards intoxication. Cheltenham Racecourse had many vast open spaces and yet the majority of the crowd were corralled into packed paddocks and stands, everyone murmuring, chattering, laughing or scowling and anxiously studying form before making (costly) decisions. Standing amidst the throng it was a maddening array of trilbies and bowlers, tweed or moleskin caps and ladies in Dutch-style crocheted affairs or ultra-stylish berets on the younger women, whilst the ever-popular headscarf made a good showing around the deeply jowelled lines of stern matriarchs. The Irish were out in force in their tweedy greens and browns, Racing Posts tucked under their arms, maintaining a confident banter punctuated by endless cigarettes. They were probably making bee-lines for the nearest bar or beer tent, but the observant would notice their enthusiasm for a 'wee' drink did not prevent them from casting observant eyes on the ground underfoot and the odds signalled by the tick-tack men.

Into this confusion strode Kane and Abel. Confidently aware they could blend in with consummate ease. Both enjoyed a flutter on the horses and slipped into the role of racegoers so effortlessly they could brush shoulders with a plain clothes detective or tip a hat at a grinning young bobby with no fear of attracting attention.

Abel was wearing a pair of black-framed glasses in a rectangular shape that looked thoroughly modern and quite altered his face. A trilby with a pheasant feather tucked in the band and a camel top coat over a charcoal-grey suit and regimental tie made him look quite the man-about-town down from London. He probably frequented one of the more exclusive jazz clubs on a Friday night and treasured a perfectly assembled collection of long-playing records that included Fitzgerald and Coltrane.

Kane was in suit and tie with a Fedora and a woollen overcoat worn unbuttoned with a scarf dangling untied around his neck. A cigarette, unlit, remained a fixture in his mouth and bobbed up and down when he spoke. Leather driving gloves flopped from a pocket. Both men sported binoculars and leather cases around their necks. They had the appropriate passes allowing entry to both one of the more exclusive stands and the winner's enclosure, not that they were going to allow such trifles stand in their way of going wherever they wished.

They walked through the collection of horse boxes and trailers gathered to the Winch Hill side of the ground, weaving amongst the owners, stable lads, anxious trainers, the slightly-built jockeys. Some of the latter were still in civvies and others in riding boots and breeches underneath bulky top coats to keep them warm before the weigh-in and making them look top-heavy on their sparrow thin legs. Everywhere was fuss and bustle and the pungent smell of horses, sweat and anticipation.

'The nag is called Money For Nothing and Buckrose has purple and green quartered silks.'

'Over there...' Abel used his unlit cigarette to point. 'The colour combination is an absolute abomination!'

'Just keep yer eyes out for his Lordship or the trainer. We need to get him somewhere quiet.'

'If I'm not mistaken, that's Coldicott.' Abel used a subtle twitch of his head to indicate the trainer in his boots, tweeds, checked shirt and olive drab tie, now striding purposefully towards a lorry-mounted horse box backing into the enclosure. 'Another of his steeds being delivered...'

'Then he's occupied. We've got a few minutes to work in.' They walked across to where a horse wearing a blanket and blinkers was being tended to by Joe Biggs. They were tucked away behind a corral of empty horse boxes. Biggs was fussing the horse's ears and whispering to him.

Kane stood nearby and nodded approvingly. 'Lookin' good. Is he running well?'

'Yeah, he's in good form and the going today suits him.' Biggs gave a satisfied smile whilst checking their tags. These two had full access so were probably friends of another trainer or owner and so posed no threat. As it was, he was in a good mood and looking forward to a decent bonus. He sensed a win on the cards with Money For Nothing and had passed the hot tip on to a couple of appreciative acquaintances with a promise of a share of any rewards.

'He's attracting a lot of attention. He'll run as favourite at this rate.' Kane spoke calmly, not wanting to startle either man or beast.

'I'd heard something along those lines, but I've not had a chance to see how it's shaping up. Got more important things to be doing...' Biggs did a good job at appearing disinterested in the betting odds. Lying came naturally.

'Miss Paget must be getting worried. She's got high hopes for Buckingham.'

'Nice horse that, but Mr Coldicott reckons its between Money For Nothing and Great Eliza.'

Abel strolled over, a full pail of water in his gloved hand. Biggs gave him an odd look. 'Hey, what's that for?'

'He looks thirsty.'

'What'd the Hell do you know? You tip that away right now!' Biggs stood away from the horse but with one hand on the halter.

Abel placed the bucket in front of the horse. 'There you go old boy, have a good drink!'

'No you bloody don't!' Biggs made to kick the pail over but found that Kane had placed a hand squarely on his chest and was pressing him back with considerable force.

'It would be in everyone's best interest if this horse came second. We'd all be better off. You included...' Kane slipped what was obviously two crisp ten pound notes into the top pocket of Biggs' shirt. 'Let him drink or we'll be seein' yer later. In the dark when nobody's lookin'...'

'Let go, you bastard!' Biggs looked alarmed, but whether for fear the horse would take in too much water and run slower or from the very real menace of Kane, it was hard to tell. The horse was now tossing his head, perhaps eager to slake his thirst, but Biggs held the halter firm despite the pressure on his chest and refused to let the horse lower its massive head.

'We're friends of Lord Buckrose,' Abel spoke quietly. 'We're following orders, dear boy. Just do as we ask, and it will be all smiles after the race. His Lordship will be especially grateful...' He blew smoke in Biggs' face.

Kane backed off. 'A sly little drink, then tip the rest away. Nobody is any the wiser. Buckrose will be most upset if his horse was to win...'

'Sod off!' Biggs kicked the pail over despite their threats and glared angrily at them as the water slopped out. He was scared, but still felt the urge to do the right thing.

'Have it your way. That was just an insurance policy - against winning.' Kane's expression was enough to make Biggs quake. 'It would be awkward if word got out you've been passing inside gen on for money...'

'I never! Now piss off!'

'Toodle-pip!' Abel gave a cheery smile.

Trainer Coldicott was approaching but too far away to have heard the exchange. He gave the two men barely a glance as he called for Biggs to lend assistance with the horses about to be unloaded.

'We've scared him.' Kane muttered. 'He'll want to speak to Buckrose as soon as.'

'We just watch and wait...' Abel looked content and continued to enjoy his menthol cigarette.

'I want to get the measure of this Buckrose. Work out his game before we close in.'

'He's new. A fresh face and putting a few noses out of joint. I won't be sorry to have a few crossed words with the cad!' Abel wafted menthol scented smoke away from two giggling young debs walking by, arm in arm. The men leaned against a handy fence rail and waited, watching Coldicott and Biggs and the others preparing their steeds.

'We need to lure him away from here. Somewhere nobody can hear him squeal.'

'Too many coppers around today. And he can't be so dumb as to have the rock with him...'

'We make him an offer he can't refuse...?'

'We do.'

'Which part of this job do I love the most?' Abel closed one eye the better to focus on the distant figure of Biggs with his stronger eye. 'Weaving a veritable spiders web to lure victims in, or the precision application of pain...?' Abel's smile was chilling, his eyes cold like two ice cubes clinking in a glass of vodka and tonic.

*   *   *   *

Vignoles and Mellor threaded their way through a crowd focused on a race just started. This made progress a little easier as there was less uncoordinated milling about as most were now standing and watching or seated high in the grandstands. Countless twin lenses of binoculars were raised to eyes tracking the racing horses. The thunder of hooves was surprisingly loud, and the ground vibrated beneath their feet.

They stopped at a fortuitous gap, peering between shoulders, hats and vigorously waving gloved hands and watched the closing moments of the United Hunt's Challenge Cup steeplechase. A gaggle of punters were urging on horses called Old Glory and Purse Strings. Neither sounded promising titles for potential winners to Vignoles' way of thinking. But what did he know? He'd noticed one horse was called Tingle Tangle and the name appealed. However, this poor beast was completely out of the running, not unlike the sickly 'Lympney Grange.'

A huge roar of cheers mingled with groans now filled the air.

'Yessss...' Mellor hissed his quiet celebration, a balled fist making a short punching movement. It was not ostentatious, but Vignoles noticed. He looked over the rims of his glasses at Mellor.

'St Coleman!' was the reply to his unspoken question.

'You backed the winner?'

'Just a few bob...'

Vignoles shook his head. There was still much to learn about his new DS.

'We might get a sight of Buckrose in the parade ring. They bring out the runners in advance so you can get a good look at them. He's likely to be there with the other owners.' Mellor spoke like a man who knew his way around a racecourse.

Vignoles grunted assent. He'd never been to a race meeting before, as neither he nor his wife Anna had felt the need to spend their hard-earned salaries on backing losers - he knew nothing about racing form and would simply choose a name he liked and undoubtedly lose as a consequence, a point perfectly proven by his (thankfully purely theoretical) 'backing' of Magnifico in the Birdlip Selling Hurdle. To his surprise, after voicing his opinion about the inherent futility of betting, Mellor didn't disagree.

'You can try to know more than anyone else and spend your days studying form and horse anatomy and appreciating how the ground underfoot affects different horses, understand the style of each jockey and so on, but in the end, it's just a lottery. Most of the people here will swear otherwise and convince you they have the 'inside knowledge' and are making wise investments.'

'There are a lot of people studying newspapers and those race cards they keep trying to sell us.'

Mellor proffered his. 'My tip would be Rosenkavalier. But I'd hate to see you throw your money away on my recommendation. Still, has to be a better prospect than that nag you picked earlier!'

'I was surprised it even finished...' Vignoles watched the horses and attendant stable lads, trainers and owners and realised he had no idea what he was looking for.

'Most lose more than they win. So, you're in good company,' Mellor laughed.

'Is that so?'

'Nobody tells you about the times they lose. It's a mug's game, but with a thrill attached.' A pause. 'I'm quite partial myself... A decent win once in a blue moon is a blast, 'specially if you're with a bunch of mates.'

'And then you go to the beer tent and blow your winnings.'

'If you have a skinful you're less likely to tally up what you lost along the way!'

They both laughed. It felt like they were finding common ground.

Vignoles was glad. He could do with someone watching his back. He realised how much he missed Trinder, but Mellor just might prove an adequate replacement, given time.

Vignoles lit his pipe and finding a space to lean on the parade ring rail watched the horses snort steam and twitch their heads as they were led around. A young woman was leading one of the horses and he was struck by how many owners were women. A surprise shaft of sunlight brought a welcome dash of cheer as it illuminated the jockeys in their intense and many spangled colours amidst a scene weighted heavily towards a wintry palette of blacks, greys, dark browns, fauns and faded greens.

'Any clue as to who might be Lord Buckrose?'

Mellor was using his field glasses to get a closer look at the figures in the centre of the ring. 'Dunno... Trouble is, we don't actually know what the cove looks like...'

* * * *

Lord Buckrose stood in the loose group of owners along with wives, husbands and other select hangers-on. They were on the muddying grass at the centre of the parade ring. He was feeling confident of bagging a share of the prize money. The conditions were favouring his horse.

The slight thaw was producing fresh mud to stain his, and everyone else's footwear, effectively concealing the signs of wear on brogues that should have been replaced long ago. He smiled at how mud and the cold was such a leveller. Muffled in scarves and buttoned in warm coats and bowler hats pulled low, the gentlemen owners all looked the same. The woman in the outrageous leopard skin coat and white beret with diamonds dangling from her ears was an exception. She was a countess from Luxembourg but did not own a horse and attracted little attention from those he was now engaging in easy conversation. Talk was on the hard going, on the possibility of it cutting up into mud and complaints about trainers and their extortionate fees and the flightiness of jockeys. It was the cagey sparring of rivals sizing up the opposition, but all done with the strictest sense of decorum and good manners.

Every owner wanted their horse to win, but there were so many variables with which to contend that could influence a race it was obvious there was a longer game to play in this business. Few, if any, got rich quick from racing. Keeping in the good books of one's peers on the other hand, might allow access at preferential rates to a fine stallion stud, thereby hopefully bringing into the world a future champion. Gentle wheeling and dealing and the smoothing of business and family connections took place between their observations on a particular horse and the sharing of views on a specific trainer's methods.

Buckrose was a master of this kind of talk. After a season of carefully introducing his name and bogus title in a manner he hoped sent nobody scurrying away to ask awkward questions, he'd wheedled his way into the upper echelons of society. He was close to charming his way into the boudoirs of a number of impossibly well-bred young ladies of low intelligence but firm bodies honed on the show-jumping circuit and significant disposable income - large portions of which, he hoped to convince them to invest in spurious 'fail-safe' schemes and thereby line his various bank accounts. It was a slow process requiring time and patience and considerable skill, but the payback could be significant.

It also took a hefty amount of capital and that was something Buckrose was rapidly running short on. However, he'd drawn a decent wedge from the bank in Cheltenham and was comfortably set for the next two days of racing and the bulging wallet inside his coat gave him confidence. He just needed that darned weasel in London to deliver on his promise about that rock... If he got the thousand pounds he'd been promised, then he'd be home and dry. But what could be taking so long? There was an unpleasant knot of fear in the pit of his stomach that just refused to unloosen.

But that was not the end of his worries. Buckrose rarely read local papers, preferring to scour the social columns of The Times and The Daily Telegraph for useful tidbits of information he might exploit to his advantage. The more informed he was, the better he could fool others he was a legitimate member of Society. However, the headlines on a local paper he'd found lying on a table in a cafe this morning had stopped him in his tracks.

Chapter Twenty

Murder In Broadway!
Local jeweller found dead at the quiet country station.
Police baffled by the identity of the sinister strangler who took the life of Cheltenham jeweller, Peter Krast.

Krast dead? The newspaper suggested the motive was likely to be robbery, although the police apparently were neither ruling that in, or out. A typically evasive answer from the authorities, implying they might have other ideas but were unwilling to share them with a reporter.

Buckrose could not understand what this meant but he'd felt a horrible sensation like iced water was being poured through him as he read the article. Perhaps it was just an unrelated act of pointless aggression...but from the little he could glean from the sparse report, this sounded like a calculated attack. Carefully orchestrated right under the eyes of the station staff. And strangulation was so cruel and slow.... Buckrose didn't want to admit it, but he was starting to feel very scared. It was just too much of a coincidence that the man who'd gullibly entrusted the diamond into his care, was now dead.

He'd scrunched the paper up in frustrated irritation and tossed it aside to be blown across the frost-whitened fields of the Cotswolds. If only he could toss away the mounting sense of menace so easily. Everything was starting to weigh on his mind and distract his attention when he most needed to remain alert whilst he verbally fenced with the great and the good. He must ensure the skillfully constructed facade of his persona remained in place.

The horses were being led out of the enclosure, and Buckrose watched as Coldicott's head lad walked Money For Nothing towards the exit gate. He exchanged some polite words of mutual encouragement with the owner of Prudent Star, then made his excuses and headed for the stands.

*　　*　　*　　*

His feet were getting cold on the frozen ground and Vignoles was wondering what they were doing here. Looking for a needle in haystack. 'If his horse wins, we'd be able to find him easy enough. If I understand this

131

betting system, his horse is looking a contender?'

'A decent chance... If he's placed between first and third he'll be with his trainer and the jockey to celebrate after, in the winner's enclosure,' Mellor replied. He'd put his glasses away in their case and was lighting up. He too was sharing the same frustration. They'd got no closer to Buckrose. 'It'll be a squeeze to get close, but if we stake a place early, we'll have a chance.'

'Catching Buckrose when he's celebrating might be good. Catch him off-guard when flushed with the adrenaline rush of a win.'

Mellor grinned. 'I like your style, guv.'

'Don't call me that.'

Mellor ignored the command. 'What time is the race?'

'Four-Thirty.'

'Then there's time for a swift pint.'

*   *   *   *

'Lord Buckrose?'

He gave the two well-turned out gents a questioning look and waited. Buckrose was feeling twitchy and concentrate hard on maintaining his fake aristocratic persona. *What might they want?*

'We understand you're the owner of Money For Nothing?'

'So I am.'

'A fine horse!'

'My trainer and I share that opinion...' Standard race-day banter. He relaxed. A few minutes of empty pleasantries would help distract his aching head from the alarms constantly ringing like unattended fire bells.

Coldicott had only recently informed him about the brazen attempt at race-fixing that Biggs had averted. It was scandalous. Quite shameless the dirty tricks people would attempt to gain advantage. At least the lad had the intelligence to report it. It sounded a poorly planned attempt, but all the same, what was swirling around Buckrose's head was that Biggs claimed the two reprobates said they knew him. Said they were friends and working on his instruction! It was both bizarre and deeply disquieting. Why in God's name would he send people to try and slow his horse to and leave him out of pocket. And why would he ensure they declare that *he* was behind the plot? The Jockey Club would throw the book at him. The inescapable fact he did not wish to consider was that someone had rumbled him. Someone was trying to queer his pitch. Taken on top of the shocking news he'd read about Krast, Buckrose was fighting hard to maintain his disguise. He needed some jovial horsey banter right now.

'He's coming out a favourite with the bookies.' Kane observed, sagely.

'One enjoys that vote of confidence. But there is stiff competition and the going is likely to be tricky for both horse and jockey.'

'On the back of three straight wins, your horse looks a dead cert,' Kane gave his rolled copy of the Racing Times a wave to indicate that he was up to date with current form. 'He's come on well.'

'Just minor races...they were hardly a test.' Buckrose flapped a hand dismissively, but he was enjoying the adulation. The wins had been small but presented him with some much-needed fighting funds. 'A far sterner test today. One will get a true measure of the horse. However, I prefer to keep my powder dry and not declare my expectations. A win gives one a boost, of course.' *And a most welcome cheque.* His unpaid bills were mounting and Coldicott was not going to be fobbed off much longer. 'But I'm approaching this as much as a litmus test as anything.'

Abel proffered his pack of cigarettes and Buckrose gave them a doubtful look. He was low on the Sobranies and needed a smoke, so he took one and graciously allowed Abel to light it. As their heads drew closer, Abel spoke.

'We're a little concerned...'

'About what?' Buckrose narrowed his eyes as he drew in a lungful of sharp, fresh menthol. Disgusting.

'This sudden improvement in form...' Abel clicked his lighter shut in a deft movement and dropped it back in his pocket. He blew perfumed smoke as he spoke. 'A good friend of ours assumed it was but a blip in your nag's erratic form?'

'Nag? How dare you!' Buckrose was about to launch into a tirade, but there was something menacing about how the two men were standing close and boxing him in that made him adopt a more conciliatory tone. 'My horse is much improved thanks to hard work and good training. I hope your friend is not implying anything?'

'Heaven's no. What sort of fellows do you take us for?' Abel fluttered his eyelids in mock outrage. 'It's simply that our friend has put quite a lot on Money For Nothing *not* winning today.'

'We came here with the intention to win. It is quite simple. Each man must decide whom he backs and at what price, but one does *not* race to order! Now, if you please, I have things to attend...?' Time to beat a hasty retreat. This was starting to take on an unpleasant aspect. Somebody was very keen his horse didn't win. Perhaps the horse didn't need encouraging in that department, but even so, Buckrose felt an unpleasant prickling of his skin on the nape of his neck. Were these the men who'd tried to nobble the horse earlier?

'Lord Buckrose, this *mutual* friend of ours, to quote Dickens, is most anxious you appreciate the importance of achievin' the correct result...' Kane spoke quietly but clearly. There was no mistaking the implied threat.

Buckrose stared at Kane. Mutual friend? Who the hell could that be? He was desperately trying to place their faces. He must have met these two before and it was vital he dredged this information up and rescued the situation. He realised that Kane was now proffering a small business card. Buckrose took it, mind still racing. It simply bore the words:

Money For Something.

He made a slight laugh. 'Forgive me for not remembering the name of our shared acquaintance - but I'm afraid he is misinformed. He's got the wrong horse!' Buckrose felt a surge of relief. This was some foolish nonsense and he was going to make his excuses.

'Turn it over.'

'Eh?' He read the three words on the reverse, *Something For Money*. 'Look here, I have no idea what your game is, but I am rather busy...'

'Mr Slatter sends his regards.'

'Slatter. Ernest Slatter?' Buckrose stopped short. He dropped his voice so it would be lost amidst the noise and chatter all around. 'Are you working for that gentleman?'

'We come bearing *gifts*...' Abel blew smoke into the air and winked. 'He's most anxious you oblige in return.'

'You have what Mr Slatter and I agreed as part of our trading deal?' Buckrose felt his heart race. It pounded like the rhythmic vibrations of the cold earth as a clutch of horses pounded around the course accompanied by a rising hubbub of cheers and the frantic voice of the commentator broadcast over the Tannoy. *Slatter had delivered on his promise! He'd come through with the money!* Buckrose fought hard to stop his face cracking into a wide grin.

'Not about our person...' Kane explained.

'Far too risky...There might be pickpockets about! Abel completed, with an arch raising of an eyebrow.

'And too many eyes to see...'

'Naturally. Of course, of course...one cannot be too careful.' Buckrose was fighting to maintain his equilibrium. 'Just me get this quite clear. Our friend here has secured the necessary...er...*investment* funds?'

'He has. In full. But he's put one condition upon delivery. Payment only if your horse loses...'

'That's outrageous! Then you are the bounders who tried to water my horse!'

'Keep your hair on, old boy, we don't want to cause a scene.' Abel kept his voice low and level.

'I should report you both this very instant!'

'But you won't...' A trail of scented smoke irritated Buckrose's eyes. Abel's expression was inscrutable. The blue eyes seemed to bore into his head like a gannet's gaze penetrated the sea for prey. 'You want what we have. You'll do as we say.'

Buckrose wasn't going to call the police or the race officials. That was the very last thing he would or could do, and these thugs knew it. The rising din of chatter continued all around. There were cheers and groans as a race ended. Useless betting slips ripped in half. More drinks being necked. Nobody noticed the three of them in conversation, and nobody cared.

'He is a most unusual fellow. You should indulge him.'

A dirty, conniving rat, more like! Buckrose kept his thoughts to himself.

'He wants to see a certain level of co-operation before allowing us to proceed to close the deal.' Kane explained.

'You rotten...' But Buckrose was cornered.

'We shall meet tomorrow.'

'I-I shall need a little time to make arrangements...'

'Likewise.' Kane looked at the horses in the parade ring. 'Two-thirty in the afternoon. At Belas Nap'

'What the Devil's that when it's at home?'

'A burial mound.'

'Neolithic, and dreadfully interesting...' Abel chortled at Buckrose's confusion.

'What? I've never even heard of it!'

'We bought you an O.S. map. It's marked in red. There's a place to pull your car over...' Abel was turning away.

'Why two-thirty?' He'd have preferred the cover of darkness.

'Everyone will be distracted by the Gold Cup. Now I think it's time you went to see your horse...' Kane winked. 'Remember. Get the required result or the deal is off!'

Buckrose stared at their backs as they melted into the crowd of dampening wool beneath the fug of combined breath and tobacco smoke hanging like a thin cloud. He turned the little card over in his hands. He was scared and angry in equal measure. They'd caught him unawares and were now tugging his strings like he was a wooden-headed puppet. He hated the sense of losing control.

On the other hand, Slatter was going to deliver. The sly fox. On the telephone, Slatter had stalled and it had been frustrating and disheartening, but now he'd sent these two goons along with the dosh. What a turn up for the books. Buckrose was smiling to himself. He was about to become very rich. Tomorrow afternoon he was about to get his hands on a wedge of freshly 'laundered' money in exchange for a stupid little stone he cared nothing for.

Then the race could go hang! His horse could fall and break its bloody neck for all he cared. He could pay off his bills, sell the horse if it survived the jumps and live the life of Riley somewhere hot and very far away. It was ironic, but Money For Nothing actually stood half a chance of coming first and there was not a lot he could do about it. Unless...

His jockey was a shifty fellow he didn't trust. The little man was always whingeing about never having any money. Buckrose had a crisp pair of fresh tens in his wallet. That should ensure his man didn't encourage the horse too eagerly. With the tricky conditions underfoot, nobody would suspect foul play if it faded in the closing stages.

Chapter Twenty-One

Derek Coldicott was giving the jockey a hard time. Short angry bursts of stinging vitriol fired from his mouth like staccato bursts of machine gun fire.

'Why did you ease off! I saw it clear as day! Don't argue back, you lazy idiot. Why do I pay you if you're going to chicken out of a jump?'

The jockey was still breathing hard and there were beads of sweat on his brow despite the plummeting temperature, courtesy of the bitter late afternoon air now rolling off the hills that overlooked the course. He gave the impression of a man who'd expended every ounce of effort. Between the verbal assaults, he was trying to plead his case, but Coldicott was having none of it. Placed third meant a smaller share of the purse and the trainer needed Buckrose flush so he could pay off a substantial portion of his debts.

Lord Buckrose however, was all smiles and trying to convey his satisfaction with the jockey with a twinkle in his eyes, whilst patting the horse's giant head. Biggs was attending to the steaming beast and giving both owner and trainer anxious looks. He hoped nobody was going to point the finger at him. He'd stopped the horse from taking on too much water, but it had been a strange affair and he desperately hoped no-one was going to suggest he'd had a part to play in it.

'Don't be so hard on the fellow, Derek. I think under the circumstances we can feel mighty pleased with third.' Buckrose was all smiles. 'It was a jolly close haul. Buckingham pushed us all the way...'

'He should have given him more whip!' Coldicott was not mollified. 'We were neck and neck coming out of the last jump.'

'You know best...' Buckrose turned away in response to a voice he heard close by and magnanimously shook hands with Mr Cooper, the trainer of Great Eliza, who'd won by a nose on Buckingham. 'Good show, sir!'

Cooper offered his hand to Coldicott and they exchanged a few words of mutual congratulation before returning to his own party. Mrs Hope Collins, the owner of the Broadway Novice's Steeplechase winner was waiting to have a photograph taken with horse and trainer.

Buckrose was feeling a warm glow of satisfaction. This was playing out better than he'd dare hope. Placed a narrow third was no disgrace and the jockey had played his part perfectly. The perceptive Coldicott sensed there had been a win in the offing, but despite haranguing the jockey, the margin was small and it could never be proven as anything other than bad luck. Buckrose would soon mollify Coldicott by passing over all the winnings. It would hardly make a dent in the outstanding invoices, but the trainer would be pleased by the gesture. Buckrose could afford to be generous. He was going to collect a payment that rendered a hundred pounds little more than small change. By tomorrow afternoon he would be rich. He searched the excited faces looking into the enclosure and hoped to catch a glimpse of the two delivery men sent by Slatter, but there were just too many pale ovals of faces under hats in the failing daylight for him to pick them out.

Two men were entering the ring, a gap being made by a uniformed policeman and a race official. Long coats, hats pulled down, one with a pipe, the other a cigarette, both with black leather gloves. They looked like the law. Buckrose turned away and enthusiastically clapped the jockey on the back and started to offer a more positive appraisal of the race, hoping they were headed elsewhere.

'Lord Buckrose?'

This was the second time his false name had been used as an opening gambit in as many hours. He felt his stomach give a nervous twitch. He turned about and smiled.

'DCI Vignoles and DS Mellor. Might we have a word, sir?'

'About what may I ask?'

'We are making enquiries about the murder at Broadway railway station on Monday evening.'

'Good God, what on earth has that to do with me?' Buckrose glanced at Coldicott, as if for support, before angrily confronting Vignoles. 'I find your timing outrageous. We are on public show and with the press to hand.' A flash bulb went off behind them.

'Then I suggest we withdraw somewhere more discreet...'

'I see no reason why I need to answer any questions. I know virtually nothing about this murder!'

'But you do know *something*...' Vignoles gave him a knowing smile.

'I read the daily papers!'

'Lord Buckrose, the horse needs...' Coldicott butted in.

'Of course, Derek. Take him away. I shall rejoin you shortly after I have dealt with this. It won't take long.'

'There is a steward's tent we can use,' Vignoles indicated.

Once inside the small tent, Buckrose folded his arms defiantly. 'Fire away but make it snappy. I have a great deal to do and a trainer and jockey to deal with.'

'We consider murder important,' Mellor snapped back. 'Sir.'

'Of course. I-I didn't mean to suggest otherwise.' Buckrose cleared his throat. 'Forgive me, gentlemen, we hit it off on a rather sour note. If you believe I can be of assistance, I will do my level best. I'm just not sure how?'

'Do you know a jeweller from Cheltenham by the name of Peter Krast? He has a shop on Royal Well Place.'

'Never heard of the fellow.'

'But perhaps you know the shop? A small, well-appointed establishment that attracts the more well-to-do citizens of this town.' Vignoles was going for the charm offensive.

'I regret I do not. You are forgetting, or perhaps unaware, that my estate is not close. This is far from my stamping ground.'

'Where is your estate?' Mellor was taking notes.

'The East Riding. We're Yorkshire blood through and through, although the accent has lapsed. Eton and Cambridge does that to one!' He laughed.

'This estate has a name?'

'Sledmere Hall. A 14th Century pile, although we suspect Norman footings to the tower and the moat is perhaps older. It comes with forty acres of...'

'Where were you on Monday 7th between 6 and 7pm?' Mellor cut him off mid flow.

'Monday? Ah, now I was in town. At my club by 7.30pm at the latest. So that means I would have been braving the rush hour traffic at the time in question.' He gave an arrogant lift to his chin.

'Town?' Vignoles queried.

'London...'

'Your club would be able to confirm this?' Mellor was writing as he spoke.

'Of course. But look here, my secretary can make the appropriate page in my appointment diary available for inspection. I can place a call to arrange it if you insist on having some kind of proof? I see no reason to trouble my club. We're a most respectable group. Mainly judges, QC's, bankers and surgeons - and the occasional *senior* police officer...' He smiled. 'I can allay any fears you may have that I was grubbing around killing someone in Broadway without the need to fuel unfounded tittle-tattle at the club.' He risked a hard laugh.

'The name of your club?'

'The Wellington. But look, I do think this an imposition...'

'When did you travel down to Cheltenham?' Mellor was dead-pan and gave no indication of whether he believed what he heard or not.

Buckrose hesitated a fraction too long and the detectives noticed. 'I drove myself.'

'And when was that? When you drove yourself here...?' Mellor tapped his pencil in a deliberately irritating manner on his notebook.

'Late Monday. Very late, actually. I had an appointment with Coldicott the next morning and wanted to see my horse safely loaded for transporting to Broadway.'

'You motored all this way after an evening at your club?' Vignoles sounded sceptical.

'I dined there in preparation for the drive.'

'What car do you drive?'

'A Bentley.'

'Not an Alvis?'

'Heavens, no!' This was more promising. They were barking up quite the wrong tree. Buckrose felt himself regain safer ground. He'd not been near Broadway station and certainly not in an Alvis. He started to feel more comfortable. The gears of his devious mind were now engaging smoothly. He'd stumbled over the date and time of travel but reckoned he could still recover from that...

'Did Lady Buckrose accompany you?' Vignoles asked.

'There is no-one of that title, at present.' He sniffed contemptuously.

'I have answered quite enough questions on personal matters that have no bearing on your investigation, but if you care to furnish me with an address, I shall have the relevant page of my engagement diary mailed to you, first class.'

Vignoles handed him a card.

'Leicester? Rather out of the way...'

'The long arm of the law stretches even this far,' Mellor replied.

Vignoles pulled out the copy of Miss Wolfe's line drawing. 'Do you know this man?'

Buckrose replied in the negative and made to walk away.

'Please consider the general appearance of this man. It may not be a good likeness. He was dressed in typical country garb of working tweeds and deerstalker hat.'

'I don't know him.'

'How odd, because he claims to know you.' Vignoles gave a twitch of a corner of his mouth.

'Then it is a poor likeness. What is his name?'

'That's what we would like to discover.'

'With no name and just a cartoon, I am unable to help.' A smarmy smile.

'This person in the company of another and driving an Alvis, called at Broadway station on Monday night to arrange the delivery of one of your racehorses, would that jog your memory?'

Buckrose looked genuinely confused. 'That makes no sense. I don't understand...'

'He claimed to represent yourself and was seeking to book the unloading of a horse on Thursday. Failing to find an available slot, he was directed to Winchcombe by the ticket clerk, who telephoned through whilst this fellow waited.'

'What an extraordinary tale?' Buckrose stared confidently at Vignoles. 'Complete humbug of course. Money For Nothing was unloaded yesterday at Broadway, accompanied by two other horses and by a prior appointment made by my trainer, Mr Coldicott. I have no horse running tomorrow, so the arrangement you describe would be nonsensical. You might like to check at Broadway, under Coldicott of Acre Vale Farm. They will confirm all I have just told you.'

'Shall you attend the Gold Cup tomorrow - even with no horse in action?' Vignoles wanted to establish where this man was likely to be and thereby satisfy one element of Badger's ranting request. He could not, as yet, find any good reason to detain Buckrose, let alone arrest him.

'I cannot see that is any business of yours. However, since you ask, I have a seat reserved alongside the Royal party...' Buckrose left that hanging in the air for a moment. 'Now, if that is all?' He handed over a gilded card whilst speaking. 'My club. They can field telephone calls and hold mail, but I would be grateful if you contact me only if an absolute necessity and based upon robust police work and not some silly cock and bull story.'

*   *   *   *

'Do we trust Lord Snooty?' Mellor asked.

'Only as far as I could ride his bloody horse...'

'You ride?' Mellor was surprised.

'On a donkey at Bridlington, when I was eight...'

'He's lying about something,' Mellor exclaimed.

'But not about being at Broadway station on Monday evening.' Vignoles looked at the card he'd been handed. 'His confidence grew as we became more specific and I suspect his alibi will be strong during that time-period. He wasn't there. But I wonder if his alibi is robust enough to stand up to scrutiny in other aspects? There is something not right and we need to dig deeper. Call his club and ruffle as many feathers you like. I don't care if his QC friends give him disapproving stares when he next drops in for a snifter of twenty five year-old brandy.'

'Gladly!'

'Let's see what the trainer has to say about our man on shoulder-rubbing terms with the Queen...'

*   *   *   *

'Can you spare a few minutes?'

'Not really.' Coldicott had lost none of his irritation from earlier. He glanced at their warrant cards and realised he had little choice. 'Take over!' The young man Vignoles recognised as Biggs, accompanied by another, took over rubbing down Money For Nothing.

Coldicott gave a glance at what they were doing and apparently satisfied, stepped away and thrust his hands into the pockets of his jacket in an attitude of casual indifference. 'Before you ask, I was at my place all Monday. We brought the string in from the gallops about four-thirty. I was in the yard and office until after ten, then I turned in. We start the day early in this business, so late nights are out and pointless jaunts down to Broadway are something I avoid.' His self-satisfied grin shouted out - *So there!*

Vignoles had the feeling Buckrose had primed him. 'That was not why we are here but thank you for clearing that up.'

That removed the smile. 'What do you want to know then?'

'Lord Buckrose is the owner of this horse?'

'He is. And about to pick up a nice cheque in return for being placed. What of it?'

'When did you take the horse into your establishment?'

'Eight months ago. What's this to do with that murder?'

'Nothing as far as I am aware...?' Vignoles wanted Coldicott to feel less confident. It was clear the trainer was used to issuing orders and asserting control and if Buckrose and Coldicott had agreed a strategy, he needed to steer around it and get him into more uncomfortable territory.

'Why do you think we wish to talk to you about murder?' Mellor cut in.

'I heard you speaking to his Lordship...I heard the name of the man who was killed.'

'Indeed? And can you help us?' Mellor continued.

'Of course not. I train horses...'

'Why did you send one of your employees down to Broadway Station on Monday evening?'

'I sent nobody anywhere that evening. Everyone was at the stables and can prove it.' He stared confidently at Mellor.

'Do you get on well with Lord Buckrose?'

'As good as any trainer with any owner. We have our ups and downs, as any might. It's a job, not a friendship.'

'I saw you were angry your jockey didn't drive the horse harder...' Mellor asked.

'Nobody wants to come third. What's this got to do with your investigation?'

'Do you often lose you temper?' Mellor gave his meanest stare.

'What sort of a question is that?'

'When did Buckrose arrive here from London?' Vignoles asked.

'Monday night...' There was a flicker of doubt in the trainer's eye. Vignoles wondered if this part of the story had not been rehearsed.

'What time did he arrive?'

'I've no idea...'

'You did not see Lord Buckrose on Monday evening?'

'No...'

One of the stable lads paused in rubbing down of the flank of the horse and his eyes looked across at Coldicott, before continuing his work.

'So how do you know he came down on Monday?' Mellor queried.

'He told me.'

'You believe him?' Mellor was once again taking notes and managing to make the act look mildly menacing.

'Obviously. One develops trust between trainer and owner.'

'He didn't telephone to say he was in the area?' Vignoles and Mellor were trading verbal blows with Coldicott.

'No.'

'Or call in at your stables? I imagine an owner would be keen as mustard to see how his investment was holding up!'

'Are you doubting my word, Inspector?'

'Can you explain why someone came to Broadway station on Monday evening to arrange the delivery of one of Lord Buckrose's horses tomorrow?'

'What? He's only got one horse! That one - and I made the arrangements last week to bring her in on Tuesday.'

'If not on Monday, when did you and Buckrose meet?' Vignoles changed tack.

'Yesterday morning. It was agreed by telephone the previous Friday. A meeting at eight to discuss our prospects in the race, then get the horse loaded up to take to the station. As I have just explained...'

The stable lad on the far side of Money For Nothing had a troubled look on his face, but when Coldicott glanced across to see how they were getting on he bent his head down and gave more application to his work.

'Have you ever met a man called Peter Krast?'

'No.'

'Has his name come up in conversation with Lord Buckrose?'

'No. The first I heard of him was in the paper this morning.' He folded his arms in a gesture of defiance.

'Have you seen this man?' Vignoles showed the line drawing.

'Nope.'

'He claims to be representing Lord Buckrose.' Mellor continued. 'This is the man seeking to arrange delivery of a horse. That implies he's one of your employees. Take a closer look.'

Coldicott gave it barely a glance and shook his head. 'Nobody from my staff was at Broadway. End of discussion. Now I need to load this valuable horse into the van and get him on his way...' He pulled out a set of ignition keys and strode off towards a row of motorised horse boxes parked along the perimeter.

Mellor stepped closer to the stable lads. 'You heard some of that conversation?'

The two young men looked up and stopped their grooming. Biggs looked nervously over his shoulder towards the receding figure of Coldicott.

'Biggs, isn't it?' Vignoles recognised him.

'Yes, sir.'

'And...?'

'Sid. Sid Pearson.'

'You both work for Coldicott?' Mellor asked. They nodded and tried to look busy with the horse.

'You looked worried, Sid. I saw your expression.' Mellor's voice was conversational and relaxed. 'Is there something on your mind?'

'No...'

Mellor opened a pack of cigarettes and shook it, so a number protruded. 'Go on. You've got a few minutes before he's back.' Both lads took a cigarette and accepted a light from Mellor. 'You're not in trouble...'

Mellor joined them and casually exhaled smoke. 'I bet he runs the place like a regular Tartar?' He winked and the lads laughed.

'Not half! He'll give us one 'ell of a bawling out if he catches us talking.'

'Why would he do that?' Vignoles asked.

'He told us to keep our mouths shut. He doesn't like stable business shared around. Says its private.'

'Because you know something?' Mellor asked, keeping a watchful eye on the line of parked vans.

'I've nothing to hide!' But Biggs looked guilty.

'Being circumspect is reasonable, but we are investigating a serious crime,' Vignoles spoke. 'We can interview anyone we choose. Not that this is an interview, just a friendly chat...'

'Although not answering our questions could make us jump to conclusions...' Mellor added.

Both young men looked uncomfortable but remained silent.

'Alright, we'll haul you down the station and do it there...' Mellor made as if to step closer.

'They had an argument.' Pearson mumbled. 'A big flare up.'

'When?'

'Monday evening.'

'You're sure it was Monday?' Mellor quizzed.

'Yes.'

'What time on Monday evening?' Mellor gave him a hard stare.

'Six - or thereabouts. I saw Buckrose and the boss going for it big guns in the yard. They made up soon after, and Buckrose left. I guessed he parked his car down the lane, out of sight.'

'Did you witness this argument?' Vignoles asked Biggs.

'No. I was dealing with Chicory Blue at the time. But I saw him. Buckrose was there. Hanging about the yard about the time the string came in off the gallops.'

'What is this string?' Vignoles queried.

'That's what we call the line of horses taken out for exercise.'

'Thanks lads. We'll keep this under our hats - for now,' Mellor tipped his. 'We'd best be off, guv...'

The headlights were on and the engine fired up in one of the vans. In the distance, locomotive whistles sounded as impatient steam engines urged inebriated passengers to stagger and wobble their way down to carriages awaiting their return in the cutting below. Racing was over for today.

Chapter Twenty-Two

Buckrose abandoned his attempt at sleep when an attack of cramp in one of his feet caused him to scrabble urgently in the constricted space to get hold of his foot and pull it hard to stop the searing pain. Aside from the agony of cramp, he was chilled to the core and felt a wave of uncontrollable shivers wrack his body. Breath streamed from nose and mouth as he huffed and puffed like a steam locomotive whilst he eased the cramp and gave his foot a cautious wiggle.

The rear seat of his Humber made a poor bed, requiring him to twist his back and keep his legs bent all night. He now sat upright and tried to look out of the windows with their thin veils of ice patterns at the silvery world outside. He'd been a dud at physics and had no proper understanding of why a car offered so little protection. The scything wind that troubled the lank grasses on the verge and wheedled its way between the gaps in the drystone walling was held in check by the metal and glass, but the cold was just as deep and intense inside. He might as well have lain on the steel-hard ground outside under a coat. This was a cold that made his bones ache deep inside.

He staggered out of the back of the car and made tentative steps as he stiffly worked the circulation back into his complaining legs. He stretched, took a lungful of easterly wind and immediately dived into the driving seat and fired up the engine. The heater was on full and he sat hunched and shivering as he waited for it to take effect as the motor gently rocked the car.

He needed a cafe and a supply of coffee. Hot soup or a bacon roll would go down well. Something to reignite the spark of life, which at the moment felt more like a sputtering candle.

However, despite his physical complaints, creased suit and yesterday's shirt and the dispiriting view of a gaggle of Cotswold of sheep staring at him uncomprehendingly through the bars of a metal gate, he was feeling happy. Ludicrously happy! There was a joyous madness coursing through his body and desisted from blowing on his fingers for a moment to throw back his head and laugh out loud.

'You did it! You clever bastard!' His accent was now more Southern streetwise than Eton College and it sounded harsh within the confines of the car. The sheep stared back impassively mouths temporarily motionless. They had no comprehension of what was happening, but it made a diversion from a long day of munching on frosted grass that snapped like glass.

'Not quite the way I'd planned it, but that's the name of the game. You take a chance when it lands in the palm of your hand and run with it!' He grinned like someone crazed, his hair flopping over his brow adding to the effect. He made a series of idiot faces in the rearview mirror, then, almost reluctantly, started to comb his hair into something more respectable. His days of sleeping in frozen cars before fastidiously creating an impression of wealth and fine breeding were over. Once he'd done the deal to end all deals that afternoon he would cut and run and become whomsoever he liked. He would change into someone quite different - and easier to live with. Lord Buckrose would be dead. He would vanish like a puff of smoke, with just his clothes offered to a jumble sale. Or might it be better if he made a celebratory bonfire and warmed his hands on a funeral pyre to a man who never was?

He'd start dreaming up a new name over that frothy coffee he was thirsting for. Think out a new identity. A wealthy business man from the South coast perhaps? Somewhere closer to home so he didn't have to watch his accent and where the places his character was supposed to inhabit would be familiar. He could be a man who'd made a mint in the motor trade. That would be easy enough. As long as it got him a new passport and an airline ticket to somewhere distant, that's all that mattered.

Having felt the benefit of the heater, Buckrose stepped out of the car once again, this time to better straighten his clothes and brush down his overcoat. He needed to maintain the illusion of Lord Buckrose long enough to get some breakfast inside and then meet those two gents at their ancient archeological site.

The warm glow of conceit and over-confidence seemed to act like a buffer against the wind on this upland stretch of road. Buckrose looked down into the valley and in the distance could see a towering plume of startlingly bright steam, like a skein of white wool, issuing from a locomotive puffing along the valley bottom. A railway station! They often have a refreshment room. And sell tickets to far off destinations. That's what he'd do. Find himself a cosy station to properly thaw out and over a hot drink sketch out his new life and buy a ticket to London or Liverpool, where he could get a new passport. He'd ditch the old car once the deal was done and hop on a train.

It might be wise to lose that odd couple as well... Duck and dive and blur the trail. It was always best to cover one's tracks. He needed to get himself a new jacket, hat and coat and a ticket on an express train and he'd soon shake them off.

Chapter Twenty-Three

Elsie Gable was sitting on a bench alongside two girl friends on the platform at Winchcombe station. They were all dressed in British Railways issue coveralls, stout work shoes and the almost obligatory headscarves tied around their hair. Winter overcoats had been slipped over their workwear whilst they took their lunch break away from cleaning the rakes of carriages brought up from Cheltenham Racecourse.

They had snap tins opened on their knees, although Mary Joyner had one of the new plastic Tupperware type with a nifty air-tight lid in bright red. This was the cause of some admiration along the bench as they tucked into their modest lunches. As they ate their fish paste sandwiches from beds of greaseproof paper, Elsie Gable and Suzy Simmonds were appreciating how their own careworn enamelled tins in cream and dark blue or bearing a Scottish winter scene with a stag, looked awfully old fashioned in comparison.

'It was not terribly cheap...' Joyner raised a perfectly trimmed eyebrow. Gable inwardly groaned and gave Simmonds a sly glance. Gable considered Joyner a friend and she could indeed be terrific company, but Joyner did have an annoying trait of deriving enjoyment from 'getting one over' her friends, especially if it was something new, fashionable and unaffordable to those not walking out with a man flush with spending money. Joyner never seemed happier than when she could show off a new lipstick that was 'in vogue' and made by one of the expensive brands Gable and Simmonds could not easily afford. Last Friday night, Joyner had met the girls wearing her lovely woollen coat, but now off-set by a trendy white felt contrivance that reminded them of those Dutch women in a Bruegel painting. And yes, it was just like the one worn by Olivia De Havilland and also the fashionable choice of the prettier young ladies travelling to the racecourse earlier, a fact Joyner had delighted in pointing out. Joyner had lapped up their praise about how charming she looked (she did, there was no denying it...) and delighted in being asked once again how much it had cost (far too much...). Gable could just about stomach this with her senses pleasingly dulled by a G& T or a rum and cola on a night out, but now, whilst desperate for some much-deserved lunch, she was discovering that even a humble box for sandwiches had now trumped their war-time tins that served admirably. Until today, none of them had given a second thought to whether they were smart or modern until the moment Joyner had proudly brought her new acquisition out of her bag with an ostentatious flourish. Gable now understood why Joyner had insisted they sit on the platform bench and risking a ticking off from the stationmaster, who preferred staff to take their breaks away from the public gaze.

Gable bit into her salmon paste sandwich and watched as 'Oldlands Hall' piloting a glamorous beast named 'Earl Cawdor', stormed through the station towards the Midlands with a long rake of coaches behind. The double-headed express made a stirring sight. She and her gang had cleaned those carriages now disappearing in a drift of smoke and rush of sound and her body was feeling the after effects. But never mind the complaining knees and chapped hands, one day soon she would give Mary something to talk about! And it would be a darn sight more exciting that a snap top Tupperware box!

Once Ian got the ring back (another silent prayer that the police would find it soon) she had planned how to obtain the maximum dramatic effect. When they were all seated, but before Mary had time to launch into telling them about another new acquisition, Gable would slowly slide her glove off (which she would make a point of wearing all morning) and watch as the light caught in the many facets (a new word recently learned) and see their faces. Gable took comfort in the fact that whilst their plans had hit a nasty bump in the road with this awkward business of the jeweller and the humiliation of being caught snooping around the dead man's house, at least Ian wanted to marry her. She had no doubts about him in this regard and indeed, for all their lack of money and the frustrations of both living at home and in different villages, she was lucky. For all the fancy clothes and super-duper Tupperware, she'd not trade places for anything. She had no idea why, or *how*, Mary could want to take up with a far older, and *married* man. He wasn't even good looking...

It was quite shocking really, although it gave them plenty of salacious entertainment, especially as Mary was hardly shy about telling her friends of her supposedly secret rendezvous. Yes, he bought her lovely presents, but the fleeting liaisons and stolen moments over lunch were starting to sound rather grubby and unexciting to Gable's way of thinking. She knew Suzy felt the same. Gable may have been grilled by the police in an excruciatingly embarrassing episode, but their foolishness had been driven by an honest desire to get back what was theirs and do the right and proper thing.

And she would never let Ian do anything like Mary claimed she got up to! Well, not quite... She was determined to wear a white wedding dress and Mary Joyner could jolly well stand in the church as bridesmaid in an off-white number and think what she wanted!

Gable snapped out of her none-too charitable reverie as she realised Joyner was asking her about these same marriage intentions. 'So, come on Elsie, when *are* you getting hitched? We want a spring wedding!'

Gable was momentarily flustered. 'Soon.'

'Why the wait?'

'Well...we're still saving up.' It seemed a valid excuse.

'Well hurry up about it! We want to get choosing our dresses. You do still want us as bridesmaids? Please don't say you've changed your mind and haven't the heart to tell us!' Simmonds clapped a hand to her mouth.

'Don't be silly, Suzy! It's just that what with all the trouble there has been here this week...'

'What's that got to do with anything?' Simmonds was puzzled. 'You've been telling us for weeks and weeks that Ian was going to make an honest woman of you and now you're telling us that a murder is stopping you?'

'How on earth do you work that out, Else?' Joyner chimed.

'Well obviously it has nothing to do with us...'

'I should hope not!' Simmonds exclaimed. 'But I heard the police came asking for you? Can that be true?'

'Is there something wrong?' Joyner sensed this was not a time for frivolity. For all her love of bright things and pin-up good looks, she was not immune to picking up signals on her emotional radar. There was a softer soul hiding behind the lipstick, expensive scent and silly hats.

'Everything is fine. Really, it is.'

'No, it's not. I can tell when you have something on your mind.'

A large 'Prairie' tank engine reversed into the station at a fair lick amid much steam and rhythmic clanking as it hauled more empty coaches up from Cheltenham Racecourse. More work for the afternoon shift being delivered. This was made up of smart-looking stock, much of it first class and with Eastern region numbers. It had probably brought the high-rollers in for a day's racing down from the North-East.

Gable did not answer Joyner, but instead took a sudden intake of breath and clapped a hand over her mouth.

'What is it?' Simmonds wondered if the sudden release of the safety valves on the locomotive had made her friend jump, although they were all long used to the noises of the railway. It was waiting for the signal to drop to allow them to propel the train onto a siding. The crew of the engine seemed more interested in someone further up the platform, and the fireman dared a wolf whistle under the cover of the screaming safety valve.

'Talk of the Devil...' Joyner looked down the platform in response to the whistle, and with a trace of competitive envy, watched a blonde ponytailed policewoman in a tailored coat and with a hat set at a rakish angle approach.

'It might be news...' Gable felt a thrill of excitement.

'About what?' Simmonds was even more puzzled.

'Miss Gable. I hoped I might catch you on your break,' WPC Lansdowne gave a friendly smile. She introduced herself to the others. 'I wonder if I could have a few words?' Lansdowne gave the others a quick glance that suggested they might like to absent themselves.

'They can stay. I want them to stay. I've nothing to hide.'

'Are you sure?'

'Have you got news for me?' Gable sounded pitifully hopeful. 'About you-know...'

'I have not. I'm here about something else. I need you to help identify someone.'

'You mean in a parade? A line up like in the films? Have you found who did that to Mr Krast and you think I know them?' Gable looked aghast. Her friends were silent, transfixed. What on earth was unfolding before their eyes?

'Nothing so dramatic!' Lansdowne smiled to reassure Gable. 'It's probably unrelated to the murder investigation, but we must follow up every angle, even if it leads nowhere.' The prairie tank now heaved into motion with much hissing as it propelled the coaches onto the sidings and the crew reluctantly turned their attention away from Lansdowne and the three cleaners.

Gable fell silent and her face took on a sullen expression. She'd felt a jolt of excitement that the diamond had been found, but this hope had been dashed. 'What do you want to know?'

'We have been speaking with Mr Twister. He was telling us about an evening you spent together in Cheltenham a couple of weeks back.'

'What about it? It was just a meal and a drink, and I was home by ten.'

'Nobody is suggesting anything inappropriate,' Lansdowne remained reassuring.

Joyner fiddled with the Tupperware lid but seemed disinclined to look at Lansdowne.

'Mr Twister said you saw somebody in the same restaurant who you knew. But...' Lansdowne now looked at the other two women as she was talking. 'You told Mr Twister not to stare and pretend he had not seen them. Do you remember?'

Apart from the gruff huffing of the 'Prairie' tank, followed by the squeal of brakes and the 'chonk' of the signal returning to danger, an uncomfortable silence fell. Simmonds was looking at Gable with expectation of a thrilling revelation. She was holding her breath. Joyner had become fixated with the surface of the platform, her jaw muscles tensing.

'I'm not sure. When was this?'

'Monday. I am sure you can remember as far back as the start of the week. Mr Twister remembers clearly. You saw a girlfriend with another man. An older man.' Lansdowne was carefully observing the three women.

There was a sharp intake of breath from Simmonds. Joyner's throat was turning blotchy crimson despite the icy air.

'I told Ian to mind his own business and ignore them.'

'That is what Mr Twister told us. You were a model of discretion.' Lansdowne was aware of Joyner's discomfort. 'On the train home you told him your friend had a secret lover and you swore him to secrecy. He only told us because this is a police investigation and we take a dim view of secrets when investigating serious matters.'

'She's not doing anything wrong...'

'We have no interest in your girlfriend nor even that he might be married ...' Lansdowne looked at Joyner who was now in the grip of almost mortal embarrassment. 'She may even be unaware of his marital situation. Men are known to lie about such matters. Our interest is purely in the identity of the man. Do you know his name?' The question was aimed at all three.

'Colin. Colin Jeffries.' The words were almost a mumble from Joyner.

'Is that the man working in the jewellers?' Simmonds exclaimed. 'I read his name in the paper today! Oh my, you never told us he worked there!'

'Miss Joyner, am I correct in understanding the man you were seen with at Locarno Restaurant on the evening of Monday 7th at approximately 9.30pm was Colin Jeffries, senior sales assistant at Krast Jewellers?'

Joyner nodded her head. 'We have met for a number of weeks. On Mondays. Just for an hour or two. Nothing more. It was quite innocent. It's not what you think!'

'Did Mr Jeffries buy you presents?'

Joyner stroked the Tupperware box and looked into the distance. 'Sometimes...'

'Did he ever buy you jewellery?'

Joyner was aware her friends were staring at her. 'A brooch. And a silver bracelet...'

'Don't forget those lovely earrings...' Gable added, then stopped herself.

'Nice presents for a man to buy an innocent young friend.'

'I resent that!'

'Are you denying having an affair with Colin Jeffries? Before you answer, remember this is part of a murder investigation. We will uncover a lie, so it would be wise to tell the unvarnished truth.'

Joyner glared at Lansdowne with anger in her eyes. 'That depends on what you consider an affair...'

'Romantic meals for two, lovely gifts... You understand exactly what I mean.

Chapter Twenty-Four

'So, Jeffries was getting his leg over on a Monday night with a pretty carriage cleaner from Cheltenham? There's worse he could be doin'...' Mellor dragged on his fag and gave a lecherous laugh. 'Look, I know it don't sound proper, but his home life was miserable.'

'That is no excuse,' Lansdowne retorted.

'His extra-marital affair is of no direct relevance. Whatever one thinks of his behaviour, spending time with Miss Joyner is not our concern. What *is* relevant, is Jeffries appears to have been stealing from the business and covering up the paper trail.'

'Cooking the books.'

Vignoles shook his head sadly. 'I suspect so. It will take the Cheltenham Constabulary's experts in financial fraud to confirm our suspicions, but it looks like his actions are partially, if not wholly, responsible for Mr Krast discovering his business was in dire straits. Krast was in trouble all thanks to a man he trusted.' Vignoles was angry. 'That makes my blood boil. Actions have consequences and Krast found himself in desperate straits. Worry and despair allowed temptation to take hold, and when that diamond was presented to him on a metaphorical plate, Krast seized his chance. He would give Gable and Twister a pretty ring that neither would suspect was anything other than the one they found. It could even be argued they might be better off, as the real rock was liable to draw the interest of extremely dangerous criminals...'

'Very socially minded of Krast!'

'You know what I mean, Mellor.'

'I understand the logic behind Krast's thinking,' Mellor agreed. 'It was wrong, but he was trying to keep them content whilst selling this dodgy diamond to rescue his business - and keep the likes of that sneak Jeffries and the lovely Mary Jephson in employment. Trouble is, it got him killed.'

'Jeffries might not consider himself responsible and a decent lawyer will argue a strong case. He might stand trial for fraud and theft, but Jeffries's actions led to the murder of Krast. He's guilty by proxy.'

'I never liked the man from the start...' Mellor pulled a face. 'But if not Jeffries, then who the heck *did* kill the old man? And where's that bloody diamond?'

* * * *

'Slatter...'

'We need to talk...'

'Who is this?' Slatter frowned as he tried to recognise the voice down the telephone.

'Mr Jeffries. We...um...have an arrangement...'

'What the bleedin' Hell are you doin' callin' me? Are you nuts? Get off the line!'

'No, listen! You need to understand that it's getting out of control down here. I never agreed to you-know-who being killed.' He was speaking so quietly it was hard to hear what he said. 'There are police crawling over everything... going through all the papers from the safe and in minute detail. They're going to find out. It just a matter of time before I'm rumbled. I want it to stop.'

'Ring off and don't contact me like this ever again!' The phone line remained connected. 'Look, I'll see yer right. I'll get this sorted. But you've got to keep yer trap shut and yer head down. Deny everything.'

'I want no more trouble...'

'Bit bloody late for that. We've got trouble and we need to fix it. Now don't call me again. I've got someone looking into this.'

Slatter slammed the phone down and rubbed his temples. Was the line tapped? Had they said anything incriminating? And was he able to fix this mess? He had his doubts...

The door clattered open. He hoped it wasn't more trouble coming knocking.

Chapter Twenty-Five

'Sir?' It was WPC Jane Benson telephoning from the Detective Department offices in Leicester Central station. 'Any luck with the case?'

'We're making headway, but there is much I remain puzzled about.'

'Perhaps I can help? I've found something...'

'Go on.' Vignoles gripped the receiver that bit tighter.

'It's this Lord Buckrose.'

'Don't tell me; he really *is* a lord and with friends in high places stirring up trouble for me?'

'Far from it! He's a complete bounder. A charlatan. Blencowe has been trying to unearth some background on this character but with no success. You know what he's like when he gets the bit between the teeth, he never gives up.'

Vignoles smiled at the analogy. Horses seemed to be everywhere these days. Benson continued. 'He was hard at it with his head in a mountain of books on genealogy when Badger visited the office...'

'Chief Superintendent Badger.'

'Sorry...'

'Walls have ears, Benson.'

His impolite nickname for the boss was catching on across the department but it was dangerous to become carefree. Benson did not deserve the ticking off she'd get if the man in question overheard her.

'Chief Superintendent Badger was quizzing us both, and Blencowe explained about your interest in establishing the legitimacy of Lord Buckrose's title. The incredible thing is that the Badg...The Super, had heard of him.'

Vignoles gripped the phone tighter. 'What? He knows of Buckrose?'

'It was two years ago. The Super was attending a swanky event in London. The Lord Mayor was hosting a gala reception and the guest list read like Who's Who, as the Super was happy to tell us about, at length.'

'I bet he was...'

'It was strictly invitation only and any number of Lords and Ladies and even minor Royalty were there. None of whom matter to the story, except that the Super remembers the evening vividly and particularly an altercation that took place as Mrs Badger and he were arriving. A man was having cross words with a footman about his invitation. He was a smartly dressed gent, with a plummy accent, but there seemed to be a muddle about his name being left off the list. He clearly identified himself as Lord Buckrose. Before the Badgers could enter the dining room, they overheard Buckrose demand that some high-ranking member of the gentry came to his assistance and vouchsafed his right to enter. Things threatened to turn ugly for a moment until help arrived and he was escorted off the premises. As you might imagine, this was quite the talk over champagne and canapés and the name of Lord Buckrose was on everyone's lips. During dinner our Super was in conversation with one of his peers in the Met and they decided to make discreet enquiries. They felt it their duty to see if this man posed any kind of threat.'

'And did he?'

'No. He was not identified on any lists as a possible trouble-maker, nor with any connections to undesirable countries and regimes. He didn't turn up anywhere as it transpired, much as Blencowe discovered. The Met found this suspicious and brought in Scotland Yard and it was they who made a connection between Lord Buckrose and, wait for this, a third-rate pickpocket and small-time fraudster called Terry Grinal of Southampton.'

'That name lacks the gravitas of Lord Buckrose of Sledmere Hall...'

'Doesn't it just?' Benson laughed. 'He'd defrauded money from elderly ladies around his hometown and tried dipping his hand in the pockets of passengers off the ocean liners. But he was strictly small time.'

'How does his alter ego of Lord Buckrose come in?'

'Grinal was suspected of boarding the luxury Cunard cruise liner 'RMS Caronia' with the intent of stealing from the wealthy passengers. He used the bogus title of Lord Buckrose to book a first class berth and embark. However, before they sailed, the Head Steward was unhappy with some aspects of this man's story and details that didn't tally and was becoming suspicious. Then came an accusation that Grinal had been seen leaving a cabin not his own. After the occupants were alerted, personal items were found to be missing. These were soon discovered wrapped in a cloth behind a lifeboat and as Grinal had not being caught in possession, charges were not pressed. The passengers were foreign, and the ship due to sail and it was easier to just leave it be. However, the Chief Steward and the Captain were sufficiently unhappy to have Grinal, aka Buckrose, escorted from the ship.'

'Would CS Badger recognise Buckrose-Grinal?'

'He would. But better still, the Met hold a photograph of the imaginary Lord, a copy of his passport photograph was attached to the passenger registration documents he used to get aboard the 'Caronia.''

'Bingo! What a prize fool to provide us with a photograph. Can they send it across, urgently?'

'It's in hand. The super asked for copies to be made and will get his man to drive them straight down to you once the prints are dry.'

'Splendid work!' Vignoles hung up feeling more pleased than he had since they'd arrived at Broadway.

The news was welcome, because neither Mellor nor he were satisfied with the man they should perhaps now call Buckrose-Grinal. His alibi for the time of Krast's death was suspect. The Wellington Club in London denied all knowledge of anyone answering to that name, whilst both Pearson and Biggs claimed to have seen the bogus lord at Acre Vale Farm early Monday evening arguing with Coldicott; who in turn, had lied about this meeting. Both detectives felt inclined to trust the testimony of the stable lads and Wilcox had sent a constable off to question more of the staff at the farm with an expectation of establishing further corroboration. The question was, why were both men lying about this encounter? Neither could be accused of murdering Krast, because thanks to the testimony of the stable lads, they effectively gave each other an alibi. They were up to something, just not strangling elderly jewellers.

It was however, becoming clear that someone else had made use of the bogus title of Lord Buckrose in order distract the ticket clerk. This curious fact could not be coincidence. This was also the only connection they had so far between the killers and the horse racing fraternity at Acre Vale, but it was enough for Vignoles to decide that Buckrose-Grinal would not get within a country mile of the Queen. The man had boasted of a seat in the Royal Box and Vignoles was going to put a stop to that idea the moment they set eyes on him. Badger wanted potential suspects banged up in cell and out of harm's way and Vignoles was going to do just that. Terry Grinal the petty thief could stew on a wooden bench whilst the Queen enjoyed the racing.

Could he bring Coldicott in whilst he was at it? There were no grounds to do so. Perhaps just ring-fence the man with uniformed constables and if he made one false move, they could bang him up? Vignoles was not convinced any of this brought him closer to solving the question of who killed Krast nor indeed any closer to the missing diamond, but Vignoles felt better for being seen to be acting on the orders he'd been given.

Vignoles used the telephone in the bar at the Lygon Arms and put a call though to Cheltenham Constabulary HQ. He may call upon whatever resources he wished, and if yesterday's racing had seen a hefty police presence it was going to be nothing compared what they brought out today. A pen-picture and the names Lord Buckrose and Terry Grinal would have to suffice whilst they awaited delivery of the photographic prints, but if he dared show his face, they'd nab him.

*   *   *   *

Vignoles and Mellor stood at a respectful distance from the welcoming party gathered around the red carpet laid across the platform leading from the station building door to a set of special steps retained at the Bishop's Cleeve station for this particular duty. There was a hushed murmur of voices heavy with expectation and nervous excitement.

A high-ranking member of the SAS advised Vignoles and Mellor where he expected them to stand, and whilst polite, made it abundantly clear there would be discussion about this arrangement.

Vignoles was carefully inspecting the various men in suits and unbuttoned overcoats on yet another chilblain inducing day. Amidst the ever-present Scots pines, men in camouflage lurked with field glasses deployed and ready to react to their eagle-eyed commander's signal. An Alsatian dog barked in the distance. There was a good chance Buckrose-Grinal would turn up, unsuspecting of the hot welcome waiting. Not that Vignoles expected trouble. This chancer was a fraudster at heart, but his casual comment that he intended to rub shoulders with the Queen during the Gold Cup had sent Badger almost apoplectic - and the response had been overwhelming. They were back on railway territory at least, and Vignoles was technically the most senior police officer present, but it was clear he should leave everything to the secret service and those intimidating SAS men who clinked ominously with the sound of heavy weaponry.

Failing an arrest at the station, Vignoles had the dispiriting prospect of spending the greater part of the day maintaining a discreet distance from the Royal party with instructions to signal recognition of their quarry to any number of plain clothes police, secret service or special forces men whilst respectfully deferring to a DCI Silver, who had been brought in from Divisional HQ in Gloucester. Vignoles was trying hard to maintain the belief he had any meaningful influence over what was now more like a military protection exercise than a murder investigation.

The reception committee fell quiet in response to an unseen signal. Like a flock of sheep, it took only one to issue a subtle note of warning for all to cease what they were doing and stare. The Stationmaster was in full regalia with top hat gleaming in the flat light that promised a break in the clouds. His pristine white gloves held a watch polished until it dazzled. Any minute now...

A signal fell. A murmur in response, a shuffling of leather soles on the coarse surface of the platform. A throat cleared. The Alsatian whined. A whistle on the still air and then pale clouds of steam billowed above the trees just moments before the locomotive appeared, hardly making a sound as the regulator was now closed as it coasted gently, respectfully, into the station.

Number 7037, 'Swindon' had been polished by the cleaners in Plymouth Laira depot the day before. Evidence of the pride and delight that an engine bearing the name of its birthplace and the 'spiritual home' of the former Great Western Railway, was honoured with hauling the Royal train from the South West where the Queen and The Duke of Edinburgh had been attending other events. Both footplate crew sported white shirts with collars and ties over railwaymen's 'blues' that looked new, unlike their regular sets washed to a pale memory of the original colour. The footplate inspector was immaculate in dark top coat and bowler hat. A rose in his button hole was an affectation, but his stern face and watchful eyes brooked no dissent to his wearing this on the footplate of one of Swindon's finest at the head of the Royal Train.

The gleaming coaches painted a colour like that of damson jam, came to a rest almost silently and the stationmaster gave a little nod of approval to the Royal equerry beside him, noting how the steps were perfectly aligned with the door the Royal party were to use.

There was a subtle readjusting of position as the door opened and Vignoles and Mellor found themselves being muscled out of a clear view. This was a State Affair and the Secret Service were taking no prisoners. The young Queen appeared and Vignoles saw her blue hat and a matching coat, a pale glimpse of calf and dark shoes as she stepped down. A handbag, a flash of red lipstick as she gave a smile whilst shaking hands with the stationmaster, who was doffing his top hat. The Duke in a practical but perfectly tailored coat and a tweed cap followed. A clutch of Royal hangers-on followed and in less than a minute were all moving into the booking hall and thence to the waiting cars. The Queen was here to watch the racing as relaxation. Protocol had to be followed but only in its most pared back form. Once the tedious official introductions and obligatory handshakes and were out of the way at the racecourse, the Queen would be marking her race card and bending the ear of her trainer, wishing her jockey good luck and cheering on Devon Loch in the Cotswold Steeplechase before settling down for the main event of the day, ending with her own horse, M'as-Tu-Vu running in the 3.45.

No sign of the bogus Lord, however.

Vignoles was relieved, although he sensed Mellor's disappointment. They clambered into the car provided by the Cheltenham Constabulary and followed the line of vehicles making the short trip to the racecourse.

*   *   *   *

Buckrose pulled over at the remote road junction and peered at the map. He traced the narrow lane he must follow to the spot marked with an underlining in ink. It was a barely navigable dirt track between fields that offered little sign of human habitation for miles. It was good job he had the map.

It's in the middle of sodding nowhere...

Chapter Twenty-Five

He let out the clutch and proceeded slowly, the suspension creaking as he bounced over the ruts and pot holes. He dragged heavily on a Player's and concentrated.

Perhaps it made sense to come out here? There would be no-one around. It was hardly day-tripper weather out here and this was no route for coach parties. That meant nobody would see them make the exchange. He grinned with the cigarette gripped between his lips. They'd need a hefty suitcase for all that lovely dosh! He'd want to click open the lid and inspect the bundles of five-pound notes tightly packed inside before he did the trade. So, yeah, they needed to be sure nobody could see them.

Ah, but he could almost smell the money... He removed the cigarette and made a dramatic show of inhaling noisily through his nose. Soon he would be lovingly flipping the grubby notes through his fingers, smelling the accumulated grease and grime; the cocaine some wags claimed could be traced on the bigger notes of the realm and inhaling the glorious stink of ill-gotten gain. He'd be swapping this for the sweet smell of warm sun-oil on a paradise island with a big-breasted dolly bird squeezed into one of those bikini things they were wearing in the French fashion magazines... Yeah, come to think of it, a God-forsaken hill fort was a good place for the exchange. He liked their style.

He had another desire to reassure himself the diamond was still where he'd put it. It would never do to turn up and find he'd lost the blasted thing. He patted the envelope in his jacket pocket. Felt for the tiny hard lump inside. He grinned and smoked and put his foot down and made the engine roar as he bounced along the rutted road. It was funny really, but he didn't care a damn about the rock. A silly bit of sparkly nonsense...Leave it to Marilyn Monroe and Jane Russell to harp on about diamonds being a girl's best friend. Personally, he couldn't wait to convert it to hard spendable cash.

'Money is a man's best friend...' He sang the words aloud.

Having said that, a bird like Jane Russell would be nice...

* * * *

'Any sight?'

'Nothing, guv.' Mellor had been scanning the crowds with his binoculars. 'Plenty of plain clothes doing the same...'

'We'll go to Coldicott. He's got two running and there's a chance our man will exchange greetings with his trainer.'

They made their way into the enclosure behind the stands where the horses were unloaded and made ready for the parade ring before their race. Vignoles was conscious they had a tail. One of those stern-jawed men from the Ministry who didn't button up his coat. The eye contact was fleeting, and both knew not to speak nor show recognition, but both understood the deal. Vignoles would identify their quarry and the agent and his companions close by would deal with Buckrose-Grinal.

Coldicott was standing beside a beautiful horse together with a jockey and the stable lad Pearson. The trainer saw them approach.

'Getting the racing bug, Inspector? You can't keep away.' He did not seem delighted.

'We're looking for Lord Buckrose.'

'Not seen him.' Coldicott spoke confidently and gave Vignoles a look that dared him to doubt his word. 'Not expecting to. This isn't one of his...' His hand patted the neck of the horse.

'When did you last see him?'

'Yesterday afternoon, about the same time you did.' He gave a knowing look at Vignoles that challenged him to say otherwise. 'He didn't come back to the stables with us.'

'I'm surprised.'

'Why? His horse came third.' Coldicott shrugged his shoulders. 'I got the winnings before we left, which was decent, and we shook hands. I've two horses to prepare for today so had more than enough to be thinking about. Yesterday's race is done with.'

'This horse is...?' Mellor asked.

'A'kira Kungota. One of our best.' Coldicott was growing in confidence as he spoke. Vignoles sensed that the further they drew the conversation away from the dodgy Lord, the more relaxed he became. 'Biggs is bringing the other out now.' Coldicott nodded towards a horse that had just been led out of a motor horse box.

'Were these the two that came into Broadway on Tuesday?' Vignoles asked.

'Yep. That's Chicory Blue. Destined to be in the chasing pack today, I'm afraid. She's still young, so we've high hopes for next year.' Coldicott noticed that Mellor was interested. 'Not that I'm offering any inside tips, Sergeant.' He grinned for a split second. 'So, gents...If you don't mind...?'

Vignoles thanked Coldicott. 'If you see Buckrose, tell him we need to speak to him at the earliest convenience. He can make himself known to a race official or a policeman on duty.'

'Is it anything I can help with?' Coldicott was trying not to look interested. Pearson was staring at the detectives from the other side of A'kira Kungota.

'A private matter.'

As they walked away Mellor was eyeing up a jockey who walked past them.

'That was Dick Francis...'

'And he is...?'

'Only one of the best jockeys. Whatever he's riding is worth a punt.'

'The only tip I need is whether to pull Coldicott in and get him out of the way. I can't think on what grounds we can justify doing so.'

'Me neither. He can't be the killer. His alibi is too strong.' Mellor checked his watch. 'We'll try the parade ring. Devon Loch will be in. It'll be a heck of a crush. But if that creep is going to turn up anywhere, it'll be when the Queen shows her face.'

*　　*　　*　　*

Buckrose edged the car into the tiny lay-by that apparently served as a vestigial car park. There was nothing to indicate he was in the right place except an iron finger post that indicated a gap in a hedge and a straight track across a wintry field towards a curious elongated lump about 200 yards away.

'That must be the long barrow.' He squinted at the map.

Was he disappointed nobody was waiting? Had he expected to see two men standing on either side of a car with the boot open, both smiling as they lifted the lid on a suitcase to reveal the contents, like game show hosts? Of course not. That was a foolish conceit. No, it was better to arrive first and select the most advantageous spot to park so he could make a clean getaway. Not that the springs on the old Humber were going to hold out much longer. He took a moment to plan his escape route. That was the Grinal method. Or should that be the 'Buckrose method'?

He stood for a moment and studied the distant form of the earthwork. There was something faintly menacing about this weird grassy lump. The curving shape was covered by yellowing grass like the fur of a sleeping beast. Everything about this place was inexplicable and alienating. He walked along the track and was disturbed by the sight of a hideously deformed rabbit lolling slowly across the field, its eyes milky white and weeping sores blistering the skin. He shuddered and looked away only to see the fresh corpse of another equally disfigured rabbit lying in a shallow gulley. A number of flies lifted from the poor creature's eyes as he passed. He hurried on towards the barrow, his sense of disquiet heightened by the myxomatosis riddled rabbit dying a slow and painful death.

He came to an ancient stone doorway leading into a small, dark place. A shaft of sunlight would probably work wonders, but beneath the leaden sky the barrow was gloomy and unwelcoming. The woods behind formed a towering wall of black and brown branches, some showing the first dots of budding leaves, and these clattered in the wind. A single magpie made an ugly cackling sound.

He shivered.

Get a grip and don't lose your nerve...

* * * *

Vignoles was starting to worry about whether he should be worried. Buckrose-Grinal had not shown his face, which was unexpected. It came as no surprise that the Queen's equerry confirmed none of the Royal party were aware of someone by that name, let alone expecting him and the men with guns lurking in wait would soon put paid to any such ideas if the duplicitous chancer showed his face. Someone by the name of Lord Buckrose had reserved one of the most expensive tickets in the grand stand, but the ticket remained unclaimed. Despite the cost, the ticket would not get the bearer within any distance of the Royal party, but it was hard evidence their man had intended to be there. The afternoon was still young, so he might still turn up.

The crush around the parade ring had been as tight as Mellor predicted. Devon Loch had been shown off to the salivating crowd of the great, good and inebriated - and a number of undercover agents. The Queen had offered a dash of colour in the centre, absorbed in watching with friends as the horses circled them like a scene from a bizarre Western movie. Mellor had become animated at the sight of Dick Francis beside his ride, Saxon King and slipped some money into the hand of a man on a Tote stand and got a betting slip in return. This gamble aside, it had been an unproductive exercise for the detectives.

The Queen Mother's horse had duly won the Cotswold Steeplechase to general approval and now Vignoles and Mellor were now awaiting the conclusion of the penultimate race before the Gold Cup itself. The heaving mass of cheering punters was giving off wafts of steam as arms waved and fists punched the air. The roar was deafening as pounding hooves made the stand shudder.

He and Mellor were high in the main grandstand leaning on the sidewall, with a good view of the jam-packed crowd and the finish line. Vignoles had decided a pint and a pipe was needed and Mellor had been happy to concur. The police presence was intense and the recent delivery of a wad of freshly printed photographs of Buckrose-Grinal had boosted everyone's morale. Armed with a good likeness, the probability of apprehending their man was high. Vignoles could afford to rest his eyes which were tiring from hours of studying every face, both close and far, in the mind-muddling throng.

'We've got this wrong, Mellor. We're wasting time here whilst this character is in all probability miles away and laughing at our stupidity. Why did we take something he said as credible?'

'I reckon you're right. And we're just spare parts in the operation here... They don't want or need us.'

Vignoles drew heavily on his pipe. Mellor was not making him feel better.

'But what choice did we got? We've orders to protect Her Madge at any cost and that's what we're doin'...'

Vignoles was still not used to Mellor's use of disrespectful language and pulled a pained expression.

'She's safe and there's a small army keeping an eye on her. Job done if yu ask me.' Mellor cracked a wry smile. 'Still, I backed a winner!'

Vignoles was not interested in Mellor's betting results. 'We should have left this to DCI Silver and his men. We're here to find out who killed Krast, not waiting for some horses to run around a freezing racecourse. I've made a miscalculation somewhere...' Vignoles was feeling uncharacteristically low.

Mellor was training his field glasses on the loose collection of horses being walked in a skittish and excitable manner towards the start line. 'The Gold Cup riders are assembling...'

Vignoles gave a sigh of resignation and downed his beer. It helped knock the edges off his sombre mood. He was in the wrong place at the wrong time. But they were hemmed in by thousands of punters with one of the biggest races of the year about to start so they might as well stay until it was over. A few more minutes would not make any odds. Talking of odds, Mellor had convinced him to place five shillings on a horse in the big race. Completely unknowledgeable on the subject he'd stuck to choosing a name he liked. The horse's name Pointsman reminded him of the railways, and despite being warned by Mellor that it had 'no better than a 100-1 chance,' he placed his bet.

'Probably more chance of it winning than us finding our man...'

*   *   *   *

Buckrose considered himself unmoved by the mysteries of the spirit world, benign or otherwise. The only noises that went bump in the night that concerned him were those made by men able to inflict harm with their fists, knives and guns. And yet, despite his cynicism and the proximity of a flock of harmless and steadily munching sheep on the other side of a low barbed wire fence, he was feeling increasingly ill at ease.

The layout of this curious structure meant he soon lost view of the track leading to Corndean Lane where he'd parked the Humber and discovered there were two separate entrances, both equally uninviting. The larger of the two at least offered some protection from the scything wind and allowed him to stand upright against the drystone construction of the wing wall to the entrance. He waited whilst observing the field edge and a long stand of trees to the right dipping away towards Winchcombe.

Was he at the right place? Or were they playing games with him? Leaning on him to fix his horse and then make him trail all the way out here. Was this some kind of test? These dark thoughts were starting to play tricks with his equilibrium, not aided by the distressing image of that dying rabbit limping slowly closer. He spat on the ground in disgust.

Was that scrawny little toe-rag Slatter leading him a merry dance? He took out the card he'd been handed yesterday. Money For *Something*. He understood the meaning clearly. Slatter was prepared to trade and had sent these two monkeys along with the money in return for the sparkler. Clear as day. He'd even done what they'd asked. He'd nobbled the jockey. He'd played the game. Come on...Where are you? He idly jammed the card between the stones in the wall and dug out his packet of cigarettes. His throat was raw with smoking too much, but he needed another.

'Good afternoon, your Lordship...'

He nearly jumped out of his skin. He'd not heard so much as a foot crunch on a dry twig. He tried to regain composure.

'...or should I say, *Terry*?' A pause for a beat. 'Or d'you prefer 'Tel'? More friendly...' A gloved hand was extended. 'The name's Kane. We never properly introduced ourselves yesterday. Most rude.'

'Abel...' Another hand proffered.

'Kane and Abel?' Buckrose laughed. 'You jokers or summat?' He let his stilted accent slip.

'You hear that Kane? He called us jokers!' Abel was staring through his monocle which was making one eye larger than the other. 'I don't take kindly to being called a joker.'

'Are you here to trade or just wasting my time?' He was feeling like a tightly wound spring and their odd manner was prickling him.

'Our Lordship's voice is betraying a rather more earthy note since yesterday...'

'Straight from the gutter, you mean?' Kane curled the corner of his lip and stepped close, his nose just an inch away. 'Terry Grinal from Southampton. You should 'ave stuck to robbin' old ladies.'

'I have no idea what you are talking about. The name is Buckrose and I resent your tone...'

'Cut the crap, an' 'and it over.' Kane snarled.

'Hang on! Not so darned fast. A deal cuts both ways, don't you know...'

Kane's bad breath was blowing in Buckrose's face. A vice-like grip encircled an arm. 'We know who you are and what you are, so don't piss about. We're here to collect the diamond not stand around playin' games. Understood?'

Buckrose tried to wriggle free but failed. 'Well, if that's how you want it, then hand over the money!' He was trying to sound brave.

'I say, what *is* he talking about, Kane?' Abel spoke as if bamboozled by the outburst. He was standing a step away, cigarette in one hand. His stance was effete and his wrist limp, but the eye behind the monocle was cold and unwavering. There was something decidedly unhealthy and very dangerous behind that staring blue iris. 'What money could that be?' The sugary words and baby-smooth face with the idiotic monocle had a dreadful effect on Buckrose. He realised in a moment he'd been duped, and these men meant him harm.

Kane also feigned innocent surprise. 'We ain't got no money.'

'But...but yesterday...on that card...'

'No idea, Tel.' There was the soft schlick of a blade flicking out of its guard. It flashed before Buckrose's face. 'But I've got one of these...'

'W-what's that for?'

'To encourage you to tell us where've you got the diamond...'

Buckrose blanched but said nothing.

'Now look here, be an awfully good fellow and hand it over,' Abel chipped in. 'Otherwise it will just take longer and hurt *so* very much more.'

'Let go!' Buckrose tried again to break free, twisting his body and lashing out with a forearm at the hand holding the knife. Kane was too quick and lifted the knife out of reach then allowed his captive to twist like a marionette dangling on a string as he raised Buckrose's arm high as though he weighed nothing. Abel had now produced two more knives from the patent leather doctor's bag he'd placed on the ground when they first arrived. This matching pair had long thin blades, cast metal handles and looked hideously sharp. Without warning Abel made a short jabbing movement with one of them, moving like an expert fencer. Buckrose squealed and watched as his free arm hung uselessly at his side, a trickle of bright crimson colouring his sleeve at the shoulder.

'A cut in just the right place...like so... and your arm is useless! It won't move again unless you get medical help.' Abel was grinning like a child at Christmas. He threw the matching blade to Kane, who unceremoniously let go of Buckrose and took a step backwards in order to expertly catch the lethal weapon by the handle as it spun through the air. Buckrose now had his back against the yawning mouth of the ancient monument, with two men dancing on nimble feet before him armed with razor sharp blades. He had nowhere to run, no weapon and nothing to shield himself from their merciless points.

'These come from Sicily...' Able thrust the vicious blade towards Buckrose who shied away, his one functioning arm clutching at his shoulder and trying to stem the blood.

'Stilettos!' Kane added, helpfully.

'Like the ladies' shoe...' Abel teased at Buckrose's face, making him throw up a guard with his hand.

'Used properly they make deep and neat cuts...' Kane without warning, speared Buckrose's thigh then removed the stiletto again in a jabbing move that took but a second, leaving his prey to gasp in pain, face draining of colour. 'Easier to handle in confined spaces.'

'Now...That lovely little diamond.... We really *do* need it, old boy.' Abel pranced on delicate feet, jabbing and stabbing but deliberately not striking home. 'Mere flesh wounds so far. They will heal...'

Buckrose was rendered furious with the pain and humiliation, one shoulder pressed against the stone wall, blood dripping onto his shoes, body rocking backwards and forwards as he tried to avoid the vile metal points taunting him. Now he knew how a bull felt in the ring and why the bull fought back despite having no chance of escape. He needed to do something; find a way to express the anger and hurt boiling up inside. He lunged at Abel, frothing at the mouth with hatred for this prissy, mincing creature mocking him.

His leg failed and he fell with the full weight of his body onto his knees in a bone-crunching crash that would leave lasting damage. Blood trickled from the back of his thigh.

'The Hornet, or we'll leave you to bleed to death like St Sebastian with a thousand cuts...'

'Go...to...Hell!'

More piercings followed, then a series of scratches on his cheeks designed purely to humiliate and break his spirit. Abel delivered a vicious slash to the Achilles tendon that left Buckrose lying on his side gasping for air. He was broken. He begged for mercy and promised what they wanted. The diamond was extracted from his jacket pocket in an envelope now stained scarlet.

'Simply divine...' Abel was pretending to swoon at the beauty of the stone as he peered inside the scarlet letter.

'Nice doin' business.' Kane tipped his trilby, then wiped the blood from his blade by sticking it into the grassy bank. 'If you get to a hospital in the next twenty minutes or so, I reckon you'll live. Staunch the bleedin', get a transfusion. Might have trouble walking, but in the scheme of things...' He started to walk away.

'Help me...please...I gave you what...you wanted. Please...' He was fading, the cold and the blood loss and searing pain were sucking the life from him.

Abel was also cleaning his weapon. He collected his doctor's bag from the ground. 'Oh golly gosh, Kane, by my reckoning the nearest hospital is a good half an hour away. And the ambulance needs to get here first which means at least an hour...'

'Awkward.' Kane sucked air through his teeth. 'And not a telephone kiosk for miles,' Kane shrugged his shoulders as he looked pityingly at Buckrose. 'Oh well.'

'Your car...'

'And bleed all over our seats?' Abel rolled his eyes in mock horror.

Kane suddenly turned and stepped closer and hope reawakened in Buckrose for a brief moment. 'You've just met The Debt Collectors. And you're a nobody called Terry Grinal. Out of your depth, mate. We've collected the debt, and we appreciate that. But you're not our problem now.'

They walked into the wood, taking a narrow track towards their stolen car parked on an even narrower lane on the far side, casually straightening ties and readjusting the lie of their hats as they walked. The weak cries for help were drowned by the bleating of a lost lamb and the harsh croaks of gathering carrion crows.

* * * *

'Who predicted that? Any punters backing that rank outsider must have cleaned up!' Mellor was half enjoying the completely unexpected win by unfancied Gay Donald and fulminating that his horse of choice, A'kira Kungota had come in a lowly tenth. Mellor's modest winnings from yesterday were overwritten by today's loss. 'Rubbish name as well...'

'It's the name of a winner. Unlike our two failures! Come on, I want to get out of here.' Vignoles was impatient and frustrated that whilst the day had gone smoothly and the Queen and Duke were soon due to make their way back to the waiting train escorted by a small army of men to protect them, they had achieved nothing in regard to solving the case.

'DCI Vignoles?' A uniformed constable enquired, with a salute.

Vignoles instantly sensed something in the man's voice. Mellor similarly abandoned thoughts of A'kira Kungota's dismal running.

'You're needed on the telephone. It's urgent.'

'What is it?'

'A body. In the hills some distance from here. A car is waiting once you've fielded the call.'

They hurried as quickly as the cheering, laughing, lurching and staggering crowds allowed.

'A well-dressed man beside an ancient long barrow. A couple of hikers discovered the body. A remote location and tricky to find. It sounds nasty.' It was sergeant Wilcox on the line. 'The lads we sent up there reckon it could be this Buckrose, but best not assume anything until you take a look.'

'Buckrose?' Vignoles spoke the name for the benefit of Mellor. 'Where did you say the body was found?'

'A burial mound.'

'That's ironic...' Mellor laughed.

* * * *

A uniformed constable was standing guard beside the finger post indicating Belas Knapp. A tatty car was pulled hard into the hedgerow at the side of the short lay-by and a row of police vehicles pressed to either side of the lane. An ambulance and 'Black Maria' were stopped in the middle. The lane had been closed off at both ends by simple road blocks manned by uniformed officers. DCI Silver was waiting for them at the edge of the lay-by. He looked almost pleased to see them.

'It's an odd one. Not seen anything quite like it. He's your man though.' Silver had a fresh photographic print in a gloved hand. 'These came through as I was leaving and it's a match.' Silver made no obvious move of escorting them to the body. 'Is he a material witness in your murder case?'

'We are still trying to understand the relationship to the Broadway murder victim, but we understand they had contact.'

Silver gave a curt nod of the head. 'Then you will want access to the body, the PM report and any items found at the crime scene?'

'If we may?'

'As you wish. Wilcox!'

'Yes sir?'

'Ensure anything requested is processed as priority. My orders.' Silver touched the peak of his expensive hat. 'I shall leave in your hands, Vignoles. You won't want me breathing down your necks, eh? I have work demanding my attention in Cheltenham...'

Wilcox was pleased to assist and led them along the footpath to the long barrow. A police forensic team were working close to the larger of the stone entrances. A doctor was re-packing his bag.

'It's Buckrose-Grinal. That explains why he didn't show for the race...' Mellor observed.

'You know him?' The doctor enquired.

'In one of his guises...' Vignoles replied. 'What have we got?'

'A most fascinating case. I have never seen anything like this. A most curious set of wounds...'

'This is murder?' Mellor was giving the inquisitive sheep on the other side of the wire fence odd looks as he spoke. 'Nothing else could do that?'

'Unquestionably this was a sustained assault. Deliberate and expertly handled and with no other possible outcome. Just look...here and here...

and here...these are deep piercings made by a sharp and very narrow blade that would be distinctive and most unusual. You should look for something with a blade less than half an inch wide, maybe less. These are carefully chosen strikes designed to incapacitate and cause considerable suffering. The slashes to the face are merely superficial. Disfiguring and unpleasant, but not life-threatening'

'Was this...torture?' Mellor looked aghast.

'You must decide, but it was a slow death and very painful.'

A police photographer was setting off flash bulbs as he took a series of views of the body slumped to one side with legs folded underneath and an arm thrown forward as if in supplication, face in an ugly, frozen grimace.

'The back of his ankle has been cut?' Vignoles observed.

'The Achillies is slashed. That stopped him running. The tendons in one of his arms have been expertly severed which would have rendered the arm useless and if you look at the back of his thigh, this incision would have sliced through the...'

'He was incapacitated. Made helpless, then finished off?' Mellor interjected. He didn't need to hear more of exactly how the man died.

'A reasonable interpretation of the assailant's intent,' the doctor cleared his throat. 'The PM report will provide the full list of injuries.'

'Sir?' The photographer indicated the area of flattened earth in front of the dead man's outstretched hand. 'You should see this. I've photographed it from all angles, and it might be clearer on a print with some dark room trickery.'

A word had been scratched into the hard earth. Clogged fingernails told of the effort expended in the last moments spent trying to write in the unyielding surface.

'Slate...Slater...'

'I think that could be a double T. Could it be Slatter?' Vignoles and Mellor exchanged puzzled looks. 'He was trying to tell us something.'

'The name of the killer?'

'Can you tell if one or more persons inflicted these wounds?' Vignoles asked the doctor.

'Hard to say from a cursory inspection. You should await a more detailed report, that might be able to enlighten you.'

'There are a number of footprints and it is all a bit confused...' Mellor was continuing to study the ground. 'Perhaps this scuffing and those lines where a shoe has slid...just there...and again here...suggest more than two?'

'Two were involved in the attack on Krast,' Vignoles offered.

'But a different *modus operandi*. Strangulation and now *this*...'

The doctor peered over his half-moon glasses at Vignoles. 'What sort of people are you looking for?'

'Very unpleasant ones...'

'This sounds daft, but how did he die?' Mellor asked.

'An intelligent question. From blood loss, sergeant. None of these cuts would kill outright. Excruciating, but not immediately lethal if considered individually. He was left to bleed to death with traumatising internal injuries. He was unable to seek help. I suppose we should find comfort in the fact the cold would have hurried the end that bit quicker.'

'They didn't intend murder?' Mellor questioned.

'He would have needed urgent attention to survive. I suggest those who did this knew he could not receive that in time and even if medical help had arrived, they would have found it close to impossible to save him.'

'Who found the body?' Vignoles asked Wilcox.

'Two ramblers. The Atkinsons, husband and wife. They're sitting in the police van down the lane waiting for you.'

Vignoles nodded. He and Mellor would complete their inspection of the crime scene before the daylight grew much dimmer.

'Anything on the body?'

'A wallet with five pounds in fresh notes, a cheque book and car keys.'

'Presumably for the car parked by the stile?'

'The Humber.' Wilcox replied. 'We've finger-printed the doors and only one set show clearly, but best to wait to see what they reckon once back in the lab. The car was given a bit of a rub and polish recently, so there's few prints and all fresh. We've left the contents of the car for you to look at.'

Vignoles and Mellor gave the crumpled body another glance then decided the car was potentially the more rewarding area to investigate. The boot proved especially interesting.

'Changes of clothes, some needing a wash, but pretty decent clobber.'

'Spare shoes...Wash bag...'

'And cheque books for three other banks and all under different names...and a pack of *Carte d'Visite* in the name of Lord Buckrose of Sledmere Hall.' Mellor brandished them with a flourish.

'Terry Grinal meets his demise... Bag all this up, Mellor. I'll talk to the couple.' Vignoles walked down the lane to the 'Black Maria' with the rear doors standing wide. A young WPC was offering comfort to a couple dressed in hiking clothes seated on the back edge of the van. After introducing himself to the Atkinsons he wasted no time getting the questions out of the way.

'I understand you found the body?'

'It was a distressing discovery,' Mr Atkinson replied.

'Just horrid. Who on earth could have done *that* to him?' His wife added.

'What time was this?'

'Two fifty or thereabouts. I regret I neglected to check my watch. It had quite an upsetting effect on us,' Mr Atkinson replied.

Vignoles nodded understanding. 'I presume you walked here?'

'Oh yes!' Mrs Atkinson responded. 'Michael had what looked like a splendid programme for the day mapped out.' Her husband gave an approving nod and tapped the OS map protruding from his windcheater.

'Your route here was from where?'

'We detrained at Winchcombe having travelled down from Toddington. Only a short ride but a splendid view of the Vale. Are you familiar with the line, Inspector?' Vignoles smiled and indulged them for a moment. Both would be feeling the after effects of what must have been a very unpleasant shock and now seeking solace in recounting the mundane aspects of their day.

'We explored Sudeley Castle, which we had virtually to ourselves, then struck off in a south-westerly direction finding some excellent footpaths.'

'We saw nobody all the way. And we'd feared the Cotswolds was getting over-run by tourists,' Mrs Atkinson added.

Vignoles noted the absence of other walkers. They were unlikely to find more witnesses. 'Did you notice if any cars were parked in the lane when you arrived?'

'The vehicle your officer is inspecting was there. We assumed it must belong to…the deceased.'

'You didn't see another car leaving or driving on the lane?'

'It was very quiet.' Mr Atkinson replied. 'We wondered where everyone was.'

At the Gold Cup probably, Vignoles thought. Intelligent timing by the assassins. Virtually every policeman in the county and a hefty percentage of the local population otherwise engaged. 'Did you move or touch the body?'

'Heaven's no!'

'That is not strictly true, Michael. I told my husband to check his pulse. One has to be sure… On the outstretched arm…' Mrs Atkinson visibly shuddered. 'I could not bear to go close.'

'I rested my finger tips on his wrist, Nothing more. I have done a first aid course, so I knew what to do. I could not find a pulse.'

'Was the body warm?'

'I would say it was a little.' Mr Atkinson paused. 'But it was his eyes. They were staring and not blinking.' He coughed. 'I judged he was not alive. I hope I have not done wrong, inspector?'

'There was nothing either of you could have done. Once you checked for a pulse what did you do next?'

'We went to the lane, consulted my map and we struck off together at a fair lick to find a telephone and call the police.'

'Thank you.' Vignoles asked the WPC to take details of their home address and where they were staying locally.

Mellor had finished bagging the contents of the car and gone back to the barrow accompanied by two ambulance men with a stretcher. He was now waving at Vignoles to join him.

'What is it?'

'I found this. Pushed between the stones in the wall. There was also a fresh cigarette butt on the ground that tallies with the brand in his coat pocket. I reckon our chum was having a fag whilst waiting and giving this card some consideration.'

'Then pushed it there to conceal it?' Vignoles turned the card over. 'A play on the name of his horse.'

'Money for something rather than nothing…' Mellor looked chuffed.

This was a significant find. They just had to tease out the significance. 'He had something valuable enough for them to do that to 'im.'

'And met them to close a deal for it?'

'Reckon so, guv. I mean, nobody's comin' out here on a whim today. Dedicated hikers aside... It's hard enough with one of these...' Mellor fished an Ordnance Survey map from his overcoat pocket with a triumphant flourish. 'I found it on the passenger seat of his car. It's been folded to show this place, with the start of the lane and the barra' marked in red.'

Vignoles nodded. 'Then it was pre-arranged. This map is brand new, as if bought for this one purpose.' The contrast with the much-used example the Atkinsons possessed was obvious.

'But once he got here, the deal soured? They argued...got into a fight and they tortured him until he handed over what they were after...' Mellor was trying to think through how it might have played out.

Vignoles was polishing his glasses with a cloth and considering his response. 'You said something earlier. How the MO differs between victims.'

'They are.'

'On the surface, I would agree. That might indicate two very different assailants. But look at it from the angle of *why* these two men were killed, not the method used and I'm wondering if the same people are responsible.'

'You reckon?'

'Krast was slowly throttled, as all strangulations by their nature, are. It's a method that can be controlled, the pressure eased to allow the victim to speak or respond to a question. It can be a means to extract information...'

'And this was also a slow and tortuous death... Both done to extract information or gain what they were after?'

'Precisely. Get this card and the map checked for fingerprints. The map cover is glossy and might hold a print.' Vignoles handed the card back to Mellor, thankful both were wearing leather gloves. 'The killers are surely the same two who killed Krast, and what they wanted was Elsie Gable's diamond.'

'We need to find who this Slatter is.'

'If we knew where to look...'

Chapter Twenty-Six

'Mrs Devlin. I'd like to ask you some questions.' WPC Lansdowne approached the stern-faced woman busy making notes on a clipboard of papers, an unlit rollie between her pinched lips. She was at the bottom of the same set of moveable wooden steps leading into more carriages being prepared for their return journey later that afternoon. There was little sound coming from inside the carriage except for the occasional clank of a handle on a zinc pail.

'You here again?' Her voice was harsh, but there was a dart of something like interest in her eyes.

'Following up enquiries.'

'I thought you might be back.' There was a mischievous twinkle in her eye.

'What makes you say that?'

'Stands to reason.' Devlin gave no explanation. 'Want a cuppa?' It was an unexpected invitation, and Lansdowne suspected motivated more by curiosity than friendliness. 'I've got fresh tea mashing.'

'Please. One sugar.'

'The girls are cleaning this rake and better not show their faces for another twenty minutes.' Devlin poured the strong tea into two mugs with "GWR" on the side and spooned in sugar whilst she spoke. 'When you came around the first time, I knew there was something up. I wasn't taken in by that soft-soap about a private matter.' She darted a sly look at the WPC. 'There's a few trouble-makers in the gang. When you get a group of women together that's what happens. Rivalries, jealousies even cat fights. I've seen the lot!' She handed the mug across to Lansdowne and indicated one of the mis-matched chairs nearby.

'There is a lot of trouble?'

'Not a lot, but it flares up every so often. My guess is you've found a few things out and want my opinion. From someone who knows the girls better than most...' She gave a conspiratorial wink and blew on her steaming tea.

'What do you believe would interest us?' Lansdowne feared Devlin was just a nosey-parker who traded in idle gossip. Once she got up steam she might start tittle-tattling about all manner of inconsequential nonsense. Or she may have useful information, but Lansdowne's challenge was to restrict the deluge and keep focus. 'We are investigating a murder at Broadway, nothing else.'

'I've read about that in the paper. But what about the one yesterday? What's going on? Is it the same man doing it?'

'I could not pass comment...'

'I don't take fright easy, but I'm wondering if it's safe? With killers on the loose...'

'You are not surprised I am back,' Lansdowne needed to rein her in. 'Do you know something that might have bearing on the investigation?'

Devlin sat back in her chair and sipped her tea. 'There's this man. He works at the shop owned by the gentleman as was murdered. The *first* one...' An admonishing look from Devlin as if it were Lansdowne's fault two men were now dead.

'At Krast Jewellers?'

'That's the one. Not that I'd ever been there. Well now, this Mr Jeffries is somebody you should be looking at.'

'We interviewed him as part of the investigation.'

'You did? So perhaps the penny has dropped.'

'Sorry?'

'Seeing as it was Jeffries' boss that's been killed, it got me wondering why you came here to talk to Elsie and not Mary,' she gave a knowing look. 'Because we all know they're carrying on!' She raised an eyebrow as she slurped tea, the roll-up now alight and smoking between the fingers of the hand holding the mug.

'Mary?' Lansdowne knew where this was leading, but wanted to hear Devlin's viewpoint

'Mary Joyner.' She curled up the corner of her mouth in a disapproving manner. 'She's a tart. A pretty thing, and don't she know it, waggling her hips and showing off her big bosoms all over the place.'

'How might Mary Joyner have any relevance to the death of Mr Krast?' Lansdowne was keeping an eye on the massive bulk of the carriage close by. It would not do for the cleaners to be listening in. Any fears of eavesdropping were being eased however by the loud and almost continual hissing of an approaching tank engine dragging more coaches into the station.

'Ah well!' Devlin looked pleased. Her face could switch from sour disapproval to triumphant delight in a moment. 'They've been carrying on. Mary and that Jeffries, who works in the old man's shop. On the sly - or so they think! An older man with that brazen little tart...' She folded her arms across her flat, sparrow chest. 'He's like a dog trailing after her. It's pathetic!' She waggled a finger at Lansdowne. 'You *do* know he's married?'

'I understand he has a sick wife.'

'Even worse!' Devlin was filled with righteous indignation.

'If Joyner and Jeffries are having an extra-marital affair, what connection could this have with our investigation?' Lansdowne had already established there was a relationship of some kind between the two but wanted to discover if there was anything more than salacious gossip behind Devlin's talk of an affair.

'He's connected to the dead man and he's up to no good. He's a cheat. A bloody liar. They think they're being careful, but they've become casual. Taking romantic train rides to Honeybourne or Stratford together, holding hands thinking nobody notices or cares.' A knowing nod of the head accompanied this last sentence.

'But you noticed?'

'Mary is part of the gang Elsie hangs out with. Giggly young things the lot of them.' Devlin looked morally outraged but in response to Lansdowne's penetrating look, modified her statement. 'Elsie is not such a bad 'un. A sweet girl really. No, it's that Mary who's the trouble-maker.' Devlin returned to her tea and her smoke with obvious relish.

'How long do you think this relationship has been going on?'

'Six months at least, perhaps nine. Fawning all over the girl. He should be ashamed of himself. Mind you, Mary Joyner's as much to blame!' Devlin was enjoying discussing this arrangement far more than she ought. 'So, you come along asking I don't know what of Elsie Gable, but it seems to me you and your Inspector got the wrong one; its Mary who's dropping her knickers for Jeffries and as he worked for the Krast fella...well...it stands to reason.'

Once again it was unclear what stood to reason in Lansdowne's mind, but this was interesting. Jeffries was clearly trying to impress a younger woman. He was perhaps an unlikely candidate for Joyner to choose as a lover. Hardly an attractive man, especially to a young beauty such as Joyner, except perhaps for the fact he worked in a shop selling enticingly expensive jewellery. Had he been buying her lavish gifts, then dipping his hand into the stock and fixing the records when his funds ran short? That had been the sergeant's thinking...

It was time to lean harder on Joyner.

'Where can I find Mary?'

'Finish your tea and I'll take you to the carriage she's working in.'

'Can I have a word?'

Joyner looked at Devlin, then Lansdowne with a worried look on her face. 'Why? What have I done wrong?'

'I just want to clarify a few points.'

'You mind you tell the WPC the truth, Mary Joyner! Any nonsense and you'll be getting your marching orders. I won't have disreputable behaviour around here!'

'I'll take over now, Mrs Devlin. Thank you...' Lansdowne closed the compartment door. 'I want to ask you about Mr Jeffries.'

Joyner flushed.

'Let's not waste time. You've already told me you have been seeing Mr Jeffries as a friend, but your insistence it is innocent is not going to wash. I suggest you answer my questions more honestly this time.'

'Oh...' Joyner sat heavily on a seat.

'How long have you been seeing Mr Jeffries?'

'Depends what you mean by 'seeing'.'

'Don't be smart. You *are* aware he's married?'

Joyner nodded.

'You have been meeting a married man and spending time with him in what could be construed as romantic liaisons. Does that help clarify my question?'

'There's nearly always others there as well. A group of us. It's not like you think.'

'Tell me what it *is* like?'

'A drink...sometimes dinner. That's all.'

'With other friends?'

Her silence was all the answer Lansdowne needed.

'How old are you, Mary?'

'Twenty-one.'

'And he's over fifty.'

'Exactly!' Joyner laughed. 'You can't really think that I would do... you know what... with someone like *him!*' Her face formed an unattractive scowl and she spoke with a dismissive callousness that shocked Lansdowne.

'He has a wife ill in bed at home yet finds time to leave her to meet with a young woman.' *And a good-looking one.* There was no denying Joyner's obvious sexual allure, even in grubby coveralls and a headscarf. 'It takes no effort to imagine why he is interested. But what is your motivation for meeting Mr Jeffries?'

Joyner shrugged her shoulders. 'Just a bit of company...'

'A young woman in the prime of life with a jolly group of girlfriends living in and around a town like Cheltenham. I'm sure you can find plenty of 'company' more suited to your age.'

The 'Prairie' tank engine had come to rest outside the carriage compartment window having delivered the coaches. The fireman was grinning at the two women through the window glass. The allure of Miss Joyner was undeniable.

'He needs company... Just talking...' Joyner was trying not to react to the cheeky fireman, but it was obvious she was far from annoyed or offended. Lansdowne gave the man a hard stare until he reluctantly turned his attention back to his engine.

'I know his wife has cancer. I'm not heartless. What sort of girl do you take me for?' Joyner tried to summon up a convincing show of outrage. 'She never goes out and he works all day and is stuck at home every evening - except when we meet. I mean, it's hardly a marriage, and besides, we just *talk*.' Joyner stopped.

'How long have you been having sexual relations with Jeffries. Is that question clear enough?'

'I've never with him!' She actually looked shocked.

'You expect me to believe that?'

'Yes!' The look of horror on her face was either that of a superb actress or it was genuine.

'Where and when do you meet for your innocent, companionable times together?' Lansdowne was finding it hard not to sound sarcastic. She must not allow her feelings of antipathy for this silly girl blur her judgement.

'Wednesday afternoons. It's half day in the shop and I can get the time away from here most weeks. We work all manner of days and hours, so Mrs Devlin lets me take a half on Wednesdays.'

'And in the evenings?'

'Mondays. Just Mondays.'

'What time?'

'We meet at nine.'

'Where?'

'It varies. A pub. A restaurant...We decide on the Wednesday where we shall go the following Monday night.'

'Jeffries takes you and your friends out to a restaurant for - conversation?'

'Well not exactly...it's just...'

'Yes?'

'Just me and him.'

'Romantic...'

She shrugged this off as if it were not important.

'And after your candle-lit dinners for two, you go where?'

'Home, of course! On my own. I'm not that sort of a girl!'

'What sort do you mean?'

Joyner turned to look out of the window. The cheeky fireman wolf-whistled loudly. Thankfully the engine then steamed out of sight.

'You are happy to be seen with an older, married man? People could jump to the wrong conclusions.'

'Like you are now?' She tried to give Lansdowne a fierce stare, but her nerve was failing. 'Look, I go home alone. Honestly. He goes back to his wife.'

'Do you kiss?'

Silence.

'A man wines and dines you then walks you to your door...'

'The end of the street. I won't let him go closer.'

'You walk to the end of the street, where you hope to evade being seen by your family and neighbours and you don't even let him kiss you? Or slide his arms around your waist? Are you quite sure?'

'Once or twice...'

'So, there is a romantic element.'

Silence.

'That is a very fine bracelet. It looks expensive. As do the earrings.' They sparkled attractively as Joyner moved her head.

'What if they are?'

'Who bought them for you? And don't tell me you bought them on a carriage cleaner's wages.'

Silence.

'Mr Jeffries gave them to you?'

She nodded.

'Has he given you other jewellery?'

'A little...' This was barely a whisper.

'Call me cynical, but when a man buys an attractive girl expensive jewellery, he is looking for an awful lot more than a peck on the cheek under a lamp post. Which hotel do you use in Honeybourne?'

'Sorry?'

'Or is it Stratford? An hour or two in a seedy place that won't ask awkward questions about 'Mr and Mrs Smith' wanting a room for the afternoon. Out of town and away from gossiping neighbours and girlfriends? Don't lie, as I'm a good policewoman and I will find out.'

Chapter Twenty-Seven

They were back at the Lygon Arms. Seated in armchairs on either side of a crackling log fire with pints to hand and a cloud of blue smoke around them. Two detectives deep in thought. Both Vignoles and Mellor had notebooks open trying to tease explanations from their observations. WPC Lansdowne was sitting nearby sipping a Babycham.

What were they to make of the day's events? A vicious murder with all the signs of being a professional 'hit' by a pair of especially sadistic killers. Whilst differing in style from the killing of Krast, both detectives were now in agreement they sensed a link. The calculating cruelty on show suggested the same men were responsible. In all probability the two seen departing Broadway in a car, one in a balaclava and the driver's face captured in an artistic impression. Neither of these men were Terry Grinal in the role of Lord Buckrose, or not.

WPC Lansdowne had reported back on Jeffries. She'd made excellent progress uncovering evidence he'd lied about his movements on Monday evening, but stealing off to rendezvous with Mary Joyner was hardly motivation for murder. It was possible that as a result of trying to impress this young lady, Jeffries had been taking items from the shop. If this was so, it had landed Krast's business in dire straits and possible propelled the old man into making questionable decisions, but Vignoles found it impossible to directly link Jeffries to the death of Krast. It was even more improbable that Jeffries was responsible for the murder of Buckrose-Grinal. If for no other reason than Jeffries surely lacked the imagination to use bladed weapons with such nightmarish skill. Due process however demanded Lansdowne establish Jeffries' whereabouts that afternoon and delve deeper into his affair with Joyner.

'It just might throw something up. Question Joyner's girlfriends. Find the hotel they shack up in...'

'I still don't like the man...' Mellor observed aloud to nobody in particular. He had been interested in Lansdowne's description of the salacious Mary. He was idly wondering if he could think of a reason to interview this woman himself...

'Dislike is not enough to arrest him.' Vignoles closed his notebook and removed his glasses, rubbing the bridge of his nose. He was feeling tired and missing his wife, Anna. It would be good to get the case closed and head home. 'I'm going to speculate. Not something I encourage.' He replaced his glasses and peered over them at Mellor. 'We work on facts and theorising can be dangerous, but it can't hurt to run through a series of imagined events to see if they work...'

Mellor and Lansdowne were listening.

'We're on safe ground arguing our killers came here to get a specific and valuable diamond.'

'Following orders?'

'We must consider the possibility that there are other forces at play further up the command chain. They believed Krast could lead them to its whereabouts.'

'They thought he had it?'

'He did for a while, thanks to the unsuspecting Twister and Gable. But despite a slow death that would induce most people to confess, he could not tell them where it was.'

'But why didn't he save his skin? Keeping schtum and getting killed makes no sense.'

'Because he no longer had it nor could he say where it was. I suspect Buckrose had taken it. Charmed it away from Krast. Telling fabulous stories about being part of the aristocracy, about knowing the Queen...It was an elegant confidence trick, but for all the carefully contrived stories and fancy clothes and accessories, this was a conman tricking a gullible man into handing over what he wanted.'

Mellor lit up and nodded. 'So Krast told the killers about Buckrose-Grinal. It was all he had left to trade?'

'I suggest the killers already knew about Grinal pretending to be Buckrose, so maybe this came as no surprise and they deliberately used the name Buckrose on the Monday evening.'

'Why did they do that?'

'Good question, Lucy. Maybe to muddy the waters and deflect attention? Whatever the reason, they had little choice but to kill Krast.

He'd squeal, if not to us, then warn off Buckrose. They searched office and home and failed to find what they wanted. Sometime between Twister and Gable handing the diamond over and before Monday evening, Krast entrusted this stone to the hands of a charlatan.'

'But how did Grinal as Buckrose learn about the diamond?' Mellor asked.

Vignoles chewed this over for a moment. 'Maybe he didn't... He just chanced into the shop intending to start a confidence trick and take whatever he could charm away from Krast? His shop is full of tasty goods.'

'A fishing expedition?'

'It could be. It might have taken weeks of carefully courting Krast and winning his confidence. Confidence trickery is as old as time. If it was easy to see through, it wouldn't be happening every day, everywhere.'

'Fair point.'

'Whilst being charmed by this Lord Buckrose character, Krast had the idea of swapping Gable's diamond for a cheap substitution and so Grinal as Buckrose found himself perfectly placed to help achieve this sleight of hand.'

'That could work!' Lansdowne agreed.

'Or...Buckrose-Grinal came there by the same route that brought our hitmen onto the scene? '

'Slatter!' Mellor exclaimed. 'His dying act was to write that name in the dirt. He was set up, tortured, robbed and left to die so he tried to tell us who's responsible...'

'I agree. That name has meaning.'

'The killers have gone back to this Slatter with the rock. They're well away now...' Mellor drank some beer as he chewed this idea over. 'Know what, guv? Professional killers after a rare diamond? That's unusual. A cut above your average. They're from the Smoke. That's where I'd start looking for these two...' He tapped his empty glass in an agitated manner with his fingernails.

'I'm gonna call some mates back on my old manor. Put the word around.'

'What have you in mind?'

'We've got the name Slatter. I want to see if anyone on the front line has heard of this geezer.'

Ten minutes later and after a lot of urgent talking on the phone and a stack of coins dropped in the paybox, Mellor was back. Two fresh pints foaming in his hands as he crossed the room. He was grinning like the Cheshire Cat.

'Bulls Eye, boss! Got 'im! We've got a bead on Ernie Slatter.'

'He's known?' Vignoles was surprised.

'Got a mate in the Flying Squad who knew him straight off.'

'You know officers in the C8 Department?'

'Yeah...' He looked pleased at Vignoles' evident surprise that he had a way into one of the more famous, if not notorious, departments policing the Capital. 'They've had their eyes on Slatter for years. He's a fence. Deals in top notch stuff. Gold, platinum, silver, proper jewellery. Also launders money...'

'And he's not behind bars?' Lansdowne was shocked.

'His type are clever. The Sweeney know what he does but can't pin nothing significant on 'im. Nothing to send him down long enough to make it worth their while. And besides, they don't mind a fence. They don't do the nasty stuff. They don't hold up banks and mail trains and don't carry shooters and cosh security guards. They just sit tight and trade and are well-connected. They keep their ears to the ground and know what's goin' on. There's not a fence alive who don't trade in information as well as goods to ensure he has an easy - and long - life.'

'Selling some of his clients to the police?' Vignoles queried.

'Yep. Takes nerve and an expert hand, but the loss of small fry against trading with the big boys makes sound business. The heavy-hitters know the fences feed us a trickle of minnows and that gives 'em space to do their business.'

Vignoles drank his beer and shook his head. 'I won't pass comment on that...' He'd heard all manner of stories about the notorious Flying Squad or the 'Sweeney Todd' as Londoners would insist on calling it. 'They think Slatter is the kind of man to make a deal with Buckrose-Grinal?'

'He is. Slatter's the sort who could fence this diamond then split the profits. Well, that would be his promise...'

Vignoles was interested. 'It was Slatter who put the killers onto Krast you think? Dropped in the name Buckrose as well? Slatter sent them with a message in the form of that card offering 'Money For *Something*' He was double-crossing the double-crosser?'

'Yeah! I like that! They lured Buckrose-Grinal in by offering to close the deal: cash for the diamond. But they killed him and just took it.'

'We're closing in...' Vignoles was puffing on his pipe. 'Good work, Mellor.'

'I should get down to London on the earliest train and jump in with the Flying Squad on a visit to Slatter? Like I said, these two-timing rats will sell their souls for money and liberty...'

'It's the best lead we've had since we opened the case. I'll give you two days. Telephone the moment you hear anything. I'll tidy up here then get back to the office. I've two consecutive inquests in the morning and then need to hand Krast's shop over to his solicitor to wind the business up and square some paperwork with DCI Silver.' Vignoles didn't look thrilled at the prospect of a morning filled with due process and tedious paperwork and silently envied Mellor's dash to Paddington.

Chapter Twenty-Eight

The Flying Squad roared through the early morning London traffic the blue lamp mounted on the radiator grill attempting to forewarn other road users of their rapid approach, although the squeal of rubber on tarmac and the throaty roar of the Jaguar engine was enough to startle most into pulling aside.

The streets were filled with an unhealthy smog of coal smoke and exhaust fumes pressing heavily on lungs and leaving a vile slime in the backs of throats. Staring through the side window from his seat in the rear of the car, Mellor watched people stop as they coughed painfully or to tie their mufflers that bit more securely around their faces. Some held handkerchiefs to their mouths, the cotton stained like nicotine by the time they reached their offices. The sickly-yellow of London stock bricks only made the atmosphere appear even less appetising. Buses loomed from the gloom, black cabs at traffic lights coughed diesel fumes whilst street lamps vainly tried to cast their light. Car headlamps sliced through the enveloping air like searchlights.

Mellor loved it. He was back. They were someway off his old 'manor' around Paddington, but it was still London and he'd missed it. Glamour and squalor in close proximity; big roads lined with store fronts glowing with new neon signs in contrast to new blocks of ugly flats and the fenced-off bomb sites between crumbling squares and sad corner shops, unwelcoming pubs and dodgy billiard halls. There were the Roxy and Gaumont cinemas, ailing theatres hosting third-rate comedy stars in the twilight of their careers and the huddles of men on street corners. Always shifty and watchful, hands in coat pockets and fags dangling from mouths. Who were these men? How did they live? It was all a far cry from sheep in frosted fields, pretty country pubs and narrow lanes splattered with cow pats, although Mellor conceded he might miss the snorting racehorses and the grandstands filled with roaring punters and rich women smelling of expensive perfume.

At heart, the low-life of London was his world. He was sharing the car with three of the Sweeney; mean and eager to a man; Sergeant Mills behind the wheel was handling his machine like a true pro, taking corners at speed, shooting red lights and letting the big engine growl as though he was Mike Hawthorn.

Mellor knew Sergeant Mills and sought his assistance yesterday. Mills and his men had listened with mounting interest as he explained his interest in Ernie Slatter.

'Any excuse to put the thumbscrews on Slatter!' Mills approved the plan. 'Does no harm to keep him on his toes.'

'Count us in.' 'Jock' McAlistair and Phil Hodges were just as enthusiastic. 'He's been too quiet these last months. Pay him an early morning call?'

'Catch him with his pants down!' Mills grinned.

They'd all laughed and downed another round of pints in the tatty pub that actually welcomed men from the 'squad'. They could talk freely here.

Mellor showed them the photograph Chief Inspector Badger had copied from the bogus passport Terry Grinal used as part of his pretence to be Lord Buckrose.

'Fancied himself. Not the usual gorilla we see around here.'

'Proper Dandy in the Underworld.'

'But he was playing with fire...' Mellor explained the extraordinary circumstances of his death.

Hodges whistled. Even he was surprised at the graphic details.

Mills exchanged a look with his men. 'I'm getting more interested by the minute. Nasty job that... We need Slatter singin' like a canary bird...'

Their car squealed to a halt outside the unprepossessing shop front in Grimsby Lane.

'Shutters closed...'

'Still in bed with some slag...'

'He'd be lucky - unless she's blind as a bat!'

'Aye, we'd best wake him up and see.' 'Jock' McAlistair hammered on the door with a gloved fist. 'Open up, Ernie!' He hammered again and rattled the door on its hinges. 'Get down here or we'll kick it in!'

Between thunderous knocks and the rumble of a train passing on the viaduct, they could now hear a whining voice and feet sliding on a stone floor in loose-fitting footwear. Chains clinked and the door was opened a chink.

McAlistair rudely pushed it with considerable force and the little man had to step backwards to avoid being tipped over as the door flew wide. 'Don't mind if we do. Thanks for the invitation.'

Slatter glared miserably at the men as they piled into his dark and cramped shop.

'You out of shillings for the meter? Get a light on!' Allen barked.

The unhappy Slatter clicked a Bakelite switch on the wall and a weak bulb cast a light on their hats. It gave the police the effect of having dark hollows for eyes and sharply accented noses. It did nothing for their looks.

Slatter shuffled to his place behind his untidy counter. 'I open at nine. What's with all the noise and impatience?'

Sergeant Mills leaned on the counter. 'This is Detective Sergeant Mellor. He's been hearing things about you - and a certain posh gent you've been trading with.'

'I run a shop. I get lots of people in here.' Slatter's eyes shifted uneasily between the four faces. 'I trade with folk, posh or otherwise.'

'Pull the other one, Ernie. Nobody comes in here unless they're up to no good.'

'That's a scandalous lie, Sergeant Mills!'

'And you're a nasty little toe rag who trades in stuff a lot more valuable than the junk on your filthy shelves.'

'This place needs a clean...' Hodges wrinkled his nose as he ran a black leather gloved finger along a grimy glass shelf.

'You've been in the wars, Mr Slatter,' Mellor decided it was time to take a more active role. 'What happened to your hand?'

'Nuffink.' The shop started to shake from a heavy train rumbling across the bridge, making everything rattle. It felt as though the entire building was quivering.

'"Nuffink" does not make you bandage a hand like that. Must make it hard to do your work?' Mellor continued. 'You wouldn't do that without good reason...'

'Someone lean on you?' McAlistair leered.

'No!' Slatter was now protecting his heavily bandaged hand by keeping it close to his body. His eyes seemed drawn to his soldering iron, although this looked cold and unplugged.

Mellor showed Slatter a photograph. 'Do you know this man?'

'No.'

Mills leaned closer to Slatter. 'Take a proper look.'

'I told you, I don't know him.'

'Posh. A bit snobby. Calls himself Lord Buckrose. Ringing any bells?' Mellor continued.

Slatter remained silent and looked miserably at the bench in front of him. McAlistair was inspecting the items on the shelves, lifting some for a closer inspection. He deliberately dropped a porcelain figurine of a shepherdess and it shattered on the floor.

'Oi!' Slatter lifted both hands in the air in anger. 'You watch what you're doin'! That needs paying for...'

Mills grabbed the wrist of his bandaged hand. 'This must be sore...'

'Ow! Let go...' Slatter implored. He screwed his face in pain.

'Did Buckrose do that?' Mellor asked as Mills pressed the fingers of his other hand around the bandages and gave a squeeze.

'He never laid a finger on me!' Slatter's eyes were watering.

'So you *do* remember him?' Mills released his wrist and slapped the little man on the side of the head. It was not to hurt as much to humiliate. 'It's early and you're just waking up.' Mills sounded almost friendly. 'You need a nice cuppa tea and then your addled brain will get working, eh? So how about you tell my good mate DS Mellor everything 'e wants to know and old butter fingers there will stop breaking stuff, and we'll leave you to your tea and toast.'

McAlistair laughed and dropped another figure. 'Ooops...!'

Slatter winced, but probably because of his hand throbbing rather from any concern about the matching Staffordshire figure lying on the floor without a head beside the shattered remains of the shepherdess. 'He was a gent. He never laid a finger on me...'

'Someone did.'

'I had an accident.'

'Who?' Hodges took his turn.

'More than my life's worth to say!'

'We can look after you.'

'As if!' Slatter snorted with derision. 'What, a bobby standing outside my place makin' sure I lose all my trade and when he buggers off, the heavy mob call around...'

'Change your name, get you a place to live away from here...' Mills added.

'I didn't know you cared...'

'What was the deal with this man...' Mellor jabbed a finger at the photograph. 'This gent.'

'Why you interested?' Slatter fired back.

'He's dead.' Mellor replied.

Slatter looked shocked.

'It was a nasty way to die...It took a while.' Mellor stared at the little man. 'Very painful and very slow...'

Slatter looked scared and tried to moisten his lips. 'Hey, now look it weren't me! I never done it! I'm not in that line... Come on! This is the first I heard about him being dead!'

'We're not pinning it on you,' Mellor retorted.

'But we could...' Mills sneered.

'We've established you knew the deceased, so tell us when he came to see you.'

'Couple of weeks past.' Slatter mumbled the words and looking furtively around the shop as if to check there was no-one else there except the Flying Squad. 'He just came in like. Said he had something to trade.'

'Had he?' Mellor asked.

'I never took it. That's God's honest truth. He took it wiv' 'im.'

'Keep your hair on.' Mellor gave Slatter what approximated a smile. 'What I need to know is exactly *what* he was offering that's got you and so many others worked up.'

'What others?' Slatter looked nervously towards the door of his shop, but it was barred by the bulk of McAlistair. 'Who said anything about others?'

'The two that killed Buckrose for starters.' Mellor replied.

Slatter's face twitched.

'That's the posh gent,' Hodges sneered. 'Lord Buckrose. Is that how he introduced himself?'

'I didn't know he was dead, honest.' There was fear in Slatter's eyes. The strong beat of an express train departing Liverpool Street station could be heard deep in the cutting and the burble of a van passing on the street with a leaky exhaust. The sound of people going about their lives, riding a train to the flatlands of the East or delivering the morning mail. Slatter glanced at the telephone on his desk as if wishing he could call someone. Mills noticed and drew closer, crowding him.

'Do you know this man?' Mellor showed a reproduction of Miss Wolfe's drawing.

'Very nice I'm sure, but I don't deal in Fine Art.'

'Don't play funny games...' Mills growled.

'I think you do know who this is. You gave this man and his mate a card to pass on to Buckrose. A message on the card agreeing the deal.'

'Eh?' Slatter looked confused.

'Money For Something?' Mellor spelled it out.

'I've no idea what you're on about.'

Mills had been idly toying with a heavy Chinese bronze. He suddenly brought it crashing down on the back of Slatter's bandaged hand with all the force he could muster, releasing a deafening howl of pain. 'Stop stalling you little creep. We've got you trading with the dead man. We've got your message on a card handed to the dead man by his killers. Buckrose even wrote your name in the earth as he was dying. Tell us what you were trading and who with and we'll leave you in peace.' Mills lifted the bronze away and let Slatter nurse his wounded hand. He was whimpering and sweat was beading on his forehead

'It was a rock.' He gasped for air and scrunched his eyes closed for a moment. 'A good one.' He voice was a croaked whisper.

'Worth how much?' Mellor asked.

''arf a million. Maybe more.'

'Strewth!' Mellor looked stunned. The others fell silent for a beat. A locomotive whistle could be heard in the distance.

McAlistair shook his head slowly. 'Aye well, that changes the complexion of things.'

'Are you pissing us about?' Mills was angry. He didn't believe Slatter.

'No! Straight up, it's as hot as it gets. Too hot. Far too hot for me! I don't want nuffink to do wiv it!' He groaned again as pain swept through his arm. 'Come on lads...' He had a whining wheedling tone to his voice. 'I keep my head down and I never work with gangsters... This was too dangerous.'

'How d'you mean?' Mellor asked.

Slatter leaned back in his chair and took a few deep breaths. 'This Buckrose. He wanted to sell it, but I told him it was not that easy. I don't carry that kind of money. I needed to ask around, carefully. I made a picture of it, with his lordship staring over my shoulder the whole time. That way I could be sure of what I was dealing with. Not as I'd forget...'

'Show me,' Mills snapped his fingers. The others drew closer.

Slatter opened a drawer fixed to the underside of the counter and extracted a small book of watercolour paper. It was thick and the waviness of some of the paper edges told of the use of water-based pigments. He flipped it open with his good hand, careful to keep the damaged hand underneath the counter and away from Mills.

'What on earth...' Hodges was amazed.

'Portraits of every decent diamond I've had the pleasure of studying.'

McAlistair laughed. 'Selling under the counter...'

'*Handling* is the word I use.' Slatter seemed more relaxed than he'd been since the Flying Squad had so brutally forced their way in. He'd commanded their admiration, if only for a few minutes.

'You painted these?'

'I did. Under high magnification and knowing what you're looking for...' Slatter carefully turned the pages, deftly ensuring he showed only a fleeting glimpse of most of the intricate drawings with their coloured highlights. 'That's the one Buckrose has.'

Mills peered closer. 'Alright, so it's a diamond. What makes it special?'

'That is 'The Hornet's Beauty'. A diamond in a million. Well, 'alf a million any road. It went missin' for a while. There's a bounty for the finder.'

'Not from us!' Mills gave Slatter a hard stare.

'I can't say who's offering. I didn't want to get to close enough to find out. I'd never try to collect even if I had it and that's the God's honest. Too dangerous.' Slatter made a strange grimace almost as if he were laughing.

'It's out of my league. I wish I'd never seen it. When that Buckrose wanted to sell, I told him I needed to make notes, make this picture...so I could be sure of getting him a decent wedge.'

'Did he know what he had?' Mellor asked.

'No. But he knew it was good and wanted me to cough up a decent wedge.'

'How much?' Allen asked.

'Two thousand, used notes.'

'Selling him well short. You never change...' Hodges laughed unpleasantly.

'I didn't trade.'

'You'd make a killing from the deal. So why didn't you?' Mills challenged.

'I was tempted, but I knew this was too dangerous and I'd end up dead.' Slatter replied, miserably. 'I'd need to call in a lot of favours to raise that capital and questions get asked.' Slatter glanced nervously around. 'I don't want to talk any more...'

'Why should we believe you don't have it?'

''cos the man who thinks it's his property sent men around to do this to me.' He showed them his bandaged hand. 'I know when I'm beaten. Now leave and don't let anyone see you.'

Mills gave Slatter another cuff to the side of the head. 'You best not be messin' with us!'

'I don't know their names. Just two vicious bastards who made me understand not to mess with what's not mine. And I didn't.'

'Were they the men who delivered your calling card?' Mellor asked

'I don't know anything about that! What card?'

Mellor leaned closer to Slatter. 'Let me put it this way. Whether you admit to writing that card or not, your name was scratched in the sand by the man it was given to. That's why we are here.'

Slatter fell silent.

Allen leaned closer. 'Names. Descriptions of the men who did that to you...'

'No...'

Mellor stepped aside on the signal of Allen as Mills pinned Slatter's arms to his sides whilst McAlistair landed a vicious punch to the side of his head. Yet another commuter train rumbled over the viaduct and partially masked the cry of pain. The fist was ready to strike again. 'Nobody is going to hear a thing...'

'All right! But...this never came from me! You've got to make sure it never came from me...'

Allen shrugged his shoulders. 'What d'you say lads? We were never here...'

Slatter barely whispered the words, as if by talking quietly he could convince himself he'd not just betrayed the identities of two of London's most evil killers: 'The Debt Collectors.'

'Eh?'

'Kane and Abel. Kane with a 'K'. Like in the film. That's all I know. They call themselves The Debt Collectors, and they frighten the daylights out of me...'

Allen patted Slatter on the shoulder and winked. 'Two names. That'll do us. Have a long life...'

They left the shop.

Chapter Twenty-Nine

'Guv?' It was Mellor on the telephone. 'You need to get up to London.'

'May I enquire why?' Vignoles was still trying to get used to his DC's mannerisms.

'We've found Slatter.'

'That is news.'

'And the diamond. It has a name – 'The Hornet's Beauty' - which is -.'

'A locomotive -.'

'A racehorse -.'

They both spoke at the same time.

'The locomotive is named after the Derby winner,' Vignoles added. 'To give a diamond such a name means it is distinctive, valuable and has history?'

'Not 'arf! It's worth a mint! I've work to do on the history and provenance, but Ernie Slatter is a fence and snitch known to the Flying Squad. He handles the tastier stuff on the black market. He's a valued source so they turn a blind eye in return for information.'

'The old argument of allowing one person's illegality to help catch bigger fish...'

'He's a seasoned operator, but even he baulked at this. Said it was too dangerous. He's scared.'

'Who offered it to him?'

'Lord Buckrose. He wanted to sell, but Slatter stalled. Said he needed time to research the diamond and find sufficient funds to trade. Now you won't believe this, but Slatter even made a drawing of it. Really detailed, highlighting the unique aspects of the stone and the cut. Everything.'

'I presume Slatter does not have 'The Hornet's Beauty'?'

'Buckrose kept it.'

'And got himself killed as a consequence... But are you saying the killers were not acting for Slatter? They were not getting it back so he could sell it on?'

'It is looking that way. Once Slatter started puttin' feelers out, it caught the attention of the sort of people you don't want to mess with, Slatter included. Slatter gave us names of two individuals who look suspects for the murders. They came to see him and gave him some grief until he told them about the Lord and his diamond. They go by the names Kane and Abel. Like in the Bible.'

'We've not heard of them?'

'New to me, but some of the lads on The Flying Squad said they'd heard rumours. There are stories about a particularly vicious pair of killers, but they're crafty and evade detection. The Squad also discovered there's particularly unpleasant character holed up in the Scrubs who thinks he has the right to call the Hornet his own. He's a psychopathic head case with influence outside his cell. Nobody messes with this geezer without gettin' their fingers burnt. Or chopped off. He's famous for that.'

'If he's banged up, he didn't kill Krast or Buckrose-Grinal.'

'No. He'll have bought someone in for the job...'

'The two professionals we suspect are behind everything...' Vignoles agreed. 'And we have a drawing, no matter how imperfect, of either Kane or Abel.' Vignoles chewed this new information over. 'There's a chance these two will not have found a way to get the Hornet back to their paymaster in Wormwood Scrubs. They probably wish to take it carefully before making contact.'

'That's the opinion of the Sweeney. They reckon the killers would keep their heads down for a few weeks before making the next move to let the dust settle and see how the land lies. The Governor at the Scrubs has been alerted and they're tightening up procedures during visiting hours and limiting the chances of anything getting across.'

'I'm on my way.' Vignoles reached for his hat and glanced at this wrist watch. If he hurried there was a train to Bristol due shortly and that meant he should be able to catch the perfect train to whisk him to London in record time...

Chapter Thirty

Vignoles stood under the beautifully arched cast iron trainshed of Bristol Temple Meads and admired the train waiting to depart for London Paddington. He'd made the connection with enough time to walk along the curving platform towards the head of the train where a magnificent locomotive was steaming in the cold air. A real treat.

'The Bristolian' was the *non plus ultra* of the Western Region of British Railways, closely vying with the 'Cheltenham Spa Express' as one of the fastest regular passenger services in the World. If the 'Spa' just pipped it to the post for speed, the 'Bristolian' won out for its importance connecting two great cites and the Herculean task of thrashing the engine for one hundred and nine minutes of non-stop galloping along Isambard Kingdom Brunel's high-speed 'bowling green' of a line to London.

As Vignoles expected, the Western Region had rostered a 'King'. Only their most powerful express locomotive would be good enough. Recently painted into British Railways Brunswick green it looked very like it would have done before the war. It just needed the words 'Great Western' on the tender in gold leaf to complete the illusion that Nationalisation had effected little change to this magnificent beast now standing in a station also not much altered since the day it was built.

'King Edward I' was gleaming like a new pin. The men on the footplate were calmly making final checks to the fire and water level, monitoring the steam available whilst running rags in their gloved hands over all they touched to ensure the inside of the cab also met the standards expected of this prestigious service. Vignoles wondered if they gave as much time to cleaning inside their own homes.

Giving the powerful engine a last glance and a wave to the driver, he climbed aboard his carriage, noting with pleasure that he'd bagged a seat in one allowing smoking and settled down to enjoy the exhilarating high-speed haulage whilst he turned over the events of the week.

What to make of it? Two bodies. One a respectable jeweller. A man who should have been looking forward to a comfortable retirement in his pretty Cotswold village, but instead had found his business floundering and in desperation turned to deceit as his way out of the mire. The other, a trickster and serial conman sleeping in a tired old car with a suitcase of unwashed laundry. A pathetic little man in many ways and yet he must have had times of great plenty from his ill-gotten gains as a fake member of the aristocracy because he owned a racehorse.

What linked them was 'The Hornet's Beauty.' A diamond that drove men to murder such was their desire to own, or at least profit, from it. A diamond so valuable it scared men who 'fenced' stolen goods for a living. Anyone prepared to make deals in the London gangland had to be tough and not easily frightened, yet Mellor said Slatter was scared.

Vignoles heard a whistle blown and his watch said 4.30pm. They were on their way, exactly to the minute. The immense power of 'King Edward I' pulled the fully-laden train into motion almost effortlessly. It was a smooth start with no slipping and the hard barks from the chimney suggested an engine expertly under control. Vignoles looked out of the window and allowed himself to put aside the case for a few moments and reflect that his job, for all its demands and time away from his wife, had its rewards. He filled his pipe with tobacco and struck a match. The locomotive wailed a warning whistle as 'The Bristolian' clattered through a succession of points, the carriages swayed and the beat of the exhaust and the tickety-tack of the wheels increased as the train sprinted forward.

Back to the case. There were two killers on the prowl with a diamond in one of their pockets...But they now knew their names. The nooses were not exactly around their necks, but they were being prepared...

Vignoles smoked and pondered. He was seated beside the window, the other occupants concentrating on their newspapers or important-looking documents opened on their laps. He stared out of the window, but whilst vaguely aware of the white steam tumbling past and the house backs of Bedminster flashing by, soon replaced by open fields and trees, his mind was whirring like the spinning driving wheels on the locomotive.

There was something about this case that sparked a memory. Why was he being reminded of the Palmer-Charlton case? He'd worked this with Trinder in the weeks before Christmas. Dear old Trinder! He missed his familiar side-kick, perhaps more than he'd dare admit. When this business was over, he must telephone and see how Trinder was getting on in North Wales. Or perhaps this evening? Trinder had largely run the investigation and arguably was more *au fait* with the finer points. Vignoles had been quite preoccupied with family issues at the time...

The note of the locomotive whistle stretched long on the air. The train was veritably flying, the motion exhilarating, the carriage rocking pleasantly as the countryside flew past the window in a blur.

What was it about the Palmer-Charlton case that wouldn't let him push it aside? The case had broken open when a young girl had been kidnapped from a hotel in Manchester. She'd been found alive and unharmed whilst complaining bitterly about the two 'horrid men' who had stolen a bag of sparkly coloured stones she was particularly fond of. A strange story in many ways. They had been so relieved Daisy was alive and unmolested that the bigger issues underlying her distressing experience had been pushed towards the back burner. WPC Benson had spent time coaxing Daisy into talking about her experience and offer descriptions of the men who'd abducted her. In so doing, Benson had pieced together with the help of Daisy's mother working descriptions of the men. However, they came with caveats: one man was described solely by a young and distraught child, and mother and daughter had differing memories of the other, forced the police into accepting these two were quite possibly masters of disguise deliberately leaving a confused trail behind. Disguise. A trait shared with Terry Grinal and his alter ego Lord Buckrose. Vignoles chewed this over.

Mellor reckoned the two hired killers were good at evading detection. The oddly named Kane and Abel might also be masters of disguise? Undeniably the abductors had evaded capture whilst the police celebrated the safe return of Daisy. The biggest sticking point in the weeks that followed had been trying to understand why Daisy had been targeted in the first place. Her mother had with her a considerable sum of money she'd stolen from her grandmother's house, yet this had not been the focus of the demands from Daisy's captors. They wanted something specific - yet had left it unnamed.

The train slammed into the wall of air pressure with a wallop as it dived into Box Tunnel. The world turned black outside the carriage window. Darkness. An inability to see the light at the end of the tunnel.

That had about summed up their feelings about the Palmer-Charlton case in December. They had made some progress and unravelled a number of other strands, but the two major perpetrators and the core motivation for their actions had eluded them.

Trinder then said his goodbyes and left for a new start at Llandudno Junction, whilst the newspapers ceased telling evermore lurid tales about charming Daisy and her undeniably attractive mother, both of whom made perfect fodder for the front pages. There had been a brief media circus around these two in a dreary week after Christmas until the next multiple car smash-up and the imminent threat of snow caused everyone to lose interest.

Vignoles decided he needed to reacquaint himself with the details about the little velvet bag of 'jewels' that Daisy had filched from the 'secret drawer' of her murdered Great Grandmother. Once the contents of this bag had been discovered by her abductors, it ensured her immediate release. Daisy has been unceremoniously abandoned on a train...

Could it be possible...?

What if...?

Vignoles smoked a second pipe. An idea was forming. It was so far-fetched he was glad he didn't need to share it until he could gather supporting information. But was it possible these men, two *professional hitmen*, had been after The Hornet's Beauty?

These men had taken a bag of what had been supposed were just pretty cut-glass paste, but later suspected to be real diamonds, emeralds and sapphires. Presumably of only fair quality and modest value, but the perfect hiding place for one very special stone. But then what? Had Daisy inadvertently lost the Hornet from amongst the others? Dropped it down the back of the carriage seat whilst she cried and fretted and worried about the two 'bad men' taking her away from her pretty mummy in Manchester? Benson had clearly understood that Daisy had tried to amuse herself and find comfort with her doll and these pretty stones...

* * * *

'The Bristolian' rolled to a gentle halt just before the buffers at

Chapter Thirty

Paddington station. Almost immediately the doors were flung open as businessmen replete from a meal and a few drinks strode purposefully towards the exit gates and onwards to the London Underground or taxi rank. There was a smattering of women in smart coats and hats, some accompanying their husbands, others carrying armfuls of shopping bags. As Vignoles stepped down and re-adjusted his hat, he noted the absence of families and specifically young children. It was not that kind of train. It served in the main to whisk men of business between two important commercial centres at the highest possible speed. For that matter, he had his own urgent business to attend to.

He joined the rapidly marching throng striding past 'King Edward I' now gently sighing at the platform end, wisps of steam rising from somewhere around its wheels and looking for all the world like one of the racehorses in the winner's ring at Cheltenham. It was hardly surprising so many locomotives were named after these creatures. Perhaps more surprising was that a diamond could also take the name of a Derby winning horse...

He looked for Mellor amidst the crowded concourse. His DS was leaning in a languid pose against one of the massive supporting columns of the train shed roof with his hat at a rakish angle and the obligatory cigarette dangling. Did the man think he was in a film?

'Evening, guv.' Mellor touched the brim of his hat.

'I told you not to call me that. We'll walk and talk and find somewhere I can place a call.'

'The refreshment rooms are best. They've got phone booths.'

Vignoles nodded assent to the idea.

Chapter Thirty-one

Vignoles stepped into the tiny telephone kiosk and rootled in his trouser pockets for coins. Mellor held the door ajar so he could listen in.

'Benson? Yes...At Paddington...This is priority and everything else can wait. Dig out the case files on the Palmer-Charlton case. Refresh yourself on the salient points, specifically everything to do with the kidnapping of the girl. The testimony of the mother Rachel Corrigan, her description of the man who befriended her in Manchester and subsequently abducted her daughter. Everything from Daisy, especially the descriptions of the two men. Focus on the abductors, on their movements once they left Manchester. Get Blencowe and Howerth on this. Establish the exact trains taken, their place of origin and destination that day. What stock was used...I want specifics. Yes! Type of coach, the numbers of each vehicle. I realise that...it will be hard. I want to know where the rake of coaches went after Daisy was recovered. Maintenance schedules, transfers to other depots or regions... Also, look for any mention of two names. We were unaware of the significance so possibly slipped through the net. Kane and Abel. As in the Old Testament, except Kane is spelt like in the film...Everything for my eyes as fast as possible.'

He rang off.

'There's a link to an old case?'

'It's a hunch and hangs on the slenderest of threads. We need to box clever here. We're up against agile opponents who cover their tracks.' Vignoles removed his glasses and gave them a polish. 'I'll give you the salient details over a pint.'

Chapter Thirty-Two

Perhaps the strangest aspect of Mary Joyner's testimony was that she was, fundamentally, telling the truth. Lansdowne questioned her friends at length and built up an accurate assessment of Joyner's personality. Joyner was all-too aware of her physical attraction and when feeling confident and bolstered by a drink or two, was prepared to flirt outrageously and lead any number of men a merry dance... And yet, her friends were adamant, she knew when to stop. Most of the time.

Yes, she had a few weeks of something saucy and just possibly naughty, with 'Alan' last summer and then there was 'Clive' who was apparently still hoping to get another chance to unbutton her blouse as he'd once managed to do one cold Christmas Eve, but despite her flirtatious nature and a small army of men desperate to take her to their beds, she did indeed go home alone to the house she shared with her parents. She was full of life and sexuality and eager to express it, she knew the limits of what society would take. Cheltenham was a conservative town and not so large she could hope to act under a cloak of anonymity. Regularly sleeping with a married man from the same town would not escape notice and all the evidence suggested they had not spent any nights together.

Despite her initial confidence on the matter, Lansdowne had not found a single hotel in Stratford-upon-Avon or Honeybourne that had offered a room to Jeffries and Joyner under any name or pretext. Joyner's was a memorable face, and nobody had seen her. Joyner's protestations seemed to be borne out as truth.

The dispiriting reality was, Jeffries and Joyner did take regular train journeys together on Wednesday afternoons to Honeybourne. Sitting quietly and companionably close, as observed by a number of guards and porters, and whilst there seemed to be a slight frisson of attraction between them, it never over-spilled into anything overt. They had never been seen to kiss, although a surreptitious entwining of hands may, or may not, have taken place. All rather dull and to Lansdowne they sounded like an elderly couple enjoying a simple jaunt in the twilight of their years. This was becoming a puzzle, but hardly motivation for Jeffries to become involved in a murder plot.

At Honeybourne they sat in the refreshment rooms and took a high tea, consisting of triangular sandwiches of questionable quality and scones served with Robinsons Strawberry jam and faintly rancid cream. Lansdowne knew this, as she had mistakenly tried one. Joyner and Jeffries acted like two people whiling away the late afternoon waiting for a train connection. The proprieties of the refreshment rooms had come to the conclusion they were actually father and daughter! The age gap aided this misconception and Lansdowne was forced to accept Joyner's ardent denials that they never had sex might be correct.

But did that matter? Jeffries was besotted with Joyner. He had to be. Why else would he risk being seen with her and sneak out every Monday evening? He'd given her a surprising number of very expensive presents. Items well in excess of anything a carriage cleaner might expect and despite appearances, Lansdowne was sure Jeffries intentions were carnal. He'd may not have managed to get her into a hotel bed, but he was surely trying. Jeffries was deluded and acting without any common-sense or dignity.

Joyner had probably been flattered at first and boasted to her friends and considered a kiss under a street lamp an easy price to pay. Lansdowne believed Joyner considered it almost a game, but the magic was wearing off. Joyner had no intention of reciprocating beyond politely sharing a meal or a quiet train ride together. Jeffries was in for a rude awakening and not just from the threat of imminent arrest: 'Clive' had reappeared on the scene in recent days and from what Elsie Gable and other friends had intimated, he was 'in with a chance.' Joyner was losing interest in her prim and unimaginative older man.

All of which was faintly depressing. But what, if anything, did it mean to the murder investigation? Vignoles and Mellor were in agreement Jeffries had over stretched himself buying more extravagant gifts in the hope of winning his way into the arms of the bright young thing he'd fallen for.

'Which brings us back Krast finding his business in dire straits and gambling on the lucky find by Gable...'

Vignoles agreed with Lansdowne as they talked on the telephone.

'I suggest Jeffries inadvertently set into motion the chain of events that lead to Krast's death. Ironically, making himself unemployed - and heading for a jail sentence.'

'It's hard to feel sorry for him,' Vignoles replied. 'I've spoken with the Gloucester Constabulary and they're sending in a man to go through the accounts and prepare the case against Jeffries. You've done good work Lansdowne, but he is no longer the focus of our investigation.'

'There is one other thing, sir...'

'Yes?'

'Sergeant Wilcox and some of the local constables lent assistance in door-to- door work in Cheltenham hoping someone had seen Jeffries and Joyner together. Belt and braces, I suppose...'

'That was good of Wilcox.'

'Something cropped up that has me interested. I'm not sure if it has any bearing but you should be aware. A late dog walker, a baker's assistant off to his ovensand a porter at St James all identified Jeffries talking with another man. Someone different to anyone we have in our sights. This was on the Sunday night. The 6th. Jeffries and this man were first seen at St James station at about 8pm. Now that is odd, as he told me he was home all evening...'

'Go on.'

'Jeffries lives nearer Lansdowne Road station and always walks to and from his house and has offered no explanation for why he was meeting someone at St James, which is some distance off beam.'

'Did you learn what they did after meeting?'

'They went separate ways, apparently. The porter said the meeting lasted no more than a minute and was perfunctory.'

'More a rendezvous than old friends reuniting?'

'Could be. Later that same night, a man wearing broadly similar clothes was seen outside Krast's shop. Just standing, smoking and looking around. The dog walker did not recognise him and claimed there was summat he 'didn't like about the fella' and hurried on. At about 4am, the baker's assistant saw a man, who again seems to match the other descriptions, walking briskly, almost jogging, with his head down past the Bayshill Inn away from Krast's shop, or at least from that end of the street.'

'None of which is conclusive of anything, but odd all the same.'

'That's what I figured.'

'Ask Wilcox if he can arrange for the local men to question Jeffries about this meeting. We need to know who this man is. It may be nothing or something. Throw Kane and Abel's names into the mix and see if they illicit a response. I was going to call you back to Leicester but stay there a while longer until they have questioned Jeffries.'

'As you wish!'

Chapter Thirty-Three

The shop door clattered setting the bell jangling and two men walked into the dingy shop bringing a swirl of stinking smog with them. A lorry rumbled past on the cobbles, but the noise was muffled as the door was firmly closed behind them.

'Ernest, how you keeping, old chum?'

The telephone receiver was slammed back on the holder, but it swayed for a telltale second.

'The hand getting better I hope?'

Slatter croaked something he hoped sounded polite. He couldn't get his face muscles to form a smile as he hunkered deeper into his chair. This was trouble. His call had been too short and brief to summons help.

'We heard you had some friends around?' Kane had his hands in his pockets and whistling a tuneless melody.

'People come and go all the time.' Slatter tried to stop his hands from shaking. 'This is a shop.'

'No, it's a *front*. The only people who come in here are as bent as my friend Abel.' Kane snarled. Abel rolled his eyes in mock outrage and walked to the side of Slatter's counter to block any means of escape. 'Or, they're the police...'

'What? Give over!' His smile had an air of desperation about it.

Kane leaned on the counter, strong hands gripping the wood. 'Just chatting were you, all friendly like? About this and that...'

'A nice cup of tea together and next thing, you're blabbing stuff you shouldn't...'

'I never!'

'Never what?'

'Told them.'

'Told who?' Kane growled.

'You're getting me confused...'

'They were here then?'

'I don't know who you mean!'

'The Sweeney! Came in to see how their old mate Slatter is gettin' on?' Kane spelt it out.

'Did you tell them how beastly we were? That poor hand...' Abel rolled his eyes.

'I've always got 'em on me back! They give me a bloody hard time, but I protect the lot of you! I tell 'em a load of baloney and send them on their way!' Slatter's laugh came out as an ugly croaking sound.

'That who you were calling?' Abel winked and blew a smoke ring. Slatter remained silent. 'We heard four very big and rough men were in your shop with the door closed behind. What on earth brought those brutes here I wonder?'

'That's a lie!'

'I don't think so, Ernie.' Abel bent closer. His eye magnified by his monocle. 'We have it on good authority they came to see you about a diamond...' He slowly blew a stream of smoke in Slatter's eyes. He blinked furiously but forced himself not to look away. He must show no fear. 'It would be most unfortunate if the diamond in question was The Hornet's Beauty.'

'I never said nothin'!'

'You must have told them something.' Kane was not impressed.

'I denied all knowledge, I swear. I never said a word.'

'Not even about your good friends The Debt Collectors?'

'What d'you take me for?'

'A cheating, swindling idiot!' Abel blew another smoke ring. He was enjoying himself.

'Do you like trains?' Kane stood upright and his voice now light and conversational.

'Do I what?'

'Up above and down below. Thundering past all day. I reckon they'd either drive you nuts, or you'd fall in love with'em.'

'I never give a thought to trains...'

'We love trains, don't we Abel?'

'Since I was a little boy! So big and powerful and yet there's something so very *dangerous* about a railway. Do you not think?'

Slatter was pale. He'd heard the rumours. Nothing concrete, but The

Debt Collectors were believed to choose railways as their preferred place for... He closed his eyes for a moment and tried to keep the bile from rising. He was cornered. A slightly-built man who smoked too much and had a bad cough. He had a knife under the counter but Kane and that Scottish thug from the Sweeney had both managed to render his knife hand useless. They'd nobbled him. He needed a gun, but he doubted his swollen finger would even get around the trigger.

'Come along old chap!' Abel's smile was sickly.

'Get yer coat and we'll take a little walk. Train spotting in the dark! There's nothing quite like it.' Kane laughed. A gun with a silencer fitted on the end was now in his hand. He waggled it. 'This will be pointing at your back, so don't get any ideas.'

Abel flashed the metal casing of a flick-knife in his free hand. 'And there is always this to pierce the spinal cord...'

Slatter dragged himself to his feet. Was this what it felt like when they came to a condemned man's cell?

'Just the three of us and those lovely big trains that keep on rolling...'

The evening was thick with smog and the sporadic street lamps made fuzzy luminous balls above their heads that cast little useful light for walking. They had to stare hard at the uneven slabs of the pavement to find their way, footsteps muffled, the sounds of the city blanketed and rendered down to a low mumble. A Foden flatbed lorry grumbled along the narrow cobbles of Grimsby Street, twin headlight beams trying to pierce the soupy air. It was impossible to see the driver in the cab and they in turn must have been just shapes looming out of the stinking air for a brief moment, the torch beam in Abel's hand playing on the ground. Nobody would recognise them.

Slatter stumbled onwards like a man sleepwalking. Was a cold night tasting of sulphurous coal and engine exhaust going to be his last memory of life on earth? He pleaded, offered any number of valuable goodies squirrelled away in his shop. 'I've got two grand in used notes! Untraceable...'

'Nice...' Kane's voice came from the side and half a step behind. The unseen gun making Slatter's back ache with the dreaded anticipation of a bullet. 'We'll go back and pick it up. After...'

They had stopped on a slender Brick Lane footbridge high above a cutting crowded with railway lines. The bulk of the brick viaduct that carried trains into Broad Street lay somewhere on the far side of the cutting where the footbridge descended. The pin pricks of signal lights in the cutting looked like Christmas fairy lights changing from red to green and back again as an almost unceasing succession of trains roared past. The electric passenger trains to Shenfield were just strings of yellow lights like elongated liners on a dark ocean that whooshed past with barely a sound. The steam-hauled expresses and urgent suburban trains were all noise and ethereal clouds of pale steam demonically illuminated by flashes of orange and yellow as fire doors opened, offering brief visions of stick figures on the footplates.

'Dante would have been inspired...' Abel observed.

'Don't know 'im...' Slatter had nothing left to fall back upon except trying to prolong the conversation in the hope he could find inspiration as to how to escape. Perhaps someone would come past, but just when he most needed London to be crowded, the footbridge was deserted. The three leaned against the chest high metal girder and peered over, Slatter between them. Like three friends looking down on the passing trains. The gun had dropped into Kane's pocket. Was this promising?

'Can't see the numbers in this filthy smog...' Kane offered Slatter a cigarette. 'Last fag?'

'Last...?'

Kane lit one from his own and shoved it into Slatter's mouth. He then took another unlit cigarette and pushed it carefully into the little man's top pocket. 'One for the road.'

'Generous!' Abel observed.

'Right, up yer go.'

'Wha...?' Slatter was confused.

It was the cue for the two men to grab a skinny leg each and in one deft move haul him up and over the side, leaving him dangling head first as they held his ankles.

Slatter waved his arms in the hope of finding something to hold on to, but all he could feel was cold dank London air. A stream of coins trickled from his trouser pockets.

'Get me back! Get me back! This ain't funny!' His voice barely travelled and he was shouting down at empty rails.

'I find this rather amusing...' Abel observed.

'Ernie, by my reckoning you should be get a grandstand view of a real beauty. Any moment now...'

'Chris'sake pull me up!' Slatter stared in horror into the gloom and tried to interpret what lay below. They were just trying to scare him and surely would stop this stupid lark and bring him back onto the bridge. He'd confess. Tell them all. Promise to work with them and get the Hornet back. Or could he hope to land on the stony ground below with just a broken arm and play dead long enough for them to leave?

A whistle wavered in the thick air. A pale billow of approaching steam.

'Right on time!' Abel was peering at his wrist watch.

'Can't fault British Railways!' Kane grinned. A flash of teeth in the pea-soupy mix. 'Fast express to Norwich...Should be a lovely big engine on the front!'

'Pull me back, I-I'll do whatever you want...We can sort it out!'

'What d'you think to Mr Slatter's offer?'

'Too late I'm afraid. Should have got everything into the open the first time...' Abel gave an apologetic look.

'Shout out the name of the engine if you see it!'

They released his ankles.

The locomotive stormed under the bridge, enveloping them in a warm cocoon of soft steam that smelt of hot baby oil. Slatter fell. He may have called out but dampened by smog and with the roaring sound of the powerful engine clattering away from Liverpool Street, it was heard by nobody. The body of a skinny man made no noticeable impact as it struck 95 tons of accelerating 'Britannia' class pacific. Slatter's body lay like a rag doll, crumpled on the locomotive's front footplate below the smokebox, his skull smashed.

'Neatly done, if I may say so?'

'Fancy a pint?'

'G & T for me, if it's all the same...'

A man peeled away from the brick-built rain shelter at the far end of the footbridge. His dark clothing and a Homburg hat pulled low over his eyes helped him blend into the impenetrable gloom. His view had been imperfect, but he'd seen enough. He felt a twinge of regret that Slatter was lost. He'd not seen that coming. But everyone had their time in this game...

And the time bell was soon to ring again.

The Debt Collectors were losing their touch.

Chapter Thirty-Four

Vignoles and Mellor were at Marylebone House, the headquarters of the British Transport Commission and the location of Chief Inspector Badger's office.

Vignoles had briefed Badger on the latest developments in a fractious meeting during which both men were equally anxious to 'crack on' and not sit facing each other in an office. However, between interrupting each other and Badger's not unreasonable complaints that Vignoles's hypothesis was 'threadbare and potentially flawed,' they agreed that some progress had been made. Badger would request the Flying Squad be brought in on a more formal footing as their ability to work across divisional lines within the city was vital in a case unconstrained by any one locality. More pertinently, whilst a number of points tied the case to the railways, others strayed far away from their field of jurisdiction.

'By rights, this should be handed over to the Met or Scotland Yard. But I'm prepared to chance our arm with the Flying Squad for a day or two and see if we can't get this licked! I can't say I like that outfit.' Badger sniffed. 'It attracts an uncouth and ill-mannered lot who strut around with a disdain for seniority and rank that is deplorable. But needs must...' Badger made no attempt to hide the fact he wanted the kudos that would accrue by closing this case. His peers might desist from making snide comments about his men 'playing trains for a week or two.'

'I told you Mellor wouldn't let you down! He's done sterling work, I must say.' Badger looked self-satisfied. 'His no-nonsense approach has much to commend it, Charles.'

Mellor was Badger's 'man' and Vignoles wondered if he was going to be reminded of this fact for as long as he and Mellor worked together. There was a part of him prepared to counter Badger's unconstrained approval as he'd learned more about Mellor's open admiration for the Flying Squad's questionable strong-arm methods of coercion. But time was pressing, and whether he liked it or not, Mellor and his intimidating chums had obtained vital information. Vignoles resigned himself to taking comfort that if any complaints were registered by Ernie Slatter, then Badger could jolly well deal with them.

Following the meeting Vignoles and Mellor were ensconced in a small room across the corridor from Badger's office. Vignoles now had WPC Lansdowne on the telephone having digested an interesting report from WPC Benson. The handset was getting hot from the talking and orders issued.

'We need the exact date Gable discovered the diamond. She won't have forgotten...cross check with Mrs Devlin. Devlin will have records of the rakes they cleaned. She strikes me as the sort who maintains excellent records. Try the stationmaster and the signalmen. Between them they will know what came from where. Benson has done good work establishing the carriage Daisy Corrigan was abducted in and I need to know if this could be the same one Gable cleaned...'

He rang off.

Mellor had been handed a note whilst Vignoles was talking. Mellor's face suggested trouble.

'What's up?'

'A stiff. Found on the front of a steamer called 'Geoffrey Chaucer' last night. Signalman spotted it at Stratford and the train was stopped. Nobody saw the body fall, and hardly surprising, as the smog was like soup. The doc reckons a caved in skull from striking the engine was the cause of death.'

'Suicide?'

'The doctor thinks the man was held by his ankles. Considerable force needed to hold the man upside down.'

Vignoles considered this a moment 'He was lowered head first over a bridge?'

'Could be. Intimidation that went wrong or murder. But there's more, guv. The dead man is Ernie Slatter.'

'We need to get to Stratford!' Vignoles was already standing up. 'Can you get one of your chums to run us there in a fast car? It could be quicker than hacking across to Liverpool Street and jumping a train.' Vignoles swept up his hat and scarf and patted his overcoat pockets as he shrugged it on to check he had his pipe and tobacco. 'I'll leave notice in case Lansdowne or Benson telephone in.

'The marks on his ankles are faint, but your interpretation is correct. Someone got hold of him by his ankles with his full body weight in force.' Vignoles stared at the body laid on a blanket in a store room at Stratford station, away from prying eyes. A forensic team had arrived at about the same time and the lead officer had offered his informed verdict. This chimed with the local doctor who'd first had sight of the body.

'The lack of anything in his pockets perhaps also indicates he was dangled upside down. And there are rubbing marks of rust and soot on his trousers consistent with coming into contact with a railway bridge parapet.'

'Mellor, you said his shop was unlocked and the lights on?'

'Yeah...' Mellor looked shaken. 'They heard he'd talked to us. They killed him because I got the lads to lean on him...'

'He died from severe blunt force trauma to the back of the skull. It would have been instantaneous.' The forensic talk continued whilst Mellor tried to take in the reality of the dead man before them.

'He struck the locomotive, rather than was struck first and then dropped over a bridge?' Vignoles queried.

'My initial findings suggest as much.' The forensic officer was careful with his words. 'There is evidence of oil and dirt around the wound and on his body that could have come from striking a locomotive. Once I do a full PM, I hope I might be able to give you a more accurate assessment. It might be worth getting the front of the engine checked over.'

Vignoles looked at Mellor who said this was being done. The DS was standing some distance away, smoking and listening and looking oddly discomfited. 'Payback...That's what this is. Kane and Abel are one step ahead of us.'

'But just one step. We are catching up.'

Smoke whistled from between Mellor's lips in a jet. 'Damn!'

'He was part of the underworld, Mellor. He knew the risks. Where was Slatter's home?'

'He lived above his shop on a back street called Grimsby Road, near Brick Lane. It's surrounded by railway. There's a cutting right outside his door and a bloody great viaduct in front of his bedroom window.'

'Start there. Look for fresh marks of rubbing on the parapets and get men on finger-tip searches below every bridge between his place and

Stratford. There's a chance we find whatever he had in his pockets...'

*   *   *   *

The men who had driven them to Stratford had been called away on urgent business, so Vignoles and Mellor were now being hauled back into the capital on a fast suburban stopping train hauled by a chunky N7 type tank engine that still bore the legend 'British Railways' in cream on the ageing black paintwork. Now liberally coated in a patina of London smut, railway grease and brake dust wiped into every crevice and corner, it presented a work-worn, but far from unloved sight. This dim echo of a colour scheme was like a time-travel machine back to 1948. The rolling stock it hauled was unique to the line, being wooden bodied and pre-war, consisting of four coaches mounted on three shared bogies to reduce weight. This was one of Sir Nigel Gresley's famous 'quad-art' sets and Vignoles was delighted to sample riding one for the first time. Designed for ferrying vast numbers of commuters in and out of Liverpool Street station they were built for speed and allowed rapid ingress at each platform. Not that either detective had much time to consider the finer points of the compartment they were seated in. They had plenty to discuss.

Vignoles was peering out of the window taking note of any bridges they dipped beneath whilst they talked. Mellor had telephoned Marylebone House before they departed Stratford and learned that both Benson and Lansdowne had news. As they returned to Liverpool Street, he passed on what he had learned. 'Benson works quickly...' Mellor sounded surprised. 'I didn't have her down as a detective, but she's done some decent work.'

Vignoles said nothing.

'I was sceptical she'd be able to handle everything you asked her to look into. Thought it too much for a girl, but as we've got our hands full, I let it go.'

'Very magnanimous, Mellor.'

'Not that I meant anything...'

'She's an excellent policewoman with the mind of a true detective. The sooner you appreciate that and learn to use her abilities, the better for us all. The same goes for WPC Lansdowne. Sermon over. What have they found for us?'

'Benson's traced the coach the Corrigan girl was found in. The case files included a set of photographs of the compartment and the outside of the coach. The photographer was thorough. She's got the coach number and compartment and even where the girl was seated.'

'Has she traced the present whereabouts of the coach?'

'Yes, and this is where it gets interesting. The rake was moved to Worcester Shrub Hill. It now works around that area and gets rostered for the extra race traffic to Stratford-Upon-Avon and Cheltenham...'

'Gable cleans stock on race days...'

'And said the coach needed a thorough clean and spent more time on it. Benson passed all this to Lansdowne who told me the firebrand looking after the cleaning girls keeps meticulous records and everything tallies.'

'As I thought she might.' Vignoles actually smiled. 'Then we can place Daisy Corrigan with a bag of gem stones in the same carriage Elsie Gable found 'The Hornet's Beauty'.'

'We can. We're waiting on Lucy reporting back from Gable, but...'

'We've found the link. The missing what-ever-it-was that underpinned the Palmer-Charlton murder case which eluded us at the time.'

'The cases are one and the same?'

'Only if we take the desire to own 'The Hornet's Beauty' as the root cause of the misery that followed. A gang leader with power and influence thinks the diamond is his. But it goes missing, as much through accident as design, but he can't know that, banged up in the Scrubs, and probably wouldn't care either way. He sends men to Leicestershire to track it down and collect. But they draw a blank despite some nasty attempts at persuasion. These two unsavoury characters then realise that another part of the Palmer family has done a runner with a significant haul of laundered money. This is Miss Rachel Corrigan, mother of Daisy. They presume Corrigan has taken the diamond as well. In fact, it's the little girl who's taken a bag of 'pretty stones' to play with. The perfect place for Corrigan's very dubious grandmother, Jane Palmer, who we now know was another fence to the underworld, to conceal the Hornet. Corrigan assumed this bag of sparkly stones were all paste, as might anyone, and let her daughter play with them to keep her quiet.'

'But these heavies take the girl?'

'As a bargaining chip to get Corrigan to offer the Hornet. But she can't. She has no idea what they want and hasn't got it. She swore blind she'd never heard of the Hornet - and we believed her.'

'Meanwhile the daughter was using it as a plaything...' Mellor shook his head in disbelief.

'One of the men snatches the bag and looks inside? They don't have magnifying glasses and watercolour paintings of the Hornet, but they see diamonds and other precious stones and assume it's in there?'

'I think so. However, in the most bizarre twist of fate, Daisy has inadvertently dropped the very stone everyone wants down the back of the seat cushion. Unaware of this, they leave Daisy as she is of no further use, step off the train and vanish...'

'Only to come back...Slatter's questions about the Hornet get back to this Kane and Abel who we now know have unfinished business.'

'There are blanks to fill, but we're close to squaring the circle.'

'Can we pin any of this on these thugs, even if we pull 'em in?'

'Not yet. There's work to be done. But we'll get them. Killing Slatter feels like an act prompted more by fear than logic. Slatter offered us their names and I think they're scared. We've rattled them because they know we're closing in.'

Mellor stared at Vignoles, his jaw muscles working. 'We'd best tread carefully...'

'Can you handle a gun?'

Chapter Thirty-Five

Badger had thrown over the use of his office, with its impressive view onto the train shed of Marylebone station, to the investigation.

'This is a council of war!' Badger somewhat melodramatically described it. Aside from Badger, Vignoles and Mellor, they had called in Allen, Mills and McAlistair from the Flying Squad and an unsmiling gentleman from Scotland Yard. His name was Grey, and he said nothing, barely managing a perfunctory nod as a greeting. He looked mildly bored, as if unconvinced of why he should be present at this hastily convened meeting. It was obvious the man from the Yard commanded respect even if he lacked the easy-going banter of the Flying Squad and Badger's overwhelming, if slightly pompous, self-confidence. Three senior members of the Transport Police based in London were also present, including Mellor's old boss, Inspector Howell from the Paddington division.

Mellor was trying not to show he was impressed by the turn out. It was rare for the Transport Police, unfairly perceived by their peers as one of the minor forces, could exert such influence. Many thought they did little else but chase pickpockets and escort prostitutes and drunks from waiting rooms and move animals from the line. DCI Vignoles ably assisted by CI Badger evidently pulled more weight than he'd imagined.

Vignoles was in full flow summarising why they'd convened the meeting. It was a complex series of events spanning a period of four months, but by the time he reached the death of Slatter, Mellor could see that even the dour Detective Inspector Grey was taking interest, or at least stopped twiddling with the cap on his cigarette lighter in a most irritating manner.

'DS Mellor and I have identified the bridge over which we believe Slatter was dropped. A short walk along a quiet street lined with poor shops and small warehouses on a foggy night, and everything closed up. We're not expecting witnesses. There is evidence to suggest he may have been dangled over the railway to get him to talk - or it was a straight-forward killing.'

'Not much straight-forward about that!' Allen observed.

'Perhaps not, but I suspect it was made to look like a suicide or an accident, although the marks on his ankles are a give away.' The low murmur suggested all agreed with his analysis.

'It was the work of perpetrators who know how to kill efficiently and have nerves of steel. We've found no evidential trace of their presence - as yet,' Vignoles looked towards Grey. 'Perhaps those more skilled in this area will discover something we have not... We need the evidence, but we already suspect Slatter was killed by two men who go under the pompous name of The Debt Collectors.'

Allen and Mills exchanged knowing nods of recognition. 'We've heard rumours for a few years but never been able to nail them. They're clever and careful to let nothing slip. However, Slatter told us they're called Kane and Abel after we persuaded him to talk.' There were more murmurs around the room. 'The names are funny, but their reputations are no laughing matter. It's possible Slatter had fallen out with these geezers and wanted a bit of payback so slipped us the names...'

'And equally possible The Debt Collectors found out and assassinated him,' Vignoles added. Another murmur of assent. 'What I'm interested in is following up all deaths on the railways throughout Greater London. Look at suicides, accidental deaths and especially the unexplained and unsolved. Discount anything categorically ruled as suicide or rail accidents with no whiff of suspicion. We want to identify other killings by The Debt Collectors. Start to make connections. We reckon they like the railway as the preferred location for their executions; exploiting the inherent danger, especially at night or in poor visibility to mask their murderous activities. In the Palmer-Charlton investigation there was the time-served platelayer who stumbled over a discarded shunter's pole in fog and was crushed by a row of wagons shunted in the yard. An accident, or was it a clever plan to make us believe so? He was a potential witness and long used to walking beside the line.'

'People like him develop a sixth sense and don't as a rule fall between moving wagons,' Inspector Howell nodded. 'Clever, but we in the railway business know different.'

'You reckon he was done over by the same pair as finished off Slatter?' Allen asked.

'It is possible. I'm looking for cases that appear explicable, but deep down you smell a rat but could never prove it. Cases where the investigating officer suspected foul play but there was nothing to lead to a name let alone a conviction.'

'How long back, sir?' It was the Transport Police sergeant.

'Let's say five years.' Mellor took over. He knew the man from his time at Paddington. 'It is a lot of work gents, but we need to see where else this pair have been working. We might make connections.'

'I can see what you're grabbing at, but people kill themselves all the time on the railways. It could be a lot of wasted work and for what?' Allen was starting to sound sceptical.

Grey surprised everyone by suddenly speaking up. 'What was the name of the body cut to pieces before Christmas? Over Waterloo way, on the third rail electric system?'

'Oh yeah.' Howell remembered. 'I heard. Fried first on the power rail. Right where it hurts most!'

Faces scrunched up as they imagined the pain.

'Then sliced and diced by a suburban set rolling over him.' It was a DS from the Southern Division of the Transport Police. 'It took us a few weeks to work out he was one Thomas Leach.'

'What was the outcome?' Vignoles asked.

'There was concern about the burns to his lower regions. Very nasty. They seemed to be targeted to cause maximum pain. Not what you'd expect from tripping and falling on the power rail.'

'You'd imagine defensive burns to the forearms, the side of his body, even a line across his face if he stumbled.' Howell observed.

'That was our thinking but there was nothing at the scene. Leach was a shady character and we suspected connections to gangland in London. But we drew blanks everywhere. We've left the case open.'

'We need to see the case files straight away.' Badger was interested. 'This is exactly what DCI Vignoles is seeking.'

'I'll get them sent straight over, sir!'

'Why was he wandering about near an electric rail, or any railway, for that matter?' Allen looked sceptical.

'We couldn't answer that at the time. He appeared respectable. He wasn't sleeping rough or a drunk who'd lost his way...'

'We'll make more enquiries about Leach...' Allen was intrigued

'Then all hands to the pumps. Gather everything as quick as possible. We'll review everything to see if they can be linked to common perpetrators.' Badger barked the orders. He believed in keeping meetings short.

'Send everything to Scotland Yard. I will assemble a team to review all case files. Get them to me by tomorrow at the latest. We cannot have two sadistic executioners throwing people off bridges and under trains.' Grey stood up. 'Gentlemen...' Without further ado, he left the room. It would appear the meeting was over. Badger looked mildly discomfited having not called the meeting to a close, but even he must defer to Scotland Yard.

Vignoles however, was pleased. Scotland Yard could bring their extensive resources to bear on what could be a lengthy process. The Yard would take the credit in the end, but he would take comfort knowing it had been their detective minds that had brought them to this significant juncture. Mellor and he would continue to gather information and analyse anything they found, but he suspected it was going to be something of a waiting game from now on.

However, unbeknown to everyone gathered in Badger's office, someone else was working equally hard to bring their own form of (rough) justice to bear on The Debt Collectors. The wait was going to be a short one.

Chapter Thirty-Six

'Goodnight, Jesse.' Lionel Beauchamp refrained from anything more than a handshake. Just smiles exchanged in the soft light of the hallway. Everything was less easy now the dangerous and judgmental world outside was made visible by the opened door. When the door was locked and heavy velvet curtains drawn closed, everyone felt secure enough to relax and do as they wished. But harsh reality was once again biting like the tingle on the throat and pressure in the lungs of the foetid London air filling the street.

Abel reached forward and tied Beauchamp's silken scarf more snugly around his neck. 'Don't want you to catch your death...'

'Thanks for a lovely evening. It was awfully fun!' Beauchamp stopped. This sounded trite. The proximity of the street made him shy.

Abel laughed. 'You are a dear. I just hope we lived up to expectations...' He raised an eyebrow.

'Of course!' Beauchamp turned away. He must hurry for the tube. He could not afford a cab and the walk was too long to contemplate. As he reached the gate, he glimpsed fingers waving a subtle goodbye as the door was closed.

He stopped and buttoned his duffle coat, then fished out a cigarette for the road. His face glowed in the flare of the match as he allowed himself a self-satisfied smile. It had been *quite* an evening. He was feeling giddy and foolish and perhaps a little guilty, in equal measures.

Beauchamp was a student in the London School of Economics, down to the 'Smoke' from sleepy Bedford and tentatively entering a very different and dangerously risqué world; one hitherto unknown and barely imagined. He started walking with a spring in his step and, unfortunately, not a care in the world. He should have remembered that there were forces on the street that didn't like men such as he.

The Teddy Boys looked menacing. Lithe and muscled with hair glossily slicked with generous applications of Brylcreem then combed into artfully sculpted 'duck's arse' flick-overs that glinted in the street light. Their suit jackets were long with garishly contrasting lapels, their trousers tightly straight-legged with deep turn ups and Crepe soled shoes that made no sound on their feet. Chains hung from waistcoat pockets, bootlace ties dangled from their necks like nooses. They wore heavy rings that could inflict damage to soft flesh. All were smoking and strutting in tight circles with a mix of nervous tension and bridled excitement, like so many jay birds under a park tree.

There was a fifth man, but he hung back in the shadows. Older and dressed soberly in a dark coat and suit and the brim of his Fedora obscuring much of his face. He held no desire to become a 'New Edwardian.' This craze stalking London and causing newspaper editors to fill extensive column inches on the 'degenerate youth of today' was of little interest aside from the knowledge that a small section of these 'Teds' had aggressive tendencies that could be encouraged and channelled for his own particular use. Their dandyish 'clobber' was expensive to have tailored and these street fighting lads always needed a few extra pounds in their pockets. This hunger for money combined with the boiling energy of frustration and anger towards a strait-laced society they wished to rebel against was just waiting to be vented. And he had the perfect excuse to stoke their prejudices before unleashing their ill-formed rage at a society they believed rejected them in return for a fistful of 'readies.'

He was using these flashy, but intellectually unimaginative, Teds as pawns in a clever game of strategy against canny and dangerous men. A pair of professionals at the top of their game. Cruel and merciless, they demanded extreme caution. A mistake would be fatal. But these two had moved in and taken something from right under his nose! They'd even killed the old cove who was supposed to have it. He spat on the pavement in disgust. If that was not bad enough, they'd killed Ernie. Slatter was a crabby old sod but fundamentally decent - for a crook. Ernie would have seen him right if he'd got his mitts on that bloody diamond first... No, killing the little man was just nasty and uncalled for. Well out of order. It was time someone put a stop to their antics. But he was no fool and had taken the time to research his enemy, just as a general might, waiting until he spotted a weakness. So now he was going to drive a wedge into that fault line and burst it wide open.

The indirect approach was a nice touch. Nobody, not even Jesse Abel with his pathetic monocle and disgusting scented cigarettes would suspect that what was about to unfold was carefully stage-managed. The police would assume it was just a bunch of yobs doing over a ponce for vicarious fun before running off into the dark with his wallet. Taken on face value, it was a typical night time occurrence. But it would have ramifications...

He noticed the twitch of a net curtain across the road. Eyes were watching as he had hoped they might, but just far enough away to make identification of individual faces close to impossible on a smoggy night. He heard a front door close. Saw the tiny flare of a match.

'That's him. Hurt him so he drops, but no more! We need the cops here and the lad blabbing.'

'Got it...'

He gave the command for 'action' then stepped into the shadows and allowed the story to unfold.

They carried concealed knives and lengths of chain, but these would remain unused. Tonight, they only needed the hate in their hearts. Two minutes of crazed punching and kicking and Beauchamp was left bleeding in the suburban gutter. His head resting prone against the skeletal trunk of a sad London plane tree, like a figure from a Caravaggio altarpiece with badly cut eyes, a split lip and a broken nose. Blood made artful trails down his face. He moaned and shivered. His insides were screaming with the bruising.

Mrs Lawless, despite her ironically inappropriate name, fretted constantly about the type of people in her street. She was a naturally nosey and suspicious sort who spent much of her waking hours (and she slept fitfully for only a few hours each night) observing her neighbours and making it her business to know everything she could about each of them. Invariably, some fell short of her demanding ideal; she could find fault in the clothes they wore, their choice of hat or handbag, an untrimmed hedge, the inferior marque of car some elected to purchase and (horrors!) net curtains that did not meet her expectation that such essential aids to the inquisitive also be blinding white, despite the ravages of the polluted air.

She had been harbouring concerns about the single gentleman who lived opposite for some months. Mr Abel was always immaculately dressed and his shirts were starched and pressed to standard that met with reluctant approval. However, his choice of pale suiting was unconventional and whilst visibly made-to-measure by a gentleman's outfitters of superior quality, there was something about the whole ensemble that offended her deeply conservative eye. A sober charcoal or a dependable black would be so much better. Even dark navy... And then there was the monocle. A throw-back to pre-war days and although not in itself a *crime,* of course, when taken with everything else it lent the man a dangerously dandyish air. Her husband would never have approved. Lionel was long dead, but he had been a strict follower of convention, always wearing the obligatory striped trousers, morning top coat, bowler and armed with a tightly furled umbrella, all essentials that came with being 'in the City'. A stockbroker all his life, Lionel Lawless had known how to present himself in a manner that ensured everyone understood his standing in society. He'd had no time for foppish types. He'd once told his wife in the build-up to the Munich crisis that 'this type were a security risk' and would gladly see them all sent for incarceration on the Isle of Man for the duration of the war. Or longer. Mrs Lawless had (silently) considered this excessively draconian, but nonetheless developed, and retained, a suspicion about men who didn't exactly conform to accepted social mores.

However, despite the silent voice of the long-departed Lionel in her ear, she could not fault the manners of Mr Abel, nor indeed his impeccable pronunciation. She did like a man who enunciated clearly and not mangle the English language like so many did in the working-class districts. What did put Lawless in a fractious tizzy, were all those young men who came to visit on one of Mr Abel's Bridge evenings...

'Bridge! Twelve men regularly playing Bridge and never any ladies to partner? Did that mean the men always paired off? She made the idea sound almost sinful. Mr Abel never asked anyone on the road to join them. Not that she played Bridge nor had any desire to learn. It was the principle! There was something exclusive about the set up that had her nose twitching. Her mistrust of anyone outside the Darby & Joan Club kept her awake and always ready to peek between her front room curtains.

Her worst fears and imaginings were now being fulfilled. Lawless watched in mute horror, one hand held to her opened mouth, inhaling in sharp noisy breaths as each hard punch was thrown or kick viciously administered. Her hand was on the telephone the moment the thugs ran off, laughing. It was fortunate she'd had the GPO move the telephone into her front sitting room so she need not go into the hall. Whilst speaking with the Police desk sergeant she stared at the crumpled figure of Beauchamp, who looked like a marionette with cut strings, her expression communicating outrage that such a ghastly act could have taken place on *her* road rather than compassion for the injured man.

Beauchamp had hauled himself into a sitting position against the tree, legs splayed out in front, arms hanging limply at his side as the blood soaked into his scarf and coat started to congeal and turn dark. He was shivering and losing consciousness, too weak to call for help.

The Flying Squad Jaguar car screeched to a halt and the throaty engine stilled. A ringing bell could be heard a few streets away. The ambulance would soon be there. Beauchamp would live, but he would need time to recover from the shock before the police could hope to get much more from him than mumbled words, thick with blood and a broken tooth. As soon as the injured man was in the hands of the ambulance crew, they would start canvassing the street for witnesses.

The nosey neighbour who'd placed the call was first on their list and whilst waiting for her to answer their knock they noticed her parlour windows had curtains parted an inch or two, but no light on. Perfect for watching unobserved.

Mrs Lawless gave passable descriptions of the assailants as 'those awful Teddy Boys in their garish clothes and quite ridiculous haircuts,' but when pressed further, it was clear that in her eyes, 'one looked much the same as another.' They would put out a search for four men meeting this general description and with a bit of luck they might round up likely suspects. Mrs Lawless went on to describe the victim's actions just prior to the attack. She was at least clear from whence he'd come and not reticent in voicing her concerns, even if not obviously relevant to the crime. She had little empathy with Beauchamp, who was now being lifted into the back of the ambulance.

'A house party. Once a month Mr Abel has these gatherings. They claim to play *cards*.' She managed to make the activity sound salacious and her voice heavy with implied meaning. Much nodding of her head. The Flying Squad were eager to move on, this was not going to help catch the four men responsible. The ambulance was now departing with the as yet unnamed man, so it made sense to enquire at the house party. They should be able to at least ascertain a name and address. The old lady was starting to become annoying, repeating herself without offering any new information so this was the perfect excuse to cut short her list of imagined wrong-doings behind the oaken door of the substantial residence opposite. The house in question was well-maintained with a neat front garden and exude a feeling of genteel wealth and solidity. They expected the oaken door to be opened by the well-to-do parent of the young man.

'Got some friends over to play a few hands of poker, I reckon.'

'Nuffin' wrong with that...'

'I sometimes do the same...'

They did not expect the smell of Indian incense and marujana that hit them as an effete man dressed in a Paisley patterned smoking jacket cautiously opened the door. There was the sound of quiet laughter from another room. As Jesse Abel enquired, 'How might I help?' with a note of caution in his voice, a young man, naked to the waist appeared at another door across the hall...

Chapter Thirty-Seven

The secretive and carefully controlled world of The Debt Collectors started to unravel with surprising speed. What started as an innocent door knock, rapidly escalated into a suspicion that drugs were being smoked and an uneasy sense that this all-male gathering in the salubrious suburban house was not quite the innocent bridge party it claimed to be. Mrs Lawless had a good instinct for trouble. When the two officers from the Sweeney stepped inside, ignoring the protestations of Abel, they noticed some of the men looked like they had dressed very quickly, with the odd button unfastened and ties askew, all wearing expressions that varied between surprise, alarm and jaw-clenched fear. The man without a shirt claimed he had spilled red wine on his and was washing it out in the bathroom, but this was quickly proven to be a lie despite a ham-fisted attempt to retrieve his shirt and appropriately stain it. If they were prepared to chance being caught in the act of lying about a wine stain, then there was something wrong.

The Flying Squad were occupied trying to trace the gang of Teddy Boys who'd battered Beauchamp, but another squad car was soon summoned, followed by a 'Black Maria' van with more uniformed officers and soon eight party goers were herded inside and sent to the local police station for questioning. Jesse Abel, the house owner, demanded his lawyer be called, but to no avail. He too was driven away. The police might not have a warrant to search the premises, but with everyone on the way to the local nick and a strong suspicion that illegal activities had been taking place, the opportunity was seized to collect evidence. Several partially smoked 'reefers' were discovered, and a number of beds were rumpled as if recently used, but all this rapidly paled into insignificance when an alarming discovery was made.

A young constable called his superiors into the master bedroom, where he had found a large leather doctor's bag and various curious implements and weapons tucked inside a heavy wardrobe.

'He likes knives...'

'Are these daggers?'

'They're very thin. Nasty looking things. They'd do you a lot of harm...'

'What's in the bag?'

'Gauntlets... Made of rubber and heavy-duty. For industrial use, I reckon. And electric cables with hefty clips on each end. I reckon these could be used to kick-start a tank...'

'Do tanks get flat batteries?'

'Here! Look...' A small box was opened to reveal a set of blades and a surgeon's scalpel. 'Why would you have these and gauntlets and jump leads...'

'Is that a pass for the races? The Gold Cup...He'd hardly need all this having a flutter on the horses?'

'Is he a vet?'

'Nah. There's something wrong about this. Right, get everything bagged up and down the station. I'm calling in the forensic boys. And Scotland Yard.'

Chapter Thirty-Eight

Vignoles was back in his familiar office at Leicester Central.

It was good to get his feet under his trusty desk, even if it was uncharacteristically tidy thanks to the efforts of Mellor who liked everything signed, sealed, posted or filed in its proper place. Much as Badger had promised, Mellor would take on any amount of this routine work and have it processed in the time Vignoles had taken to smoke his second pipe of the day. It perhaps edged towards insubordination for his DS to enter his office and clear his desk, but that aside, it was not a bad arrangement. It gave him more time for what he considered really mattered: serious, concerted thinking time; time to process situations and consider implications and possible stratagems and solutions...

However, at this moment he was contemplating the ageless and rather gorgeous form of the 1930s Spelter figurine of a scantily dressed female dancer that had resided on his desk since the spring of 1946. Mellor had better keep his hands off her. Come to think of it, there was a passing resemblance to Miss Jephson... Not that Vignoles had seen her dancing topless of course...It was perhaps a good thing Mellor was no longer in Gloucestershire, as Vignoles suspected his laddish detective sergeant had been warming to the idea of taking the poor girl out.

He was snapped out of this reverie by the arrival of Mellor himself, striding confidently into the office with barely a knock. 'Sir! Scotland Yard have let us get a look at the stuff hauled in from that pansy, Jesse Abel.' He handed over a sheaf of photographic prints.

'A ticket for the Gold Cup Festival.' Vignoles nodded appreciatively. 'The day Money For Nothing ran...'

'Spot on! Abel was there same time as Buckrose-Grinal. Kane as well, I bet you. They met at the races, Abel or Kane handed over that card from Slatter, then they set up the meeting at the burial mound.'

Vignoles nodded agreement. 'It is a lot to assume from one race ticket though.'

'Wait, there's more... They've found all kinds of knives and weapons and surgical scalpels and even a pair of long thin knives. They're Italian or Sicilian...' He passed across some prints.

'Stillettos. The heels of the shoes Anna likes are reminiscent... They make small incisions but can reach deep inside to pierce vital organs. The knives, not Anna's shoes.'

Mellor grinned.

Vignoles studied the prints. 'Something similar killed Buckrose-Grinal. Remember those incisions all over his body?'

'How could I forget? I'll get them to send the stilettos across to forensics and show them to the pathologist who looked the corpse over.'

'Do so. Have you got a photograph of this Abel?'

Mellor looked pleased. The news about the race ticket and possible weapon match had gone down well with his new boss, now he was about to deliver the *piece de la resistance*. 'Look at this!'

Vignoles stared at a photograph removed from Jesse Abel's house, then without saying anything turned to his desk and picked up the original drawing by Miss Marjorie Wolfe. 'It's close enough...A passing resemblance, and when taken with the stilettos and Gold Cup ticket. It could be a match.'

'It must be the same man, sir! And how many Abel's are there in London? How many with knives that shape who go the Gold Cup? He's got to be one half of The Debt Collectors. We need to show Knight the photograph.'

'Get down there immediately. I'll talk to Badger and make sure Scotland Yard know Jesse Abel is one of our suspects. He's safer in a cell than on the street.'

'Surely he wouldn't try anything after being grilled for a day in the nick?'

'For his own protection, Mellor. There are people out there terrified he'll squawk. We need him in court to stand judgement for his crimes, so we need to protect him before someone slits his throat or puts a bullet in his back.'

'His accomplice is roaming free...'

'Watch your back. Have you got the service revolver they issued you?'

'I do.'

'Give it to Lansdowne.'

'Sorry?'

'She won a bronze in the London Olympics as a pistol shot. She'll handle it better than both of us together. That's an order.'

Mellor just gave a short nod of acceptance with a look of stunned shock on his face.

'Once you've confirmed Abel with Knight, I want you both straight back here.'

Chapter Thirty-Nine

Mellor and Lansdowne were at Broadway station. Knight was on duty in the ticket office and professed to be pleased to see them back at his little glass window. 'You have news?'

'News is for newspapers,' Mellor responded. He was still smarting from having handed over the pistol and a box of shells to WPC Lansdowne. On the trip down, when alone in his compartment he'd felt good feeling the weight of the ominous black firearm in his hand with its mysteriously menacing smell of oil and cordite and he'd started to believe he was the equal of any hard-boiled man from The Sweeney cruising the streets of London in a big car with a loaded gun tucked inside his coat. But Vignoles had made it an order and Lansdowne, when pushed, had confessed she 'knew how to handle it.' He'd watched in fascination as she'd cracked the firearm open, inspected it, cleaned various parts then made a trial loading of a shell.

'It needed that, Sarge. It was filthy. Just from lack of use. I doubt this has seen action in years.' She gave Mellor a serious look. 'Failure to inspect and clean a firearm is likely to result in killing yourself, not your target.'

'It is?'

'Many felons don't have a clue. The gun jams and blows their hand off - if they're lucky. Or it blinds them. Or both.' She gave a sweet smile.

Mellor whistled. He'd no idea. Still, it didn't feel right that a junior rank, and a blonde pony-tailed girl at that, was carrying the shooter. He just prayed it wasn't needed so he didn't have to suffer the indignity.

'Mr Knight. Take a look at this photograph. Do you recognise this man?' Mellor leaned down to speak through the window.

'Yes, that's the man who was trying to book a space in the horse dock. The one who said he worked for that Lord Buckrose.'

'You are quite sure?'

'Absolutely. But what's the story about Lord Buckrose, Sergeant? It said in the paper he'd been found dead! It sounded unpleasant, although the papers were a bit cagey about the specific details. Suspicious circumstances they said, and that got me wondering...'

'I cannot discuss an active case. Have you seen the man in the photograph anywhere else at any other time?'

'No...He never came back. I went to the trouble to call my chum in Winchcombe and get him to...Oh, but... you don't think he killed Mr Krast?'

'Thank you Mr Knight.' Mellor touched the brim of his hat. He stood up and addressed Lansdowne. 'We'll show the picture to the others working here. See if it jogs memories.'

WPC Lansdowne had been listening to the exchange. 'I could ask at those houses out the front. They look onto the forecourt and someone inside might have got a good view.'

'Do so.' Mellor strode off to find the stationmaster.

A boy was just leaving one of the semi-detached houses as Lansdowne approached, a burst football under his arm. 'Oh dear, that's been in the wars!' She smiled sweetly.

'A train ran over it.'

'No wonder it's a mess.'

'I managed to get it back into shape and stuffed it full of newspapers. It won't bounce.' He demonstrated. It fell with a dull slap on the ground and didn't move. 'Dad says I can't get another until my birthday.'

'When's that?'

'July. Worst luck.' He picked up the ball and looked at it sadly, then suddenly gave Lansdowne an angry look. 'Are you another policeman?'

'A police*woman*.' She laughed.

'Are you going to buy me a new one?'

'Why would I do that young man?'

'Because that policeman kicked mine on the track. It was his fault. He ruined it!'

'A policeman did that?' Lansdowne was surprised.

'Yes. He had a dark blue hat and suit and a scar on his face and blue eyes like a jackdaw. He kicked the ball right over the station!' The boy was angry.

'When was this?'

'Wednesday last'

'A scar on his face?' Lansdowne was puzzled. 'How do you know he was a detective?'

'Told me.'

This did not match Vignoles or Mellor, and neither were likely to deliberately damage a young boy's football. 'Was he a local policeman?'

'Never seen him before.'

'Well, I'll jolly well give him a piece of my mind when I find him!' She kept her voice light.

'Oh...' The boy now looked worried and unhappy to hear the fierce detective was going to be challenged. 'But I never said nothing! Honest. He said I mustn't say a word and Scout's Honour I never!'

'Tell who about what?'

'About what happened when that man was killed. About the men in the car.'

'You saw men in a car on the evening Mr Krast was attacked?'

He nodded as if scared to say it aloud.

'Now listen. I don't know who this man was, but I am a police officer and my detective sergeant is inside the station building. We can prove who we are.' She pulled out her warrant card. 'We are railway police.' Lansdowne hoped this might sound more appealing to a boy who had grown up in the shadow of the station. 'It is very important you tell me what you saw, and don't worry about anything that other man might have said. '

The boy's eyes widened. A mixture of fear and excitement taking hold.

'You won't get into trouble I promise - and we might even be able to get you a new ball.'

That sold it. 'They stopped right outside. Two men got out and went to the station for about ten minutes, then they came back and drove off.'

'Have you seen this man?' Lansdowne showed the boy the photograph of Abel.

'That's him. He was driving. The other was in black and I didn't see his face at all.'

'Was this the man who told you not to tell anyone? The man who kicked your ball?'

'No! He was a detective like I said...'

'Oh.' Lansdowne was puzzled. 'Have you seen this detective with the scar again since then?'

'Of course! He was here about half an hour ago. I thought he was with you...'

'Here, just now?'

'I was up in my bedroom...' He indicated which one. 'I saw him outside. He stared at the house and looked angry. I was nervous and kept my head down and made sure he didn't see me. Then he went to buy a ticket.'

'Sarge!' Mellor had just reappeared at the gateway leading from the platform. 'We've got something!'

Chapter Forty

Kane flung himself down on the carriage seat and stared out of the window. What to do? He was on his own now and trying to plan a strategy to stay alive with little information to work on.

Abel was in a cell, and Kane could be sure that the police were not going to go soft on Jesse. They may resort to violence. It was not uncommon for prisoners to be badly bruised by the time charges were pressed. The question was, how long would his partner hold out? Abel was tougher than he looked, but everyone had their limit.

The trouble was that Kane had not discovered why his partner was under arrest. There was talk of a raid on the house whist Abel was having one of his infamous parties. Kane angrily lit a cigarette, making his lighter snap shut with a sharp click as a manifestation of his pent-up frustration. Things could be worse. There was every chance Abel would be released on bail and hauled up before a beak on charges of indecency or something similar. It would be inconvenient, but manageable.

But what if the police had searched his house and found his equipment...

A cloud of smoke and steam enveloped the carriage window like a temporary fog. He was flying in the dark. Out on a limb and unsure just how serious the threat was. Being out of town had probably been a wise move, albeit a fruitless one. Kane had travelled back to Broadway and Cheltenham in the hope of establishing who had muscled in on their debt recovery scheme. Kane still had 'The Hornet's Beauty', safely tucked in his jacket pocket, which was the one good piece of news, but it was becoming obvious that Slatter had been double-crossing them.

Slatter had put someone else on to Krast and whoever this upstart was, he'd entered Krast's shop on the Sunday night. They'd found nothing for their trouble but had put Krast on his guard. Kane had suspected as much when he'd throttled the old man. He had clutched at the strong hands slowly crushing his windpipe and when allowed to gasp a few words, accused Kane of being in the shop safe. The old man even managed a last triumphant accusation that 'he'd not find it there!' Just a futile attempt to spare his life, or at least, that was what Kane had tried to convince himself at the time, but it looked as though someone really had beaten them to it. His investigations had drawn a blank however, not aided by Krast's shop and house still being guarded by constables on sentry duty.

And then there was that pesky boy... He should have wrung his bloody neck! But there had been no sight of the lad and too many people milling around the station so he'd no choice but to admit defeat and return home. A loose end...

He'd collect some things together and find himself new digs a long way from Ealing. He needed to lay low and gather information and establish what the threat level was then plan how to realise a decent return on the little stone in his pocket...

*   *   *   *

'He's just gone this last twenty minutes. He stuck in my mind because he wanted a ticket to Broadway - *Ealing* Broadway!' Knight laughed.

'West London...' Mellor looked at Lansdowne as if for confirmation. 'Not far from Abel's neck of the woods.' He turned back to Knight. 'Did this man have a scar on his face?'

'Yes. He looked like an ex-soldier as he was wearing a regimental tie. Commando if I am not mistaken and had a Southern accent.'

'It could be him... What connection is he getting in Bristol? Quick, get a timetable! We need to catch him up!'

Knight reached for the Bradshaw, but it was obvious this was superfluous. He knew the timings of the main connections by heart. 'I've got it all in here.' Knight tapped the side of his head with his other hand. 'If you have a car you can get to Cheltenham Malvern Road in time and hop on his train there.'

'Wilcox! We need your car!' Sergeant Wilcox had been hanging back, not wanting to intrude on a case that no longer fell within his remit. A speedy drive to Cheltenham was an unexpected request, but he was happy to oblige.

'Glad I was in civvies,' Lansdowne adjusted the collar of her coat.

They were anxiously waiting the imminent arrival of the train to Bristol that should also have the man Mellor was now convinced was Kane, onboard. 'Yeah...' Mellor dragged on a fag. 'We board the train acting like man and wife and keep our heads down. We mustn't spook him, so no silly stuff!'

Lansdowne was miffed by his comment, but dutifully remained silent, wondering if using the pistol presently weighing down her shoulder bag constituted 'silly stuff.'

'We let him change trains and board an adjacent carriage. Don't let him catch you looking his way. He must not clock we're on to him.' Lansdowne patiently listened to Mellor's commands and refrained from mentioning that she'd gained over ten years of experience and knew how to handle the situation. 'The guvnor will have a welcoming party ready at Ealing Broadway. When we're close to Ealing, we close in so he can only exit through the one door.'

Lansdowne nodded understanding.

* * * *

Vignoles and Benson were on their way from Leicester to Marylebone, where they would cross over to Paddington and thence to Ealing Broadway. The phone call from stationmaster Roberts had set many wheels into motion. Badger was busy pulling strings like a puppet master, Scotland Yard were on full alert and the Flying Squad already in place accompanied by a handful of Transport Police constables, although all were under instructions not to present an obvious visible presence. The trap was set.

Vignoles was willing their train on, reassured that he was in the agile hands of one of Sir Nigel Gresley's 'racehorses of the rails', A3 pacific Number 60107 'Royal Lancer', with a local Leicester Central crew who promised to coax the best out of their top-link steed to make a spirited dash to the capital (signals allowing...).

* * * *

Kane was snoozing as his London-bound train rocked him gently. The stress and strains of the past week were catching up. At first, he'd chain smoked and paced the corridor in an aid to remaining awake and alert, but eventually succumbed to leaning against the corner seat in a compartment with his hat tipped over his eyes and allowed himself the indulgence of closing his eyes. Waves of drowsiness washed over him. *Don't sleep... must plan next moves...*

A jolt and momentarily opened heavy lidded eyes.

The train just passed Didcot...miles before Ealing. Just a short nap...

His breath slowed and hands relaxed as the warmth of a pleasantly steam-heated compartment lulled him asleep.

Kane's dreams were confused, coloured by the sound of wailing whistles and huffing trains, screaming men falling from bridges - or was he doing the falling? Blood, knives and violent sparks of electricity flashing from the end of a cigarette Abel was smoking, whilst grinning like a madman... Policemen in uniform were marching towards him...along the narrow corridor and sliding the door open. Silver buttons on their uniforms, razor sharp creases in their trousers, truncheons at the ready...

He sat up and hastily pushed his hat back into place. He blinked the sleep and sense of disorientation from his eyes.

He was no longer alone. Four Teddy Boys were sharing the compartment. Two seated opposite, one close beside him and the fourth standing with his back to the compartment door that was closed. The train was restarting and turning to look out of the window Kane watched a running in board slide past that declared they were leaving Southall. Damnit! So close to home and he'd allowed himself to be hemmed in by these yobs. The sense of menace was thick in the air, like the blue cigarette smoke curling from their lighted cigarettes.

The Ted seated opposite was leaning forward, elbows on his drainpipe trouser clad knees, his face unpleasantly close in the narrow compartment. He was deliberately blowing streams of smoke into Kane's face, challenging him to react. His friend, dressed in an emerald green drape coat with a black velvet collar was lounging back in his seat, one leg crossed over the other to reveal a blue suede shoe with a thick sole.

'Smoke not annoying you, grandad?'

Kane remained silent, trying not to blink despite the acrid smoke. He stared back at the man with the long side burns and impressively combed and greased hair. He was dressed outrageously in magenta and black and a good twenty years younger than Kane. They were all much younger, but each looked like they could handle themselves. Four were too many, and in a cramped space he had no chance. The man leaning against the compartment door was idly allowing a vile looking switch blade to slide out of its casing, before pushing it back into place. Over and over, he repeated the action.

A bony elbow jabbed into him. 'Want a fag?' The man grinned and proffered a crumpled pack of Navy Cut.

'No. Thanks all the same.' They were in a mean enough mood already.

'Nice tie.' It was said with heavy sarcasm. The Teds all laughed.

'Army is that?' The slouching Ted in green made a mocking salute. 'Stand by your beds! Ready for inspection!' More laughter.

The train rocked and rolled onwards. Not far to go. Kane just had to keep the aggression under control a while longer. He took in each face and memorised them. Not now, but one day, when the odds were favourable and he wasn't blocked in a corner he would give them pay back. He felt a trace of smile form on his lips as he imagined the hurt he'd cause each of these arrogant peacocks. Upstarts! Dumb kids with too much money and a bad attitude, but he suspected they had no proper street-fighting skills. They could kick and lash out as a group, but they didn't have the skills to take him on down a back alley. One or even two at a time... He'd show 'em!

'What you so pleased about?' The leaning Ted spat the words out. 'Find us funny, grandad?'

'Hair too long for you, *Army* boy?'

A chain clinked. Fingers drummed impatiently on the moquette.

'Where you gettin' out, old man?' The standing man didn't look in a hurry to slide the compartment door open.

'I don't see that's any of your business.' Kane kept his voice flat.

The man next to him pushed his face close to Kane's. His breath stank of beer and his teeth were rotten. 'He asked you a question. Tell him - or I knife yer!'

Kane's mouth was dry. If the fist now pressing too hard against his kidney contained a flick knife, he was in trouble. It might not be fatal if the blade was short, but he'd lose a lot of blood...

The lounging Ted flicked his still burning cigarette through the air so that it landed on Kane's trouser leg and instantly started to burn the fabric. He flicked it away impatiently.

'Hand it over or the blade goes in...' The voice hissed in his ear.

Kane said nothing. Ok, it was just money they wanted. Robbery with menace and all dressed like peacocks. In a busy train and broad daylight. He had to admire their bare-faced cheek.

* * * *

Mellor and Lansdowne walked cautiously along the corridor. They knew which coach Kane was in, but not the compartment. It was time to get into position ready for the imminent stop at Ealing Broadway. Mellor had a strange tingling sensation of unease coursing through his body. He'd seen the four Teddy Boys board the train at Southall and noticed they had chosen the same carriage Kane was in. It was happenstance surely? How could they know Kane was there? But he'd read the reports on the arrest of Abel and the beating the student had taken by four Teds. It felt too coincidental for comfort.

'The shooter...?'

'I'll take the safety catch off, but...' Lansdowne sounded concerned.

'Those Teds look trouble. A warning shot will sort 'em out!'

'On a busy train, Sarge? It could go through a compartment and injure an innocent passenger.'

'Yeah...I guess so,' Mellor winced at his own idiocy. 'The threat alone should be enough.' They were minutes from Ealing. With back up on the station they might be able to control the situation just by showing they had a weapon.

* * * *

Vignoles and Benson were waiting. Dressed in civvies and looking like passengers, they could afford to stand on the platform the train was due in. Two Flying Squad also pretending to be waiting passengers were positioned in front and behind, with all the uniforms out of sight on the covered footbridge or inside an office. The presence of the constables was drawing some attention from the steadily increasing numbers of passengers assembling. Vignoles had forgotten just how busy London stations could get and their sight lines were constantly being compromised by more and more people pressing down on to the platform. Nobody would be able to move swiftly with so many people and their all their hand bags, brief cases and other luggage acting like a veritable forest of tank traps to impede the progress of the police. It was going to be a nervy few minutes as they tried to confront and remove Kane from the station with the minimum of fuss. It was best not to consider the possibility Kane was carrying a firearm and willing to use it.

*　　*　　*　　*

'If you will excuse me?' Kane was speaking through gritted teeth. He stood up, a movement not easy to accomplish with these idiots crowding him. He trusted his move to stand as they approached Ealing Broadway would be enough to stay the itchy fingers on the safety catch of the flick knife. He swayed and had to steady himself as the man opposite also tried to stand, but there was no room.

'My station!'

'Ours too.' The Ted guarding the door spoke with an unsettling sense of eager anticipation in his voice.

'Oy, make room for the gent! He wants to get off!' The lounging one pulled his friend's drape coat tails and made him drop back into the seat.

Kane pushed past the legs and suede shoes only remembering to grab his holdall from the luggage rack at the last moment. The other three stood up once he passed and again these strange gaudy creatures smelling of beer and Brylcreem and sweat crowded in on him. Their false bonhomie didn't fool Kane. He sensed they actually wanted him to get off at Ealing. The gate guardian slid the door open and stepped into the corridor, bumping into a man and a woman about to walk past the door. Without an apology, he extravagantly indicated that Kane step into the corridor with a mocking grin between his carefully sculpted sideburns. Kane observed the station rolling past the carriage window. The platform was busy. Could he duck and weave through the crowd and shake them off?

He felt something hard and metallic press against the small of his back. 'Hand it over...' A voice hissed in his ear. 'Now...'

'My wallet is in my bag...' He walked forwards hoping to pull away from the blade waiting to pierce his skin. The train brakes were squealing. He reached the outside door and hauled the window down. The hard shape was pressing harder into his spine, now meeting bone and starting to hurt. He felt anger swelling inside. He'd like nothing better than to slit this bastard's throat...

'Give it, or I slice yer.'

'Let me get on the platform and take that bloody knife out of my back!'

'We don't want your money...'

The door swung open before the train had completely stopped, the momentum making it fly wide and it narrowly missed striking a woman who managed to step backwards in time to save her nose. Kane leaped into the space she vacated and as he did so, twisted around and slammed his holdall into the hand with the knife. He'd bought himself a few seconds, but in the time it took to regain his footing after colliding with a man waiting to board, the Teddy boys were already piling out of the carriage. The waiting passengers gave cries of dismay or alarm and pulled away, creating a rapidly expanding semi-circle of space. Kane reached into his coat pocket and pulled out a pistol, but before he could level it, a length of motorbike chain whistled through the air and struck his forearm, one end wrapping around with a nasty wrench. He winced with the pain but managed to retain his grasp on the gun.

The red draped Ted landed a haymaker of a punch on the side of Kane's head, but he rode it, ducked, then lashed upwards with his pistol hand, striking the chain thrower full force in the throat. The gun barrel didn't pierce the skin, but the man made a horrible strangulated howl and fell to the floor clutching his neck, mouth opening and closing as he gasped for air.

'Hands above your heads! All of you!' Kane yelled at full voice. He levelled the gun and started to swing it from one Ted to another.

Vignoles watched in mute horror. He was unarmed and rightly wary of the gun in Kane's hand. He could see Lansdowne standing in the open carriage doorway with her own pistol held with both hands and a look of complete stillness and concentration on her face. But she could not discharge a firearm in this crowded place whilst the three Teddy boys still standing were circling Kane, lashing out with switch blades flashing in the late afternoon light. Kane fired a shot that made ears ring with the explosion. The shot struck the ground beside one of the flashy shoes of the Teddy boy in green, stopping him in his tracks. The crowd of onlookers started to run in a mad howling frenzy, colliding with the uniformed police coming in the opposite direction.

The platform was, mercifully, emptying at least. Kane was standing quite still now, breathing hard, his gun hand not quite steady, but enough at this short distance to draw a bead on a potential target. He was holding the side of his body, blood oozing between his fingers. A knife had struck home.

'It's over Kane! Drop the gun!' Vignoles called out.

'Run lads!' One of the Teds yelled, his face pale with fear, and without waiting to see if his friends were following, made a dash for the footbridge only to be manhandled to the ground by a burly constable, face pressed into the concrete whilst a knee rested in the small of his back.

'Stay where you are! All of you! Don't run!' Kane cautioned. 'Or I'll shoot you!'

The two standing Teds were backing up against the train, their injured colleague in obvious distress on the ground, twitching his legs whilst his lips started to turn blue.

'You back off!' Kane levelled his gun first at Mellor, then Vignoles, then a young constable.

'There's nowhere to run. You don't have enough bullets to stop us all. Put the gun down...' Vignoles urged.

'I know how to handle this!' He waggled the barrel menacingly and Mellor froze. Kane's face was going pale, but his eyes were filled with fury. Bright drops of blood splashed on the platform.

Vignoles could see Lansdowne tracking Kane with her own gun, but worryingly both he and one of the Flying Squad were in the firing line, with Kane between them. She could do nothing, and Kane knew it.

'Put it down lady or one of these takes a bullet. I mean it! Now!'

'Do as he says, Lucy!' Vignoles ordered.

Lansdowne slowly placed the gun on the floor of the carriage then stood up again.

Kane laughed. 'I can handle all of you! Come on! Who's big enough to take me on now eh?' The gun moved around the semi-circle of stationary police officers, taunting each in turn. Nobody moved a muscle. The sound of stampeding feet and more distant shouts and screams of fear, started to diminish. The station was starting to fall quiet with a tense, uneasy feeling of watching and waiting.

'You've got five bullets left. You can't shoot your way out of this.' Vignoles called out.

'That's five more dead than you want!' He pointed the gun towards Lansdowne. 'Shall I take her first?' He suddenly swung the gun at Benson. 'Or what about her?' He pulled a strange expression, half grimace, half smile. The blood was flowing freely. 'Do as I say, back off and let me through or the pretty girl gets it!'

'You're going nowhere. Abel blabbed everything. We've got you both for three murders!' The high-ranking Scotland Yard officer yelled.

'You're lying!' Kane twitched the gun and fired, but the bullet only ripped his coat at the shoulder and sent the man from the Yard staggering backwards with the impact. There was a collective intake of breath and a new cacophony of screams from the footbridge

Vignoles pulled backwards, making sure he stood in front of a retreating Benson as he did so. They needed to bring calm to the situation, not goad the man further. Those who could, tried to seek protection from a roof support pillar or a Nestle's chocolate machine mounted on the wall or a massive weighing machine.

A train was approaching the opposite platform at speed. A non-stopper for Bristol and it would hurtle through the station with a screaming whistle and drift of steam. There seemed to be a collective intake of breath as the train steamed closer. Kane surprised everyone by sprinting across the platform through a space now cleared of people, away from the stationary train and only stopping once he reached the white painted edging stones of the far platform. He turned about and waved his gun hand in an uncoordinated manner whilst reaching inside his jacket pocket for something.

'Hey! I can see you!' A shot pinged off a wall as one of the Flying Squad dived to the ground to avoid the shot, his pistol skidding across the surface.

'Nobody move!' Vignoles bellowed. 'What do you want?'

'I've got to deliver it...' Kane was shouting but his voice was losing power and his face was deathly pale. 'It's what we do... I-I...' He swayed, his gun arm swinging wildly, but with so many targets so close, the threat remained real. The shape of a speeding train was now visible, a desperate sustained whistle screaming from the rapidly approaching engine, a pair of faces of the crew peering out of the cab.

'This what you want? Come and get it...then...' Kane deliberately placed the gun to his mouth. 'The Debt Collectors always deliver...'

'No!' Mellor hollered.

Lansdowne had taken up her gun once again and tried to take aim on Kane. Was the weapon accurate over this distance? Could she shoot the gun from Kane's hand or hit his shoulder? She needed a moment to steady her hand, slow her breathing. Kane was swaying as if about to faint...

Too late. There was sharp crack, and Kane's head was flung backwards as a cloud of red exploded in the air. His body seemed to lift from the ground and catapult backwards as his arms spread wide, his fingers loosening their grip on the gun. He was dead whilst still in the air. He disappeared over the edge of the platform and landed between the track below just as 'King John', passed overhead in a storm of steam and whirling connecting rods. Kane might have survived if he'd not blown half his head away first. As it was, these same speeding wheels missed most of his body, only slicing off a hand, later found still holding a little red box containing a diamond.

A stunned silence fell for what must have been just a fraction of a second. When they talked it over later, all agreed it had felt more like a minute. It was as if a film had been paused on one frame for an extended period before the projectionist allowed it to run on.

As the noise and melee erupted, an unremarkable and unremembered man who'd watched the whole sorry scene unfold to its bloody conclusion turned away, adjusted his Fedora and walked towards the District line, where he melted away into the evening crush of the city.

Chapter Forty

His jaw was set firm. He'd lost the Hornet. A shame. You win some, you lose some. It would have done his credibility good, but in the face of overwhelming odds there was little he could do. But The Debt Collectors had made a final reckoning. One was dead and the other would swing. And for that, he felt he deserved a few celebratory whiskies in strip club in Soho.

'Out with the old, in with the new...'

Chapter Forty-One

Vignoles, Mellor and Lansdowne were gathered in his office at Leicester Central. A stack of reports lay before them, the contents of which they were digesting.

'Abel will hang for his crimes and seems happy to sing like a canary bird before he does. A callous individual who amassed considerable wealth from his vile profession. Now it is over, he seems to be revelling in taking as many others as he can to the scaffold at the same time.'

'So much for honour amongst thieves...'

'No such thing, Mellor. A selfish world devoid of morals. Anything romanticised as honour is motivated by the selfish consideration of whether remaining silent will aid their own survival and the further aggrandisement of illegal gains.' Vignoles tossed the Scotland Yard report on the questioning of Jesse Abel, onto the desk. 'We'll leave him to his fate. The only aspect of Abel's testimony that need concern us is his denial that neither he nor Kane entered Krast's shop that Sunday night. They killed Krast on Broadway station and took his keys so they could search his house, but they left the shop alone as they were sure Krast would not try to conceal the Hornet in such an obvious place.'

'Why's this important, guv? Krast, Grinal and Slatter are all dead. Kane's killed himself, the diamond's recovered and Abel is going to the scaffold...'

'Because *someone* entered the shop and searched it. And I want to know who - and why.'

'A loose end...' Lansdowne added.

'I don't like loose ends. It means we've missed something.'

'I might have something that could help...' Mellor was holding an envelope filled with typed transcripts.

'In a moment, sergeant: Lansdowne - talk us through your report on Jeffries. We've cast him aside with all the chasing around London and the shoot-out at Ealing Broadway, but I think his story is important.'

'I pulled together what I feel is an accurate description of Jeffries' life from those who knew him, witnesses on and around the railway and most significantly from Miss Joyner...'

'His bit of skirt?' Mellor exhaled cigarette smoke and laughed. 'The old Devil!'

Lansdowne ignored the interruption. 'I confronted Jeffries with the evidence and he caved in and talked. He seemed relieved. Desperate to unburden himself.'

'Adultery and fraud, cooking the books...he's got a lot to admit to,' Mellor interjected.

'He has. But...' Lansdowne hesitated. 'This may sound odd, but I almost feel sorry for him.' Mellor snorted contemptuously, but Vignoles nodded his head as he lit his pipe, indicating he wanted to hear her reasoning.

'His life has not worked out well. He's moderately bright, quick with numbers and is presentable, but has ended up in a small shop and similar salary and a terminally ill wife. Quite dreadful for her, of course. We can sympathise with her suffering, but her needs are demanding. They sleep apart and he does most of the laundry, cooking and housekeeping. He can only afford help one day a week and whilst the neighbours also lend a hand, when coupled with a job six days a week, it is a terrible burden.'

'Seeking a few hours respite does not seem unreasonable?' Vignoles asked.

'He just needed company. Time with someone to get away from his personal woes. A young, pretty and hopelessly inappropriate young woman. She never had any intention of consummating the affair. There was never any long-term prospects for the two of them. I suspect he had immoral intentions, certainly at first, and plied her with extravagant presents he could not afford, but in the end all he was buying was a few hours of fantasy.'

'You actually *believe* that?' Mellor was scathing.

'I do, sergeant. Deep down he is not a bad man. Foolish, lonely, over-burdened and short of money, but a long way from people like Kane and Abel. He was vulnerable. And then, someone came along who offered him the prospect of a lot of money. Money that might help solve some of his problems. This person exploited his weakness. The lure of money can be compelling to man in his situation.'

'The mysterious man who arranged to meet Jeffries at St James Station?'

Vignoles asked.

'Yes. We know of Grinal posing as Buckrose targeting Krast, eager to get his hands on the diamond, but it seems there are others out there just as keen...'

'And just as clever...' Vignoles blew a smoke ring. He was feeling relaxed at last.

'Jeffries told me about someone who introduced himself as 'Mr Jones from Scotland Yard' who paid him a call. Jones was another trickster, and nothing to do with Scotland Yard of course. He claimed to be working undercover on the trail of a stolen diamond and explained how their investigations had led them to Krast. A story that was, substantially, correct.'

'All the best lies are based on truths...' Mellor added. 'We said the same about Buckrose-Grinal.'

'Mr Jones had done his research. He implied Scotland Yard would be appreciative and understanding towards Jeffries' misdemeanours in regard to falsifying the business records in return for allowing them to secretly search the shop, and most importantly, the safe. Jones needed Jeffries with him to ensure they were thorough and careful and left no trace. A substantial reward was promised upon receiving the diamond.'

'It was Jeffries who let him into the shop. But this Jones didn't kill Krast?' Mellor queried.

'That was at the hands of Kane.' Vignoles interjected. 'We've got a description of Jones from Jeffries and shall pass it on to all relevant authorities. He'll have gone to ground, but we'll get him in the end.'

'I do wonder, can we be sure this Jones really exists and is not a fabrication by Jeffries to help exonerate his actions?' Lansdowne asked.

'He exists. Consider why was Slatter killed? Why would Kane and Abel make such a crude assassination of a trusted cog in the London underworld unless for a very good reason? They panicked because they suspected Slatter was dealing with Jones for the diamond, behind their backs. Jeffries posed no threat.'

Mellor dragged heavily on his cigarette. 'Yeah, an' we've further evidence of this person's existence. I've got here transcripts of the interviews with the four Teddy Boys.' He passed the folded foolscap papers across to Vignoles. 'The Teds were put up to the beating they gave that pansy. Paid by a bloke who never gave a name or an address. The same man paid them to threaten Kane on the train and steer him off at Ealing. This same unknown man had a network of telephone kiosks he called into at set times of day. They loitered about, menacing anyone who came near, until it rang and took instructions. They got a call from Didcot with the time of the train Kane was on so they could join it at Southall. They were on a promise of ten quid each if they gave Kane a hard time - and - and relieved Kane of a diamond. If they delivered the said diamond, there was a hundred smackers each...'

They all fell silent for a moment.

'This man has to be the same Mr Jones. Write it up Mellor, including everything from Lansdowne and pass it over to Scotland Yard.'

Mellor and Lansdowne stood up. The meeting was over.

'There is one other thing.' Vignoles picked up a telex print out. "The Hornet's Beauty'. We now know some of the history of the stone. It belongs to a millionaire in the Cayman Islands. He loaned it to an exhibition in Geneva in 1951, from where it was stolen as part of a raid. But there is an ironic twist. The millionaire still has his diamond, safe and sound on his paradise island. Despite the reassurances and a hefty loan fee, he was unwilling to risk the diamond and secretly had a fine reproduction made. They can do wonders these days. He loaned the replacement without telling anybody and nobody doubted its authenticity.' Mellor whistled low in surprise.

'Then it really *is* paste?' Lansdowne was shaking her head in disbelief.

'Exceptional quality - but a fake,' Vignoles agreed.

'Perhaps Elsie could have it back? After all, she found it.'

'And I bet that millionaire claimed insurance on the real diamond,' Mellor added, bitterly.

'I shall ask if Miss Gable can be reunited with it. Although it comes with an awful lot of misery and heartache. Perhaps not the most auspicious stone for their engagement.'

'Perhaps not, sir. But I still think Elsie would be happy to get it back and announce her engagement. It might bring a touch of cheer to a long and sad story.'

Vignoles swivelled his chair so he could look out of the window onto the platform outside. An A5 type tank engine was gently steaming at the platform with a set of suburban coaches in tow. He recognised this as a regular engine on the down 'stopper' to Nottingham Vic. He and Anna would be catching a later version of the same service. The engine was a powerful beast and Vignoles rather liked them, but they were getting long in the tooth and his shed master friend at Woodford Halse reckoned it would not be long before they were withdrawn and replaced with new 'Standard' designs. He would be sad to see the old engines go, but all things must pass, and change was not always bad. It was not unlike replacing Trinder with Mellor, except that Trinder had a bright career ahead of him rather than a one-way trip to the breaker's lines at the back of an engine shed.

He puffed on his pipe. Mellor was taking some getting used to but given time they would adjust. And at least he got the job done, just as those ungainly new steam engines would get the job done in their own way. He might even come to like the arrangement.

There was paperwork still to do, reports to write, any number of tasks to tie up due to their involvement in this long and complex case, or should that be in the plural? It felt like a sequence of cases, not one. He stared at the folders waiting his attention. He could set Mellor onto some of this. Mellor could type almost as fast as Mrs Green who acted like the office gate guardian behind her monster typewriter, tip tapping away all day long.

Vignoles glanced at the station clock. An hour to go before his wife left her desk in Goods Despatching. Anna had a tiny diamond on her own engagement ring but he was not aware she cared one jot about the carat or monetary value. There were more important things in life than killing for a diamond the fraction of the size of a pea. So much misery caused by something so tiny.

He gave a deep sigh. He was tired and irritated by all this pain and greed and death over a stupid little stone. He needed to forget it all for a while and concentrate on what really mattered. He'd suggest to Anna they head straight into town and have a slap-up meal and a decent bottle of wine then get a later train back to their cosy house in Birstall filled with furniture he now realised had been designed and assembled in Broadway.

But they wouldn't light the fire tonight, nor listen to the radio or even warm up the television (better not tell Mellor they'd acquired one of these...)

Instead he'd suggest they had an early night and take his lovely wife to the bedroom...

THE END

The Inspector Vignoles Mysteries

'The best of the railway detective novels on the market.
The series continues to grow from strength to strength with
every new release. First rate.'
Steam Railway

Smoke Gets in Your Eyes (1946)

The Murder of Crows (1947)

The Torn Curtain (1948)

The Marylebone Murders (1949)

The Last Train (To Brackley Central) (1950)

New Brighton Rock (1951)

Blood & Custard (1952)

The Mountsorrel Mystery & Other Stories (1953)

Cold Steel Rail (1954)

Murder In Broadway (1955)

Coming in Autumn 2020: The Signalman's Daughter (1956)

Available from all UK booksellers and from The Vignoles Press direct via Amazon.
The GCRly shop in Loughborough Central stocks all titles, as does the GWSR
shop in Toddington, Vale of Rheidol Rly and the North Yorkshire Railway, all sales
of which actively support the respective heritage railways.

Books direct from the author.

Signed copies are available for £12.00 (including p&p).
Email Stephen.done@gmail.com to arrange bank transfer or to obtain address to
send cheque.

Any book suppliers interested in stocking the Inspector Vignoles Mysteries, please
get in touch and I can arrange attractive rates.